BRED

A COMING-OF-AGE LOVE STORY
INSPIRED BY GREAT EXPECTATIONS

by
GINGER SCOTT

*For my fellow "And, Or, Nor, But, Fors" – you know who you all are.
And for the woman who taught us so well.*

"I have been bent and broken, but—I hope—into a better shape."
— *Charles Dickens, Great Expectations*

CHAPTER 1

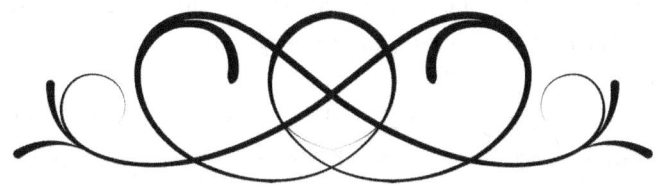

"Lily! Make sure you run the brush through your hair! And hurry...we're late!"

I've brushed my hair six times, and my scalp burns from the sharp teeth of my comb. We're always running late. Alice and Collin aren't my parents. They aren't really my aunt and uncle either, though that's what we tell people. Alice was my mom's cousin...like second or third? I don't know how to count that stuff, but their grandmothers were sisters, so we're whatever that makes us. They're the only family my parents really talked to, at least about me and where I should go...*if*.

Seven months ago, a police officer showed up while I was asleep on Alice and Collin's couch, a ring of chocolate caked around my lips, and several empty cans of carbonated sugar left as evidence on the coffee table. My parents went to a show in the city, and this was how Alice and Collin babysat—they gave me all of the things my parents never would.

They were young—still are...to have a thirteen-year-old, at least. Alice is twenty-seven, and Collin twenty-eight, and because Alice doesn't want people thinking she had a baby when she was fourteen, she's constantly telling people I'm not really hers. I don't mind. They're not really mine, either. We all just live together.

With the water running in the sink, I pass my toothbrush underneath to soften the bristles and make Alice's gross toothpaste a little weaker. I'm just about to spit the foam from my mouth into the sink when I feel the door push into my hip at my left.

"Lily, we're going to miss the train if we don't leave right now," Alice says, leaning across me to turn off the water. She makes eyes at me in the mirror, her silent reminder that I shouldn't keep the water running. *Water costs money.* Sometimes I think it's the only fact she really knows.

"Spit," she says, gesturing to the sink and reading a text on her phone. I do as she says and drop my brush in the cup, too nervous to turn the water back on to rinse it off.

I wipe the extra paste from the corners of my lips with the hand towel just as Alice tugs at my sleeve. I don't feel ready for whatever this "important opportunity" is. I don't feel ready for lots of things, though, so I guess I'll make the best of it. I do like riding the train, and at least we'll be able to do that for an hour all the way into the city.

We dash through the front door so quickly that my tulle, flowered skirt catches on the rotting doorframe wood, tearing the side of the fluffy part of my skirt up to my waist. The sound makes Alice pause, and her panicked eyes widen when they glance down to see the threads dangling along my knee.

"Lily! You're supposed to look nice. How are we going to fix that? We don't have time…" She bunches her bangs in her fist and rests her knuckles heavily on her forehead. I can see the sweat forming, and I swallow my nerves.

Alice is usually really nice. She's bossy, especially about the water, but she's nice. Ever since she got the call about a possible job at that rich, fancy lady's house, though, she's been…well…*mean!*

"I'm sorry. I was trying to hurry," I say, my bottom lip showing more of a tremble than I want. I gulp down air and wish away the sting of tears in my eyes. Alice does the same thing, her eyes falling to my feet as she draws in a heavy breath through her nose.

"It's fine. I'll fix it on the train. Just…let's go," she says, turning and holding my wrist to keep me close.

I have to take two steps for every one of hers, and I start to memorize the pattern my feet make between the cracks on the sidewalk.

We get to the station just as the train is about to leave. Alice searches for our passes in her purse and lets go of my hand as we trample quickly up the steps. I slip a little, and my black tights snag at the knee. I cover it quickly with my palm, walking bent at the waist so I can keep the hole hidden until I sit down and can bunch up the material enough to hide it.

Collin left for work early this morning. He's a dishwasher at the Blue Bird, the only semi-nice restaurant in Heywood. I like it better when Collin rides the train with us, because Alice always takes the window, even if it means I have to sit somewhere else, by a stranger. There are only two window seats open today, and my tummy fills with dread as we get closer to the rows because I know Alice is going to give me the one facing other people.

"Here, Lily." She guides me into the first open spot, startling an older man with a wild-looking white beard and deep, red marks on his face. He was sleeping, I think. He grumbles when I slip through the space between his kneecaps and those of the man dressed in a business suit directly across from him. His dirty pants are torn near his feet, and his shoes lack laces. He smells like the bathrooms at Collin's restaurant, and I'm so afraid he's going to talk to me that I only look down, at the hole in my tights, or straight ahead at the man who looks like he's about my dad's age—or how old my dad *would* be. This man is gripping a newspaper, and he glances at me for a second without smiling before pulling the paper up higher to shield his face.

"Lily, here. When he comes, hand him this…" I feel something lightly slapping at the top of my head, and I look up to see Alice's hand and a worn-out transit card.

"Okay," I croak, taking it in my palm and clutching it against my body.

As soon as the train begins to move, I set the card on my lap and lean forward, reaching to my ankle to pinch at my tights to bring more material to my knee. My mom taught me how to do this; I miss her a little doing it now.

"Tickets!" I pat my card against my belly at the sound of the conductor making his way down our aisle. When he gets to our row, I expect him to have to throw my neighbor off at the next stop, but the man fishes inside his front pocket and pulls out a bent card that's nearly full of stamps. I hand him mine next and lean back as the man across from me leans in for his turn.

I stare at the words scratched into the metal of the armrest for the remainder of the ride. Someone spelled the F-word wrong, leaving out the C. I wonder if it was Shay, whose name is carved near the end. Probably not—the writing looks different.

Old homes give way to old buildings on the streets outside as we crawl closer to downtown Chicago. I know we're getting close to our stop when I start to see people dressed in suits, and University sweatshirts. The trees outside still have their leaves, so when the train passes along the park, the shade dims the sun through my window where the reflection bounces off the lake. There are lots of boats out there today.

When I see the sign for the museums, I move to the edge of my seat, ready for our exit, and I push past the smelly man next to me before we come to a complete stop. Alice's hand is on my shoulder, gently pushing me to walk faster, and when I leap from the bottom step to the station platform, she nudges a little harder.

"We're late. Can you jog?" She starts to pick up her steps, so I do the same. We slow at the start of a deep-green iron fence that looks like a perfectly straight line of arrows jutting up from a garden. I pant loudly trying to catch my breath.

Alice pushes a button above a mailbox that doesn't match the enormous home gated behind it. The box has cracked paint and a red flag poking up high through some overgrown ivy, but I can't imagine mail ever getting delivered here. The leaves have overgrown so much. Nobody answers, and the more seconds that pass, the more Alice's hands touch her face and long brown hair. She runs her palms down her shirt and over her thighs a few times before huffing out "I knew we were going to be late…"

Her eyes flit to my dress, the skirt still torn, and she sucks in a sharp breath, immediately kneeling in front of me and tugging the torn shreds together to tie in a bow at my waist. She jerks down on the remaining part of my skirt to make it look even, and starts to shake her head when she realizes it's not going to work. I look silly with a bow anyhow. I'm an eighth-grader. I wanted to wear jeans, but Alice told me I had to look like we went to church. This dress is the only church-like thing I own. It's three years old, and every stitch of it is juvenile.

"This is a disaster," she says, looking down between her knees to the sidewalk. I follow her line of sight to a thin row of ants trailing between her feet and mine. Some of them are carrying crumbs. Alice kicks at them as she stands, and I watch for a few extra seconds while they scatter.

Alice pushes the button again the moment I look up, and this time, only a breath passes before a buzzing sound crackles through a speaker almost entirely swallowed up by ivy.

The gate releases and begins to fall open, so I take a step forward. Alice halts me with her arm in front of my chest, though, quickly taking a few steps until she's in front of me and staring me in the eyes.

"This is really important, Lily. I need this job. We need this job. When you get inside, just find a place to sit that hides your dress. Please." Her eyes plead with mine, and my skin burns.

"I'm sorry I tore it…" I say, feeling the need to cry. Alice's palm runs along my cheek just in time, and her other hand runs over my hair, tucking one of the golden curls behind my ear.

"It's not your fault," she says through a heavy breath. Her mouth curves in an almost-smile before she stands and reaches for my hand. We haven't held hands since I was little, but I take her palm in mine now and lock our fingers tightly. I don't want to be here.

She climbs up the brownstone's steps first, her hand slipping from mine, and I trail a level or two behind. The sound of the door unlocking *clicks* loudly, and the first thing I notice as the towering iron and glass door swings open is the heavy chain that swings at the door's edge. My eyes move to the woman standing in the open space next.

"Ma'am," Alice says, taking a bow with one of her feet behind the other. I watch her carefully and try to do the same, holding my skirt out to my side with my fist gripping at the ripped spot. We both look awkward, and the woman stares at us briefly, a tiny, unimpressed dent between her brow and a sour curve to her lips.

"Come in…you're late and I only have a few minutes…" The woman walks away with the door open behind her, and Alice looks down and back to me, where my feet feel like magnets clinging to a metal floor.

She gives me a crooked grin and lifts her eyebrows before heading inside. My feet somehow follow, but my heart starts to pound loudly the deeper we get into this woman's house.

Some kind of piano music is playing throughout the house, echoing from somewhere; it reminds me of the haunted house I refused to go inside—at that amusement park I went to with my parents just before they died.

Alice and I follow the woman down a long hallway that seems to split this house into two halves. None of the lights are on, and the farther inside we get, the more the darkness makes the woman look like a witch. She's wearing a long black dress that touches the floor where her heels *click* against polished wood. Her sleeves are long, and the neck of the dress is high, like those turtlenecks Alice made me wear when I first came to live with them. Those shirts choked me.

"Who are you?"

I gasp when a boy who looks to be about my age steps from one of the rooms along the never-ending hallway and cuts off our path. My heart thumps inside my body and my stomach suddenly feels sick from the rush of being scared. My hands are clutched at my skirt, and I catch his eyes dipping down and noticing the rip in my dress. He smirks, then pops his gum, pushing his tongue through the center and blowing a giant pink bubble that hides his face from view.

"Henry, can you show our guest to the music room? Her mother and I will only be a moment…"

"Oh, I'm not her mother…" Alice begins, just as she always does— quick to correct people about our relationship. Her explanation trails off though when she's met with an instant scowl. The woman who let us in is tall—somehow, she seems a full foot taller than Alice, and she tucks her chin into her neck slowly and lifts her right hand to slide her glasses to the tip of her nose. Her eyes move from Alice, to me, then back again.

"I see," she says, the tiny sentence dragging out with a sort of *hiss*. "Come on. Henry…the music room." The woman continues her march down the hallway, and Alice stumbles a little to catch up to her, stopping just long enough to wave her hand low, urging me to go with the rude boy who smells of old bubblegum.

My back is pressed against the wall so hard the chair rail is slicing into my shoulder blades. Henry, I suppose is his name, casually leans against the opposite wall and crosses his arms. I instantly notice the whiteness of his crisp dress shirt. His sleeves are rolled, and the gold and blue tie he's wearing is knotted perfectly up close against his neck. My dad used to wear ties like that; he said he'd learned to tie them from my grandfather.

"You wanna see the piano?" A blonde wave of hair slips down across his forehead as he nods toward a room behind me. He's my height, but so many things about him seem so much older. He reminds me of the high schoolers that live on our block, the ones that sit on the corner to smoke and throw rocks at the stop sign late at night.

"Sure," I say, moving an inch or two away from the wall. I roll my shoulders back to make my chest look bigger—so I feel older, like I belong here.

Henry stares at me for a second then laughs, but only on one side of his mouth. Instantly, my hands fold together nervously at my waist.

"Come on," he says, nodding his head in a way that says "follow me."

He draws open a pair of pocket doors that slide into either side of the wall and open up to a room that makes me dizzy with its riches. Somehow, the wooden floors seem shinier in here. Floor-to-ceiling windows look out over the lake, broken up only by floor-to-ceiling bookcases filled with a rainbow of book spines. My fingers are instinctively drawn forward to touch them, tracing the golden titles embossed on the sides. They look so old, yet also brand new.

"You must read all the time," I say with wonder, smiling with my back to Henry.

"I hate books," he says. I roll my eyes and groan a little louder than I intended, but before I can take it back, Henry picks up on it.

"Let me guess…" he says. "You *love* reading, especially books about princes and princesses and love and all that shit."

My eyes flare. It's not that I've never heard someone my age swear. I hear it all the time at school. I mean, I grew up near Chicago! My dad always said we used the best adjectives in this city. It's more that Henry and I only just met. And I don't know…maybe it's also the way he's dressed and the way his hair is combed away from his eyes, minus that one strand, and how he suddenly smells less like gum and more like aftershave. I feel like he's supposed to be proper.

He smirks at me again, seeing my surprise. I'm embarrassed by it. I must seem like such a baby to him.

"Actually, I love reading about adventure. And thrillers. Something about getting inside the mind of a killer." I hate thrillers really, but I wanted to shock him—that's why I said it.

"That's sick," he says, twisting his lips at me with disinterest.

I blush harder as my stomach tightens. I even lied poorly. This day has been a disaster from the moment the toothpaste hit my brush.

"Play for me." He flips open a wooden panel covering the keys of an ornate grand piano.

My eyes travel along the beautiful row of black and white.

"I don't know how." I swallow, wishing I did. If I could sit down and play something spectacular, it would make him stop treating me like a baby.

"Here…I'll show you," he says, sliding onto the bench and moving to the far side to make room for me. When his pants rise above his ankles, I notice the color of his socks—gold and blue, just like his tie. I take the seat next to him and study his hands as his fingers stretch wide over the keys.

"You go to a private school or something?" *Or something*…I sound so naïve.

"I go to Richmond Prep." Leaning his weight forward on his hands, he presses down firmly on several keys that somehow sound perfect together. I look from his fingers to mine, one at a time, trying to find keys that match that I can press on my own.

"Oh. I go to Public Thirteen." In concentration, I suck in my bottom lip until it disappears then press my own set of keys. My sound is off. I can tell instantly.

"Here," Henry says, adjusting two of my fingers and moving them over a key. His hands don't feel rough like the boys at my school. I bet he doesn't play football in the street or climb over walls like they do. He probably just sits in this room and does nothing but make fun of his fancy books and play this piano.

I lean forward again, this time my sound matching his, only lower.

"Ah!" I turn my head until my eyes meet his and I smile wide, showing most of my teeth.

He laughs, so I start to curl my fingers. I stop when his hands cover mine.

"No. Don't...I was laughing because you seemed so excited. That's all," he says, half chuckling. I make a nervous sound that matches, but sounds nothing like his easy laugh at all.

"I always wanted a piano," I admit.

Concentrating on my fingers again, I try to repeat the chord.

"Elena used to play. She taught me a few things, but she doesn't use this room much anymore. If your mom gets the job working for her, I'm sure she'd be all right with you coming over to practice."

I press the keys a few times, changing a finger placement here and there to see what the difference is. The sound isn't always bad.

"Who's Elena?" I sneak in the question between a good note and a terrible one.

Henry laughs the same way as before. I sit back and pull my hands into my lap this time.

"She's the one who let you in? The reason you're here? She's the CEO of Havisham Industrial, and she just lost her personal assistant. People have been interviewing all week. I hope your mom gets it, but honestly...she doesn't really look like the kind of person Elena hires."

My head shakes automatically, trying to compute the information and keep up.

"She's not my mom," I say, answering the easy bit first. Of course, next comes his questioning look.

"Sister?" he asks.

I should probably just say yes, or say *aunt* like I usually do. But for whatever reason, I give Henry the truth. "My parents died in an accident. Alice is like my cousin or something. We don't have a big family. I...I live with them now—Alice and her husband, Collin."

I brace myself for a harsh response, similar to the one he gave me about hating books when I complimented this library.

"I'm adopted. Elena...she adopted me when I was five from the Catholic Sisters of St. Agatha. I was the oldest one in their care. She *saved* me...so she likes to remind me constantly."

Henry shifts on his end of the bench; I do the same until our knees accidentally touch. My stomach dips with a falling sensation.

"Sorry," I say, quickly scooting back a few inches.

I twist my lips and look around the room, now incredibly silent compared to a minute before when our hands were pounding on the piano.

"You don't call her *Mom*..." I say, finally filling the silent gap. I glance up at him, and he shrugs.

"She's just Elena. I guess that's like Mom. I don't know. Hey...you call your cousin or whatever by her name too. We're the same!" Henry's mouth finally curves on both sides equally, a real smile—like the one I made over playing my first chord.

"We kinda are." I smile back.

His eyes are both a little brown and a little green, and a powder of freckles connects them from one cheek to the next. His teeth are super straight, not like mine that turn in on both sides. I bet he'll never need braces. I'll never get them because we can't afford them.

I try to hold his stare long enough to notice more things about him, but it starts to feel weird between us—almost warm and a bit like drowning without water.

"Isn't Havisham the soap company?" I see their commercials on TV all the time. They make everything that's used to wash anything. Henry's rich. I was right about that part.

"Soap and paper, mostly." His answer is short, and that strange, warm quiet begins to stuff my ears again.

His attention slips back to the keys, but this time he barely strokes them, his fingers climbing closer to me one key at a time, pressing them in so softly the sound is essentially a piano's whisper.

"What's your name?" His voice breaks at the end, and he covers it with a quick clearing of his throat. His eyebrows draw in to a pinch, too, but his hand continues to trail down the keys toward me.

"Lily." His fingers slow when I speak, and I part my lips to share more—*Julienne Ames* runs through my head but never leaves my mouth.

"What do you think of the music room?" The woman's voice behind me causes my shoulders to draw stiff. I instantly turn so my body is facing away from Henry and toward the piano again. I look to my left nervously as I stutter.

"I...love it. I...it's I mean. It's a great room. Especially the piano. I... I have always wanted to learn to play." My gaze catches on Alice's face behind Elena, and she looks nearly ill. I'm guessing this first is also the *last* time I'll ever touch a piano. There's no way Alice got the job judging by her expression.

"I think everyone should learn an instrument," Elena says, waving her hand toward Henry. I feel his weight leave the bench. Elena moves closer and takes his spot. I bring my fisted hands to my thighs, tucking them under my legs and hoping nobody notices.

Elena's hands stretch out like Henry's did, only she presses the keys softly at first, almost as if they're alive and sleeping and she doesn't want to wake them with her touch. Her hands move like they're dancing, swaying up toward the high notes then back down to where I'm sitting. It's almost like waves passing, and my mouth falls open at the way her hands cross over one another effortlessly.

"Would you like to learn?"

I sense her eyes on me before I turn to meet her gaze. Somehow, her hands are still moving, making perfect music without looking.

"I would...very much." Alice is going to kill me. Elena is probably going to offer lessons, and then explain how much they'll cost. Alice is going to have to tell her no, right after telling me no, right after not getting the job she came here for in the first place.

"Can you start on Monday?" The music continues as Elena's chin tips up and her eyes move to Alice who is stalled in the doorway just beyond my shoulder.

I twist and look Alice in the eyes, both of our pupils wide, confused looks on our faces.

"I suppose…yes…I would love to." My guardian swallows loud enough I hear it over the melody Elena is creating. Her hands finally stop and she brings them into her lap. There's something about everything she just did that felt professional—*rich*.

I'm not sure how long she was studying me, but when I finally lift my eyes to Elena's face, I get the feeling that it was for several seconds.

"You can come here after school, or when you don't have school. Henry will be doing homework at that time, and the music won't bother him. It gives you three hours a day. That's perfect."

The time that passes feels short, maybe only a breath, but my answer didn't come fast enough for Alice, who steps closer to me and holds me still where I sit, her hands on each of my shoulders.

"Thank Mrs. Alderman for her offer." My eyes crinkle because I was about to, and I hate that now it looks like I was just told. So insincere.

"Thank you, Ma'am." I catch Henry's stifled laughter behind Elena, and I instantly know *Ma'am* was the wrong word.

"Oh…ha ha ha." Elena stands from the piano as she pushes out forced laughter. She pauses with the wooden cover propped up with her fingers, nails longer than I've ever seen someone grow them. It takes me a moment to realize she's waiting for me to step away from the piano. She's putting it away.

"Sorry, ma…" I stop myself.

"You can call me Elena. Ma'am…" She waves her hand in the air between us. "It sounds so old. And I'm not married, which *Miss* would always remind me of, so Elena is what I prefer. You can both call me that."

She looks over my shoulder to Alice, who had just called her *Mrs.*

"Elena. Okay," I nod. "Thank you, Elena."

I repeat her name just to force it into habit. At the feel of Alice's hand on my arm, I turn into her and move a few steps away from the piano. I hold my hands in front of my body, my right clinging to my left. I can feel my pulse in my fingertips.

"You'll want to wear comfortable shoes, good for walking, but not sneakers. And your dress should be…" Elena's eyes scan down Alice's body. "Nice dress pants and blouses work well. You'll be driving a lot, and taking some of my appointments. I'd like you to look like my brand."

Beyond her, Henry mouths the word *brand* and lifts his mouth on one side. I pull my lips in tight to hold in my laugh.

"I can do that. I'll be here bright and early…" Alice starts, but Elena interrupts.

"Seven. There is no need before seven. But no later."

"Seven," Alice repeats.

I've gotten used to getting myself up for school, and I know that seven is going to be hard for Alice. She's not an early riser. Her last job was in the evening. I should probably get as much time in with the piano as I can before she gets fired for being late.

"Thank you…again. I'm very excited to begin," Alice says, her palm stretched forward. Elena takes it but her eyes move to me.

"As am I. And please, be sure that your daughter comes along…"

"She's not my…"

Elena corrects herself before Alice can, holding up her hand and ending their shake. She shakes her head quickly and blinks her eyes several times, which is the first time I notice the thick black that coats her lashes and shades her almost teal-blue eyes.

"My mistake. Your niece…be sure she comes."

Niece. I see Alice went with the easy lie. I should have, too, but I'm strangely glad that Henry knows the truth; especially if I'm going to see him again.

I hold my open palm up with my fingers stretched to say goodbye to him as Alice tugs at the shoulder of my sleeve for me to follow her from the room. The brightness and humor that was on his face seconds ago has disappeared, and his only response is to shove both of his hands into the pockets of his tan pants.

My stomach fills with sand, weighing me down as I follow Alice out the door of the room first, then the home second. The steps outside seem grander now, and I swear they multiplied. We aren't in a rush like we were on the way in, so I glance to my right and left to see what flowers I must be smelling. They look like tulips and maybe rows of lavender. Bees flit from bloom to bloom, and perfectly trimmed grass swerves around newly washed bricks, forming a path back to the gate we came in through. We wait at it until we hear it *buzz*, and Alice pushes it open. I step through behind her and turn to look over my shoulder at the grand brownstone that I somehow get to come back to in a few short days.

I walk backward, secretly hoping the door will pop open once again and Henry will wave goodbye...and smile. It remains closed though, and that heavy feeling of sand in my gut returns.

CHAPTER 2

A lice picked my outfit before I left for school today, so I'm stuck wearing a sweater that makes my armpits itch and sweat. I've spent most of the day tugging it away from my chest in short bursts to create a breeze. It hasn't done much good.

She stuffed my Metra card in the deepest pocket of my backpack, worried I'd lose it or someone would steal it. I've lost two at this junior high in seven months. This girl Everly says some of the other girls trade the cards for drugs, but I think they just like the rush of stealing something. I bet they use it once then throw it away.

Besides, a thirty-dollar Metra card wouldn't buy much on the street. My dad was a drug counselor, so I know more than I should about these things. I'll never use, though—I've literally seen what the bottom looks like and I don't think I'd survive it.

The hidden Metra card and awful sweater are doing quite the job on me right now. I need to swipe it to make the train, but I can't reach it underneath all of my books, and the panic is making me sweat.

Finally giving up, I dump my bag upside down right on the other side of my turnstile and yelp with joy the minute the bright pink card flashes and draws my eyes.

I begin to scoop my things back into my bag when a group of boys walk by and jump over the bars next to me, one of them stopping just long enough to kick my algebra book through the gate and nearly over the edge into the tracks. The pages fly open and my homework, already done and folded, ready to be turned in, tumbles into the dark pit below just as the train rushes into the station.

"Hey!" I shout, fumbling with my card and my barely together backpack, still unzipped in my arms. I'm holding my things together like a poorly made taco, and a woman next to me stops to help me swipe my card and make it through the gate.

"Are you all alone?" Her eyes are narrowed with concern, and for whatever reason I lie.

"No...no." With a deep breath I pull myself together...*ish*, and roll my shoulders back as I smile. "My friend is on the train. She's saving our seats. Thank you though."

"All right." The woman smiles, leaving satisfied. I wait a beat before walking toward the back of the train, several cars away from her—to the car that the assholes went into after they amused themselves with me.

Plopping down near the door, I turn myself so I can keep my eyes on them, my taco bag still hugged to my chest. Two of them are standing, the other two sitting, and they're flicking a lighter off and on against one of the pole grips. After a few seconds, they move on to trash they find near empty seats, burning up pieces and letting them fall to their feet so they can stomp them out and stain the floor.

I glare the entire time, just waiting for one of them to look my direction and feel a glimmer of guilt. They get off three stops later, never noticing me.

Left unsatisfied, I carry my mood all the way to my stop, thirty minutes later, and by the time I get to the Alderman gate, I boldly push the button and march toward the front door. Alice is waiting for me just inside, and she slips out to meet me at the steps.

"You look awful. And why are you scowling? Lily...this is important. If you didn't want to come here, you never should have said so when Elena invited you during my interview." Alice brushes away a loose string from the shoulder of my sweater and tugs it near the collar to straighten it. I hate this sweater. I'm just glad I got out of the house in jeans instead of the khaki *slacks* Alice was trying to get me to wear. I think she was trying to make me look like I went to a fancy private school too. I don't, though. I go to a school where a boy was locked in the bathroom today for being gay, and where someone cut away the chains on the swings before the year started. A thousand kids ages five to thirteen all cram into two rows of classrooms. It is not the kind of place one wears khakis.

"I want to be here. The train was just…"

Alice has already moved on, uninterested in anything more than getting me inside so she can keep her job. We haven't talked about it, but we both know that Elena liked me more than her and that's why she got the job.

I follow her inside, closing the door behind me when she glances over her shoulder and lifts a brow. I double up my steps to catch up to her. She slows down just outside the music room.

"So what kinds of things are you doing for her?" I whisper.

Alice bunches her lip in thought and looks to our sides.

"Random things. It's really weird. I brought her a bunch of boxes of old photos this morning, and she spent an hour sitting at the dining table and moving them around, like she was organizing them. She sent me out for lunch at noon, and by the time I came back the photos were all packed away again in the boxes, and she had me put them back on the highest shelf in her bedroom closet."

"That is weird, I guess," I say, wondering if Elena was looking for one photo in particular or if she just wanted to revisit her past. "Maybe she's making a slideshow for something, or a history book for the company."

Alice shrugs.

"I don't know, but if she's going to pay me thirty-five bucks an hour to help her sort her closet one box at a time, I'm game. This beats washing dishes."

"What if she makes you wash dishes?" I joke.

Alice smirks and jerks with a silent laugh.

"For thirty-five bucks an hour, I'll wash her dishes. Besides…no way she doesn't have one of those fancy dishwashers that basically does everything but put them away."

"True," I agree.

Sliding the doors open, I bring the piano into view and move toward it instantly. I've been dying to touch the keys again ever since we left last week. It's even more beautiful than I remember, the wood a deep mahogany and a spotless silver rod holding up the top that covers the strings. I kinda want to find Henry so I can ask him to push in the keys and let me watch the strings.

"I should go check on Elena to see if she needs me. Don't break anything," Alice says, leaving with a spin, her hair punctuating her exit with a flap against her shoulder.

My fingers are itching to touch the keys, but all I can think about is that hour-long algebra assignment now lost in the depths of the Heywood train station. I consider looking for it when we get home. Our station isn't very big, and the train times are spaced far apart. With my luck, though, the six or seven trains that will pass between now and then will have picked it up and carried it in a wind down the town streets, dumping it anywhere. *Anywhere* is a much less specific place to search for something.

I move to a small desk tucked in the corner where two of the tall bookcases meet and drop my bag on top, letting my things slide out to the sides. I busy myself sorting through my mess first, putting papers back in folders, books back in order, and pencils where they belong. I'm struggling with the zipper when Henry walks in and drops his backpack next to my algebra book.

"Hey, what's up?" He talks to me as if we've been friends for a while. Naturally, I start to sweat.

"Hi, Henry," I say, tucking my hands under my thighs and smiling up at him. Right back to feeling like his kid sister. He gives me a crooked smile that makes one eye squint a little.

"Hi, Lily." There's a teasing tone to his voice. I'm relieved when his eyes leave my face and look down at my algebra book. He spins it with his finger and flips it open a few pages, leaning down and resting his elbows on either side.

"I miss this stuff," he hums, flipping several pages by at a time. He stops on one of the unit intro pages that I doodled a heart on and the initials PJ.

"PJ, huh?" His lips pucker and I flush.

"It's an old book. I didn't write that," I lie, flattening my palm on the page and turning the book back toward me.

"Uh huh...sure," Henry says, standing tall again and moving toward the piano. My eyes follow him, wondering if he's going to play. I already feel envy that he might. I should have started at the piano, taken it for mine before he could insert himself.

He grips the bench on one end and drags it across the floor to the other side of the desk, sitting on it and bringing a book from his bag up on the desk.

"Chemistry?" My eyes flit from the book to him. At my school, we just have *science*. It's a little bit of everything, but nothing very in-depth.

"Richmond is a pretty academic school. We have a class on water harvesting, too. It's a hippy class, though, so no one really takes it." He chuckles as he flips his book open, and I wonder what water harvesting even means.

"Oh," I say with a slow nod, faking it. I probably should have laughed like he did, found the joke about hippies funny. Alice and Collin are kind of hippy-like, though, so I'm also a little offended—even if I don't really know what water harvesting is. I think Henry might be a snob.

I force myself to concentrate on my work, slipping a blank paper from my packet in my bag that's now resting by my leg. I write my name and the date in the upper corner and begin with the first problem. I get through the first three before the fast scribbling sound of Henry's pen forces me to look up.

"You're left-handed," I say, that small fact not really why I'm looking at him. He has the pen gripped in a fist, and he's scratching out letters with tiny numbers, like formulas for God knows what. Maybe he's water harvesting.

"Yep," he says. His lips smack shut at the end of the word and his eyes glance up briefly, amused by me.

His hand continues to scratch away at the paper, so hard I think he might tear it if he keeps up this pace. He gets to the bottom of the paper and begins to flip it over when he looks up and catches me still staring.

"What?" His forehead is dented between his brows.

"You're uhm…kinda loud," I say, pointing my pencil's eraser to his pen.

He leans back in his chair, dropping the pen as he does. His hand flexes wide then joins his other palm behind his neck, elbows bent out on either side.

"Sorry," he says, smirking for a brief second. "I rush through the stuff I don't like."

"You don't like chemistry?" I flip his paper over and scan the rows of formulas.

"It's my second time taking it. Failed the first time through," he says. I realize that means he probably took chemistry in seventh grade. My school is an embarrassment.

"You seem to have a good grasp on it now," I say through a half smile.

He shifts in his seat and leans forward again, his hands folded on top of his book.

"I get bored, I guess. I don't know. It sounds so typical, but sometimes I just *act up*, I guess. I don't know…" He trails off, staring at his paper for a few seconds before squinting with one eye again and looking at me, his tongue pushed in his cheek.

"You have to do that right now?" He points at my homework.

"Sadly, I do. Four dickheads at the train station kicked my backpack and my homework took off to who knows where." I sigh heavily at the visual replaying in my head. When my eyes move up to meet Henry's, I catch the amusement on his face. "What? You think those guys were funny?"

I feel myself starting to stew all over again.

"No…you said *dickheads*. Just…you don't seem like the kinda girl who talks dirty," he says, biting the tip of his tongue as if he's stopping himself from saying too much. I'm glad he stopped.

"They were jerks," I say, flipping my book closed with my paper inside. "And I can probably do this later."

"Thata girl," Henry says, doing the same with his book and paper.

He pushes his bench back and stands, taking a few large steps toward the door. I linger by the desk, a little disappointed that we're not moving the bench back and playing the piano.

"Well...you coming?" His thumbs are hooked in his pockets, the bottoms of his pants rolled up to show off his ankles. I don't know how anyone can wear shoes without socks, but I admit that Henry looks cute this way.

"I guess," I relent, dropping my pencil on top of my closed book. I follow Henry through the music room door out into the hallway, past the sitting room that Alice is in with Elena. Neither of them notice us walk by, but I hurry up my steps, feeling like I'm breaking some rule by leaving the one room I was given permission to be in.

Henry stops in a massive kitchen, nothing in the room out of place. Pans shine spotless from a rack above a center island with large burners, and rolls of linen towels sit on top of a small stack of plates, as if a server is due at any moment.

"Do you guys have a cook?" I ask as Henry opens a heavy silver door to a refrigerator, pulling out two bottles of sparkling somethings.

"Sometimes," he says. "Only for parties or things. Usually, I order delivery and eat on my own. Elena doesn't like to go out."

Sometimes. My mind stretches to try to understand this life. We don't even go out to eat for special occasions. Most meals are sandwiches, or soupy things that sat in the crockpot all day. We all get excited when Collin comes home with leftovers from the restaurant, but the fries are always cold and never reheat quite the same.

Henry hands me one of the bottles and walks back down the hallway, past the room Elena and Alice are in. I figure out that I'm holding something alcoholic about a second before we pass by, and I feel my heart fly up to my throat when my eyes meet Alice's through the doorway. Our gazes catch just long enough for her chin to tilt and her brow to wrinkle. I tuck the bottle against my side and keep walking, muttering to myself with every step.

"*Shit, shit, shit...*"

I'm expecting us to walk back into the music room, but instead, Henry moves closer to the front door, turning into the foyer and taking the spiral staircase up two steps at a time. I stall at the bottom, my thumb rubbing away a bead of water that's formed on the chilled bottle in my hand.

"You coming?" He slows his climb and leans over the railing to look down at me. I lift my chin and crane my neck in an attempt to see where we're going. I know it's his room. And while the rule-follower knows she should just turn around and go back to redoing her homework, the thirteen-year-old girl thinks following a cute boy up to his room is kind of exciting.

"Yeah. Be right up," I say, giving in and rushing up the steps before Alice comes down the hall and sees me.

Henry beats me to his room by a second, and he's already sprawled flat on his back on his bed when I step through his door. I lean against the wall just inside, drawing a limit to how daring I plan to be. Henry sits up and pulls a bottle opener attached to a few keys from his pocket. His drink fizzes as he pops it open and gestures for me to hand him mine. I do, even though I don't really want it, and he scoots forward to hold his bottle between his knees while he pulls away my cap.

"Cheers," he says with a laugh, handing it back to me.

I hold it up with a little tilt, my eyes watching his, trying to read this dare. He wants to see just how far I'll go with this—if I'm really just a little girl, like I seem. I bring the glass rim to my lips and lift, the sharp carbonation coating my tongue in a flavor that's both sweet and bitter at once.

"It's almost lemon," I say, trying my best not to frown as I swallow.

"It is lemon," Henry says, chuckling again before taking a large swig of his.

I look at the label, noting the word HARD before the lemonade.

"Almost," I repeat, taking another small taste. If I can stretch this out slowly, I think I can stomach drinking a quarter of it before it's time to go home.

Henry rolls his eyes at me and shakes his head as he stands. He sets his bottle down on top of a dresser before he begins to yank away the tie that still hangs around his neck. I nestle myself into the corner of his room, against the wall but in a place where my elbow can lean on his chest of drawers. I'm going for relaxed, but instead I look like the world's worst undercover spy.

I force myself to take another sip, but the moment the liquid hits my tongue, I pull the bottle away and gasp. Henry's unbuttoned his shirt and pulled it from the waist of his pants. His shoulders can't possibly be the same age as mine—they're too toned and...and...big! He has biceps where most of the boys in my school have pale skin and zits, and his forearms are marked with a line where a muscle rolls while his fingers work.

Henry turns to face me when his arms are fully free of the cotton button-down, and I turn to the side with a blush. His laugh is quiet, but it's there, which only makes the red on my cheeks crawl down my neck and up my ears.

"I hate wearing uniforms," he says, giving me an explanation.

I cough to clear my throat.

"Oh yeah...I mean, I would too. Not that we have uniforms. Alice made me wear this sweater...which is kind of like a uniform, so I can understand. I wish I could change out of this thing..."

"You can," Henry says, and my head jerks to look at him. My wide eyes make him laugh hard.

"No, I mean...borrow one of my shirts. Hold on..." He steps into his closet and shuts the door, giving me enough time to tug my sweater away from my now-damp chest and arms. The cable knit is heavy, and the yarn is scratchy—this sweater is a product of Satan.

Henry exits after a few seconds, now wearing a pair of jeans and a long-sleeved, navy blue T-shirt. He tosses one that matches at me, and I grab it as it hits me in the neck.

"You can change in there if you want. Or...I could just turn," he chuckles, slowly spinning until his back is to me.

"Closet is fine," I answer quickly, not giving him a chance to tease me more. I rush by him and shut the door, pulling the knob hard and searching for a lock. Makes sense that there isn't one, but I still wish there was.

I back into the corner of his closet, behind the door, so even if he were to open it, I could hide long enough to do something. I realize how stupid I'm being after a few long seconds of standing in here alone, though, so I strip away my sweater and consider tossing it high up on one of Henry's shelves. Knowing Alice will ask me about it, though, I don't, instead dropping it at my feet and unfurling the shirt Henry gave me.

The front corner is crested with his name, both first and last, and the back has a large yellow circle with the words: SATIS HOUSE CREW TEAM. I run my thumbs over the printed letters and wonder what Satis House is. I pull his shirt over my head and breathe in, smelling only fabric softener. The shirt's a size or two too large on me, so I gather it around my waist before I pick up my sweater and step out.

"Thanks. I'm already a million times more comfortable," I say.

Henry is tucking his wallet and phone into his back pockets as he looks up at me, his hair less perfect than it was when he was dressed for school. Messy curls flop along his forehead, and I think how his color is almost the same as mine. I like his hair better this way.

"Hey, looks good on you. Wanna join the rowing team with me?" His lip raises on the right as he bends over and pulls a shoe over his heel.

"I'm pretty sure I would be the worst rower in Satis House history," I joke. "I can't even do one pullup. I'm going to fail PE."

Henry laughs, so I join him, though I wasn't actually kidding about that last part. He slips on his other shoe and moves back to his door, grabbing his bottle in his hand and nodding toward mine. I was hoping he'd forget about it.

"Oh...yeah. I'm actually kind of full, so..." He sees right through my excuse, and with a mocking hiss he takes my bottle in his hand and takes a long drink as he walks out his door. He carries both bottles down his front steps as I follow. When we round his house toward the backyard, he drops the half-filled one that was mine into a recycling bin.

"I had a feeling you were a goody two-shoes," he says.

"I'm not...I've just never really had anything with alcohol, so..."

"Goody two-shoes," he interrupts me, turning to walk backward through yellowed, thick grass. "No...Lily two-shoes! That's what I'll call you!"

"Great," I respond, my lips flat and my gut heavy.

My face deflates when he laughs loudly at my expense.

"You know what? I really should do my homework...I'm just gonna go back," I say, turning with every intention of leaving Henry alone here in the shadow of his enormous house and the Chicago skyline.

"Don't be like that," he says, the tips of his fingers brushing against mine as he tries to stop me. The slight touch jolts me, like that feeling my muscles get when I'm about to drift off to sleep and suddenly wake myself at the sensation of falling.

"I'm sorry," he says when I turn to face him. His hand is still a little outstretched toward me, and my fingers, now buried in my pockets, twitch at the offer. His palm falls away quickly though, and I regret jerking away in the first place. "I won't tease anymore...at least not today."

His cheeks dimple with his grin as he draws a cross over his chest. I hesitate, but it's just for show. When he turns to move closer to the iron fence wrapped with ivy and dividing his yard with the one behind him, I follow. When he begins to climb over, I accept his offer to help me first with a boost under one foot, and when we both land in a yard that isn't either of ours at a house that's marked for sale, I follow him inside.

"This place has been on the market for a year. Elena says they're asking too much for it." Henry pulls his shoes from his feet one at a time, stepping on the backs, but leaves his short socks on before sprinting through the sitting room we entered through. He stops when the hallway begins and slides a dozen more feet toward the front of the house, laughing, for once acting like the younger one of the two of us.

"Your turn," he says, flipping his waves of hair back and away from his eyes. He's positively juvenile, but yet happier than he's ever seemed. I wonder if perhaps there are two Henrys.

"I doubt I'll slide very far," I say, trying to avoid his request by stepping forward instead of running.

"Ah!" He flashes both palms to stop me. "Shoes off. Your turn."

I take a deep breath and let it out through my nose. Coordination of things like legs and arms and knees is not in my skills set. I don't need

Henry rushing back over the fence to call an ambulance when I break my arm.

"I don't run very fast," I say, offering another excuse.

He just holds up a finger and slides as if he's on skates back to me.

"I'll pull you," he says, holding his hands forward. My eyes go right to the fingertips I wished I'd held a few minutes ago. My heart drums an offbeat and my toes begin to curl in anticipation of me putting them through something mildly athletic.

"Fine," I relent, sighing one last time and pulling my shoes from my feet just as Henry did.

With his arms outstretched, he slides back a few feet, just out of reach. I let my head fall to the side, mad that he's teasing me again.

"Relax, I'm just giving you slack. You'll catch up to me and I'll pull you to keep your speed going. Come on. I promise you'll have fun."

A wry smile sinks into the corner of my mouth. There's no going back now.

"All right," I begin, letting my arms dangle at my sides, swinging forward and back in my silent count to three.

"Go!" Henry shouts, somehow on the same count with me, and I push myself forward, slipping a little at the start but running toward him and catching up to his hands after the first few steps.

His grip is immediate. There's nothing awkward about it on his end, once again as if he and I have done this before and often. He's instantly comfortable, playfully shouting and encouraging me to go faster as he pulls me forward and off balance. My feet rush to keep up and just as we hit the hallway, he slingshots me past him. I slide sideways on my socks, haphazardly surfing across the shiny grain while my arms, no longer under his control, flail around my body for balance. I go a few feet farther than he did, crouching down and eventually getting to my knees just in time to move to the side as Henry races toward me. I roll on my hip as he slides by, lowering himself to his side like a baseball player reaching for second base. He coasts the complete length of the hallway this way, stopping only when his toes reach the front of the house.

"Woo hoo!" His arms stretch up and out, and he kicks to his feet quickly, grabbing my hand as he runs by so we can go again.

With every attempt, my grip becomes less awkward, and my muscles relax more. I run faster, sometimes on my own, and I slide low with my knees bent, trying to beat Henry's best distance. I never do. But I constantly try. I slide on socks in a house that isn't mine with a boy who seems to like to break rules so he can smile and act his age with no one around to tell him not to. I wonder how often he comes here alone. I wonder if he'll ever bring me back.

CHAPTER 3

ONE WEEK BEFORE FRESHMAN YEAR

The rain has soaked through my shoes, and every step makes my toes feel colder. I hug my music book to my chest, my coat folded over it tightly.

Elena gave it to me a month ago, and the pages are yellowed and crisp. I've learned almost every song inside, so even without the book, I could play them. But I still don't want the pages to be ruined. Not like my shoes.

Something about the piano was easy to me, easier than any math or English class ever was. I don't know how it all makes so much sense, but it does. I picked up sight-reading sheet music within a week, and Elena says my technique is flawless. She told me I've learned more in six months than most students of the piano learn in six years. She never calls me gifted, but I think maybe, perhaps with this, I am. And this gift…it makes me feel special, like I have a gift or something to offer the world more than a girl with a tragic story. I feel a certain sense of home when my hands are on those keys.

I've been taking a few summer classes, trying to improve my

résumé and add things like theater and art before applying for private schools. It's a longshot, and we can't really pay for them, so I'll need to earn a scholarship, but Elena thinks I can focus on my playing at one of these schools. I've never been really good at anything else, so if there's a chance that I can go to high school and mostly play the piano, I'd like to try. I'll need to look more impressive on paper, though. I've been glad to be busy. If anything, it keeps me from spending the day looking forward to the time Henry gets home from rowing. I'm too embarrassed to ask him if I can come with him to watch. I don't want him to think I'm infatuated, even if most of me totally is.

He's been rowing with some of the guys from Satis House, which I've learned is one of the city's most prestigious private schools. I still wear the shirt he gave me at home sometimes, but never to Elena's. I suppose I don't want him to ask for it back.

Alice has the day off today, but Elena said I could still come. This is the first time I'll be at the house without my "aunt" there. At first, I was afraid Alice would be mad or think that I looked pushy or desperate, which would somehow reflect badly on her. But when I told her, she got hyper-excited about it. I guess instead she felt like it reflected good on her that they don't mind having me around. I am her offering to the Alderman elite!

Either way, I'm probably going to be late now. The train was running behind schedule. Some guy in Cicero broke down on the tracks. When we finally made it to my stop, I missed the sidewalk when I started to run—sinking my feet deep into a pothole puddle. They're my only pair of sneakers, other than my old Converse which aren't much for running.

I spot the rooftop spire of Elena's house and bounce urgently at the crosswalk as traffic zips through the roadway that stands between *on-time* and *late*. It's a Friday; rush-hour traffic has picked up early, and the amount of people slipping through Hyde Park trying to get an edge on freeway traffic is more than usual.

I'm clustered with two men in long coats holding large black umbrellas and briefcases. Somehow, their umbrella points meet just above my head, letting the rain dart through and nail me while they stay dry. I try to lean to my right to sponge off the man with the bigger umbrella and smaller briefcase, but the moment I get my head underneath, he jerks to his right to talk to a woman who is even wetter than my shoes.

"Excuse me...sir...sir?" She's walking toward him with frantic eyes. The green sweatshirt and jeans she has on are plastered to her skin and heavy like washcloths. He's ignoring her, and the closer she gets, the more uncomfortable it makes me feel. There's no way he doesn't see her.

"I ran out of gas. I need to get my daughter to swim practice, and I'm running late. I don't have my wallet, but I promise...if you can spare a couple dollars, I will pay you back. I'll PayPal you, right from my phone..."

As she reaches to pull her phone from her pocket, the man rolls his shoulders and dips his umbrella, moving to the other side of me and the other businessman.

Her eyes begin to fall shut and I recognize the humiliation that colors her cheeks and pulls down the corners of her mouth.

"I have ten dollars. Here," I say, feeling in my back pocket for the soaked bill. I pull it out, folded in quarters, and hand it to her. Her hand covers mine when she takes it, and our eyes meet for a full breath.

"Thank you," she says, droplets of rain cascading from her upper lip. Her breath frosts the air between us as I nod and smile. "What's your email. I'll send you money."

"It's fine. I don't have a PayPal or whatever. Really...it's okay." Her eyes stick to mine for another second, slanting with guilt. "I have a phone. If you call me, I can give you my address or something..."

She begins nodding, handing me her phone to type my information in, shielding it from the rain with her open jacket and sleeve. I give her my full name and number. The crosswalk begins to flash behind me, and I'm bumped by the rush of bodies trying to cross to the other side before it's too late. I hand the woman her phone back, knowing she probably won't ever call but at least the guilt is gone. With my book clutched to my body, I work to rewrap myself in my coat as the wind beats against my chest while I rush to catch up before the light changes. I manage to leap up to the sidewalk over a puddle in front of the fleeing umbrella man, and he catches my arm to spin me around.

"You can't give people money like that. It's a scam. It's raining, for Christ's sake! Swim lessons...in the rain? Use your head." His dark brown eyes beam down on me from underneath thick, blond brows that match his mustache.

"She looked like she was really in need to me." I replay the look on her face in my head, and if that was a scam, I'm impressed by the commitment to her performance. I'll consider my money a tip for a job well done.

"Stupid kid," the man grumbles, rolling his eyes and shaking the water from his umbrella before turning on his heels and heading the opposite way down the street.

I wish I had a snappy comeback, but his words hit my body and make me feel small. My hands shift where I'm clutching the book and my coat, and a few pages from the middle of the book slide out onto the wet sidewalk.

I pick them up quickly, but some of the ink has already started to run. Laying them flat against the back of the book, I hug it tight again and begin to jog down Elena's street. Most of the homes are decorated for fall with orange wreathes on their doors and pumpkins clustered by their steps. The smell of burnt logs taints the air as people rush to enjoy a fire on a rainy early September night. The sky is gray enough to show off the stream of smoke above the Alderman home. I bet it's warm inside.

Just like almost every day since I've been coming here to play, Henry is sitting on the steps outside waiting for me. The gate buzzes before I reach to push it, and I take a deep breath, sucking back tears from the damn balding man who called me *stupid*. I'm not sure what part hurt more—*stupid* or *kid*.

"I wrote an essay for Satis House. Will you read it for me?" Henry stands, pulling a paper folded into fourths from his pocket and stepping out from the overhang into the rain with me. I take it in my hand slowly, noting the fringed torn edge with the pad of my finger. I tap against it. Henry breathes out a short laugh.

"Yeah, I probably should type this shit," he says, leaning to the side and spitting on the ground. His teeth make that short clicking sound as he does it. I wave my hand at him to back up under the cover so his essay—and me—can get dry.

"Why do you spit like that?" I scrunch my face and look up at him —he's gained inches on me, and lately, I have really started to notice. He leans to the side and spits again then laughs.

"Gross," I say, blinking as I roll my eyes and move to his front door.

Despite my regular visits, I still wait for Henry to open the door first. The handful of times I've beaten him to his home, I either rang the bell or waited for him to show up. I'm the help's kid, and I'm not even really Alice's child. I'm there because the courts had nowhere else to put me, and my parents put Alice and Collin on some document they filed for three hundred bucks online when I was six.

Henry steps inside first, swinging the door wide and leaving it open in his wake. I close it behind me, like I always do, then follow him to the sitting room where Elena is usually reading.

"Your shoes are sopping wet," Elena says, startling me from my trance as I work to unfold Henry's essay.

"Oh…" I wince and redden, working my feet to my toes one at a time, trying to lessen the impact my shoes have on the beautiful wood floors.

"Are you trying to hover?" Henry sniggers. I shoot him a glare.

"Well…she's not happy with you," Elena says, closing the book on her lap and leaning forward with her hands clasped together on top. She peers at me over her glasses, a sinister smile glimmering in deep-red lipstick as she puckers.

"Throw them away."

She waves the back of her hand at my feet while she speaks, and I glance down at my shoes. They're wet, but they aren't ruined.

"I'll just leave them outside," I say, lifting one foot to peel my shoe away by the heel. I stop at her glare.

"Right…leave them out where it's raining. Maybe they can smell of mildew forever, leaving you to constantly wonder where that odor is coming from. Wear other shoes. Those are done." She leans back and begins to crack open her book again.

32

"I don't *have* other shoes. Not like these. Not running shoes. And I have a test…"

Her book snaps closed again and she punches out a short laugh.

"You have a test on wet shoes? My God, Lily…what kind of summer school do you go to?"

"It's for her PE credit, Elena," Henry says, coming to my defense. My shoulders relax a little. I love what I've learned here from Elena, her books, and her piano, but more often than not, I feel like she doesn't really like me.

"Ugh," she bites out. "Then take her shopping, Henry. You need a new jacket for interviews anyhow."

This time, when Elena sits back to begin reading again, she fully commits. Her book falls open and her finger moves to the edge of her glasses where she gently moves them up the bridge of her nose.

"Come on," Henry says, bumping my shoulder with the butt of his fist. "We're going shopping."

I follow him back down the hallway, a tinge of longing burning my insides as we pass by the music room without going in. I reach for Henry's arm, grabbing hold to stop him before he takes another step, and his hand flinches to catch mine.

"I just…" My lips freeze along with my body as I stand face to face with Henry, our hands strangely linked more than palm to palm. His fingers flex and twitch at our contact, widening just enough to make room for my own, until we're locked together in this weird, intimate face-off.

My inner voice is ordering me to retreat and let go, but that daring part of me that I've slowly been uncovering over the year I've come here presses on. I stare at Henry's face. His eyes puzzle while his top lip twitches in a way that's either slowly moving to disgust or flirtation. Bold me gets knocked down a peg in a blink when Henry's eyes snap to mine and his lip lifts even higher.

"You never talk about guys or anything. We're almost freshmen now, Lily. Have you had a boyfriend yet?" His lips close when he's done, and tighten at the corners, forming the devil's smirk.

"I don't date yet," I say, pulling back and expecting my hand to fall free. Henry steps closer to me though and tightens his grip.

"Your aunt and uncle are strict? Or is that by your choice?" He's pushing me, something that I've noticed he likes to do. Henry often teases me with certain questions. Last week, it was about my bra size. But his teasing has never crossed into this type of stuff—*romance.*

"Both, maybe," I say, licking my lips and instantly regretting it.

I look down at my feet, now warm and wet in shoes I'm about to throw away apparently.

"You're afraid of dating, aren't you?"

I lift my chin defiantly, but weaken my resolve when met with his eyes. He was cute a year ago, but he's become something more over our last year before high school. Maybe it's his wealth, or the fact that he dresses like he's British royalty or a model in some *Tommy* ad. I think maybe this is what the brink of handsome looks like. Handsome, but dangerous—I feel that in my gut, too.

"I'm not afraid of dating. I just haven't thought about it much, I guess. I study a lot, and it's not like I live with my parents in some normal house, with a mom I can talk to about...*stuff.*"

I blush and look off to the side.

Henry lightly shakes our clasped hands.

"Stuff like sex?" He lifts an eyebrow, and I instantly wish for death.

"No, Henry!" My face puckers because I'm embarrassed, and now I'm upset.

He jiggles our hands again, and I stiffen my arm, no longer amused and no longer distracted by his *almost-handsome* face. He's officially made me mad.

I flex my fingers and wiggle as I take a step back, my music book still hugged with my opposite arm against my chest. Henry stops fighting me after a second and I immediately turn into the music room, pushing the partially opened door enough to step inside. I move to the piano quickly and set my book on the ledge above the covered keys, checking to see how damp the pages I dropped are. They feel cold and like they could tear easily.

"Shit," I mutter.

I feel Henry's shoulder touch mine before he speaks. The cotton of his perfectly pressed shirt tickles my stiff jacket that I'm both glad and regretful to be wearing right now.

"I dropped it. Elena's going to be mad…" I say, pointing to the smeared notes on the top page.

"She will not," Henry says, sliding the top page over to expose the next one, the ink on it blurred even worse. "Well…maybe just a little."

"Gah!" I cover my face with my palms and fall into the sinking feeling that's taken over my insides.

"Hey," he says, his hand light against my wrist. I jerk back as my hands fall from my face, and he stiffens before rolling his shoulders and putting his hands in his pockets. "I was only kidding. She won't even notice this. I promise."

I watch his eyes for some sign that he's lying, but they're nothing but sincere. His head tilts, and I sigh.

"I don't want her to think I don't take care of things she gives me. I want her to give me another one, and I'm just afraid…"

"She will. And she won't notice this. Lily…" There's something in his tone, his voice more man than boy all of a sudden. I've heard it crack several times over the last few months, but there's something completely mature about the way he's talking to me right now. His eyes soft, his smirk nonexistent, lips parted and teeth bared with his tongue held at its tip, Henry Alderman is being sincere.

"I promise." His mouth raps around the words, sealing them as if they are a secret between us. For some mystical reason, I know I'm supposed to believe him right now. And so, I do.

I nod and look at the pages one more time before stepping around him and leading us out of the room, down the rest of the hallway and out his front door. Henry trails behind, and neither of us feel out of place in those roles.

I'm used to trains. When Henry leans into the roadway—completely blocking traffic in one lane while he whistles with fingers in his mouth and holds out a hand to a line of cabs racing by—I almost reach to pull him back to safety. The last taxi through the stoplight pulls over, and Henry rushes to open the backseat door.

"Come on," he says, his youthful smile back where it belongs. The rain has stopped, but the streets are flooded, and I have to leap to make it from the curb to the car. Henry offers his hand, and I take it again, letting him propel me into the car. I let go quickly, and once again, he notices.

"You know, someday you're going to have a boyfriend…and he's going to want to hold your hand." He leans into my shoulder as he climbs into the seat next to me, shutting the door. His mouth quirks a grin. "And hold your…"

I elbow him as he breaks into a soft laugh—that *perfect* laugh I've started to look forward to. I've also started looking forward to seeing him in his crew shirts and the board shorts he rows in. The summer sun and time on the water has bronzed his skin and brightened the gold in his hair, and it's gotten just a little longer. I want to tell him not to cut it, but then he'd ask me *why* I'm so invested in the length of his hair, and then he'd tease me about it.

"I think we should practice," he says.

I turn my attention away from the taxi window and back to him.

"You know…holding hands. I mean it's not like we never have, and it would be good for you. That way when you begin at Jefferson Union High next week and I'm not there to help you through all of those uncomfortable moments when guys are hitting on you and trying to get some…"

"Get some?" I break into his words teasingly, but it's because my heart is beating so hard I'm afraid I might vomit. He's making up a reason to hold my hand. Today—*right now!*

"Oh, guys are gonna want to get some, Lily. And I'm gonna make sure you know how to fight them off." He dips his chin and gives me a serious glare.

"So, you don't want me to have a boyfriend?" The question falls out faster than I give it thought, so I try to peel away any hint of flirtation from it with a steady glare and folded arms.

Henry leans in again, his shoulder warm alongside mine.

"You'll have a boyfriend, Lily. You'll have many." His lips fall into a soft line that hints at a smile and his eyes don't blink but rather settle into this expression that feels like a mask—like he's hiding a secret.

"Doubtful," I say.

"Ha...probable," he retorts. He shifts in his seat and wiggles his head, looking out his window toward the lake as we rush deeper into the city, then turns back to face me with a broad smile and an open palm resting on his knee.

"What do you say? Who knows...maybe you'll like it."

My lungs inflate and burn with a breath I don't remember taking. I'll hold his hand. I'll do it because I want to, because I don't know what other answer to give him or any way to avoid it that won't lead to more teasing. But he's wrong about one thing—I do know. I know I'll like it. And that's precisely why I don't want to.

I form a tight smile and blink hesitantly back into his eyes and let out my breath, my shoulders forced to relax for a moment.

"Fine," I say, shaking my head as if this is somehow torture and I'm just giving in. I slap my palm against his and curl my fingers around the rough and soft parts of his skin, and the moment we connect, I feel the pounding of my heart in my belly.

"What was that?" Henry asks. I lean a few inches away from him and lift my shoulders, looking him back in the eyes.

"What?" I immediately unfurl my hold and feel the heat crawling up my chest and back. Was he tricking me just to tease me? Did he *not* really want me to hold his hand?

"You said *hold your hand*, so I held your hand," I huff.

Henry chuckles.

"Yeah, but...that's not how you hold a guy's hand. Well...if your four, maybe. Or if your buds, and goofing around. But you hold a guy's hand like that your freshman year and I will never have to worry about you having a boyfriend to fight off. They'll think you're either not interested...or..."

"Or what?" I feel sick.

"Or a wrestler...I don't know!" His laughter spills out uncontrollably, and I catch the driver's shoulders shaking with amusement too.

"Ugh!" I tighten my hold on myself, hiding my hands under each of my elbows, and flop my weight back into the seat with a sigh, shifting my attention to the railways and industrial buildings outside.

"Don't give up. Come on...that's why we're doing this. Let me show you." I feel the back of his hand on my elbow and my head jerks to look at it. His fingers gently work my arm loose from my body and I give in quickly. He spreads my palm open and rests my arm and hand on my knee, just like his was.

"Here, like this..." His eyes catch mine as he nods, then gestures to look down and watch this terribly embarrassing lesson on intimacy he's about to give me. My throat is closed, and I haven't taken a breath in what feels like a minute. I dip my chin and watch as Henry's hand gently moves over mine, the tips of his fingers grazing along my wrist, his thumb drawing a soft line straight through the center. The sensation leaves tingles in the wake of his touch, and my fingers start to curl out of my control. The weight of his hand on mine increases, his fingers now moving in unison into the open and waiting space between each of mine until somehow—*naturally*—both of our hands fall in line together.

Henry twists his hand, moving mine along with it, and then shifts his thumb to slide it against my wrist twice. My dad used to do this to my mom's, right before he'd bring her hand to his lips to kiss it. That thought drives a shiver up my arm and neck.

"See the difference?" Henry leans in again after his question, but doesn't let go of my hand.

I glance at him briefly, sure he'll noticed the bright shade of pink my face has turned if I look too long. I nod once and smile as if he's just shown me how to serve in tennis, then look back out my window with a combination of terrified, wide-open eyes and pure glee on my lips.

Henry holds my hand for the entire ride, and when we get out of the car on Michigan Avenue, he finds a way to take my hand again just before we enter the mall. We pass dozens of couples who look just like us only they're real, and I watch the girls' eyes as they swing from Henry to me, judging to see how well we match. A few times, I try to pull my hand away, but Henry keeps us intact, sometimes so we're only linked by a single finger or two. Every new position excites me, and I dread how much I'm liking this.

Finally, we get to my favorite shoe store, and Henry lets go so I can roam the stacks of shoes in search of my size. When I find a pair I like, I rush to a seat and unbox them quickly, worried that he'll kneel in front of me and try to slip the shoe on for me. I think people would stare if he did that.

Once both shoes are on my feet, over my still slightly damp socks, and tied, I stand and walk over to the mirror slanted near the ground and lift my heels one at a time.

"How do they look?" I glance over my shoulder at Henry, who's on his phone and holds up a finger.

"One sec," he says, typing out something with his thumbs then putting his phone away in his pocket. He leans forward with his elbows rested on his knees and squints at my feet, then nods.

"They look just like your old shoes." He leans back and folds his hands behind his neck as he smiles.

"Is that good? Or bad?" I probably shouldn't have asked.

"It's…shoes." He shrugs, so I sigh and look back at the reflection of my feet, bouncing on my toes a few more times.

"And they're dry," I add, deciding to be done shopping. "I'll take them, and I'd like to wear them out," I say to the clerk. He nods and puts my old, still-damp shoes in the box and walks up to the counter.

Henry pulls his wallet out and slides a credit card free with his thumb. I notice his name on the bottom, and I start to cringe over the fact that he's buying me shoes.

"I'll pay you back," I whisper, leaning in close. I miss his hand.

"Nah. Elena puts money in my account. She's the one buying these and she'd hate it if you paid her back." He smiles down at me then turns back to the counter to sign his name on the receipt.

The clerk hands the bag with my old shoes and the new box to me, and I wrap the strings around my wrist, keeping the box between Henry and me like a barrier. I thought this through in the few seconds it took him to pay, and I figured if the logistics were too hard for him to hold my hand, he wouldn't. Not that I don't want him to, but I like thinking that he's not because my hand simply isn't free, not because he doesn't want to.

We retrace our steps back to the front of the mall, and Henry stops at the pretzel store to buy a lemonade on our way out. He offers me a sip, and I decline because in my now-twisted psyche, drinking after Henry would be equivalent to kissing him.

I've gone mad.

The flash of deep blue and a rich shade of pink forces my eyes to pay attention. I stop a few steps behind Henry to stare at the short but flowy dress paired with white Converse on the mannequin in the window. I've never been much for shopping, and even when I was younger and would come here with my mom to pick out Easter dresses or things for school events, I'd let her do the browsing. I was fine with whatever I wore. But this dress—*I want to wear this dress.*

"Hey, sorry...didn't see you stop," Henry says, pausing to slurp through his straw. "That's pretty," he nods toward the dress.

I smile at it and picture it on my body, lining my head up with the form in the window to see how I look in the reflection.

"It is," I agree.

Henry makes a louder slurping noise, and I breathe out a short laugh, glancing at him. He nods back toward the window.

"Let's get it," he says, walking past me and into the store. I shake with a mix of surprise and fear, forgetting my temporary rule about shoe barriers as I grab his arm.

"No, no! It's fine. I just wanted to look at it...Henry..." He laughs me off, wiggling out of my hold and moving his drink to the opposite hand.

I trail him into the store, letting the distance between us grow while I think about bolting to the nearest restroom. Henry jets toward a college-aged guy wearing a short-sleeved white shirt and a purple bowtie with suspenders. His badge says JARED. I swallow while they talk, and my feet pool with the blood draining from all parts of my body. I shift my weight so I don't pass out.

Henry and Jared walk toward the window, and I move with them, only because I look suspicious hovering near the entrance.

"I think we have two more in the back. Let's see..." Jared turns to face me and puts his fingertips on both of my shoulders as he gazes me up and down. "Probably a medium."

I can feel the wrinkle deepen between my brow. That's where my worry lines go. I'm worried. More accurately, I'm nervous. I'm stressed. Is it too late to sprint for the nearest bathroom?

"You look like you're going to vomit. Don't throw up," Henry says, his lips closing around his straw. He smiles while he drinks.

"I'm just not comfortable with other people buying things for me... and I saw the price. How about I just try it on?" Even admitting that made my stomach tighten.

Jared's already found the medium, and he's holding it draped over both arms as if he's bestowing me with a queen's cape. "This dress is going to look great on you!" he beams.

My mouth falls wordlessly open.

"It sure will," Henry adds. I turn my head to face him quickly, my mouth still frozen. He grins and takes another drink, his cup now almost empty. He sucks the final droplets and breathes out, "Ahh."

"Ring us up," Henry says, twirling his finger in the air.

I start to shake my head and force the dress into Henry's hands. Jared has already sprinted to a register.

"Henry, no. I don't really want it..."

He stops abruptly, turning to face me, and I nearly plow into his chest. He lifts my chin with his fingertips, and our eyes lock. His pupils grow and the black deepens, bleeding into the deep lines that slash through the greenish-brown.

"It's okay to want things, Lily," he says.

I nod and start to answer with "I know, but..."

His thumb presses against my bottom lip, and my mouth quivers. He has to notice.

"And it's okay that I want to buy you something."

I blink, numb as if his touch has stung me with poison. I think maybe it has.

Henry runs his thumb along the width of my lip once and lets his hand fall away, grinning as he turns back to face Jared. I wait a few steps behind him, stupefied and madly in a crush that is going to kill me. I barely move when Henry hands me the bag with my new, beautiful dress, and I don't actually speak when he tells me the blue color is kind of like my eyes. He also doesn't try to hold my hand again—not through the mall or in the cab ride home.

I'm disappointed, yet glad. I've let myself dwell on a fantasy today, which I have never done before. I've liked boys, and I've gossiped about that stuff at school with friends. I haven't done much of that since my parents died, though, and I haven't really clicked with anyone in our neighborhood since I've lived with Alice and Collin. Not like I have with Henry, at least.

There's a deep-red SUV waiting in the driveway when we get back to Henry's house. I never see people visit, at least not during any of the times I've ever been here over the course of nearly a year. I open my mouth to ask Henry who it could be, but before I can he exits the cab, tossing money through the front window, and begins to jog over to the vehicle, turning to wave to me just before he opens one of the back doors.

"I had fun today, Lily. Just text me what you think about the essay later, okay?" Music spills from the open door but cuts off the second he slams it shut, now inside and sitting next to a girl with straight, silky-blonde hair. I hold up my palm to wave as the woman driving smiles and turns her wheel, maneuvering the car around the circular drive-way. She bunches her hand at me as if we know each other. We do not.

Like a dumbfounded fool, I gawk through the back window, watching Henry lean into the girl just as he did with me. I close my hand into a fist, remembering his touch while I imagine he plays the same game with her. I picture her laughing and knowing how to hold his hand the first time.

"Lily, did you want to play today?" Elena's voice is practically a drowned-out echo behind me.

"Actually…" I say, turning to meet her eyes. She's holding the door open, welcoming me in. I don't know where Henry's gone to, or when he'll be back, but I know I'd like to be gone before he comes home. "I'm finishing up my application for Satis today, so I really should be getting home."

"Oh," she steps forward, one foot now on her front steps. "I didn't know you were thinking of that one. How…wonderful." Her smile is polite. She either senses my bullshit or knows my chances of getting in are terribly slim. The encouragement, even if it's just to be nice, still feels good though.

"Thank you for the shoes," I say, a wave of nerves rattling through my core because I just remembered I'm holding two bags. I look like a moocher. I'm not sure if I should bring up the dress or not. I'm thankful for both. Sort of.

Elena waves her hand, and I notice her eyes glance to both bags—two store labels.

"Henry insisted I get a dress…I guess I don't have many or whatever." That could not have possibly come out more desperate.

Elena's eyes crinkle with her smile, her face shaded with a touch of pity.

"Of course. I'm sure it's lovely on you. Maybe we'll have you over for dinner, so you can wear it one night."

I swallow hard, praying that invite never comes. It sounded like one of those things people just say, so I take it as that.

"Thanks. And…thank Henry for me…whenever he gets home." I turn to leave simply so I can scrunch my eyes and chastise myself for adding that little passive aggressive bit on the end. I should have just said thank you and left.

"I'll tell him in the morning. I'm sure he'll be out late," she says, sharing a fact I preferred not to know. Now I can obsess on that, imagining an entire night of Henry and blonde beauty holding hands, and kissing. *Kissing!* I bet with her there is kissing.

Somehow, I'm strong enough to keep walking without adding more to this conversation, and I push through the gate, letting it slam to a close behind me. The iron fencing rattles all the way to the corner, the noise keeping me company as I walk quickly and rush my steps across the street. I get to the train station about twenty minutes before the next train is due to arrive heading back in my direction, and I almost convince myself to take one going the other way just to ride for a while. I know I'd only be compelled to look for him, though. To look for *them.*

When my train pulls up finally, I slip into the last car, taking a corner seat near the back where homeless people normally sleep and tuck their rolled-up sleeping bags. There are only two men in here with me today, and they're passed out drunk and unshowered. A few rows separate us, and normally I'd move. Then again, normally I wouldn't be back here hiding with them in the first place. Instead, today, I sink into the seat and open the top of the dress bag against my chest so I can reach in and feel the delicate, light fabric. I squeeze it in my palm and tuck my chin to breathe in the linen scent. I did love this dress the moment I saw it. Now, though…I'm not so sure.

CHAPTER 4

I applied to Satis House almost as a dare to myself. It wasn't even an option I allowed myself to plan for on paper, because the odds of being accepted were so slim. I had to fluff answers for most of the questions, and my essay vaguely steered close to the question. Collin helped me with it, though I wrote it after planning with him.

The question was to talk about influences in our life—meaning *people,* I am sure. On Collin's advice, I wrote about my parents' deaths and the severe turn my life took. One accident with ripples felt all over the place. It wasn't a very happy essay, but it was an honest one, and I suppose that—or the guilt that comes with denying a teenaged girl who recently lost her parents—is the reason I'm hauling a wagonful of the few things I own along the Thirty-First Avenue sidewalk toward the girls' dormitory.

The letter came exactly one week ago. I had one offer from a prep school in Wisconsin, and that school came with room and board expenses we wouldn't have been able to pay even if the three of us had six jobs apiece. I was ready for my freshman year to play out at Jefferson Union along with four-thousand other faces in a sea of adolescents. I knew the envelope was special the moment my fingers felt the paper. It was thicker than a normal piece of mail—the paper ridged and expensive, my name typed on the front.

More than just being accepted, though, somehow my financial aid application earned me enough to cover everything. Free private school education, far away from Alice and Collin—a young couple who didn't really want kids. I was going whether I wanted to or not.

And I wanted to. Even though my palms won't stop sweating today, I want this. I want this more than I've ever wanted anything.

Alice is with Elena today, so Collin switched for a night shift to help me move in. I'm glad it's him. He's less structured, like me, and I'm too nervous to have someone pointing out things I'm doing wrong today.

"Maybe this is how you earn your scholarship—one stair at a time," Collin says through a half-grunt, half-laugh. I join him, unable to see him around the box full of jeans, tees and sweaters clutched in my hands and resting on my face as I climb up the final flight of stairs.

"I bet the view from the sixth floor is amazing," I say.

"Lily, if you're stuck looking at a brick wall your stuff is not coming back down these stairs for at least nine months. And if there's an option to leave everything here for good, like a donation after you graduate, by all means, please can we do that?" He huffs out a breath as he leans against the stairwell wall and kicks open the door, holding it with his ankle while I catch up.

I smile at him as I pass, finally about to see him around the box. He's carrying things on hangers. Bedding was our first trip, and my books and laptop will be last. We came in a cab, so the front desk let us load everything near the mailroom so we could make trips.

"At least I'm not one of those girls with a lot of shoes," I say, turning back into the hallway in time to trip over what felt like a tall set of boots.

My box flies from my hands, flipping end over end but somehow remaining intact despite the weak tape holding the seams together.

"Oh my God, I'm so sorry!" A short girl with braces and long, dark, braided hair twisted down her back rushes to help me up from the floor.

"It's okay," I say, holding in the swear I almost let slip when the carpet burned away the skin on my elbow. It stings, so I avoid touching it right now.

"My brother left those out here. I asked him to bring them in, but he was trying to prove a point—something about not working for me. Anyhow, I wasn't going to give in either, and my mom will be here soon and I thought I'd drop a little hint about how he's not really helping me just so I could get him in trouble, but now that I've sabotaged you...I see how immature that all was. Here..." She grabs the thick pair of blue rubber and tan leather snow boots and flings them into the door across from us.

"That's right! You get your own damn boots!" a cracking voice shouts from deep within the room.

The girl rolls her eyes then holds out her hand for me to take.

"I'm Anya. I'm here from Boston. And I cannot wait to be away from my brother!" She yells that last part over her shoulder.

"Same here!" her brother shouts back from inside.

I laugh at their banter as Anya shakes her head in apology. I'm an only child. My parents never even talked about the idea of it being otherwise, but I used to pretend that I had a sibling. Truth be told, I had an imaginary brother-slash-sometimes-sister far longer than a maturing girl should. I liked the way people treated me when I shared stories about things my sibling did—like trips we took or holiday meals. None of it was real, except in my head.

"I'm Lily. I live on the other side of the city, so...not quite Boston. But...with rush hour it feels like it." I shake Anya's hand and instantly think of Henry. I wonder where he is? I wonder if he'd approve of this handshake? I'm giving him too much space in my head.

"Which room are you?" Anya asks.

"Six eleven," Collin shouts in a grunt. He's been standing, patiently waiting while my things slowly slip from his grasp a piece of clothing at a time.

"Yes! Sorry Collin!" I pick up my box and smile to my new friend— a *prep school friend*.

"Well, this is me. Stop in later, when you're done," she says, pointing her thumb over her shoulder.

I nod and smile.

"I will!"

Collin collapses with the heap of clothing on my bed, and I drop the box just inside the door and lean against the wall as I wipe the sweat from my brow.

"It's seventy degrees out, but it feels like ninety," I say.

"It's because it's still humid." Collin rolls and grunts as he tries to free himself from my pile of clothes. It makes me laugh, and for the first time since we accepted the Satis House offer, I feel a tinge of sadness—I'm going to miss him and Alice. Mostly him.

"You start putting things away. I'll run down and grab your computer and book bag. I'll be right back," he says, shaking out his fatigued arms.

With exaggeration, he high-steps a jog in place, bringing his knees up to his chest as he salutes me. His enthusiasm carries him right into the chest of a man whose body fills the entire frame of our door. Collin literally bounces off the man's chest with an "*Oof!*"

My eyes widen, growing bigger when I take in the truly massive man with arms busting through his T-shirt sleeves. He looks like one of those famous wrestlers, or…like an action figure.

"Dude…I'm so sorry," Collin says, shaking his head, clearly a little rattled. He holds his hand out to introduce himself, but the man only gives him a wry grin and walks the rest of the way into the room.

"That your bed?" He points to my pile of clothes, and I look back at it to confirm what he's talking about as if I suddenly don't know where I am.

"Yeah…" I stammer for a few seconds, half worried that some mix-up has made this forty-something-year-old my roommate.

"Cool. Hey, Nick…looks like you're here," he says, pressing his enormous hand on the center of the opposite mattress.

My eyes scan in a circle, searching for "Nick;" they land on a girl with jet-black, straight hair. It's shaved on her right side and hangs down to her shoulder on the left. Her eyes are practically purple, clearly accented with contact lenses, and a diamond stud glimmers on the side of her nose.

"That's fine. Okay, I'm good, Dad. You can go now," the girl says abruptly. I can almost see the resemblance underneath a layer of pale

48

makeup and thick black liner under her eyes. Despite being so opposite, there's something oddly similar between her and this man.

"What? You don't want me to hang out?" The man's voice booms, the sound growing as he laughs.

"Uhh...no," the girl says, sitting on her bed next to an overstuffed surplus duffle. She pulls the strap from her shoulder and her dad sets the bag he was carrying down on the floor next to her.

Rubbing his hands together he turns to face me, giving me an intimidating grin. There's a credit-card-sized gap between his front teeth.

"I'm Raj. This attitude behind me here is Nicki." His daughter sighs heavily, and I'm not sure if I should laugh at his joke or defend my new roommate. I pause with my mouth gaped open and Collin steps in to make things more humiliating.

"I'm Collin," he says, taking Raj's hand from the side. The giant man shakes his head and quirks a brow up to his hairline. "This lovely flower here is not my daughter...err...not that I'm some creepy old boyfriend. No...no, she's *like* my daughter. Uhm, basically, her parents died, and my wife was her mom's cousin, and we were the only close family, so...*ta-da!*"

Ta-da. Fucking ta-da.

"I'm Lily," I break in, trying to save this massively awful first impression.

I peel Collin's hand free from Raj's grip and replace it with my own, trying to make my fingers as firm as possible. Raj has enough awareness to know he could crush me, so his palm relaxes as we shake. His eyes shift from Collin to me, and the confused wrinkle dissipates and his strange smile returns.

"Nice to meet you, Lily. I notice you don't have a nose ring..."

"Dad!" Nicki growls from behind him.

Her dad drops my hand just as Nicki starts to push him in the bicep.

"You promised that you wouldn't do this—make things weird. You're making things weird. Now go. I'll see you in two weeks. You're an hour away..." Her dad stumbles playfully toward the door.

"Fine, fine," he says, hugging Nicki and swallowing her whole with his arms.

"I should take off too. I'll just run and grab the last of your things then I'll get on," Collin pipes up, standing and patting me on the back like I'm a puppy he's training with treats and affection.

"Right…well…Raj!" Collin says.

I cringe behind his back.

"You said an hour away. Are you heading south by chance?" Collin asks as the two of them head back into the hallway.

"Do you live south?" Raj asks.

"I do! Yes…I was thinking we could share a cab, unless you have a car and maybe I could…"

"I live up north," Raj interjects.

I hear Collin's sad, "Oh," squeak out as our door falls closed behind them. My new roommate and I sit in utter stillness for several long seconds, our hands mutually planted on our foreheads and our mouths hung open and unsure of how to put words to the adults who are somehow responsible for us.

"I think the important takeaway for you to know about me based on that is Collin and I share zero blood relation. Like…none. Our genes do not cross at all," I say, slicing the air in both directions with my hand gestures.

Nicki's shoulders shake with laughter and she cups her mouth. The smile on her wide lips shows through the sides, and I instantly envy her deep-maroon lipstick.

"He called you a *lovely flower*," she says through hard laughter.

"He did," I nod.

"And…*ta-da!*" She snort-laughs which only makes her laugh harder. I join in, mortified but also grateful for this icebreaker that I'm certain is not what Collin intended.

"I don't know what to say. He's literally never acted that way. I think maybe he had a man crush on your dad," I say.

Nicki chuckles and rolls her eyes.

"He gets that a lot. He's a former pro-football player. It's usually the moms that get all stupid around him. Your dad might be the first man crush." She catches herself, and I recognize it in her eyes.

She called him my dad.

"It's okay," I wave off before she can apologize.

Collin brings the last of my things up and leaves with his dignity the second time. I move to my clothes pile and begin sorting and making sense of my mess. A second or two later, Nicki does the same, dumping her bag on her bed—almost everything she owns is black or gray; my bed is vibrant with color. Our only crossover is the plaid skirt, deep-blue cardigan sweater and white-collared shirt. Where I have three sets of everything, Nicki has one. I sense her plan to rebel on the encouraged uniform.

On the surface, she and I look like complete opposites. Yet, as the day moves on, more little things reveal themselves linking all the ways we're the same. Like me, Nicki is here on a scholarship. My emphasis is performing arts, and so is hers—she is here for technical theater and set design. She's an only child, and despite her dad's lie, she grew up about ten miles away from where Collin and Alice live—though in a much nicer neighborhood. She likes all types of music, and scary movies, and cotton candy, and her favorite pizza topping is mushrooms.

We only get into my parents for a short conversation, and she's quick to understand when I'm done sharing. In the span of a single morning, I've already made more friends than I ever did at Alice and Collin's, and I already feel closer to Nicki than any friend I've ever had before.

Almost.

As if some supernatural force was alerting him that nearly an entire day was about to pass where he wasn't my sole obsession, Henry taps out "Shave and a Haircut" on our door. He opens it wide before either of us call for him to come in, and his blunt entry puts Nicki off in an instant.

"Nice room!" Already dressed in his uniform, his wrist glimmers with shiny platinum cufflinks, the crisp white of his shirt popping from the deep-maroon and blue of his vest.

"Hey, Abercrombie ad...you weren't invited!" Nicki stands and folds her arms over her chest, and Henry's eyes fall to her heavy-duty boot-clad feet.

"Right…well, I'm not a vampire, so that rule is sorta…" he winks and tilts his head to the side. His charm is not going to help here. I can tell. And I am oddly relieved that Nicki isn't interested.

Before she can launch at him, I step between them and flatten my hand on Henry's chest. I can feel every mile he rowed over the summer in his chest muscles underneath his uniform.

"Sorry Nicki…this is my friend. This is Henry. And he's sorta used to getting his way," I say, twisting my lips and scowling at him.

He holds his palms out and shrugs an apology.

"So he's a privileged asshole?" Nicki asks, glancing at me. She's joking, but she's also…sorta…not.

"He's not an asshole," I sigh out. Henry's mouth curls into a smug grin, satisfied with my stamp of approval. He falls into my bed and pulls my pillow free to tuck it behind his head as he crosses his ankles. His body barely fits.

"Hmmm, that's up for debate," Nicki says.

Her gaze drags from Henry's body to me, and when our eyes meet I try to apologize for him with my expression. She shakes her head slightly, just enough that I see it. "I'm going to run down to the common and grab some snacks. Want anything?"

"I'm okay," I smile, wondering if she thinks Henry and I are a thing and she's trying to give us privacy. I decide in a split second that I don't care if she has it wrong.

"I'll take some chips," Henry says as my roommate heads out our door. She flips him off over her shoulder and the door slams closed behind her.

"She's charming," he says with a tight smile. I sit on Nicki's bed across from him even though my entire nervous system is firing alarms that I am missing an opportunity to be close to him.

"She's actually really cool. And you should probably knock. I could have been changing," I say.

Henry wiggles his brows and sits up, tossing my pillow to the corner behind him.

"You're such a perv," I say.

"Yeah, yeah," he says, standing. He stretches his arms up high and the tips of his fingers skim our low ceiling. This building is nearly a hundred years old, and I guess less space is easier to heat, so the rooms are all tight and small.

Right now, alone with Henry, behind a closed door—it's suffocating.

"So...did you meet your roommate?" My legs swing nervously against Nicki's mattress. Henry lets his hands fall back down to his sides like strands of spaghetti and his shoulders slump.

"He's such a nerd," he says, leaning against the edge of my small desk.

"There's nothing wrong with nerds. I'm a nerd," I protest, defending this stranger. I don't like it when Henry judges people.

"Yeah, well then you live with him." He laughs at his own joke and I just crook my neck and glare at him sideways. "Sorry...you're right. Honestly, the guy will probably help me out a ton. He's an engineering focus too, and I have a feeling his math is a lot stronger than mine. I just don't know how cool he'll be...ya know."

I bunch my face and squint my eyes. *I don't know.* I maintain my puzzled expression until he explains.

"Like sneaking out and stuff, or having girls in our room after hours, or drinking. Just...stuff." He shrugs as if his version of our freshman year is what's normal and not the other way around.

"Maybe he'll keep you out of trouble," I say, standing and ushering him away from my desk. He's knocked over a few things already just by sitting on the edge. I right my pen cup and rearrange my glass bears that I've had since I was four. I can feel Henry staring at me, so I turn slowly to catch him.

"What?" I ask.

"You're strange. I think you might be OCD. Aren't those the people who have to turn lights off and on and stuff?"

I huff but go back to my desk, tucking away my notepads and leaving everything tidy. I pull the comforter even from where Henry left it askew. So what if I'm a little OCD. My mom always told me there was nothing wrong with being neat.

"I was thinking of looking around a little before practice. That's why I came by actually. I know you took the tour last week, but I thought maybe I could give you the *unofficial tour.*" Henry smirks, which makes me nervous.

"The dark underbelly of Satis House?" I joke.

"Oh…dark indeed," he says, rubbing his hands together like he's evil. He gives in quickly, though. "Nah, nothing like that. Just short-cuts, the best places to take your lunch, the door that gets you on the roof—shit like that."

"You can get on the roof?" The thought excites me. I've always envied the people that live downtown in the high rises and can look out over the lake. The water goes on forever. I'd love to wake up to see it every morning, and I'm willing to climb out on a roof.

"Yeah, come on. Grab your sweatshirt though. It's windy up there." I open the closet door to find my soft blue sweatshirt, and when I grab it, Henry notices his old crew shirt hanging just behind it.

"Hey, I was wondering where that thing was…" He says, reaching for it and pulling it free from the hanger. My stomach sinks. I love that shirt and the childish memory attached to it of me and Henry sliding around wooden floors.

"Yeah…I've been meaning to give it back, but I just always forget," I lie.

Henry's mouth hangs open, his tongue lodged between his teeth. He knows the truth, but for once he's considering not embarrassing me. His lips curl into a soft smile while he bites the tip of his tongue, eventually nodding and flitting his eyes to mine. He drapes the shirt against my shoulders and arms as if he's gauging how I look in it.

"Yeah, you know what? You keep it. I've got others, and this one's your only Satis House shirt. Besides, I like that you're our fan." He winks and my lips tingle trying to contain my grin. I know he made that up to spare me, and the simple fact that he probably senses I wanted to keep the shirt just because it was his gives me that good kind of blush—the one that warms my chest and fills me with butterflies.

"Thanks," I say, deciding to wear the long-sleeved shirt over my plain gray T-shirt. I pull it over my head and push my arms through the sleeves then pat my hand against the emblem on the front. "And I'm probably the only crew-team fan in existence," I laugh out.

Henry shakes his head with a smug grin.

"Nope. We've got a lot of hot moms who support us." He folds his arms proudly and I smack his arm playfully. Every time we act like this together, I remember the day in the car—the trip to the mall where we walked hand-in-hand. The best things with Henry seem to only happen once. The house where we skated around the floors sold a week after we broke in.

Henry wasn't joking about the wind on the roof. He took me to the newest building that houses most of the science and fitness classes as well as the gym. A small door between the girls' and boys' locker-room doors hides a stairwell that climbs four stories up. It comes out on a flat roof that faces northeast with nothing tall in front of it. The view is breathtaking.

"Wow." I gape at the water, squinting from the reflection of the sun along the choppy waves.

Henry takes a deep breath and folds his arms around his body, tucking his arms under his biceps and bouncing on his feet a few times to stave off the chill.

"It's pretty great, right? The first time I came up here I knew this would be the place I went to hide." His eyes drift out to look at the same view I was just taking in. I take advantage and look at him. His jaw works, teeth chewing at his inside and eyes flickering from the bright reflection on the lake.

"What do you hide from?" His mouth twitches at my question.

"People, I guess." His answer is too simple, but I know better than to press for more. I've known him for a year, yet what I know *of* him is so basic. He rarely shows his emotions, and sometimes I wonder if he ever gets upset. I suppose I don't share when I'm excited or upset either, but I have the luxury of knowing I feel both the highs and lows. I experience them. I don't have proof that Henry does, other than this one tiny clue that this space up here is where he plans to come to bury his secrets.

"How did you get up here before you were a student?" I know

Elena is a graduate and a major donor to the school. Her money heeds a lot of control over this place from what little I was able to read in online articles and gossip posted about Satis.

He shrugs at first, but after a few moments of silence, he snaps back to present, leaving whatever troubles he was burying behind.

"Elena thought it would be cool if I got to know the engineers on the project when this was built. I came out with this guy Lionel; he's the president or CEO or whatever of the company. He basically got the bid because of Elena, so it's not like he could say no. Anyway…I'm sure I was supposed to learn some cool technical shit that would make me uber-successful when I'm twenty-five, but all I basically took away from those meet-ups was how to get through the door."

He holds his palm open to unveil a key, and I flash my eyes wide.

"We're not supposed to be up here?" My pulse jets. All of my firsts with Henry seem to be about breaking rules!

"If that door wasn't locked, everyone would be up here. Nah…this place is private." His mouth forms a crooked smile as he pushes the key deep in his pocket and holds out both hands toward me with his palms up.

"Private, huh?" Nervously, I reach for him. He is going to feel my fear the moment our hands touch.

"I mean…I guess I could let you borrow the key anytime you want," he winks, immediately chuckling when my hands nervously cover his.

"You are still a bad hand-holder, Lily Ames!" His voice echoes off the retaining walls that we could easily climb over on a dare if we wanted to. That thought continuously runs through my mind because daring things seem to be Henry's muse.

"Shut up, jerk! I'm nervous because I didn't know I was going to break the law on my first day of school!" I grab his hands firmly, maybe a little anger in my hold. Henry just throws his head back and laughs at the sky.

"There's no law about being on a roof, Lily Ames…" His chin falls and his eyes settle on mine with all of the warmth of the sun. His teeth barely part, hiding his tongue behind the devious smile that lives on those lips.

"Quit saying my entire name!" I shake his hands once in mine as I shout nonsense at him. He's trying to goad me. He does this sometimes. I'd rather not be goaded on a rooftop though.

"Lily Ames." The words spill out in a breath, all gravely and deep in a voice that switched from young to mature over the course of our relationship. I narrow my eyes on his in a challenge, defiant only because I don't want to give in. I'm stubborn. Always stubborn rather than giving over and letting Henry bring out my joy.

He works for it, just as he does every time. Like an older brother poking at his baby sister's weak spots, he sings my name out loud, so loud I'm sure it's carried over the roof and into the corridor below.

"Shhhhh!" I say, stepping closer to him and flattening one of my palms over his mouth. I can feel his breath as he laughs, and damn him the entire thing forces my mouth to curl into a relenting smile.

"Lily! Ames! Rooftop dancer!" He howls after he declares my latest dare for the entire world—at least this small corner of Chicago.

"Henry!" I giggle out his name, my hand still struggling to cover his mouth, doing a poor job of it. Tangled arms and hands wrestle, while our feet jockey for dominant positions. I'm destined to lose—I always am with him—both because of his six-inch advantage and because my heart gives in too quickly.

My grip weakens just as his slows and grows more tender, his hands both cuffing my wrists loosely, one in the space between us and one against his cheek, a light brush of his jawline runs against my skin as he shifts my hand just enough for his lips to dust against my veins.

My constant state of vibration is making the earth move in my vision. This is the first time I've held his hand minus playful slaps since the cab ride, which was so very special. This moment right here has left that memory completely in the dust.

Henry presses a soft—no...a *precious*—kiss against my wrist before holding it firmly against his cheek. At some point we began to rock our steps, and as Henry's eyes reflect against the setting sun, the brown and green mix in a hypnotic gaze that stops my heart ever so briefly. It skips. I die, just for a breath. I die—and I come back.

"Dance with me," he says, lips falling into the casual smile a boyfriend would wear. Perhaps it's just the smile of a truly best friend.

A best friend whose lips have the power to cripple me with smiles and slight touches.

"Okay," I say, voice crackling through the word. Henry's chest quakes with quiet laughter at my expense.

"Always so nervous," he says, drawing me to his chest, pressing my right hand to his chest as he abandons it. His other hand follows the curve of my side and the lower part of my back. I fit with him, my head falling under the weight of his chin while we draw tiny circles with our feet under a beam of rays that poke holes through Midwestern clouds. The air is getting crisp, and I tuck my face against his warmth, thankful for the excuse. I smell him—his shirt like warm, pressed cotton, his cologne a wooden honey and spice. I listen to his heartbeat through his chest, through bones and skin, his body against mine.

I have no idea what we are, or why I'm the one he brought up here. I fight off those thoughts that tear me down, screaming that it will be another girl tomorrow. It doesn't matter, because today…it's me. I'm the girl in Henry Alderman's arms dancing as the sun sets, welcoming four years of a future I've dreamed of in a place I somehow was lucky enough to come.

This place is for secrets. And this shall be mine.

CHAPTER 5

Theology is not my best subject. Two months into my first semester, and I am barely holding on to my *B*. Everyone at Satis is expected to have a "well-rounded education." For a girl whose family—both the version with my parents and the life I have now—has never set foot in a place that could remotely be considered a church, a semester of theology is a lot like hell.

Not that I would know, because apparently, I have no concept of what hell is. I failed my quiz on the subject. Mr. O'Farland is letting me retake it—tomorrow. Which means tonight, while my roommates are singing off-key karaoke in the common area with everybody else, I am in the study room that painfully overlooks the fun I won't be having.

"All right, your expert on hell has arrived. What do you need to know?" Henry flops into the leather of the couch that backs up to the window, folding his hands behind his head as he kicks up his feet.

Normally, I welcome his distraction. But right now, all I want to do is get this information from this book to somehow stick in my head for twenty-four hours. I don't have time for distractions—even ones that smell like cinnamon and fire and take up the entire length of the sofa with their body.

"I'm going to fail. I'm going to fail, and then I will slip to a *D* in that class, and then I will lose my scholarship." I start to cry from panic, so I slam my book closed and ball my fists against my ears. I'm melting down in front of him. Not my best moment.

"Relax," he says, and my initial reaction is to fling my book from my desktop. Henry catches it right before it hits the floor. I deflate into the wooden chair, the railings hard against my tired back. I've been hunched over, staring at these pages, for two straight hours.

"You know this stuff…" he starts, but I interrupt with an emphatic shake of my head. When his fingers splay out over my back I freeze. I follow the path my book takes back to the place it started in front of me as Henry slides it in place, flipping open to the chapter I'm trying to memorize. Knelt down next to me, he leans closer, resting his right arm next to my left one—we are touching.

I swallow. I'm going to fail. I cannot memorize something like the varied historical degrees of differences between a Protestant hell and a Lutheran one while the master of all hotness is sharing a desktop with me. My arm hairs are literally electric, standing up and reaching to plant themselves in his skin. I've gone completely primal—my body convinced that I am the gatherer in need of this hunter.

"Look," he says, leaning in even closer and reaching to flip the pages. I barely register the movement of his thumb under a bold section of words. When his eyes catch mine still stuck on his face, I jump in my seat a little.

"Sorry," I say, clearing my throat. "I'm just overwhelmed. Maybe a little slow, too, from being in here so long."

It's partly true, but I'm also just crushing. *Crushing*—that's what Nicki calls it. She rolls her eyes every time she catches me doing it too, then labels it with that word. I crush in the dining area. I crush between classes when Henry pokes my arm with his index finger as we pass in the halls. I crush when I watch him sprint across the lawn every day at three in the afternoon, late for rowing. It's literally become how I know it's three o'clock! My body just instinctually glides toward my window at exactly 2:59. Pathetic!

At this point, we should just say that I'm crushed rather than crushing. Crushed and utterly destroyed of all pride.

I am gatherer.

"What you need to do is make up a rhyme. Something that will help you keep all of the key words in your brain so when it comes time to write them down in order, you'll have them there."

I draw in my lips and let the acid climb up my throat.

"I don't even understand *that*. Ugg, I'm hopeless," I say, letting my head fall flat against the book. I bounce my forehead there lightly while I eke out a desperate laugh at my own expense.

"You aren't hopeless." I feel the warm breath from his chuckle and smell the mint of his gum, and it's intoxicating enough without his touch, so when the warm hand slides the hair from my cheek I go full hypnosis. His fingers trace my jaw, and my head lifts from the light pressure of his hold. For a moment, I believe in myself just because of the look in his eyes when our stares meet. He's dead serious—and God, the way he's looking at me, hair all tousled, smile soft and true, cheeks lifted as if they're glad to see me.

Like a drunk, I lean closer, my lips parting and ready—my mind imagining everything I'm about to feel—Henry's mouth on mine, the graze of teeth against my lips, us standing as his arms sweep around my back before his hands rush up my spine into my own messy hair.

None of that happens.

I get an inch away from his mouth, my eyelids fluttering with nerves and uncertainty whether they should close or remain open, and Henry turns a few inches to his left, stiffening and backing away just enough to keep me from making this worse—*as if I can make this worse somehow*. The rush of heat that coats me isn't from passion—it's from humiliation. My eyes remain open just long enough to see the movement in his neck as he clears his throat. His soft smile is replaced with a hard line, drawn under the pity that slants his eyes.

I think I understand hell a little better now. It helps that I'm in it.

"I'm just tired. I…" Why I try to speak, I don't know.

"It's fine." His voice is laced with discomfort. In one blink I erased everything that was easy between us. All because of my damn fantasies.

Fine. That word—so short, so four-lettered. Such a lie. I ruined everything.

"It's the stress…and I really have been at this for a while. I think I probably need a break, or to get outside or…"

Henry stands while I stammer, pushing his hands in the back pockets of his jeans and backing away a few steps.

"No, no…I get it. Your test is tomorrow. I should probably let you keep cramming. I'm…you know what? You're probably better your way. Just keep at it. It will work. You've got this." He glances at me for a breath, flashing the smirk of a salesman. The only thing missing is the wink that seals the deal. "Your roommate is going to sing soon. I need more things to blackmail her with, so I'm gonna head down and video it. I'll send it to you."

He points at me as he swings open the door, the finger's version of a wink. I don't answer. My head says I should smile, but I'm pretty sure my face just contorts into a painful bitterness. I quit trying when his back is to me, and I groan heavily when the door *clicks* shut.

Concentrating at any point tonight will be impossible. A good ten minutes pass before I blink my gaze back to the page, and another fifteen go by before I even attempt to read the words. I'm too stunned to cry. Doesn't mean I don't want to. I just…can't.

Defeated, I flip my book closed again. I'm sure I'll get the exact same grade.

I drop my book into its space in my backpack, just between my music sheets and the geometry book that someone drew naughty pictures in the year before. I shuffle my feet to the center of the room with my bag dragging on the ground at my side, and I stop long enough to try to spot Henry in the crowd below. The common room in a giant, sunken living-room type space built into the atrium of our two dorm buildings. The study hall rooms for every floor—on both the boys' side and ours—have windows that look out over the space. Enormous wood-carved trees and leaves crawl up toward the glass ceiling. The sculptured artwork was donated from a former student who now designs pieces for celebrities and dignitaries. An Le, the name I read on the plaque, is the same person who designed the ornate pillars that welcomed me for a year through Elena's front door. Henry said that Elena's company is filled with work from the artist; they knew each other when they attended the school.

I like this piece here at Satis House more than the ones I've seen in books and at Elena's though. It's soothing. Sometimes the air inside the building touches the thinly carved leaves just enough to make them rustle like the giant cottonwood trees that lined the river my dad used to take me to for swimming in the summer. I hold my breath to listen now, hoping maybe the branches will move enough to make a sound. The air is quiet inside tonight, though. It's getting colder out, so I probably won't hear that sound for months now. Not until the air conditioning comes back on in the spring.

Henry is leaning against the thick, glazed trunk. So boyish from up above, he's talking with my roommate and tilting his head with laughter. I imagine the sound of it, so clear in my head. There are things about him I've memorized.

Crushing.

Crushed.

"Right," I say to myself, pulling my bag up over my shoulder. Henry was right...ish. I should know this stuff on my test. If I don't by now, another two hours in here is not going to help. Denying myself a little fun is just going to make me resentful. Plus, I don't think I will ever sleep if I don't somehow fix the mess I made between me and that stupid, adorable boy below.

I flip the lights off on my way out of the room and stop at my room to dump my school bag on my bed. I lock up then take the stairs rather than the elevator down to the main floor. I like the time to think, and the elevator always smells like pot, so I try to avoid it when I can. I push open the heavy glass doors and am surrounded with a Lady Gaga-like wall of sound immediately. When I search for the source and find Anya, the small girl down the hall standing on the circular stage in the very middle of the pit, I let my mouth fall way open and begin to clap.

"She's good, right? Like...she's the legit real thing," Nicki shouts in my ear.

I stare at her and nod, still in shock. It seems impossible for the sound we hear to be emanating from such a tiny frame. With every new note that Anya climbs to, we bend backward and shout "Whoa!" in synchrony. By the end, Nicki and I have decided that Anya needs to be discovered, or that Nicki and I need to form a corporation to sign her and turn the three of us into multi-millionaires.

We inch our way close to the stage to greet our friend on her way down from the stage, and I grab both of her arms as soon as I can touch her, shaking her lightly and forcing out an embarrassed laugh.

"Girl, what the hell was that?" Nicki play slaps Anya's arm. She shrugs under my grip—I'm not letting go until I understand what I'm looking at.

"You guys knew I was a vocal emphasis." Her lips pucker into a modest smile, and Nicki and I bark out a laugh.

"Anya, that's a powerhouse—not an emphasis!" Her eyes meet mine at my compliment, and they fire up for a tiny second.

"Thank you," she says, her voice sheepish. Modesty takes over again quickly, but I saw it there—just a glimpse. Anya was proud, and she was fully aware of what she did up on that stage. That wasn't her first time, and it won't be her last either.

"*Ring...ring*!" I stiffen when I hear Henry's voice, and Nicki's eyes squint the smallest bit. She tilts her head a hint with suspicion, so I give her a shake of my own and mouth the word "later." Maybe she'll be able to help me untangle the mess I made thinking Henry and I were about to kiss when clearly...*we weren't.*

"Anya...you've got a phone call," he says, stepping into the space between me and Nicki. His arm doesn't brush mine this time, but the tiny hairs on my skin reach for him anyhow. He holds out his palm with his thumb and pinky stretched out as if he has a phone. "It's the Grammys, they made a mistake and wanted to know when you could pick up your artist-of-the-year award."

Anya shoots out a laugh, which does a great job of breaking the ice that only I'm experiencing and sets off a chain reaction of all of us trying to recreate her guffaw to perfection. Nicki comes the closest. The lightness fades eventually, though, and when Nicki talks Anya into helping her pick out a song from the list, Henry and I are left alone. Awkward has a flavor —it's a mix of butter and salt, with a hint of vinegar. It's all I can taste.

"Why aren't you singing?" He swings his elbow into my arm. It's not the same as his normal playful touch. I can tell. I made it weird.

"Oh...I'm...piano girl, remember?" I feather my fingers, playing the air.

"Right...but I've heard you hum. When you're practicing at Elena's..."

My jaw tightens as my lips draw tight and I shrug.

"Yeah, but I don't know that there's a song on that list that is all humming. I'm probably more of a background girl. You know...coordinated dancing and claps?" I swing my arms on either side of my body then snap to the rhythm of the country song one of the juniors is singing right now.

"No...you definitely aren't background." He shakes his head lightly and his eyes linger on me before flitting up to the stage. I swallow once his attention leaves. I wish he wouldn't say things like that—things that are twisted with compliments when all he probably really meant was I'm a really bad dancer. There's that tone, though... the way he says things.

Do not try to kiss him again, Lily!

A tight wave grips at my insides just remembering what happened an hour earlier.

"Hey, about before...I'm under a lot of stress. That was just me panicking and freaking out a little, and I know we're friends. *Just friends.* I don't want things to be weird now, though, so..."

"Yeah," he stops my blabbering. His eyes haze as he looks up at the stage, gripping his bottom lip under his teeth as he pauses with thought. He slowly starts to nod, but he doesn't turn to face me. "No problem. Really, Lily. I get it. Let's forget about it, huh?"

He glances at me briefly, waiting for my answer. His palms are tucked in his back pockets and he's ready to move on from this conversation.

"That sounds...*great.*" That last word is barely audible when it leaves my lips. It was loud enough for him to hear it, though, and he nods with a smile, closing that chapter for good in his mind. I, however, will continue to dwell on it, probably around the same time I watch him rush across the lawn for rowing practice every day.

I'm doomed.

"You're up next." Nicki's grin is dreadfully smug, and Anya can barely hold her laughter in as she passes the slip of paper to me.

"Next for what?" My heart has instantly gone from the depths of my stomach, where it was wallowing in self-pity, to my throat, where it is fighting with rapid beats to leave my body entirely.

I unfold the paper and read the song title six or seven times, fully aware that it's an Aretha Franklin song but unable to click with the idea that my new friends think I should sing it. In front of people. Out loud. Here.

Now!

"Oh, hell no!" I crumple the paper up and take Anya's thin wrist in my hand, forcing the paper into her palm.

"You'll be great! Come on; I've heard you hum!" She begs me, and I flash my eyes to Henry who is laughing under his breath.

"What the fuck is with you guys thinking humming is anything at all like singing? There are no words in humming!"

Henry shrugs at my tirade, but his gaze is distracted on a crowd of people gathered on the other side of the stage.

"Girl, I sang earlier, and it was terrible. You cannot fail. I've already won the award for worst performance of the night," Nicki says, taking the paper from Anya's hand and pushing it back into mine.

I sigh out, my pulse no slower at all. I'm going to die from some stroke or hemorrhage or something because of this moment right now. There is nothing that could make this worse.

"Henry will watch." Nicki's voice comes out in a sing-songy tease.

The moment has just gotten worse. Damn.

I look at her sideways, and she laughs on one side of her mouth, fully aware that I won't kill her because, out of our relationship, she is the dominant roommate. In fact, I'm the sub in every relationship. I always give in, and I'm going to now. Drawing this out is only going to make it worse and bring more attention to what I'm about to do to music by the Queen of Soul.

"Fine," I huff, looking to Henry. His eyes are still scanning the crowd far away. "Are you really going to watch this? It's not too late for you to run for the hills before I ruin your ears for life."

"What?" He shakes back to attention, looking down at me. "Oh… yeah. I wouldn't miss it."

His response was a guess at my question. I can tell. Alice does that to me sometimes when she's busy with something and I need her help. Collin's a better listener.

My fingertips begin to pulse with my nerves, and I have to sway in place just to keep my feet from falling asleep or my knees from locking and buckling me to the ground. Everyone out here is dressed to impress someone else—even Nicki's eyes are painted blacker than normal, and her hair is a shiny, straight ribbon of silk that she probably spent an hour on straightening with my iron. Anya's wearing a short skirt and an enormous sweater that falls off one shoulder, and I've noticed more than one freshman boy glance at her because duh…skin!

I'm in the same leggings I woke up in and the same long-sleeved blue T-shirt that I wore yesterday. My hair is in a twisted bun that's losing pieces every time I take a step. At one point, I had a pencil tucked in there, but I lost it somewhere. Or maybe it's just buried in my knotted hair. My study hair ate it.

"Lily Ames!" Shayla, our student council president, shouts my name into the mic. My tingling fingers feel as if their ends might explode.

"That's you, superstar," Nicki says, palming my shoulders from behind and giving me slight shake and then a push to send me on my way. I step forward and glance at her over my shoulder, shooting daggers from my eyes as best I can. Henry gives me a thumbs up then begins to move to the right, toward whatever has had his attention for the last ten minutes. I look back to my path through the dozens of students that are watching me walk up to the rounded steps. I climb them one at a time, paying close attention to where my foot lands on every step. At the very least, I am not going to fall on my ass up here. I will stay standing.

By the time Shayla passes the mic to me, my hand is quivering. Maybe it will create vibrato.

"Thank you," I say to her. She smiles, scooting back to her seat on top of the large speaker. She almost looks excited to hear me. It's the song. Which I don't know very well, but I know enough about Aretha to know that this song comes with expectations.

The music kicks in and I feel the base shake the stage. My lip is vibrating, and it would be so easy for me to give in to the urge to cry right now. This is terrifying. The title pops up on the screen in purple letters – "I NEVER LOVED A MAN."

I clear my throat, the mic picking up some of the sound. A few people near me chuckle. I need to keep my eyes on the screen for the lyrics and so I don't look at anybody else. If I see there are people out there, this little bit of poise I've somehow scraped up will fall apart.

My eyes are glued to the bouncing ball, catching on to the rhythm and readying my chest to push air through my vocal cords. Please, dear God, let a slightly pleasant sound leave my lips.

With the mic barely an inch from my mouth, I follow along and utter the first pass of words. I do the humming equivalent of singing. It doesn't sound awful, but it's barely audible, and I hear a few people near the stage scream "louder!" I shake the nerves from my right hand, the mic gripped in my left, and I push harder for the next line. Someone whistles, and I laugh nervously, giggling a little through the next line of the song.

I'm not sure when I started to sway, but that little movement keeps me grounded for the first thirty seconds and slowly, my body starts to warm and the tingling turns into a tiny dose of confidence.

The chorus is coming up. I recognize this part. My mom loved Aretha, and while this wasn't the song we played often, it is the one that made her stand a little taller while doing whatever she was doing when it was on. I'm not sure if the memory is real or not, but I have a flash in my mind of my mom stirring cake batter and pausing to belt this next part into the spoon. I copy her spirit now, and when the notes come out loud enough for me to hear them through the mic, I'm astounded by the sound of my own voice.

The whistle from the crowd comes louder this time, drawing my eyes toward it, and my roommate is clapping her hands above her head and smiling wide with her black-painted lips. Anya is clapping with her, my backup dancers that nobody can see. I didn't know I could do this.

With each passing verse, I get bolder, and the crowd gets thicker, the cheering louder. There are more people watching me right now than were here for Anya, and she was amazing. I'm nowhere near her talent, but I think maybe there's something to be said about surprise. I'm…surprising.

During the last music break, I scan the room trying to estimate how many people are in here. It's really no more than a hundred, but it feels like thousands. Even with all of those bodies, though, it only takes me a breath to spot him.

Henry's eyes aren't up here. He's talking to two girls and another guy, students I don't recognize because my social circle consists of my two friends and Henry. He has several circles, though. He always has, and I've seen him with other people here at Satis. But I'm singing my heart out, doing something scary, and he's swaying his elbow into a girl who isn't me, but is just as stupid under his trance.

I'm late to the verse, so I look away from him to the screen to get caught up. The fire is gone from my voice. The magic has worn away, like Cinderella's pumpkins at midnight. I'm not off key or anything, but I'm no longer bold. I'm quiet…meek. *Diminished.*

And Henry is walking the girl who isn't me through the door, into the study hall of his dorm, and drawing the blinds. My mom's power ballad fades off, and I don't finish the last few words, giving the mic back to our hostess and sinking down the steps to get lost in a crowd of mostly strangers.

CHAPTER 6

This time, I'm the one sprinting across the main courtyard of Satis —late for my first meeting with my advisor.

Three weeks left in my first semester, and a tenuous three-point-seven grade-point average have me out of sorts. I had no idea how easy public school was, no clue all of the things I wasn't learning. The curve from there to here has been brutal. But I woke up this morning feeling an odd sort of confidence in my gut. Henry has been dating Ava for two months, ever since they got to know each other at karaoke night. At first, it kept me awake at night with a singed sensation in my chest, as if someone was holding a branding iron to my insides. But for the last few weeks, I've gradually set myself free from worrying about it.

Free from Henry.

We've hardly talked, except in passing. And lately, I haven't even bothered to be in my room at three in the afternoon to watch him race to practice. He wasn't late as often anyhow, so nothing there to see.

My morning confidence is fading fast now, though. Every step I stretch into the icy wet grass on my way to the administration building carves away a little bit of my poise and replaces it with panic and a looming sense of failure. That was the only main takeaway from the email the office sent out for our meeting times: DO NOT BE LATE.

I'm late.

I'm exactly eleven minutes late, twelve if I don't pick up the pace for the final two hundred or so yards I'm sprinting. I'm wearing two different socks and a sweater I wore yesterday and put in the "needs to be washed pile" because it so desperately needs to be washed. In my freak-out mode, though, eyes popping open to see the realization that my alarm never went off on my phone, the *iffy* sweater had to do. It went on easy and required zero thought.

My steps slow at the main set of doors. I work my fingers through my messy hair, pulling the band around tightly and twisting a few times to pull off the messy bun look. I try to catch my reflection in a few of the office windows as I walk down the long hallway to the arts division, and before I rap on the window, I suck in a breath so deep it fills my belly.

"Come in." I allow myself a second to try to decipher the tone on the opposite side of the door. I can't tell if it's disappointed or indifferent. I decide to prepare myself for a lecture, or at the very least a scowl, and I push the latch down and open the door.

My advisor's name is Rebecca Manning, and she doesn't greet me with a scowl. Instead, her back is to me and her fingers are pounding out a message on her keyboard. I slip into the seat on the opposite side of her desk while she works—as if somehow, when she turns around, I can convince her that I've been here all along.

"There," she says, punching the final return on her keyboard and spinning around to face me. She folds her hands on her desktop calendar and smiles with perfect bronzed lips and hair that has probably never seen a messy bun. She doesn't look mad, though. That's what I hold onto.

"Lily." She says my name in a way that someone familiar with me would, her head falling slightly to one side while her eyes smile as her cheeks push them up. I force myself to look her in the eyes for a few seconds, but unable to take the mystery of why she's being so quiet, I look to my lap and tuck my hands under my thighs.

"I know I'm late. There was a...well...a technical glitch, I suppose. I've never messed up my phone alarm before, but maybe because I made a new alarm entry, or maybe..." I'm yammering on like Collin does, and the moment I recognize it, I snap my lips closed and breathe in and out quickly through my nose to clear my thoughts and quiet my heart. I need to stop panting.

I lift my gaze to Ms. Manning's again, and her smile is unchanged. It's unsettling.

"It's fine, Lily. We book a whole hour for these things. And I have something I've been meaning to give you..." She leans to her left and pulls open a file drawer, taking an envelope out then sliding it across her desk toward me. It looks like a greeting card.

"Thanks." My breath holds, not sure if this is going to lead to a joke or some sort of probation letter for my scholarship. Maybe it does matter that I was late.

Ms. Manning nods toward me to open the envelope; I bring it into my hands and unfold the edge to pull out a floral note card with gold lettering in the middle.

THANK YOU

I search my memories for some sort of reason she's giving me this, and I'm coming up empty as I slowly open the card and a ten-dollar bill slides into my lap. I pick it up with my right hand and hold it between two fingers, looking at it in front of the card. I refocus on the words scribbled inside, and suddenly everything is clear.

Thank you for loaning me this money when I was so very desperate. You are so very kind.

Sincerely,

Rebecca

The woman in the rain!

My mouth falls open wide, lifting at the sides with a relieved smile plastered over the shock.

"I hope it's okay that I'm just paying you back now. When I saw you got accepted at Satis House, I thought I would give you a card here rather than some sort of impersonal money transfer or check in the mail." Her smile broadens as she leans back, her palms holding onto the edge of her desk while she takes me in.

"It's fine. Of course," I say, folding the card back with the money inside. I tuck it in the zipper of my bag. "You really didn't need to pay me back. I'm glad I was able to help you."

"Well, now…maybe I can help you in return. Let's see this schedule you have planned out and maybe talk about your goals, shall we?" She pushes her chair forward and stretches toward me, taking my folder to review my selection sheets.

She separates every list into individual years and semesters and quickly goes to work highlighting things. She highlights more than she leaves, and I push my hands back under my thighs unsure if highlighting is a good or a bad thing.

"How did you know it was me?" I ask while she finishes up, pushing the cap on the bright yellow marker. She pulls out a new set of sheets.

"I recognized your name when we got the list of applicants, and I compared your phone number just to be sure it was the same Lily Ames. It's not a very common name." She smiles at me for a beat then returns her attention to her desk, matching up new forms with my rough drafts.

"I'm glad it was me," I say, my heart rate just now slowing from my rushed morning.

"Me too," she says, pulling her course binder out and flipping to a section she has marked ARTS.

"You need more humanities…" she runs her thumb down a long list and stops at a number, writing it on a Post-it and sticking it to one of my sophomore-year forms. She repeats this about a dozen times, adding something on art history, more musical composition, and then my senior year—all performance. Well, and lit and calculus.

"There," she says, pushing her new sheets together into a line and admiring as if she's created a masterpiece rather than an impossible mountain for me to scale. I'm too thankful for her time, and maybe for her not being upset at me being late, to ask for any changes. Instead, I swallow down the fear and pull the pages together and sign the acceptance line for my future to be set in digital stone for the next three and a half years.

"I'd love to see you play sometime, Lily. I heard you studied with

Elena Alderman." She takes my papers from me and my fate is sealed. I nod, a little numb from my new expectations.

"I did…well, a little. She gave me access to her piano, and sometimes she would help me through lessons. Mostly, though, I'm self-taught," I admit. My smile is a crooked guilty one because I wrote about my lessons in my acceptance essay. Everybody lies a little on those things though, I'm sure.

"I bet it's an amazing piano to play. Elena only keeps the best." Her mouth twitches a little, and her smile slips briefly. I have a feeling Elena's involved with the inner workings of the school quite a bit, given the amount of money she donates. I wonder if she's as gruff and abrasive as she is with Alice, and with me sometimes during our lessons. She is not an easy woman to please.

"I doubt I'll ever play a piano that sounds even close to that one," I say.

My advisor nods, her smile understanding. I think she and I have a lot in common. I don't have any proof, and I'm not comfortable enough to have a real conversation, but maybe in my next visit with her.

I shake her hand as I stand from my seat, and I catch the small signal in her eyes, a wink of sorts, that lets me know someone is on the other side of her door, waiting. I recognize the houndstooth coat fabric through the office window, and I replay everything both of us said about Elena in my head before I leave just to make sure there was nothing she could have heard that might cause trouble for Alice —*or me*.

"Lily, dear." Elena greets me with gloved hands, leaning into me on one side for a rehearsed hug. These are the things my mom used to call *niceties*. This is polite, and for show. I perform just as well as she does.

"Hi. Henry didn't mention you were coming. It's nice to see you." Even though I'm not looking at Ms. Manning over my shoulder, I feel our connection and I know we are both smiling inside. Elena intimidates the hell out of me, and I'm sure she does the same with my advisor, and the dean, and every teacher employed here. She probably scares the shit out of the construction foreman putting in the new parking garage at the south end of campus.

"No, he didn't know. I was planning to come tomorrow, but Alice mentioned that you weren't coming home for the break, and I don't know...I guess I just thought it didn't seem right."

I puzzle my eyes on her.

"Thanksgiving is a time for family, Lily. You should come home. Even if Alice is working. You can have dinner with us, and stay with us if you'd like. Please, I insist." She pulls one glove from her hand, then the other, using the cloth to clean a smudge from her oversized sunglasses.

"Oh...it's just...we don't have a car, so it would be me on the train, and it's hard to lug a suitcase on my own, and Collin's going to pick up extra shifts. I thought I'd get more practice time in..." I know that she isn't hearing any of this, so I quit talking and wait for her to finish with her glasses and tuck them into her front coat pocket and square her shoulders with mine. When her palms land on my shoulders, I know I'll be eating turkey and dressing at her house in two days.

"I'll bring you home. I already told Alice I would. So that's settled. You don't have to take a train, but we will have to leave today. You'll need to be cleared for Wednesday's classes..." She gazes over my shoulder, a slight lift to her chin, and I hear Ms. Manning draw in a deep breath.

"She'll need a guardian to sign her out."

"I should be on the approved sheet," Elena answers. My eyes squint and I turn to my side, baffled. I never added her to my contacts list, so if she is on the list, it wasn't because I put her there. I can't imagine Alice did, though I doubt she'd protest, so it's possible.

Looking sideways, I catch the duel happening in my advisor's glare. Elena isn't on my list, but she'll be there the moment we leave—when Ms. Manning writes her name on the list.

"Very well," Elena says. I've come to learn this is her way of closing a deal. Arguments don't move beyond this point, and her way is *the* way from this point forward. I turn back to look her in the eyes, and her tight lips stretch into a victorious smile. "I need to wait for Henry's practice to finish. We'll leave at noon sharp. See you at the front drive."

I nod slowly, then curtsy before I leave, holding the bottom of my dirty sweater out as if it's a skirt. I catch the chortle sound escape Ms.

Manning, and I look down to hide my own snicker. Before I regret mocking the woman who has probably funded my entire education, I slip past her and slide both of my arms through my backpack straps as I rush down the hallway to the front door.

My inner voice reminds me that my dorm room is to the right, but my feet carry me past it and veer left, toward the boat house and the shoreline, along the line of trees that hide the stands and pier from my window's view. If those trees weren't here, I would be able to watch Henry row. Not that I'm watching Henry anymore. Only…here I am, marching along the wooden walkway and over the floating bridge to the place where the boats are stored each night.

Henry is in the back. There are eight boys on our team, but he's the only one with blond hair. He's the only one with curls that blow in the wind and shoulders that span the width of the wooden shell.

I've always wanted to watch them from down here. The rhythm of the oars along the water is perfect, in sync with the song I put in my head to match. Henry is the only member of the crew team I know, but that's mostly my fault. I don't venture far outside my circle. That's something I should aim for, I guess.

They sweep the water as their forms grow larger and larger the closer they get to me. It's only a few minutes past ten in the morning, and Elena said noon, so I'm sure there will be several more trips up and down the water. I'll only stay for this one. And though my legs itch to hike back up to the trees before Henry can see me, I stay. I remain in this very spot until the entire team passes by me, cutting through the shimmering water top with a quiet line marked by dip after dip of their oars.

Henry's arms flex and release, his skin pink from the effort and the sun, and his gaze is fixed on the back of the head in front of him. I note that boy for just a moment, black hair cut short and eyes that are practically the color of ice. He's handsome, and he's Henry's teammate. His stare isn't as disciplined as Henry's, and as they push away from me with one more thrust, this guy glances my direction; I lift my palm just enough to signal that I notice him. His lip tugs up on one side, and his eyes stay on me for the next hundred yards, until he's so far I can't tell if he's watching me or not.

I leave with the thought that he was looking. And Henry, he looked too. He saw his friend watching me, and he hates it—just a little. This...this is how I will survive an hour-long drive back to his home with Elena. This is how I will choke down Thanksgiving and knowing that he'll be spending spare moments on his phone with Ava. This will be the rest of my year, and maybe...maybe I'll have him introduce me to dark hair and ice eyes. This is how I woke up today—confident. A heartbreaker.

I don't stop on my way to my room, and I pile in a few sets of clothes to one of the suitcases that Collin gave me when I moved in. Nicki shows up while I'm mid-pack, and after I explain to her my hijacked Thanksgiving plans, she takes half of my outfits out of my suitcase and replaces them with a few of hers.

"I'm not really...goth." I wince because I know she doesn't like me to label her, but her clothing is so dark and her mood...hell, it matches. I love her for it, but it isn't me.

"I know you're not, but think about it. How funny will it be when they expect you to come down for dinner and you're wearing this." She holds up a black, holey sweater that goes over a gray dress and black leggings. She rolls it all together and tucks it into the corner of my suitcase then reaches under her bed to pull out one of her boxes of boots. She pulls out the black combat boots that lace up to her knees and throws those in next.

I laugh out loud.

"I definitely can't wear those!" I pick one up and hold it out in front of me. The heel is so heavy.

Nicki rips it from my grasp and puts it back in my suitcase.

"For one night? Yes...you can. Trust me, Lily. There's a reason people don't fuck with me. And sometimes you have to dress like a freak to get your point across." She levels me with her dark, smoky eyes.

"You aren't a freak." My head falls to one side.

"I know. But I'm good with who I am. I'm badass. And if I don't want to go to Thanksgiving at someone's house, I have the balls to tell them." She crosses her arms and waits for the response she knows isn't coming.

I let out a heavy breath and stare at the black boots, picturing them on my pale legs.

"We'll see," I say, adding in a plain T-shirt and jeans back to my options. My roommate breathes out with disapproval and flops on her bed, flipping through gossip stories and posts on her phone while I finish packing.

I lay my pillow on top of everything and give my side of our closet one more pass to see if I've missed anything. The only things that are really left are parts of the school uniform and the dress. My eyes have gotten used to the dress Henry bought me, the tags still on the back. If I had the guts to return it without the receipt and take the money, I would have done that a long time ago. Or maybe I wouldn't have. Maybe I like keeping this reminder of Henry's kindness, his safe-wild side—the part of him I like.

"What is that?"

I can't tell if Nicki's tone is awed or ill. I pull the skirt out to show off the fabric. I loved the colors at first, but the more I looked at this dress after it became mine, the more I loved its story. It's a painting—a famous one of flowers swirled into faces. I can only tell when I hold the material out wide.

"I've actually never even tried it on," I admit with a short laugh. Wearing it felt silly. I've never had a reason.

"Well, I think it goes in the suitcase," Nicki says, nodding her head in the direction of my bag.

I grimace.

"I don't know." I look back at the dress, pulling the hanger free and holding it up in front of my body. "It's not really a winter dress…"

"Won't matter because you'll be eating inside." She offers up a quick argument.

I turn and give her a sideways glance.

"What about the combat boots and black, moody shit you said would scare them?" My tight lips defy her to go against her own style.

"Fuck the boots. You wear that. That's very you, but it's also…not."

"Henry bought it for me," I admit.

Her smile spreads over a long breath.

"Then you *definitely* wear that."

I roll my eyes and turn to look at the dress over my body, holding it from hip to hip and tucking the top under my chin. I look to the side at the bottom of her boots sticking out under my pillow.

"Maybe I bring both," I say.

She stands and pulls her boots from my bag, returning them to their box.

"You'll chicken out on both, and then you'll just be in a damn sweater and Vans or something with jeans. Perfectly back-to-school catalogue."

I frown a little, but she's right. I like plain. I don't even really *like* it but I *do* plain. Plain is easy, and it comes with zero attention. It keeps me invisible.

Before I can overthink things, Nicki yanks the dress from my hand and lifts my pillow, folding the dress in half and layering the pillow back on top. She zips the lid of my suitcase and holds her opposite palm out toward me like a point guard on defense.

"I don't have any nice shoes," I add.

"Wear those," she motions down to my feet. "But dump the socks."

"Ugh, I hate sweaty feet," I protest.

"Your socks are babyish."

I flash an open mouth and wide eyes. She's getting personal now, and that...that was mean.

Lifting my foot to the side, I look at my white Vans and blue sport socks, a thin pink stripe along the edge, and well...shit. She's right. My socks are either *Mom socks* or meant for a third-grader in PE.

"Fine. No socks," I say, taking the ones I'm wearing off now.

Before I can put them in my laundry bag, Nicki grabs them and walks them to the trash.

"I'm clearing out the rest after you leave."

I shake my head at her with wide arms and open palms. She waves me away and lies back down on her bed, diving right back into the posts about famous people breaking up and the stabbing down the street from her old neighborhood.

With my roommate off my back for a moment, I unzip my bag and lift my pillow just enough to get a glimpse of the dress. I pinch the material between my fingers and rub it remembering how I imagined the gauzy skirt swaying just above my knees. I pray it fits nearly as well as I imagine it will in my head.

The next hour passes slowly, and I cheat on my window denials, looking out every few minutes to see if the crew team is done early.

"I'll bring back my binoculars so you can stalk the right way." I look over my shoulder and she's not even looking at me while she pokes fun.

"I'm not a stalker," I retort.

"Uh huh," she says, glancing up to meet my stare as she points her finger exaggeratingly and swipes down her phone to the next story.

"I wouldn't be able to see through the trees anyway," I admit, which makes her body shake with a quiet laugh. I join her and turn back to the window for a few more minutes before deciding it's close enough to noon for me to walk down to the front.

I stop by Anya's room on my way out and hug her, wishing her a happy Thanksgiving. Almost everyone else is out at classes or studying for final projects or presentations. I'll be missing one in my English class that I'll have to give when I return. I wasn't quite ready anyhow, so maybe there's a silver lining to my Thanksgiving plans after all.

Silver. Just like the flecks that sparkle in Ava's sweater. Her arms swing side to side while she practically twirls next to Elena. There is no dress that will be able to get me through a holiday break with Henry *and* his girlfriend—his *stunningly gorgeous* girlfriend who, I swear, walked right off of the pages of a princess storybook. Her hair is swirls of mocha, and her skin is rich and perfectly smooth with pink cheeks, matted red lips, and lashes that seem so long I don't know how they avoid tangling. The taste of bile coats my mouth and tongue as I expect the worst when I step up to them at the side of Elena's car. Her driver gets out and takes my bag, which I hold onto not quite ready to commit. I let go after an awkward exchange with him when he looks to Elena to force me to relent.

"He'll put it in the back for you, Lily."

I give up and answer with "Of course." She's already back into her conversation with the perky brunette who's covered in glitter from her holiday sweater, though.

I feign interest, and for the four or five minutes it's just the three of us, I've learned that Ava's family owns racehorses. Stables full of them. Elena once owned a few horses of her own, but she never had time to ride them. I bite my tongue when I nearly ask what she's so busy with, but I'm less successful keeping in my own horse story.

"My dad rode a horse in the Veterans Day parade once, and it got spooked and took off down Michigan Avenue. The only way he could get it to stop was by taking it inside Nordstrom's. It liked listening to the guy who played the piano." The laughter I expect doesn't come, and instead the two of them stare at me blankly while I choke down my own giggles at the memory. It's a fond one, and I'm sure my dad exaggerated parts of it. He always did that. Now I regret sharing it with people who aren't worthy. I would have been better off making up a story about shoveling the horse crap to pay for our mortgage. That would have gotten sympathy, and they would have believed it.

"Sorry, we ran late," Henry's voice sweeps over my shoulder, buzzing my skin like a feather. I'm surprisingly stable on my feet. Ava is waiting here. I expected him to show up soon, because why not? I'm over the crush—so I've told myself. Naturally, there must be a test to make sure I'm being real.

"It's all right. I've let Alice know. She's coordinating with the caterer for me." Elena's glossed lips tighten into a smile that she gives me. "Alice can't wait to see you."

I nod and move toward the car, letting myself into the back seat and blowing off the driver who frantically tries to beat me to it. "I'm sure she can't," I mumble under my breath.

As I assumed, Ava follows me into the car, taking the seat right next to me and Henry sits across from us by Elena. We all buckle up and I instantly draw my feet in under the seat and fold my arms, trying to make myself smaller. Ava's sweater is sticking to mine, and I can already see droplets of glitter on my frayed yarn. I breathe in long and slow through my nose, a technique I learned about at my old school, where we didn't have classes like theology and art history, but we did take practical things like how to render first aid and how to keep our stress in check.

"Lily, how are you enjoying your first semester?" I seize at Elena's question. I don't really want to share in front of Ava...or Henry, really, since he hasn't been very involved in my life lately.

"It's good." I lift my shoulder against Ava's glitter and shift so we're no longer touching. Elena holds my gaze for a few long seconds, waiting for me to say more. I don't want to. And I wish I were wearing Nicki's boots right now for strength because waiting out her probing eyes is hard.

"Well," she turns to look at Henry with unamused laughter. "You've been accepted to the best preparatory high school in the Midwest and your only reaction to it is what most people rate movie sequels."

"I don't know, I kinda think *Terminator Two, Judgment Day* is rather exceptional." I shrug as if this were a normal debate, and I immediately wonder if my roommate sent me off with her super powers or somehow is inhabiting my body to give me her snark and quick wit.

I glance to Henry, and his eyes meet mine for a brief smile that he masks with the side of his fist as he adjusts his posture and turns to the window. I wait until I see the corners of his mouth dimple his cheeks and his eyes flit to me one last time before I look out the window myself.

"Well, it is a very expensive school, and you were very fortunate to be accepted. You should appreciate it more," Elena reminds me. My chest sinks with guilt.

"You're right, and I'm sorry. I am very grateful...for everything." I force myself to swallow some pride and look my benefactor in the eyes. Her expression softens from scorn to satisfaction and she nods with a righteous smile in return.

"Good. You deserve it. You're quite gifted with the piano, you know. I think you may be better than me by now." I roll my shoulders and sit taller, surprised to be honored by her compliment.

"Maybe you can play for us."

I'd forgotten briefly that Ava was here. I shrink a few inches back into my seat and glance to my left.

"Yeah, sure. I'd be honored." Lies—I cannot think of anything I'd rather do less, other than to watch Ava and Henry reenact the balcony scene in *Romeo and Juliet*.

Elena's purse buzzes with a call and she holds up a finger in apology for taking a business call. It's a wonderful excuse for the three of us to remain silent and look our separate ways. Henry has pulled his phone from his pocket and has started to type, and Ava is straining her neck trying to read what he's writing. I bounce my focus between them both for a few seconds then lose interest, letting my forehead fall against the window so I can count the mile markers until we change freeways. When my back pocket buzzes, I reach into jeans and pull my phone into my lap. I'm expecting an update from Alice, or something from Collin since I texted him that I was giving in and heading to Elena's for the holiday. It takes me a second or two to make sense of Henry's name, and when I do, I slide my phone to the side of my hip out of Ava's view.

Henry: I was going to break up with Ava today. Elena did not ask me about inviting her. Help.

I have to read through the message twice to believe it, and I let myself enjoy the humor for a few more seconds before I pretend it has nothing to do with Henry and slide my phone away from Ava and into my other pocket. I go back to counting signs along the highway until Elena finishes her call, and I only half listen to her share the marketing fiasco that threatens to unravel their agreement with a Canadian papermill.

I drift back into my blissful numb place that will get me through the next four days, and I start to appreciate the fact that I'll have endless access to the piano and all of Elena's books for my final English paper when Henry ruins everything for every single one of us.

"Ava, I don't think it's going to work out."

My palm slips from my chin to cover my mouth and I expose my teeth to feel them along my hand. Why would he do this now? I'm embarrassed for her...for me...all of us.

"I'm sorry, but...what?" My eyes close because that's probably how I would react, and hearing it from the outside is cringeworthy.

"Henry, you're being rude." Elena chides him, and I push my palm against my lips with more force to hold in the laugh that wants to slip out because of the absurdity playing out in this tiny space.

"Rude is pretending you're into someone when you're not," Henry says, and the irony makes holding in my laugh unbearable. Everyone looks at me when I practically snort, and I hold up my palm to apologize, patting my chest as if I've just coughed or swallowed a fly.

"Henry, I'm packed and I'm staying with you for the weekend...I don't understand..." Ava argues, talking with her hands so violently that glitter flies from her arms and spreads around the floor of the car. She's like a holiday explosion.

"You live in the city. You can take a car, or your parents will come." Henry's head falls to the side as he feigns empathy. What's stunning is how he doesn't even seem remorseful. Everything about him screams relieved, as if he's handed in a test and just been told that the grade on it is meaningless.

I push my back into the corner of the seat and door, creating more distance and expanding my view. Ava's lips are parted and her words are stalled; Henry's head remains tilted in fake apology. Elena's eyes, however, are on me, along with a hint of a smile, and I can't tell if it's assuming I'm to blame or if she's taking credit for this youthful angst and chaos happening in front of us.

"Ava, maybe it's best that I have Phillip take you home."

Ava doesn't flinch at Elena's suggestion, but now that it's been said, it's what will be. Eventually, my glittered classmate sinks back into her seat and folds her arms, staring out her own window now, stewing and jilted.

There are no work calls to Elena to rescue us all from the next fifteen minutes of stifling quiet, so we ride with grinding teeth and flexed jaws. I tuck my hands under my legs and keep my eyes low. Henry, however, relaxes and stretches out his long legs until the toe of his right shoe taps into mine. I assume it's an accident at first, so I shift my legs and cross my ankles. His foot slides forward a few more inches, though, tapping me again, and lifting up and down in a signal. I smirk at our feet, his size eleven canvas slip-ons against my worn, vinyl clogs. Two feet that do not belong in the same car. I twist my foot sideways a few times, tapping back in response, and when I lift my chin, I see Ava's eyes in my periphery.

I should apologize, or look her in the eyes directly at the very least. But I don't move. I connect with Henry and leave my foot right where it is. Damn them all. I woke up a little different today.

CHAPTER 7

Wednesday, Henry was nowhere to be found. Neither was Alice.

The Alderman home sat dark, cold, and quiet—minus a single fire burning in the sitting room where Elena keeps her desk. She sat on that uncomfortable-looking green velvet sofa for most of the day reading the same book over and over again.

Brontë. Emily. An afternoon of *Wuthering Heights* seemed fitting for her.

I spent the hours at the piano, rehearsing for my winter test. I'm not sure if I believe in the class—technical piano. I need to earn high marks, though, because I do believe in every course that follows. I want to write my own music, and to ace all of those things that Ms. Manning put in my academic plan.

By the time Elena decided to be done reading, my fingers were sore, the joints feeling bruised and swollen. I didn't want to stop, but I knew I had to. I expected Elena to visit the music room one last time before heading up, but she didn't. I left my things as they were and went to bed so I could return to the keys in the morning.

BRED

It isn't the smell of oven-baked turkey or sweet potatoes that wakes me now. It's the banging of off-key chords. In my twisted half-awake state, I imagine the sound coming from my own hands, and I sit up quickly and ball my fists in my lap to make it stop.

It doesn't. It continues, along with a whaling type of cry and lyrics that make zero sense. Lights in the hallway just outside my guest room flip on, so I move to my door just as Elena rushes by, wrapping herself in a thick robe.

"That's quite enough," she growls, cascading down the stairs as if she's sliding on ice. For a moment, I worry she'll fall. When she disappears around the corner, I leave my room and move to the railing to see if I can hear anything below.

"I hate you so much." It's Henry's voice, only it isn't. It's garbled —sloppy.

He's drunk.

"Yes, and that's fine. But there are still rules. You need to be presentable in a few hours." The piano echoes again, keys pressing haphazardly to form a terrible, flat chorus. "I said that's enough."

A small squeak pings down the hallway, followed by the heavy thump of the piano lid falling to a close. The lights below click off, so I rush back into my room and crack my door enough to hear them as they pass. After a few stumbles and protests by Henry up the stairs, they finally seem to be moving smoothly back toward Henry's room. He was gone all day, and hearing this version of him, I'm curious how he made it home.

Fifteen and drunk.

"Why do I have to be presentable? It's not like anyone will be here. It's just going to be me and you...and *her*."

My shoulders sag and my palm slides along the wall as I let my ear fall flat against the plaster. My door is cracked too thin to see anything, but I'm the only *her* left. Ava was sent home as soon as we arrived.

"Alice will be eating with us. It's the polite thing to do, don't you think? Her husband will be working. And they are our friends."

"You don't have any friends," Henry shoots back, belching through a laugh.

"Friends are enemies in disguise," Elena says. I pause at her jaded response.

Henry coughs out an angry laugh, but he doesn't argue with her beyond that. A breath later, they stumble into his room—two doors down and across the hall. I wait, breath held and feet still, until I hear his door close, and I cover my mouth to keep myself silent until I hear Elena's door shut at the end of the hallway.

I move to my phone, plugged in and resting atop my still half-packed suitcase. If I get sent away like Ava was, I want to be ready to go. I check the time, and yawn seeing it read a few minutes after four in the morning. There's no sense returning to the bed. I'm too wired right now, too...*curious*. Nosey, really.

I walk back to the door and crouch down, resting my back against the wall as I sit and push my fingertips through the crack to open it just a little wider. I wait for something to see, anticipating a shout or the sound of something being thrown. There's nothing but the distant tick of a clock and the normal pops and creaks that come with old brownstones settling in the winter.

My phone buzzes in my palm, startling me, and I swipe to read.

Henry: Did you hear that?

I'm not sure which part he means, so I simply respond *yes*.

Henry: I'm sorry I woke you.

I try to decipher his apology for a few minutes before writing back that it's fine. I delete the part where I apologize for him having to spend his Thanksgiving with me, instead forgiving him for being drunk and saying things he doesn't mean. Only, I think I very much meant it when he told Elena he hated her.

I wait for more questions or him to need me—need someone—but after ten minutes of nothing, I give up and slide down into a more comfortable position to read on my phone for a while. My eyes are surprisingly heavy after a chapter or two; I give in and close them while I rest on the floor, figuring I'll make it back to the bed eventually.

The warm sun on my chest wakes me the second time. The open drapes let in the light from the morning sunrise, and my room glows. Windows are rarely open in this place. It's like a tomb, as if sun rays might spoil the secrets inside these walls.

My cheek feels flat on the left side, and my elbow and shoulder are sore to the touch. Wooden floors do not make for great rest. I suppose drunk teenaged boys don't either.

"You look like I feel." I rub my face and lift my body to twist toward my now-open door.

"You look like you sounded last night," I bite back.

"Touché," Henry says.

He peers down the hallway then slips inside my door, closing it behind him and kneeling down next to me with a steaming cup of coffee. I take it, then hesitate, arching a brow at him.

"Where's yours?"

"Drank two of them already," he says, his mouth frowning with a sour tinge. He can't feel good.

I blow across the top and stretch out my legs while I sit, the clanking sounds of a turkey dinner being prepared echoing up the stairs. I take a sip, which burns the tip of my tongue, then wince as I set the cup on the floor.

"How many people are cooking down there?" I bring my legs up to hug them, also to hide the childish teddy-bear shirt I'm sleeping in. I should have worn Nicki's clothes to bed.

"Just two, but Alice is here. She asked if you were all right."

I grimace, cynical.

"I think you mean she asked if I was *all right* as in acceptable." I pick up my cup again and blow into the liquid, making tiny ripples along the top.

"I think she really misses you." Henry's mouth pulls tight, his face struggling to find the right expression to sell the lie. I reach forward and let my fingers wrap along his forearm.

"You don't have to pretend. Not with me. The fact that I'm away at boarding school is a huge win for them. They get to keep the support money my parents set up through the state, and they don't have to parent."

I don't often dwell on the fact that my parents are gone. I never have, really. From the moment I was shuffled along through the system to cousins who are ill-equipped, I knew that crying and wishing wasn't going to change the hard facts. My parents were dead; I had to be all right with my new normal. I do miss them, though. I miss them most on days like today.

"Is it really just going to be the four of us?" I attempt another sip, happy to find it not quite so scalding this time.

Henry's brow draws in sharp, the confused wrinkle deep along the bridge of his nose.

"Last night…during your *episode*." His expression softens. "You said that it was just going to be the four of us—me, you, Elena, and Alice."

Henry's eyes drift to the floor between us and his mouth twists before he gives me a nod.

"It's better than it usually is. Normally, it's just Elena and me. One year, she made the caterer stay." He breathes out a laugh that masks his sadness. His normal isn't so great either.

"Where were you yesterday?" I take a bigger sip this time, mostly to busy my lips while I ward off the nerves I feel from asking such a bold question.

Henry's mouth puckers, eventually giving way to a burst of a laugh that sends his body rocking backward.

"The new neighbors," he says, nodding his head toward the back of the house.

My eyes flare.

"You mean…*the house?*"

I'm a little hurt that Henry didn't offer to take me with him, but when he explains that he was there because Elena set him up to do some work for the man who owns the house, I ease up on feeling jilted.

"He's a woodworker, makes this really beautiful custom furniture, and Elena thought I might learn something."

"I didn't realize you wanted to be a carpenter." He's actually never mentioned it to me, not once. I know that our talks haven't always been deep, but he's well aware of my musical ambitions. Career dreams aren't something people our age keep secret.

"Oh God, no. I don't," he says, clearing that up…sort of. "Elena just wants me to learn *something*. And they have a daughter, who I'm sure she wanted me to meet."

He rolls his eyes, and I draw in another long sip while envy boils in my gut.

"That's her thing, in case you haven't noticed. It's like arranged marriages, only it's arranged winter formal dates, and proms, and photo ops. It's like she wants me to be some society celebrity or something. She's always been pushing me to be where the eyes are."

"And where are the eyes?" I ask, burying my other question about the daughter he was supposed to meet next door.

"Why, darling," he begins, standing up and offering me a hand. I take it and smirk as I do. He bends at the waist before lifting me to my feet, and finishes his answer. "Don't you know that the eyes are everywhere? And those are the only ones that matter."

I scowl a little in thought as he brings me to my feet. The floor is warm where the sun has baked it, and it feels good on my bare feet. While Henry is dressed for a formal dinner in a pair of black slacks and a red sweater over a white shirt and tie, I'm still rocking the friendly bear smile on my chest and oversized sweatpants that have pushed their way up my calves.

"Why do these eyes matter so much?" I ask, not letting go of his right hand but bending down to pick up my cup. He takes it from me when I stand, then places it on the top of a dresser so he can hold both of my hands with his. He pushes me back a little and turns me into his own made-up waltz.

"Because they have to adore you if they see you everywhere." His answers come out like scripture, and I wonder what formed his opinion. He's clearly done explaining it to me, though, as he spins me out of his hold and drifts back through the door behind him.

"Now get dressed and meet me downstairs before they put us to work." He winks and closes my door gently.

My phone *buzzes* against the wall where I left it propped up last night, so I take it in my hand and move to my suitcase to pick out my outfit of the day. I can't wear the dress around the house for eight hours, so I'll need something different for now. Most of my things are casual, but I do have a few of Nicki's tops that maybe I could pair with my jeans or something. I check the message on my phone while I lay out my options, and smile when I see Nicki's name.

Nicki: It's dress day. You better own this, bitch.

I laugh quietly and write her back.

Me: I will wear it, but not until later. I need to be comfortable for the next several hours.

Nicki: Then go with Vixen.

Me: What's Vixen?

She doesn't respond, leaving me clueless for a few minutes until I unfold her long-sleeved black shirt with holes for my thumbs at the wrist. The word VIXEN is printed along the chest in black on black; it's only there in the right light. I smile at the word, ready to be a little bit like Nicki for now. It's actually just what I need.

The shirt works well enough with my jeans, and my messy hair cooperates with a little finger combing and a knit cap. Henry is waiting for me at the bottom of the stairs, his hand on the front door and his eyes trained down the hallway on lookout. He does a doubletake on me as I get close, which brings blood to my cheeks at first.

"You look like you're about to rob a GAP," he jokes, sending what was excited tightness in my cheeks down to my toes like lead.

Feeling a lot less sassy, I follow him out the door and down the front path to the street lined with cars and a faint covering of mist. He doesn't seem in much of a hurry, and like every other adventure I've been on with him, the destination hasn't been revealed.

"It's supposed to snow tonight," he says, a thin fog sifting from his lips. He pushes his hands into his pockets and I do the same with mine. No temptation to hold hands this way—no *practice.*

"They always say it's going to snow. I think that's how they get people excited about the holidays in Chicago. They mystify snow." A shiver cuts through me as we cross Henry's street, the breeze from the lake finding our bodies. I pull my sleeves down and over my hands and shove them back into my pockets for warmth.

"I take it you hate snow?" Henry smirks and tilts his head toward me, the bounce picking up in his step.

"It loses its splendor when you're the one who has to shovel it." My flat-mouthed expression pulls a soft laugh from him. I doubt Henry has ever shoveled anything.

"I suppose it would," he chuckles.

We get to the corner where his street meets a busier one, and Henry glances both ways before sprinting across and shouting for me to "come on!" My feet slip a little at first, but I shoot across the road a few steps behind him. My pulse stays steady, even several steps after I catch my breath. It's not that there were a lot of cars to dodge; the street was fairly empty. It's just the rush of it, of not knowing where we're going.

It's Henry.

We keep walking along the rail line, leaving the sidewalks for the dirt and gravel that builds up to the tracks. The dead trees and dry and dirty long grass form this dystopian tunnel around us, and soon, it feels as if we're all alone in the world.

"Snow is one of my first memories," he says, slowing his steps from the rush we've been on. He spins to walk backward and face me, his eyes locked on mine as if he's reading my reaction, hoping I'll ask for more.

I will.

I do.

"Do you remember life before Elena?"

His smile tightens just before he shrugs the shoulder closest to the tracks.

"A little. Just like...scenes, if that makes sense?" His gaze lingers just as a breeze rolls dozens of dried leaves over our steps.

"It does."

He nods, something soothing in the way his face falls at my acceptance.

We've never talked like this—about all of our *befores*. What I know of Henry is just enough to lead to mystery. I guess the little I've shared with him does the same.

"I don't know that the memories have to be old to live with you like scenes," I say, my chest growing a little tighter as I prepare to let go just a little.

"Yeah?"

The crunch of our steps falls into sync as he turns to walk alongside me, our hands both still protected from each other. We move close enough to feel our shoulders brush once...twice.

"My parents died two years ago now, and I remember so much about life with them, but that last day—it's just frame by frame." The burn seeps into my chest, my mind replaying every moment like a flip book, over and over. I shake my head as if that will shake the visions away.

"What happened?" His question slips out in a whisper, somehow knowing this is hard for me to share...but that I still want to.

"Car crash on their way home from the city. It wasn't even bad weather. No ice, no snow or rain. It was their anniversary. My dad surprised my mom with tickets to see this show downtown, at one of those fancy theaters where you dress up and stuff."

A tiny laugh catches his breath, and I realize how stupid that probably sounds to him, but for my family, fancy theaters are on one end of the list and then bargain movies and school plays are on the other. We didn't splurge much.

"My mom's best friend from high school was the lead, and my mom hadn't seen her in years. My dad was surprising her, and they had dinner before the show. My mom sent me a picture..." My breath holds as I feel for my phone and bring it in front of me to hold in my palms. I skim through the pictures to the one of my mom and her friend, both beautiful—both so young. I hand it to Henry.

"Which one is she?" His eyes dance around my screen, and I feel so bare sharing this with him. It scares me, so my hand trembles as I point to the blonde on the right with hair pulled up in sweeping curls.

"Hey," he hums, taking my shaking hand. I grip at the first hint of his touch and choke out a cry that turns into laughing. I wipe away the fast tear with my other hand.

"I'm sorry. I haven't talked about it a lot, so I guess I wasn't ready for what would happen when I did." Another tear slides down my cheek, and Henry catches this one with the side of his finger after letting go of my hand. He sweeps it from my skin with a slow and tender move, stopping to feather his knuckle gently down the side of my face.

"You're supposed to cry over things like that."

My eyes blink up to his briefly and I force a smile.

"I guess so," I sniffle, wiping my forearm across my nose. It's gross, but probably less disgusting than snot dripping to my upper lip.

"What was your mom's name?" he asks, turning my phone to hand it back to me.

"June," I mutter. "June and David. My parents…"

"June and David," he repeats, almost like he's honoring them and the fact that I've said their names for the first time in…well, two years.

I swallow.

"Her friend was Sondra Juarez, and she's a little famous…in theater, I guess. They grew up neighbors, but Sondra moved into the city after high school. My mom moved to the sticks." I punch out a laugh.

"Sticks?" Henry quirks a brow.

"Yeah, that's like…you know, the opposite of this cosmopolitan world you live in? Where people own tractors and sheep or goats as pets." I giggle, remembering my mom's stories of when she and my dad first got married. "My parents lived in this rusty trailer that froze in the winter, but they had three acres that grew nothing but fed six goats. My dad worked for the Chicago Transit Authority as a mechanic, and my mom was a third-grade teacher. She was mine. They moved to the burbs when they had me. That's when my mom and Alice got close. My grandparents died when I was two or three. I never really knew them."

I breathe out at the realization of everything I just shared, and I turn to my side with stretched out arms.

"That's me, pretty much," I laugh out.

Henry stops walking, letting me move a few more steps away. His mouth pulls in on one side with an effort to smile, but there's too much weight from other things pulling his expression down to earth.

"You're a lot more than that," Henry says. I blush off his compliment at first, waving my hand and laughing at myself as I take a few more slow steps backward. When his expression shifts into something more serious, I stop. His mouth draws in tight, his chest rising with a deep breath that he never seems to let go, and suddenly I'm lost in his eyes.

"You really *are* a lot more than just some girl from the, what do we call it? Sticks?" His serious expression brightens for a short breath of a laugh, but falls back in line with his intense stare.

"You know sometimes…"

His mouth pulls in tight on one side, his eyes wincing a little with thought, like he's not sure if he should keep talking. I really hope he does. Even though I'm so unbelievably nervous.

He shrugs, shaking his head and peering down, about to shake off wherever he was going with this, so I step in a little closer to stay in the present with him, to beg him to keep sharing. I want to know whatever it is—I want to know things about him.

"Sometimes…what?" I ask.

He licks his lips then pulls them tight with a nod, smiling but in the saddest possible way.

"Sometimes I wonder who I would be if Elena Alderman didn't adopt me," he admits.

My heart kicks. I've wondered this too, about him. Of course, if he wasn't here, then we probably never would have met.

"She's really strict," I respond, leaning my head to the side. It draws a short laugh from him in agreement.

"Yeah," he sighs, then shakes his head. "It's more than that, though. It's kinda like, I'm supposed to know I'm better than everyone else, which seems like such a dick thing to say, but I kinda am. Being an Alderman? It's like…an advantage I guess?"

I nod, a little stung from his words as I mull around the thought of him being better than me. He thinks that. I knew *I* thought that, but it's weird to hear him say it.

"It makes it hard to have friends. *Real* friends." His forehead dents with disappointment and honesty, and for the first time since I've met him, I have this vague sense of what it is like to be Henry Alderman.

It's lonely. Even when he's the center of attention.

The whistle sends a burst of adrenaline through my spine, and I jump toward the tracks before tripping over my feet in an attempt to move back. It's several hundred yards away, the glow of the light dull through the fog that's beginning to fill up our world.

"We should go," I say from the bottom of the slope, the beats growing in speed and impact throughout my body. My pulse is racing the train—trying to outrun Henry and every little trap he seems to lay for my heart. I was over him.

"Just wait for it to pass. It's safe. I promise. Stand right next to me," he says, hand outstretched like Eve's apple. I stare at his pink palm and pale fingers, chilly from the air now that they've left the comfort of his pockets. I curl mine into my sleeves as I blink at my other option for a moment.

"How do you know it's safe?" My eyes flit up to his, and I catch his hand fall back down to his side in a defeat. His gaze sinks into mine more.

"I just do," he says.

I try to read his lips—his blank expression and sure eyes. They're gambling behind their green and golden mask. I look to my right, to the tracks that are only steps away, and to the growing light in the distance. A blaring whistle rings out again, twice, and it feels like a warning for more than just this little game of truth or dare. The ground beneath me vibrates with indecision, and as each second passes, my nerves wrangle around my chest, squeezing my lungs of air. I look to Henry again, his face unchanged, so sure that I'll give in, so certain that we'll be safe here.

The thunder against the tracks picks up, the rhythm like a chase as the train races toward us, barreling at a threatening pace. I turn my back to it slowly and retrace my steps back to where I was a minute or two before, my eyes locked on Henry's. My hands are sweater-covered fists at my sides, and his are relaxed, looped by his thumbs into his front pockets. The trees around us begin to sway, sticks bending where leaves used to rustle months ago. Henry's jawline glows with the reflection of the incoming light, and my hair falls loose at the sides of my face, tangled curls slapping at my cheeks and causing me to blink. Every time I open my gaze, though, Henry is there waiting—daring.

He lifts his chin as his smirk grows, and even though my mouth itches to do the same, I'm too overcome with fear to match him. My eyes close tight just before the train rushes by, and I steady my legs, only stumbling a bit when the first gust slams into my body. Slaps of wind push against me so hard I have to lean into the force, and my chest booms with every thud of metal along metal only feet away from me.

When the sound begins to ease, I open my lids and catch the last few cars rush by. My body is sucked forward a step or two at the very end, and I stumble into Henry's outstretched palms, his hands on my forearms and a proud smile curving his mouth. My hair is flung in wild strands over my face, but before I can clear them away, Henry's hands slide up my shoulders to my neck and then cheeks, sweeping my hair behind both ears as his thumbs take gentle strokes. My skin is electrified—in an instant I've gone from one rush to the next. Raw from sharing my past and learning more about Henry, alive from adventure, and terrified by wanting something to happen next now that Henry is near.

"We should get back," he says, tucking one last blonde strand behind my ear before both of his hands fall away, retreating all the way back to his pockets. His eyes stick around for an extra breath, so I keep my disappointment buried from the surface for later. It boils inside though, and the longer I stare into eyes that hide so many secrets and feel so warm and cold at the same time, the bolder I grow. Being an Alderman doesn't mean he's allowed toy with me. It's cruel!

"Why do you do things like that?" I shout my words, breaking what was starting to become a peaceful quiet. More like a brewing storm.

His eyes flinch and my lips do the same.

"Don't act stupid. I know you're not. You do this to me all the time...the hand-holding, the rooftop, sliding around the floor. I can't tell what any of it means, and when you say things like 'I'm more than something' and you have nothing to add—it just feels sorta empty that way. It starts as a compliment, but then later...it just makes me sad."

He studies my eyes for long, quiet seconds, like he's trying to read directions to put something back together that's broken.

"I don't know what you want, Lily." His head shakes slowly and his elbows shift, his hands never leaving his pockets.

"I want to be friends..." My mouth hangs open.

I don't say the rest, because I'm not *that* strong or brave, but the meaning is there in the quiet that follows. I want to be *more* than friends. And Henry…just…doesn't.

"I told you it's hard for me. I'm not like you, Lily."

"I know…you're *better* than me."

The words leave my tongue like acid. I threw something he shared with me right back at him, and in the moment, I thought it would feel good. But with each passing second, remorse begins to take over, gripping at my chest and pushing my thoughts into a constant replay.

I've made a rule between us. One neither of us seem to like but that I need. Henry's gaze dips to my chest then waist, and finally the ground. He nods with a slight movement, turning slowly to the direction we came from. He gets a few paces ahead before I follow him home.

He opens the door and lets me pass through first, the lush scent of cinnamon, apples, butter, and onions seeping into our bodies the moment we step inside. I move down the hallway to see the feast in preparation mode, but I notice soon that Henry doesn't follow me. He takes the stairs two at a time, and his door *clicks* shut when he disappears.

I don't see him again until dinner. And he doesn't stay downstairs to watch me play after the meal is done. He leaves, out into the dark night and falling snow, just like the universe promised to deliver. A dusting covers the back and shoulders of his long, wool coat as he crosses the street outside the music room window. I don't feel much like playing Elena's piano anymore, but I know if I don't, Alice will feel like I let her down. It's less that she wants to hear me and more that she likes to see her employer take pride in what I've learned.

I like to play for Henry, though. It's been a long time since I have. But maybe that's his rule—maybe it makes him sad.

CHAPTER 8

F ate is cruel sometimes. It does things like force you to have to retake theology, and then it puts the girl you quickly summed up to be an arch nemesis in your class. The real kicker, however, is this— Ava Farmstead is unbelievably kind...despite her damn glitter obsession!

Shit.

I spent most of the start of this spring semester maneuvering seats through barters and trades due to Mr. O'Farland's penchant for shaking things up in the classroom to let us get to know each other better. He likes to change the seating arrangement on Mondays. This meant I had to be the first one in the door at the start of every week. Once, I even tampered with his seating chart and erased my name from the spot next to Ava, putting myself at the time-out chair reserved for discipline. I half convinced our teacher that he had caught me talking too much that week. I'm not sure if he bought it.

I ran out of tricks by late February, though, and when I finally shared the table with this bubbly girl who I was ready to hate, she hugged me. She also squealed when our teacher announced that this would be our spots for the rest of the year. And then told me she'd been hoping to sit next to me for weeks.

Weeks.

I dodged her for weeks.

How ironic.

In a massive pendulum swing, I've become incredibly grateful for her. She fits the gaps. Where Nicki is exceptionally jaded and Anya is equally cautious, Ava fits in-between. She's me, if I were rich and enjoyed wearing clothing that made me stand out in a crowd of thousands. I knew that of anyone, Ava would be the one to come to the first crew race of the season with. I knew Elena would be here, and Ava makes for awkward conversation. Because of that, Elena's kept her distance, sitting under a special donor tent near the finish line.

This sport isn't like the others at Satis, or even in Illinois. People don't buy jerseys or pick out individuals to idolize. They appreciate the form, and they resolute in smug confidence that one school's team is faster than all of the others—an elite among the already private elite.

Truthfully, before I met Henry and before I watched his team row, I would have made fun of the few hundred of us, mostly friends and family, sprinkled along the channel's shoreline ready to inaugurate the season. At public school, they held a bonfire to kick off the football season in the fall. We're all supposed to tip our hats. The only hat I own is a very well-worn Cubs ballcap that was once my father's. I have to keep a pin in the back for it to fit. There was a time that it would have embarrassed me not to have a beautiful sun hat to wave at the boats as they cruise by, but the version of me I am right now waves the Cubbie blue proudly.

"You know, I haven't talked to Henry since we've broken up," Ava says, as we hold our hats outstretched until the Satis boat—and Henry —cruise past the staging area, heading off to the starting line.

Ava and I haven't talked about Henry much. I think we both don't want to get into personal things when it comes to him—she not wanting to relive the embarrassment of their breakup in a limousine with me present, and me not wanting to get into the fact that the only romantic thing to come out of that weekend for me was a daring visit to some train tracks.

There's an unspoken sense, though. I feel it, and I know she does too. She knows that there's something that exists between Henry and me, and neither of us know exactly what it is. It's better off unsaid. I made sure of that on Thanksgiving, and Henry hasn't crossed the line since. Honestly, we haven't even talked other than cordial *hellos* and *goodbyes* in front of Alice and Elena.

"He's really been busy since we got back from break. I've only seen him once or twice," I say, careful to make just enough eye contact to sell this as the truth.

Henry and I did exchange Christmas gifts when I saw him last, just before school started again. I gave him a snow globe that I'd found at an antique store near Collin's restaurant because he had said he was fond of snow. He gave me chocolates, expensive ones that weren't personal in the least. I'm the one who drew the line, though, and made the rule—so expensive candy didn't push my imagination overboard. I was a convenient acquaintance, as convenient as Frango chocolates picked up at the department store.

None of my classes overlap with Henry's, and my second time through theology keeps me away from my window most afternoons. I haven't seen him rush to practice in nearly six weeks. And other than updates from Alice about life at Elena's during my weekend calls to her and Collin, my connection to the Aldermans feels like it's fading.

I see him now, though. Even hundreds of feet away, he stands out. He's like one of Ava's outfits: bright even in a row of boys who, to most others, would seem identical.

He cut his hair, only a little, but enough that the long curls no longer move in the wind. It must make him faster, more efficient with the oars.

"Wonderful that you both came to support Henry."

Elena's cold tone blankets both of us. From my periphery, I see Ava's posture sink, her skin growing a little paler as all of her blood rushes to shore up the sick feeling in her gut. I've built an immunity to her, so I turn to engage first.

"First race of the season. This is the place to be." I tip the brim of my ballcap up enough to look Elena in the eyes, and I catch the disdain in hers as she takes in my fashion choice for the day.

"I would have loaned you a hat if you wanted, Lily. All you had to do was ask."

It's strange how Elena can seem kind and conniving within the same breath.

"I didn't want to bother you," I lie. "I'll keep that in mind for next time."

Ava draws in a quick breath. She's probably been holding it and is in desperate need of air.

"Ava, dear. How are your parents? I'm so sorry we weren't able to spend time together for the holidays. Henry...he's going through that typical adolescent rebellion I suppose." Elena sings out the last part, not-so-delicately eluding to the limo ride over Thanksgiving.

Ava's frustration and panic is radiating off her as she stands next to me, shifting her feet like someone who really needs to pee. She glances down, shadowing her face with her hat, probably hiding her anxious expression.

"Aren't we all," I step in for her, waiting for her to lift her chin just enough for me to catch her eyes. I wink at her, which causes her lips to lift with hope.

"I suppose you all are," Elena hums. I'm sandwiched between my new friend and my benefactor, trying to protect them both and preserve that small piece of respect that got me into Satis in the first place.

"You both should join me closer to the water. There really is nothing better than watching the strong finish after fifteen-hundred meters. You know, most high schools don't row as far as the college prep schools in Illinois." Without waiting for us to accept her offer, Elena begins walking with her hand gesturing for us to follow toward the tent that's housing all of the school's most important people.

Reluctantly, we both follow. I'm stronger than Ava, but we are both rather weak.

We join Elena right along a wooden railing, and she reaches into her small black clutch to pull out a pair of binoculars. She hands them to Ava first, who smiles and flushes with relief to have something else to busy herself with other than this conversation.

I recognize the move instantly, though. It's a distraction. I will not get so lucky.

"Henry says the two of you don't get to see each other quite as often this semester. That's too bad." I glance at her in an attempt to read her face, but her large sunglasses hide her eyes. Not that I would be able to read them anyway. I look back out at the water, at the shrinking boats off in the distance. I wonder if I'll be able to hear the gun.

The three of us watch in silence for a few minutes, listening to the commentary playing out from the booth for the VIP crowd. I know very little about the technical nature of this sport. At one point, I wanted to ask Henry more about it, but then things got...difficult.

Rules.

I know that his job is the bowman. It's labeled on the back of his shirt. His voice carries well, which is perhaps why he got the job. He's the one who gives orders to the rest of the team. I don't know for sure what they mean.

"You like him. You've always liked him," she says, and I stiffen. She leans in close, the ends of her hair dusting my shoulder. "I could tell the moment you two met."

I don't know what my reaction is supposed to be, but the one I let out is that of trapped. I'm caught.

"He's a good friend," I say, though that isn't totally true. There are things I tell him that I don't tell other people, like about my parents. But there are things I tell Nicki and Anya that I don't tell Henry—like about my crush on him.

"Be careful with your heart, Lily. If you are going to put yourself into the game for Henry's attention, I fear you should prepare yourself for the likelihood that you'll lose." Elena's posture straightens and she takes the binoculars back from Ava. She heard that last bit. I couldn't help but glance at the both of them. Now everything is awkward and awful.

"Henry is fickle." Ava's observation does more than surprise me. She shirks her shoulders and tips her head slightly. She's sticking up for me.

"He is, Ava. Very much so," Elena says, holding the binoculars to her own eyes while she lifts her sunglasses and peers out across the water. "You can't be too careful in our world though, you know. One foolish decision could send you toppling down to the bottom of the ladder. Nobody ever makes the climb back up to where they were. Not if you let another person weigh you down."

She leaves us with this riddle, excusing herself to join a few other women her age, all dressed in long, flowing pants and light jackets. The entire tent looks like a party on Gatsby's lawn.

The boards are mere flecks out in the distance, and Ava and I both pretend we can see them in detail while we stare off in silence, shielding our eyes from the sun's reflection on the water. The brightness forces me to look down eventually, and I realize I've been clutching the bottom of my sweater so hard that my palms are sweating.

"Thank you...for coming to my rescue," I say.

Ava leans toward me a little and laughs.

"I'm pretty sure I owed you one."

I nod and smile at the ground. The gun sounds in the distance, and the voice commentary from two older alumni in the booth behind us swirls in and out of my ears like nonsense. The boats are too far to see, but I hear faint chants down the channel from people who decided to watch from different points.

"We used to board Elena's horses. That's how I met her—my family met her. We're not like her." I look up just in time to meet Ava's eyes as she turns to the side. We lock gazes in agreement.

"I know you're not," I say, guilt rippling down my insides because I actually thought quite the opposite.

"I mean it. My parents have been into horses for years. My mom was a vet when my parents met. They're older—in their late fifties. It's always been weird for me at school functions because my parents are so much older than everyone else's. Elena's older, though, so maybe that's why they clicked. She's a little eccentric, so please don't read into her gibberish. My mom taught me that."

I'm not sure what I'm supposed to offer in response, so I go with the only thing I know.

"My parents died. Alice—she's my aunt. Or cousin. Or cousin-aunt. I don't really know. She and Collin are way too young. It's opposite of you, but it kinda feels the same...if that makes sense."

Ava loops her arm through mine, a strange gesture that I'm

surprised I like. I give her a squeeze with my slight muscles, and her smile stretches as she shakes both of our connected limbs and draws my attention back to the water.

"I still can't see them very well. Which one is ours?" I ask.

She points with her other hand, counting over three spaces from the right, then squints and holds her finger steady.

"That one," she says, drawing me near enough to follow her sightline.

The anticipation is contagious. I go minutes thinking I don't really care how this race finishes before Henry's form starts to come into view. With every flick of oars that draws lines in the water, I begin to rock. My movement is small at first, but soon Ava is doing it with me—both of us bending at the knees and pushing, trying to help Henry and the other seven boys in the boat gain more power with every thrust.

His voice gets clearer, though it's still distant, carried over the water and amid such physical exertion that he no longer sounds fifteen, but more like he's twenty.

"Go half, go half, three quarters and pause..." He keeps the entire team in rhythm, and while other teams paddle furiously, our boys lean low and glide between long, fluid strokes. I begin to understand—the paddles make them go, but they also make them stop. Their speed is a delicate balance; it requires the right amount of work and patience.

"And go!" Henry's voice shouts in a raspy gargle, echoing as the edge of their boat passes the beginning of our deck.

My eyes are like zoom lenses, admiring the ripple on his bicep and forearm, the deep creases along his neck as he strains and stares at the boy with dark hair and ice eyes in front of him. Nobody breaks today —everyone's attention is forward, on this one singular task.

To win.

Better than everyone else.

And they do. They come in a full length ahead of the next team, and their celebration and exhaustion collide as they fall forward and back letting the boat glide to slow down naturally.

Everyone around us cheers, clapping and shouting the Satis House song. "Fight on, mighty commodores, aboard this battleship—hear, hear! We cry for victory, our right we take over all!"

I don't know the words, and Ava pretends to mouth them next to me, laughing with a shrug as she lets go of my arm.

"That was exciting," she whispers into my ear.

"It was," I say, forcing a smile to match hers.

Something about this moment also feels like a revelation to me. In a crowd of attendees, only two of us are quiet—Elena and I. And she has already left the tent and begun her walk up the hill. She doesn't stay to congratulate her son. She's actually never called him that. Nor has he called her Mom. He's Henry. She's Elena.

Victory above all else.

Her riddle is becoming a little clearer now, as is her warning for me.

"Be careful with your heart, Lily."

Henry has been bred to win…with room for very little else.

CHAPTER 9

SUMMER AFTER FRESHMAN YEAR

The train ride felt foreign today. I don't know if it's because I'm a year older than I was last summer, or if it's because the entire year that played out between Henry and me was so strange. Whatever the cause, everything feels as if it's happening for the very first time.

I may be a year older, but somehow Alice still sees me as this naïve young girl—*a burden.* She woke me earlier than was necessary, and when I tried to sneak in a few extra minutes of sleep before she came knocking again, she stole the quilt from my bed and tossed it into the hallway. Sleeping without a cover feels naked. So I got up, and I got dressed and then I sat at the kitchen table with a piece of toast and pretended that she and Collin weren't fighting over money.

I wish Collin was the one who had the job at the Alderman house. Or, I wish I could play a piano at his restaurant so I wouldn't have to come here with Alice to practice. I'm not even sure I really want to this summer, not that I have a choice. That offer Elena made last year for me to play her piano was a contract in Alice's eyes—a deal sealed that if I messed with would result in doom, AKA Alice would lose her job. I do love playing, though. Even in hell.

The house is eerily dark this morning. We weave through the thin alleyway between the vine-covered iron fence and the north side of the house to a small back door that Alice started using over the holidays. It's how the housekeeper arrives, and how caterers come in and out of the Alderman kitchen. It's for *the help.*

Alice's giant keyring jingles as she shakes it free of her purse, unlocking the side door then quickly ushering me inside as if she's sneaking me in or something. *Contraband.* The pantry, kitchen, and hallways are lifeless, and the temperature is cold—a sharp contrast to the early summer warmth cooking outside.

"It feels like a freezer in here," I say, feeling along the wall for a light switch. I push in when I feel one raised, but nothing happens. "Weird…fuse must be out."

"Damnit. I forgot my sweater. I brought one yesterday and it saved my ass." Alice begins to rifle through the hallway closet, pulling out a sweater that looks to be about two sizes too big. I arch a brow and catch her glance.

"What? This thing has been in that closet for months. I think the last caterer Elena fired left it here. I'll put it back." She rolls the sleeves several times to force a better fit.

I shiver and decide I can't blame her. I swear if I blow slowly enough right now, I might see my breath.

I leave Alice in the kitchen and venture to the only room I really care about in this house. Windows are drawn close, and every room I pass looks as if it's been closed up for the season, like one of those estates in Austen novels filled with noble families who only open them up for parties.

The music-room door is cracked open, so I curl my fingers around the edge and push it slowly. The sound on the keys is faint, almost as if a cat is walking from one end to the other. Henry's hair peaks out from the top, his head resting on his bent arm while his face looks down at the keys. A soft echo from one of the middle keys barely reverberates. I wonder if he's testing himself to see if he can play without any sound at all. I haven't heard him play in at least a year. Last summer, he stopped when I started to play more often. He'd always listen though.

The two of us finished the semester barely speaking. I only went to one more of his races, and not because I wasn't curious. I was deeply curious. The draw to go was strong. I denied myself because I want to be about more than Henry Alderman. And beyond him, I want to be about more than trying to either avoid or please Elena. I had to cut myself off because that's how I operate—all or nothing. Cold turkey. Deny to become strong.

Resistance.

This is how my mother gave up sugar. I just assumed it would apply to teenaged crushes, too.

I dove into the end of my freshman year, somehow repairing my failure of theology the first time around and coming out with a *B* the second time. It was my only *B*, which means my GPA is intact and my scholarship money will continue to cover *all* expenses for at least one more year.

More than focusing on my studies, though, I focused on my music for those last three months of school. I spent the extra hours—once wasted on spying out my window in search of a boy—in the practice rooms of the performance building. I'm getting better. I can actually hear it in my own hands as they work the keys.

Despite forcing myself to separate my life from Henry and Elena, though, I couldn't help but be excited to visit the Alderman piano again. I wanted to see what I could make it do.

I wanted to show off...*for him.*

"Are you waiting for me?" My voice breaks a little, the combination of my attempt to whisper and the early morning hour betraying me. I don't really know how to talk to him anymore.

Henry lifts his head enough for his gaze to meet mine. His mouth remains relaxed, his face showing absolutely zero surprise. He shrugs and looks back down at the keys, repeating the same soft sound as before.

I expect him to move over as I get closer to the piano, but he stays buried in the dark. Rather than take a seat in the small space left beside him, I move to the window and pull one of the heavy green drapes to the side, looping it through the metal hook anchored to the wall. The velvet material feels dusty, so I'm careful when I sweep the other side to the left. My allergies are sensitive to dust.

"This place looks like a museum. What's going on?" I pat my hands together to shake away the dust, then lean on the window sill to face Henry.

"Elena doesn't want me sitting around here all day, hence the uncomfortable and constant blast of air conditioning. That's the only breaker that's on, actually—the air. And she fired the housekeeper, so this place is fucking musty as hell." He presses the same key a little harder this time, letting his fingers trail up a few notes before his hand feathers out to play a full chord.

"But isn't this uncomfortable for her to live in?" I fold my arms over my chest, rubbing the bumps forming on my skin from the cold. Henry shrugs, finally looking up and moving his arms down to his sides. He grips at the bench and rocks back and forth a few times.

"That's why it's cold instead of hot. Makes it easier to normalize when she's home. Keeps Alice on task too. Besides, Elena's hardly here. She's spending all of her time at Havisham. They've acquired some big brand, I guess. I'm supposed to go there and *learn*." Henry leans forward and folds his hands together on top of the piano and leans toward me.

"Wow. That's a pretty huge opportunity for a fifteen-year-old," I say, stepping away from the window. I stop just shy of the bench, and when Henry slides to his left, I cross my ankles to signal that I plan on standing for a little while longer—until he's no longer on the bench.

Henry smirks as his eyes scan down to the place where my knee bends, then he breathes out a short laugh, blinking his way back up to my gaze.

"I guess. Though you're no judge really. I mean, you're probably going to spend this entire summer practicing runs and positioning and some sonata by..." Henry picks up a thin music book Elena must have left out for me on the piano ledger. "Shubert."

He tosses the music book to the floor. I itch to pick it up, and I can tell my discomfort amuses him. That comfort we cultivated last summer is gone. I did that.

To be fair, though...he made me.

"Do you think we can turn the temperature up while she's gone?" I shift my feet and glance around the room for a thermostat, wandering a few steps and stopping to pick up the book. Henry chuckles when I do, but I ignore him. He's pushing me, and I won't indulge him.

"Probably. I wouldn't know where to begin to do that, though."

Henry stands and I continue my path around the room, laughing a little until I realize he isn't joking. I stop and let my arms drop to my sides, the music book clutched at my hip. My mouth gapes open.

"You don't know how to work a thermostat?" I'm incredulous. I wait a few seconds for him to begin laughing, to tell me he's joking, but that move never comes. He's serious.

"No reason to ever learn." He shrugs one shoulder then drops his hands into the pockets of his khaki shorts.

"You would die in the real world," I say with an eye roll. I move out into the hallway and run into Alice, who's turned on more lights. She knows where the breakers are.

"Henry here?" She mouths the question, but it isn't discreet enough.

"Henry's here," he says behind me, not as close as he usually gets. That distance is there, and it's become permanent.

"He said we can turn the air up," I say, scanning down the hallway walls. Before I can pass, though, Alice leans to the side and stretches her arm out, pressing her palm on the opposite wall.

"Oh no. Elena told me specifically to keep this place at sixty-four until she gets home in the evening. She wants it cool all night."

"She wants me to leave the house and take the six train to Havisham," Henry says.

"That too," Alice says, pointing at Henry but putting her arm right back in my way.

"If Henry leaves, can we turn the air up?" I ask. He coughs behind me and I glance at him briefly but hold up my palm, not interested if he's protesting.

Alice squirms at the question. There's something about this job that has her beaten down. She's afraid of Elena, which I understand, but she must be getting paid enough to make it worth enduring. I can tell when she begins to chew at the inside of her cheek that there's no way this place is getting warmer today, so I decide to negotiate with Henry instead.

"We're going to Havisham," I say.

He laughs, leaning back with his hands still in his pockets.

"Oh, not just no. Hell no," he says, his shoulders shaking a few times while his laughter subsides.

I step closer, as close as he would step if I'd never made things weird. His eyes peer down at me and his mouth ticks up on one side. It's been a while, but the same flutters still rush my chest being close to him. I'm smarter about it now, though. I know that it's just infatuation. And I know Henry isn't like me, and we're never going to be anything. He told me so. Elena confirmed it. That gives me power to use his weaknesses on him. He likes being tested and playing mental games like this. I've watched him do it with other girls all semester, when he quit doing it with me.

"Well, I'm going to Havisham," I begin, my mouth curling in deep with the dare I'm about to roll out. "And if I show up without you, I'm going to find Elena's secretary, and then I'll tell her that you abandoned me to be mean and left me in the city alone."

The black of his eyes widens for a second, and his nostrils flare. He's trying to read how serious I am, and I'm trying to bluff like a mad woman. I lower my eyes on his and let my smirk grow into a *checkmate*. My only fear is that Elena wouldn't care that I'd been abandoned. It's a real possibility.

"Just go do what you're supposed to, Henry. Quit being a child. Do what your mom wants, and maybe she will stop taking this out on *us*." Alice thinks she's being stern, and this tough-talk lecturing would probably work on me just fine. But Henry is nothing like me. He's broken in a different way, and he doesn't feel things like pressure or guilt. That much I know. He barely feels at all.

His gaze lifts above my head to Alice behind me.

"Elena."

Jaw set and eyes cold, Henry holds Alice hostage with a heated glare. I heard it, too. That word: *mom*. I'm sure Alice said it on purpose, thinking it would maybe spark an emotion or make Henry soft. This is where he and I are the same, though—neither of us has a real mom anymore. I have Alice. He has Elena.

Maybe it's just me wanting to cut through the tension, or to avoid what could easily blow up into a screaming match that might just end up getting Alice fired.

Or maybe…I just wanted to.

Whatever the internal push is that makes me do it, I unfurl my arms from one another and wrap my hand around Henry's forearm, my fingers collapsing against his skin one at a time. My hold is gentle, but firm—my attempt to convey that I'm still Lily, the girl he took up on a roof and who he can trust with his secrets, even if I told him to stop sharing them.

Henry swallows, but his eyes remain set on Alice, so I tug on his limb, urging his attention to me.

"Take me with you…to Havisham," I whisper. His eyes draw away from Alice to my mouth in a steady movement without blinking. I part my lips knowing he's looking at them and let out a tiny breath. We're so close that if we were alone, he might wrap me up in his arms.

If we were alone…I might let him.

My lashes blink drowsily. It's not that I'm sleepy, though I am, but rather that I'm drunk on giving into the game. Being like this with Henry isn't good for me, and it's going to be hard to draw the line again now that I've erased parts of it. But I've been Henry. And I've been weak and given in when Alice or Collin or the world have told me that this is just the way things are. I've accepted, and I've hurt, and I've buried the suffering deep inside so I can forge ahead. If I can be here for him and help him find a way to please people, but also be himself, then maybe I can mold a little more of the new me, too.

"Let's go." I don't ask, because he'd say no. I don't dare him again because I already have, and I knew the moment I tried it that it was dangerous. It might have worked, but the avalanche of push-pull it would have spawned would have drowned me.

There's only one way to the real Henry—I have to be close. I have to put the guards down and be honest. I have to ask him innocently because the one thing I've just realized is every single time I've asked Henry to do something, really asked because I genuinely wanted or needed him to, he's done it. Even when that thing was to leave me alone.

"I can't spend a summer in another house full of people who don't like each other." I blink. He blinks back. I can hear the sharp breath Alice draws behind me, and she excuses herself a second later.

"Do whatever. Just don't piss off my boss," she says, retreating down the hallway toward Elena's office.

Henry studies me for a moment. He doesn't ask me to explain. I never have to share stories about the bickering that's happened every morning since I've gotten home for the summer. Home—I don't have to launch into all the reasons that Alice and Collin's house isn't *home*. I just had to ask. Henry understands without the rest.

"We'll get a car," he says, backing away a few steps before turning toward the front door.

I follow him, pausing by the music room since I still have the book in my other hand. He holds the door open wide, sunshine glowing brightly as it forces its way inside the cavernous hallways of the Alderman home. Dust speckles the rays, swirling with Henry's breath. I toss the music book inside the room, on the floor, and Henry smiles.

He lets me walk out first, pulling the door closed behind me but leaving it unlocked. I'm sure Alice will rush to it and lock it—just like Elena wants—the second we're out of her view. There's no way we're leaving without her eyes watching us from inside. She won't tell Elena we're coming, though, because she can't be sure. She wouldn't want to be wrong.

Henry punches in our address on his phone, calling up the closest car that slides up next to the curb in under a minute. He gets in first, moving all the way across the back seat of the white sedan. Our driver is an older man, maybe sixty, and he keeps eying us in the rearview mirror. I can tell he wants to talk, and I know Henry isn't going to, so I strike up a conversation.

"How long have you been driving?"

His eyebrows lift as he glances at me in the reflection.

"Oh, maybe six or seven months." He's wearing a visor, like a poker player, the front bill tinted green to shade his eyes. Doesn't do much to protect his thinning bald head.

"You like it?" I ask. Henry shifts in the seat, letting out a noticeable sigh. I glare at him briefly and he just lifts his brows and stares back at me as if that's going to make me stop chatting up my new senior best friend.

"It's all right. Pays for my health insurance. That's really why I do it. And I've lived here for sixty-two years, so usually I can get folks places faster than this little map thingy they put on the phone." He taps the screen where his phone is mounted to the dash of his car. I notice that it continuously reroutes as he ignores where it tells him to turn.

"Why you two heading somewhere so corporate? Shouldn't you be going to Navy Pier or Wrigley?"

"Yes, we should. In fact..." Henry's trying to make a break for it, change up the plan, so I step in.

"He has an internship. He's just a little nervous." I look at Henry sideways and give him a triumphant grin. He shakes his head and chuckles, giving up...for now.

"Internship. Wow, ain't that something! You can't start planning for your future early enough. Boy, did I learn that." The man sits up high in his seat to look around his mirrors and check blind spots as he makes a tricky turn at a five-point intersection. We dip under a bridge and the tracks of the L as a train rumbles above us.

"What did you do for work...before the driving gig?" I ask.

"I never had a real steady job. Worked in the pickling plant over on the southside, did some work at the shipyards after that, then a little security work for some of the government buildings. Nothing fancy, like I didn't have a gun or nothin'. I mostly sat in a chair by the front door and took naps."

His answer amuses Henry, and he breathes out a short laugh. I catch the smile creep around the side of his face. Staring at it, I continue my conversation.

"That doesn't sound so bad. Seems like you planned everything just right," I say.

"I guess," the man sighs. There's a long pause as he hums for a second or two with thought. I look back to the mirror just in time to look him in the eyes. "My best friend from high school went on to work for the governor. He wore fancy suits and went to all the parties.

Drove a real nice car. The funny thing was I was always smarter than him, but he just didn't get distracted."

"And you did?" I lead him and squint one eye.

"You might say I was a ladies' man." The car pulls to a stop and he reaches up to straighten his invisible bowtie. I giggle, more comfortable flirting with him than the boy my age next to me.

"Any of them win over your heart?" I ask, expecting more light-hearted answers to carry out the rest of our trip. But I've hit a nerve suddenly, and our driver sinks deeper into his seat, reaching up to adjust his mirror, putting me out of his view.

"Just one," he finally says.

The more time that passes between our words, the thicker the air feels in my chest until my lungs begin to feel bruised with every intake of air. I know the various ways his story could go. I'm not selfish enough to need him to finish it, either. He loved someone, and at one point it ended, either from life…or death.

We pull up at the Havisham main entrance, double-parked by a row of cars waiting to turn around the block. I open my door and Henry slips out on my side after me. I hold up my palm to wave thanks to our driver, whose name I didn't even bother to ask before I crushed his soul. I feel like an asshole.

"Maybe next time we don't interview the driver?" Henry teases, opening his phone to leave the man a tip. I glance at his screen to catch the name—*Chester*. I even like that.

Henry finishes tipping, then shoves his phone into his pocket. We're both dressed for summer, though Henry looks more like he's dressed for a yacht vacation or golf outing. Even his plain, white T-shirt looks like some type of designer brand. His hair is still a little fluffy from his pouting session at the piano, so I reach up on my toes and with my fingers, feather it back. The waves are soft, grown out a little from the shorter cut he got when Crew season began. It's almost as long as it was last year at this time—when I thought it was perfect.

"You know I don't want to be here, right? Like…in the worst way." He grimaces.

"What would be the best way?" I ask, challenging him. His eyes dim, unamused. I laugh his broodiness off and weave my arm through his elbow. It's a bold move that I immediately regret because instead of feeling playful and friendly and cute, it feels awkward and...intimate. Now I'm the one giving mixed signals, doing exactly what I asked him to stop. He drags for a few steps, like I'm forcing a poorly trained dog to walk, but then quickly relaxes and moves his arm around until somehow his hand is holding mine. I try to play it off while we walk through the revolving door, and I even encourage him to swing our hands as we approach the elevator. None of it phases him, though, and when the doors open and we walk in taking a space near the back, he keeps a strong hold of me.

At least a dozen people file in after us, until the elevator is uncomfortably full. A few people glance at my flip-flops and denim shorts and give me a tight smile. To them, I'm a cute school girl here to see her secretary mom. As we race up several floors at a time, waiting while new people get on and other riders get off, I start to realize how nobody is looking at Henry the way they're looking at me. He's a little more put together, sure, but he's still fifteen. Our birthdays are exactly a month apart—he's September, and I'm October.

With about six floors to go until we reach Elena's, the elevator opens to let out everybody who's left. When the doors close, the thought that we might get stuck in here races through my mind. It's a fleeting thought, almost a wish, and then it's gone. We start to slow one floor away, and when the car halts on forty-seven, a floor below our destination, I wriggle my hand to let go of Henry's. Elena's signature white coat hits my periphery first, and then my heartbeat ratchets up like a kid caught stealing from her mom's purse. Henry's hold grows firmer, and with nothing more than a blink to realize Henry wants Elena to see us holding hands, she does.

Positioned exactly between the two halves of the silver doors, her body pauses, rigid, and her gaze dives down to the very place where Henry's thumb is making a delicate circle along the top of my hand. Parts of me are continuously taking turns going numb. It's more than panic moving into my body. I want to throw up. In fact, I might.

"I'm guessing I have you to thank for making Henry show up today, Lily?" Elena enters the car completely, spinning on her heels and facing the closing doors. The long layers of her dress skirt swish against my shins.

I gulp. It sounds just like the word.

"You do," Henry says for me, again holding on with a tight clasp while I squirm my fingers around. I jerk my head in his direction and mouth "Stop," but rather than smirking as if he's enjoying teasing me, he simply shakes his head *no*.

The doors open again a second later, and Henry and I follow Elena into an impressive lobby, still hand in hand. I feel a little bit dragged around as Henry weaves around a wall-slash-cascading-waterfall, just steps behind Elena. A few people say hello to him as we pass, none of them as much as blinking at the place where our hands are now awkwardly tethered. We finally get to a set of double glass doors, and I shake him loose, quickly putting my thumbs in my pockets and taking long strides to gain a little distance. I feel like Henry is trying to prove a point, almost shoving our touch in Elena's face, and those are the things I drew the line for in the first place.

"While I'm glad you made it in today, Henry, I'm a little disappointed that Lily had to push you to come. Your future is something..."

"—to be taken seriously and requires much focus, yes...I know," Henry finishes. He falls into a metal and leather seat on one side of Elena's desk while she moves to the rolling chair on the other. The only place left for me to sit is at a chair near the ornate conference table. I actually think the base is made of soap. Glass is placed atop these waxy, ornate carvings that I'm compelled to touch. When I push my nails into the side, I can feel it soften under the pressure. It's weird.

"Well I guess I'm glad you're listening when I say that." Elena leans forward to press a button on her phone while twisting her lips into disapproval while she stares at Henry. His body is too big for the chair, and he's pulled one leg up, nearly draping it over the armrest.

While Elena taps her slender, long nails on top of her desk, Henry turns to glance my way over his shoulder. His mouth ticks up apologetically. I'm glad he doesn't say "sorry" though because it's my fault we're here.

"He's here, Maggie…yes…If you can set him up please. Next to Abigail, all right?"

It's a mostly one-sided conversation we both listen in on, and when Elena ends the call, she pushes back from her desk with a commanding roll, then presses her palms on the glass top as she stands and looks down at the boy who she's supposed to love. It's never felt like love with her and him, though. Pride, sure. She's constantly proud—like the way the Westminster dog owners are proud.

"Maggie's setting up your office. You'll be working with the community outreach team, and learning about our brand." Elena unfolds the black-rimmed glasses from her desk and slips them along the bridge of her nose, leaving them low enough to allow her to peer over the tops at Henry and me.

"Sounds great," Henry says, the words drenched in sarcasm and contempt. He skips to his feet and settles his gaze on me as he moves toward the door. There's a mixture of despair and resentment in the way they droop, and the soft but straight line that marks his lips is far from happy.

I get up from the soap table and double my pace to catch up to him. I'm not sure why I do it—maybe I feel guilty for dragging him into this —but I reach for Henry's hand. My knuckles graze along his and the slight tickle startles him when we reach the door. His head pivots to me in a flash, and his eyes question me.

Was that an accident?

My mouth pulls into a tight smile, my lips folding into each other and nearly disappearing. All I wanted was a calm place to escape to over the summer—a room with a piano and a household free of grudges and punishment. I sold Henry out for my own pleasure, and now that it's done, I feel sick.

"Lily," she calls out my name as if I'm her student. I guess I am. I became her student the moment I let myself think she was better than me.

"Yes, ma'am," I say, feeling the slight squeeze of Henry's grip on my hand. My puckered mouth itches to break into a full grin. I know Elena doesn't like *ma'am.* I was being snarky. I did it for Henry.

As I turn to face her, she lifts her chin and drops a letter she was reading back into the pile of documents on her desk. She blinks as her eyes switch from looking at me below the frames of her glasses to the space above, and she pushes the rims down just a little more to really turn her nose down and judge me.

"When you get back to the house, please have Alice call to arrange for the cleaning service to come in, and oh…let her know I would like to keep the house at seventy-four. And I'd love to see the progress you're making on your technique. You know, I'm good friends with the pianist with the philharmonic. I'm sure I could arrange a meet and greet. Henry could take you." Her eyes flit down to our hands as she pauses, and I swear there's a twitch in her lips—amusement.

"Wouldn't you, Henry?" She baits him. Her stare crawls back up to Henry this time, and there's a little warning to her voice. I wonder how many times she froze Henry in the winter just to teach him a lesson. And I wonder if she's ever baked him in the summer.

"Of course, ma'am," Henry says, following my lead. Elena's eyes twitch, but she moves on from us in a breath, waving us out the door as she returns to the letter she was reading a moment before.

Henry and I follow a slender woman wearing a deep-purple pencil skirt and matching jacket down the corridor to a huge office in the exact opposite corner from Elena's. We've passed dozens of men and women in their thirties, forties, fifties—all stuffed into cubicles that lack any personalization. I saw maybe one photo of a baby, other than that, everyone's desk was bare of anything other than the business at hand. They must want to actively hate Henry. Fifteen and blessed with the office with a view for the summer.

"Thanks, Maggie," Henry says to the pencil skirt as she holds the heavy door open with her arm. I follow him inside and let go of his hand as he moves toward the window.

"Miss, Lily?" I turn my attention back to Maggie and make a questioning expression. "Elena said you can take the train back to the house. She said you know the way."

I'm so stunned that I don't react, and by the time I'm able to form the right words—*excuse me?* —Maggie has left the room, nothing but a sway of purple hips several cubes away.

"I'm so sorry I made you do this," I say, turning back to Henry.

He's closed the distance while my back was to him, and without warning, his arms curl around me in a desperate embrace, his chin curved low into my shoulder and his nose soft against my neck. He's at least forty pounds bigger and several inches taller and wider, and by all accounts his body swallows mine whole. But right now, this one small moment, I hold him up. He clings to me, his breath heavy in an attempt not to cry, and our bodies sway while his hands clutch at my hair that spills down my back. He grips as if the strands are ropes, and he trembles desperately, holding me tight like this for a solid minute.

Henry…he missed me.

When he pulls away, it's sudden, as if morphine just kicked in to sooth him. He turns his back to me while he wipes away any proof of emotion, and he moves over to the window that overlooks LaSalle Street and the nearby Chicago skyscrapers.

"I'll have another car come. I'll put it on my phone, so just wait out front. You don't need to take the train. Elena was just being a bitch." His harsh choice of words surprises me. He's never gone that far.

"I really don't mind," I say.

"Lily," he says my name, and the way he says it is nothing like how Elena did.

His eyes hit mine as he looks over his shoulder. He's not dressed for business today, and I bet he was looking forward to taking a break from the uniform he seems to live in. He does look nice in a pressed shirt, though. He's handsome, and I can't deny that I look forward to seeing him leave or arrive back home.

I hold up my hand, relenting.

"Okay, I'll accept your car." I jokingly roll my eyes, and Henry chuckles softly, looking off to the side, his profile contrasting against the bright window behind him. A young prince standing in his future empire, Henry sometimes shows these glimpses of the man he'll be one day. He'll be powerful and a leader. He'll be loved and adored. I only hope he'll be kind.

I back through the door, feeling the weight of the dense glass against my arm as it practically pushes me out. So perfect for one of Elena's designs.

"Hey…Lily?" Henry catches me before the glass panel closes completely. I turn back slightly with a tilt of my chin.

"Yes," I say.

"Maybe when I get back today…"

I twist a bit more to see what has him lost for words. His eyes are on the wall beside me one second, and with a blink he's looking right into me.

"I'd love to watch you play. That's what I wanted to say. And…just me. You can play again for Elena, but I don't want to share what I hear with her. I know it's probably childish, but…"

"I'd love to," I say, shutting him up. His mouth rests in a smile that looks genuinely happy; it's the first one I've seen on him in ages. "I know just the song."

CHAPTER 10

I've only worn this dress once—at Thanksgiving. I kinda wish I hadn't soiled it with bad memories now, because tonight promises to be a good one. At least, I hope it turns out that way.

Every day for the first half of this summer, Elena has sent Henry to the office to learn while she's stayed behind to tutor me for the first few hours of the morning. I dreaded it at first, and I know Henry did, too. He still does, but I've gotten so much better, and he's seen me grow. Every afternoon, he slips into the music room and listens to me play. Sometimes he sits next to me on the bench, always still and never flirting or touching me, but there—to listen. He applauds me some-times, and it actually feels genuine. I'm nowhere near the level of the pianist we're going to see tonight at the philharmonic, but I'm good enough to teach someone else one day. I'm good enough to maybe help with a music program, perhaps take it over down the road. I've never had goals or dreams or whatever, but since I've started to learn music, a future has sort of opened up.

Henry and I have settled into an easy friendship. There are still times when I catch myself daydreaming, but there's no harm in that. It's human, and there's something magnetic about him that makes it hard to be helped.

He'll be here soon. I offered to just stay at his home and wait for him to return from the office, but he insisted on picking me up with Elena's driver. I'm not sure he realizes the route he's gotten their driver Phillip into, though. It's a half-hour by train, and there really isn't a freeway that's convenient for more than a few miles of the trip.

"You can borrow my shoes…if you want." Alice is leaning in the bathroom doorway and watching me attempt to brush color on my cheeks in the mirror. I straightened my hair for an hour, and it feels like silk ribbons down my back. I pause with the blush in my hand and meet her gaze in the mirror, a pair of short-heeled sling-backs in her hand.

"Thank you, but I'm going to wear my Converse," I say, remembering the mannequin I saw wearing this dress in the first place. Alice scrunches her face and rolls her eyes as she backs out of the doorway.

"Whatever," she says.

I glance at her figure as she leaves, and breathe out, letting my hands fall limp to the counter. She was trying to be nice. For a few seconds, I consider calling after her, but I really don't want to wear the shoes. I could ask her to help me with my makeup, but I kinda want to do this on my own. Eventually, I decide that one small gesture in a hallway bathroom isn't going to build a real relationship between me and my current mother figure. I've gotten on this far, and in three years, I'll be out of this house entirely and away for college. No summers at home—studies and work, straight through.

I can't wait for my sophomore year at Satis. Living there with Nicki and Anya, with Ava and hundreds of other people my age—it feels a thousand times more at home than this place ever has. I'm more at home at Elena's, in fact, and that place is a tomb.

My phone buzzes on the counter with a message from Henry telling me they're almost here, and instantly, every choice I've made about what to wear and how to look tonight is wrong. The striped pink slashes on my cheeks are more warrior than couture, the faint lipstick more little-girl than woman. I shut the blush and toss it along with the brush into the drawer I keep my hair ties and makeup in, and I turn the hot water on full blast.

Frantically searching around the tiny bathroom space, I pull the hand towel from its hook and drench it under the steaming water. I unfurl the towel to cool it first then press it against the right side of my face, smearing away any proof that I tried to look grown-up at all. My skin is pink from the heat, but after a few swipes, the makeup is gone. I do the same thing on the other side, until my face is clean.

I toss the wet towel into the tub and begin waving my hands in front of my face in a desperate attempt to cool my inflamed skin. As bad as this looks, it's better than the makeup. I keep telling myself that as I wander from the bathroom to my room, hands waving the entire time and lips contorted to blow upward at myself.

"Lily!" Alice gives me warning that my ride has arrived. I asked him not to come to the door so I hope he's waiting in the car with Phillip, just like he promised.

"Coming!" I shout back, stuffing my foot into the only shoe I'm able to find while I tuck my head between my knees and pull up my dress so I can search under my bed. If my face wasn't red from my self-torture, it's red from standing on it now.

I spot my shoe a little more than an arm's length away, so I rest the top of my head completely on the floor, my smooth hair tangling around me while my balance threatens to send me ass over neck.

"Are you hyperventilating or is there something I can help you with?"

"Oh!" I give in to the tuck-and-roll and grasp at my dress while I summersault into the middle of my bedroom floor, mortified by the act and the fact that Alice let Henry inside.

Hair wild and shading my face, I blow at it to create a hole to see through. Henry kneels in front of me, but with my blind spots, the only thing I can see are his black pants, argyle socks, and shiny, wingtip shoes. I bet he looks nice. This part of him…the right leg I think? It looks nice.

"I was being lazy, and my other shoe is too far to reach." I blow my hair again, revealing his crooked smile. He bounces with a quiet laugh then reaches forward to sweep aside more of my hair.

"Always going about things the hard way," he smirks. I'm not sure what that means, but I agree with it and scoot out of the way while he crawls on all fours and lowers himself with his forearms to army-crawl a foot or so under my bed to retrieve my shoe. He sits back on his haunches and holds my shoe out for me like a prince.

Always turning me into Cinderella. I'm the cinder girl, though. I don't think the magic really ever took.

"Thanks," I mutter out of the side of my mouth.

I start to stand, but Henry takes my hand and helps me the rest of the way. Straightening the skirting of my dress, I lean over just enough to slip my shoe on my other foot. Henry steadies me with his palm, and when it flattens on my bare back, I arch up quickly, surprised by the touch. I forgot that this dress was open back there.

"Thank you," I say, only taking direct glances at him in bits. I'm not even sure what my face looks like anymore, but his is beautiful. If a boy can *be* described as beautiful.

"No problem," he says, holding his palm out open for me to take. As many times as we've done this now, it still tangles my nerves every single time.

I rest my hand in his, and his fingers fold around me, warm but calm. His hand is never sweaty like mine is. I pray for anxieties to get in line as he walks me out of my room and toward the front door where Alice and Collin are waiting.

"Just one picture?" Collin holds up a small camera I've seen him capture hundreds of things on and never once load onto a computer.

"Why not," I shrug, knowing this image will forever be lost on some disk along with the shots he took of the golf-ball-sized hail last month and the strange cat he thought was a racoon that lived in the neighbor's trash over the holiday break.

Henry positions himself next to me, letting go of my hand so he can move his arm behind my back. I'm ready for his touch this time, and when his fingers graze the dimple of my shoulder blade, it sends a rush of fairy dust up my chest.

"Hold on," Alice says, stepping between us and the camera. Her eyes trace the form of my face and she runs her fingers through my hair like a comb, fixing the disheveled mess I made. As she steps back, her mouth falls into a soft smile, and for a tiny moment, I can tell that she adores me—at least right this minute.

"Okay, ready?" Collin holds the camera up in front of his face, steadying it and framing us between the hallway and the TV, blaring with some court show in the living room. "One...two...three!"

Alice claps as if Henry and I are children getting Easter photos taken at the mall, and it makes both of us laugh. The most natural thing happens next—Henry's hand skims along my back and he bends his arm next to me as I loop my arm through. The nerves are still there; they always are. But the movement is natural, almost habit. Henry Alderman is my gentleman.

I breathe in the smell of his cologne as we leave my house. I remember to gather up the layers of my dress as I take the few steps down the porch. Phillip has the car door open and waiting, and I let go of my escort and slow down as we near. It's the first time I look at Henry completely, and my imagination seems to have filled in all of the blank spaces correctly. The white shirt is offset with a deep gray vest, and his sleeves are rolled up a quarter, tight around his forearms. Hair—that I've only seen combed to perfection for his mother's company or blown haphazardly from crew practice or walks along the lake—is now somewhere in-between. It's touchably soft, but tousled in a way that clearly took effort and is meant to entice every girl that looks at it. I don't envy anyone who sits behind us this evening.

I tear my eyes from staring and dip my head to slide into the car, flinching the moment an unfamiliar but equally pleasant scent hits my senses. I'm not sure whether I hear him or see him first; perhaps it happens at the same time.

Eyes like ice are even bluer in person, and his dark hair is cut short on the sides, combed back into a slick line down the center.

"I'm Caleb," he says, hand outstretched to help me the rest of the way in the car. I hesitate to take it with Henry behind me, but I do. I know exactly who he is, though I haven't thought about him much since the day we made eye contact at their practice.

"Lily," I manage to answer. His lips curl and his eyes squint as he leans into me, his warm shoulder against my chilled bare one.

"I know who you are." He winks. I nod and smile, then busy myself with the small clutch that holds my phone and the emergency cash Collin gave me. Henry slides in next to me, the three of us squished into one side of the car. I'm almost tempted to bail to the other side, but now I'm not so sure if we're picking up more people. All I can do is blink at my own hands and snap and unsnap the magnet closure on my small purse.

"Do you two know each other?" Henry asks.

"Uh," I mumble, not sure how to answer that.

"We just had our formal introductions," Caleb says.

I smile toward my lap and nod.

"You're on crew together, yeah?" I glance to my right first, then quickly to my left, mentally convincing myself that I need to keep the attention equal.

"Right...yeah. I wasn't sure if you'd ever talked or anything. Caleb's in the music track, too..." His eyes glance to his friend as he leans forward, so I follow his lead and turn my focus to Caleb.

"Really. What do you play?" I know it isn't piano because I would have seen him. The number of students in our area isn't large, so really, it's strange I haven't seen him at all other than in a boat.

"Actually...it's theater. Singing and theater." He tugs at the neck of his dark gray shirt, mockingly bragging about himself. "On my way to being a celebrity."

"For a reality show, maybe," Henry snickers. His friend flips him off and hazes his eyes before returning his attention to me. His body shifts so his legs turn toward me, our knees touching briefly; I move an inch to my left—closer to Henry.

"Despite what my new roommate thinks, no...I'd like to be a serious actor, and I know that being able to sing well opens up the theater scene, so..." He shrugs, waiting for me to give him a stamp of approval. I should be impressed. It's just that I'm stuck on that other thing he said—*roommate*.

"How about you? Henry here says you can shred on the piano." He grins, and I basically spit out a laugh at his description.

"I wouldn't say I'm Elton or anything. I've only really been playing seriously for a year." Henry's hand finds my knee, stopping me.

"She's being modest. She's a bit of a genius because in one year she can already play everything in Elena's library."

"Wow!" Caleb leans back with what I think is honest awe. My cheeks burn from the compliment on one side and attention on the other, but mostly, I'm flushed because of the slow drag Henry's fingers make across my kneecap. I force myself not to look at either his touch or his face, and I wonder if he feels like he crossed some line.

I wonder how I'll feel about it when I can think and breathe again.

"I just put in the time, I guess." I snap my purse a few more times, working through the jitters tingling their way down my arms and fingertips now. By the time our car pulls onto the main road, I start to feel normal again.

"You didn't come to many races this year. Elena has her own box area. You should make her set you up. Fans make all the difference out on the water," Caleb says.

"Oh…yeah. I went to one, but I just got busy with freshman-year stuff…ya know?"

"She's lying," Henry interjects. I turn to face him and scrunch my face, wondering what version he thinks is the truth. "I made her mad; so she was protesting."

His gaze settles on mine, challenging me to say he's wrong. The longer he stares, though, the more emotions I see fill in all of the empty spaces. Anger, frustration, smugness—it's all part of his cocktail. The feeling I drown in most, though, is regret. He's sorry, and I think maybe so am I.

"I wasn't mad. I really was busy," I say with a shake of my head. My eyes blink wildly to make my lie convincing, and it seems to work on Caleb. Henry's gaze stays exactly the same, though—a dare to tell him he's wrong.

The tension eases as the miles pass, and by the time we're weaving through the city, Henry and Caleb are talking across me about other guys on their crew team and their plans for their dorm room in a few weeks. I'm a little jealous that they can talk to each other over the summer. Nicki is in Costa Rica with her dad, and Anya got into some academic program down in DeKalb. I suppose I could visit Ava, but there's still a weirdness when it comes to Henry, and I guess I've just been more invested in spending my spare moments with him over the summer.

Phillip slows to the curb in front of the theater, and Caleb gets out first, waiting to take my hand. A little confused, I slide my palm over his, and a second later, Henry's chaperoning me from my other side. Sandwiched between two boys that both tower over me and look like male models in their formal clothes, I start to giggle to myself. Not that there's a crowd gathered or anything, but there are people waiting to enter the theater, and almost all of them have turned to see who this mystery woman is walking up with two boys who are *so far out of her league.*

"Here, let me," Henry says, slipping away from my side and moving to hold the door open for me. One of the theater hosts rushes over to take over the job, and as Caleb leads me inside, Henry's fingers brush against that same bare spot on my back. It's as if they're competing for me, only I know better than that. I can pretend, though. I indulge the fantasy all the way through intermission, asking one to get me a program and the other to fetch me water. By the time the lights go down for the second set of performances, I have started to feel a little entitled.

Henry slips me an envelope, one he'd been carrying with our tickets and program, and I glance up at him curious what he wants me to do with it. I motion to my purse as if he wants me to hold onto it for him, but he leans close to whisper.

"It's for you."

My gaze hangs on for a few extra seconds as he looks away, back up to the stage, and I spend a brief moment watching the lights come up in the reflection of his eyes. He glances my way once, and quickly, just long enough to nudge toward the envelope and smirk anxiously.

My lips pucker with bashfulness, and I slip open the end of the yellow envelope, feeling a few sheets of paper inside. I slide them out, but just enough to see. It's sheet music. Old sheet music, like the kind that's been handwritten and marked on by someone who's played— someone who *wrote* it. It's thoughtful, and probably well beyond my ability, and definitely rare. But it's the thoughtful part that sits like electricity in my chest. I look at him and catch his smile on me, and for a tiny window, he's this sweet boy who brought a girl her favorite present.

The whispers are soft at first, picking up one person at a time until the small glow of the flashlight catches my eyes from the right side.

One at a time, the people in our row stand, letting someone pass, and when she reaches the man next to Caleb, I recognize the black-rimmed glasses and the perfectly sculpted nails.

"Pardon," Elena says. It's clear that the performers are actually waiting for her to get to her seat. My power was all pretend, but Elena Alderman owns a room for real.

"Henry," she whispers, encouraging him to move over a seat so she can sit down sooner. I stand to let her pass, but she grabs my arm and nudges me to follow Henry and sit between the two of them. I tuck the music away, somehow knowing it isn't for her to see, and fold my program around the envelope.

Even with her slight frame, the space around us suddenly feels tighter. It's the air that she sucks up when she enters a room.

"I didn't want to miss your experience," she whispers at my side.

"Mmm," I hum, my experience suddenly a whole hell of a lot more stressful than it was forty minutes ago.

The audience begins to clap as a man in a long, black, tailed tuxedo glides across the stage to the piano sitting in the very center. Soft lights begin to glow with a warm orange, and Elena reaches for my hand, squeezing it in some sort of rehearsed anticipation.

"Mischa is wonderful. You're going to love him. I'll introduce you when it's done." Her focus stays on the man sitting before the black and white keys, and mine drifts to her face as I try to read her. Her mouth puckers into an aged smile that shows the thin lines colored red by her lipstick, and her eyes dazzle like a schoolgirl with a massive crush.

He begins to play, the song a familiar one. It's the music Henry gave me. The *exact* music—already memorized by this great artist and passed along for me. I glance to Henry and catch the slight lift on his lips, pleased that I'm pleased, then I turn my full attention over to the man on the stage. His performance is beautiful, but my reaction pales to Elena's, and I can tell she's disappointed I'm not on my seat's edge just like she is.

"You have to admire the way he uses his entire body...the thrust and pull of his hands, it's as if he's speaking words on those keys. It's something you need to work on. You're so...frigid when you play."

I lick my lips and bite on the end of my tongue. She said that a little louder than a whisper, and she purposely waited for the applause to die down. A man behind us coughed to cover up his laugh at *frigid*. She meant it as an insult for so many things—for my naiveté, I suppose.

The music starts up again and I'm relieved at first, but my spirits are crushed when Elena leans into me to give me literal play-by-play throughout the entire eleven-minute final movement. I'm sure it was breathtaking. The little I can bring up from my recent memory of Mischa—*Micah? I can't remember what she called him*—is that his hands massaged every note, as if his fingers were moving delicate dough into a perfect crust, then thrashing it to break it into a million bits.

The rush and the slow, and the long pauses allowing the draw of the violin accompanying him to power through, were like a ballet, where the lead male pulls the female up and into a lift. It's every moment between me and Henry—*push and pull.*

I missed out on really getting to listen, though. Elena had much to say.

We all remain in our seats as the gallery empties out. I'm thrilled that Elena has started to drill Caleb with questions, though her interests in him are superficial. She asks about his family, his studies and what organizations his parents belong to. His answers must bore her because she's back to schooling me after only a few minutes.

"Now, we'll only be able to visit for a few minutes, but I would love for you to meet Mischa. Come," Elena says, standing and staring down at Caleb who sits oblivious in his seat until she clears her throat and raps the back of her nails against the outer edge of his knee. He startles to his feet and hurries out of the aisle, grabbing onto my arm after he lets Elena pass.

"That woman scares the hell out of me," he says, his voice a little too loud. I wince before it happens.

"Good," Elena tosses over her shoulder.

Henry doesn't speak, but I can feel him walking close behind me. We wander through a few people mingling near the front of the stage and Elena walks up to a man guarding the side door. She waves us up a second later, steering us inside quickly before others notice. The back hallways look strikingly plain and sterile. If someone spun me around and told me I was now in a hospital, I'd believe it. There are a few people gathered outside the door closest to the stage entrance, and we follow behind closely as Elena excuses herself and us through them all.

"This is how you groupie in classical," Caleb jokes. I turn to him to laugh silently, but when I glance at Henry, now more than a few steps behind us, his expression is unamused.

We all break through the well-dressed crowd and clanking sounds of expensive drinks and cocktail plates. I expect Elena to break through the small intimate group surrounding the man we just saw on stage, but she holds back with pause, suddenly uncertain in her own skin. It's...strange.

"I don't want to interrupt," she says, leaning back to me to whisper.

I look to Caleb and he arches a brow. I turn a little more to catch Henry's gaze, but he's no longer paying attention to the world in front of him. He's palming his phone, flipping through various pictures of pretty girls on vacation and crazy, drunken college boys doing stupid tricks on skateboards. He's detached from this moment, pulling the typical teenager move when their parent figure is embarrassing them.

Elena is embarrassing him. But why?

She lifts her hand, her program clutched in her palm, rolled tightly from nerves, and Mischa finally notices her waiting behind the group of people who seem to be close friends of his. The men peel back slowly, one taking a long sip of his drink, draining his glass then handing it to me as he walks by. I stare at it for a beat then cock my head to look at Caleb with a stunted laugh.

"He thinks I'm the help," I whisper with a lifted chin.

"Well then he should have tipped you," Caleb says. I smirk in agreement, but I'm stuck with the glass. There's nowhere convenient to discard it.

As the other two gentlemen leave, the only person left is a surprisingly familiar face—Ms. Manning. She doesn't see me until after she leaves a soft kiss on the pianist's cheek, smudging away the tiny print left behind from her deep maroon lips. When our eyes connect, she flashes through two emotions in one breath, falling from delight to trepidation in the matter of a blink.

"Lily," my name leaves her mouth nervously and her eyes flit to the woman who brought us here—well, whose tickets we used. "Elena."

The second name comes out with illness.

"Rebecca. Always lovely," Elena says, her nose tipped upward. Her hands wring the program she's already twisted until it looks like a fat blunt.

"If you'll excuse me...I'll let you and Mischa talk." My counselor hurries herself from our small circle, following the same path we took to get in and leaving the room entirely. I'm compelled to follow her, but before I can, Elena grabs hold of my wrist and drags me to stand next to her.

"You were stunning tonight. Just...amazing," she gushes. Mischa regards her with a polite smile, but I can tell his mind is on following the woman who just left his side as well.

"Elena, I wish I knew you were coming," he says, taking Elena's hand in his and kissing the top, but only because she gave it to him and encouraged it toward his lips.

"I never miss your first performance of the season. You know that." She's flirting with him, in her own, very odd way. Mischa nods with a tight-lipped smile, and his shoulders rise and fall with a heavy breath, relenting. His eyes move to me and widen, and I think maybe he's grateful he's not with Elena alone.

"You brought a student?" His brow lifts on the side closest to me and moves his open palms to take mine. I follow Elena's lead and let him kiss my hand as well. He seems to mind this less, and our touch is brief.

"This is Lily. She's studying at Satis," Elena says. It's almost a brag, the way she says it. Mischa's smile softens, and a tiny laugh breaks through.

"Of course," he says. I suddenly feel like I'm a missing puzzle piece, lost somewhere in the depths of shag carpet. I have no idea what my entire picture is supposed to be. I'm not even a corner or an edge.

"I'm sorry, I mean...nice to meet you, Lily. Did you enjoy the concert?" Mischa's body turns in a way that almost blocks Elena from our exchange, and I can see the frustration in her flexing jaw and squinted eyes.

"I did…very much," I say, answering him.

"Henry," Mischa says over my shoulder. I turn in time to see Henry nod his hello. They've met before.

Mischa's accent is hard to read with a few words, faint but heavy. It's thick when it says my name, and Henry's. But Elena slipped out as if it's been practiced several times. An uncomfortable silence starts to build, and just as Elena's eyes twitch, the man we came here to see excuses himself.

"I'm glad you enjoyed it, and I'm sorry, but there's something…" He motions with his chin toward the door, toward an escape, so I step to the side to give him a clear path.

"Thank you," he nods, moving away from us without giving Elena a final goodbye. Her eyes sear into his back as he leaves, and she remains still and speechless several seconds after he's left the room. With a slight shake of her head, she snaps awake from her angry trance, turning her focus to Caleb.

"Shoot, I didn't introduce you. You weren't essential, though, so I hope you understand," she says, tossing the now-ruined program to the floor before guiding us out of the room.

I blink with wide eyes and my mouth slowly falls open as I stare into Caleb's eyes, but all he can seem to do is laugh at being insulted.

"Better to be unessential than frigid, I guess," he tosses out, taking the glass I've been babysitting from my hands and setting it on one of the small cocktail tables along the wall on our way out.

I scrunch up my shoulders and shake my head, lost for words. We get to the front of the theater and Elena has already amused herself with a work phone call that has her lecturing whoever the poor soul is on the other end of the line. A small part of me wonders if she's faking the call, but I quickly decide I don't care because it means that she's not interested in talking to us anymore either. Stepping close to the curb, she holds up her free hand as Phillip pulls the car close. She climbs in first and Phillip waits for the rest of us to join her. I let Caleb in so I can share a brief moment out of the car and alone with Henry, just long enough to ask him what this was all about. Like Elena, though, Henry's busied himself with a phone call, too. Only his, I'm sure, is real.

"You guys head back without me. I'm going to meet up with some friends. I'll see you at move-in, and Lily...maybe Monday after my internship." He covers the speaker end of the phone and holds the door open for me, and as much as I don't want to leave without him, I also know that I can't very well invite myself to join him either. I scowl, not on purpose, and his head falls a little to the side. It's a gesture that doesn't say "I'm sorry" but instead begs me not to make this a big deal.

"Monday," I repeat. He nods, returning to the phone and asking whoever is on the other side to give him the address. His hand is wrapped around the edge of the car door, so as I get in, I purposely cover it with my own, my fingers painting down his knuckles until my touch leaves the tips of his fingers.

Henry closes the door for me as soon as I climb inside, and his phone is still pressed to the side of his face as we pull away. But before we turn completely, he draws in every individual finger on his free hand, forming a tight fist that squeezes at the ghost I left behind.

CHAPTER 11

The first two days at Satis House are my favorite. As a freshman, they were spent wandering the campus and trying to sort out where my classes were. Henry was my guide. This year, though, I am a sophomore. I know my way.

I moved in with the same two suitcases of belongings I did last year. Very little about my material life has changed.

No classes for two whole days means Satis House becomes a coed party with covert sleepovers. Boys dorms and girls dorms are separate. Hours are posted and enforced. No boys in the girls dorms after ten o'clock and vice versa. Henry says the rule used to be eleven, but the guardians who patrol the halls to make sure everyone is where they are supposed to be didn't want to stay up that late.

It's 10:02 pm right now, and Henry has wrapped himself in my winter coat and pushed himself into the farthest corner of Nicki's and my closet. While my roommate is calm and cool—seemingly able to pretend that Henry doesn't even exist—I cannot get my knee to stop bouncing while I sit at the end of my bed. I'm not sure what I'm more nervous about, though, the fact that Henry wanted to stay here for the night or that the guardian is on our hallway, making her final check on the rooms.

"No offense, Lily, but your closet looks super uptight." Henry's voice is muffled, but still too loud. I nearly pound on the door with my fist, but stop myself. Me pounding on something is totally suspicious.

Nicki snorts a laugh then tries to cover it by rubbing her arm over her nose as if that was a sneeze.

"I'm not uptight, and my clothes are fine," I say, throwing my pillow across the room at Nicki. She brushes it off her face and onto the floor before biting at the eraser end of her pencil and studying me with a quizzical squint.

"You're a little uptight," she finally says.

I hold out my palms and wrinkle my nose.

"How so?"

She's about to answer when I hear the guardian's steps near our door. In a panicked rush, I leap across my bed to the lamp, flicking it off before flying over to Nicki's bed next. I throw myself next to her and cup her mouth.

"Shh!" I force my palm over her lips when she tries to back away. She turns her head slowly, glaring at me. At least, I think she's glaring. It's hard to see in here now.

"Last call!" The guardian raps at our door three times, and I force Nicki to remain perfectly still and quiet until I hear the knock on our neighbor's door.

I uncurl my fingers from her face one at a time. She remains still, staring at me, her eyes two dark holes that are slowly becoming more defined as my own eyes adjust to the pitch black.

"What?" I ask, slipping from her bed to the lamp. I turn it back on, but only on the lowest setting. Nicki's eyes are still set on me. She doesn't blink until finally, she picks up her notebook and flops down heavily on my bed, closer to the light.

"Yeah...not uptight at all," she mumbles.

I sigh, my heart still pounding nervously with the fear of getting caught. I'm stuck for now, though, because it's not like I can rush Henry down the hallway before the guardian sees. It's a single hallway —no curves or bends. She'd see him the moment I opened my door. I won't lose the uneasiness until I hear the heavy fire door slam shut at the other end of the hall, signaling that she's moving down to the next floor.

"It's stuffy as hell in there," Henry says, using his normal, deep voice. I flash wide eyes at him, which he laughs off. "Nobody can hear me. Relax a little, Lily."

He's pulled my dark-yellow knitted scarf from the hanger and has wrapped it around his neck three times. He slowly begins to unravel it, swaying his hips like an inept stripper as he parades closer to me.

"And yes, Lily. Your closet is…uptight," he says, tossing the scarf off his body and onto my lap.

"Mmm hmm," Nicki agrees.

I glare at him before marching my scarf back to its place. I hang it next to my long winter coat, which is plain, yes, but there isn't anything about it that says snooty or unapproachable. I run my hand through the eleven or twelve sweaters and shirts I have hanging along with my uniform pieces, and then my one dress, which I *know* Henry likes because he's the one who bought it for me. Most of the things I own are blue or white, and everything is basic. My clothes are boring, but that's about it.

"I don't think you know what the word *uptight* means, guys." I turn to defend myself and find Henry now sitting on the center of my bed with his feet crossed, one of my notebooks in his lap. I write things in there, and there's a chance I maybe vented about him or wrote something about feelings. I try to play it cool while I get closer, but I rush at him when my legs reach the spot where his shoes hang off my bed. He blocks my lunge with one arm, stretching his other out far with my notebook clutched in his fist.

"Ah ah ah," he teases.

Nicki lets out a heavy groan and pulls herself up from laying on her stomach.

"I'm trying to figure out what I want to replace geology with in the course book, and you guys are literally making me ill. I am not going to referee some wrestling match over a diary." She pinches her lips and glances at me sideways before pulling her work up to her chest and grabbing the black and white flannel shirt from her chair.

"I'll be in Anya and Ava's room when you guys are ready to sneak out." She lets the door slam closed behind her, and this time, Henry panics with me. We look at each other before racing to the door and pressing our ears flat against the wood.

"I can't tell if the guardian left already," Henry whispers into my hair. His hand is on my shoulder blade while we stand in the spoon position and listen for signs in the hallway that we've been caught. I can't hear a thing over the whoosh of rushing blood in my ears. Henry's breath is stopped though. I spend the minute focusing on his warm palm over my uptight shirt that I wish was backless like my dress.

"She must be gone," he says, stepping away. I let him take a full two steps before I turn around, resting my back on the door.

Henry's in jeans, tight ones that hug his growing muscles and taper at his feet. He kicked his shoes off when he came into our room, so he's wearing short, white socks that match the bright-white T-shirt that sits right at his waist. Somehow, his boring clothes are far from boring. Even when he's wearing the school jacket or a polo shirt, he looks practically royal and amazing.

I force myself to hold his eye contact, the grin tempting my lips and jaw to move—to get bigger. I'm happy, and it's because he's here and we're alone. It's so taboo, even though I know nothing is going to happen. It's the fact that if I were someone else, or if he wanted me, something *could* happen. Lots of things could happen.

I blink.

I know I wrote some of those things in the book.

Blowing my poker face, my eyes flit to the notebook he left on my bed in our mad dash to the door. His head tilts, reading me, and we both launch for it, our hands wrapping around opposite ends at the same time. A literal—and quite ridiculous—tug of war ensues.

"What don't you want me to see, Lily?" His voice teases me, high-pitched and childish.

"Henry, that's private!" I suck in my bottom lip at the realization of how loud I am. It makes Henry laugh more, and his grip strength quickly overpowers me.

I stumble a step or two back while he jumps into my bed and wiggles his way backward until his shoulders are resting on the wall.

"Let's see," he says, licking his thumb and finger exaggeratingly before flipping the first page.

I can feel the red begin at my eyelids and crawl down to my chin, then my chest and stomach and legs. My arms get numb, and my jaw twitches while I rifle through the right words to say—the best possible plea to get him to just stop.

"Henry...please. I'm embarrassed," I admit.

He looks up at me briefly and smirks.

"Don't be embarrassed, Lily. Just because you 'saw a boy today on Henry's crew team and he has dark hair and ice eyes.'" Henry snort-laughs, just like Nicki did. My stomach sinks. A few pages later, I write some way more revealing things about Henry.

"Henry, come on," I beg. My head leans to the side, and my eyes get glassy. I let them, but truthfully, calling up tears isn't hard. I'm shaking with humiliation.

"Caleb would *love* being called that. I mean..." He points to the page in my book. "This *is* about Caleb, right?"

I breathe out a heavy sigh and shake my head. There's no need for me to answer. I decide my best move is to stare at him and remain silent, to sell him on the torture angle and find that place in him that exists and doesn't like to make me feel bad. I know it's there, even if he sometimes—often—ignores it.

"I can't wait to see what these guys look like when they're sixteen. Their bodies are..." Henry's eyes smile as he shakes with a silent laugh, his gaze scanning from left to right so quickly. I went on and on about how sexy they were—all of them. I used that word, too—*sexy*. I remember how hard it was to write the first time so I made myself write it again and again to take away the stigma. If he says the word, I'll actually die right here.

"You think we're *sexy* boys, Lily?" His eyes peer up above the note-book to meet mine, and I fall back into the desk chair, then throw my head forward into my hands, my hair cascading around me like a pathetic shield as I groan.

"Henry, I'm begging you." My words come out garbled and

raspy. I can actually feel my fingertips and face pulse against one another.

It's quiet in our space for several long seconds, and finally I hear the reassuring sound of the cardstock cover closing just before Henry tosses it on the floor at my feet.

"Fine, but we need to get you thicker skin," he says, standing and moving back to my closet. I grab my book the second his back is turned and bury it deep inside my school bag, between the biology book and *French for Beginners*.

Henry backs out of my closet with the plastic bin I keep my photos and mementos in. There's nothing in there that could embarrass me, so I breathe easier and welcome him to look.

"This is a weird thing to bring with you to school," he says, taking a seat on the floor now. He tugs the lid off the small bin and pulls up a knee so he can lean on his hip and take things out for inspection. I sit opposite him, folding my legs together, my body still warm from the torment and heavy blush.

"Collin encouraged me to bring it. I think he was afraid Alice would throw it all out by mistake. She cleans when she gets manic. Sells stuff off, or just puts it out on the curb," I say, taking the picture of me with my mom from one of the stacks. I run my thumb over it, our matching hair, before handing it to Henry. He studies it for a few seconds, and I can tell that he's really looking.

"You look like her." His mouth tugs up on one side and his thumb traces over my side of the photo.

His words sting my eyes, so I draw in a deep breath to stop the rush of feelings in my chest. Before he looks up at me, I wipe away any evidence of tears with the edge of my palm.

"Thanks," I say, taking the picture back from him.

He pulls out items one at a time. First, the fifth-place ribbon I won for the hula-hoop competition at my third-grade field day.

"I've never seen a pink award ribbon before," he says, smirking at the hula-hooping cartoon emblazoned on the front in gold.

"Clearly, you've never been mediocre at something." I take the ribbon from him and click the pin open, sticking it to the front of my shirt as I sit up tall, wearing it with pride. Henry rolls back on the floor in laughter. He shifts to lie on his elbow while he picks through more things.

My first six report cards are all bound by a rubber band. They're mostly As, though a few Bs are in the mix. That was before I had hard classes. Public school was a joke. I know that now. There's also a picture of me at the sixth-grade dance. We went in a group, though Gavin Shevski was technically my date. My class photos are all clipped together at the bottom of the bin, and Henry unfastens the clasp to sift through each of them. Somehow, he's able to point me out of every lineup. He stops at the most recent one I have—seventh grade. There are three hundred of us squished together in this photo, and I lucked out getting picked to sit in the very center.

"Uptight clothes," he says through a chuckle, looking up at me with one eye squinted more than the other.

"Let me see," I protest, leaning in and pressing my thumb next to his where it marks my spot in the front row. I twist the picture a little, getting a good view of my white tube socks that stretch halfway up my calf, bunching like legwarmers, and the tan shorts with the floral pockets on either side of my hips. The white T-shirt has matching embroidery around the collar.

"Dammit," I huff, letting go and falling back to rest my weight on my palms behind me. I twist my lips and look at Henry's elbow for a few seconds before darting my gaze to his eyes. "You're right. That time, yes—that's uptight as hell."

Henry's lips pucker and smile, his chest shaking with his quiet laugh. I stuff my tongue into my cheek and think about that photo, and the girl who was in it. I'm nothing like her. Even if my life stayed exactly the same and my parents weren't dead and I grew up with all of those same kids, I still probably would have changed, at least a little. But given all the facts of my timeline, I definitely have. I'm not the story those white socks and flowers tell, and I'm not the girl with light-blue jeans, cuffed shorts, and V-necks either.

I stand while Henry begins putting my things back in the box, and without thinking about it, I hug every single shirt belonging to me that's hanging in the closet. I rip and pull, taking a few of the hangers with me, but eventually I get the stack loose and I throw it on my bed in a pile before moving on to my drawers.

"Are we doing laundry?" Henry places the lid on my container and lifts himself to a squat, holding onto my things with both hands.

"We're donating," I say, tossing pair after pair of shorts and pants onto the pile. I don't own many things, but each one I look at suddenly fills me with this irrational rage.

"Lily, I didn't mean anything like that. You don't have to get rid of your clothes..." I hold my palm open at him and shake my head, determined.

"You didn't make me do this. Henry...you were right. And I hate these things. I mean look at this." I pick up a long-sleeved purple T-shirt and hold it against my chest, tucking it under my chin. "This says nothing about me."

"And this," I say, tossing the first shirt aside to pick up the same one, only in green. "And this," I repeat, doing it again, moving on to the peach-colored shirt.

Nothing I own is unique. It's bought in bulk with the small checks Alice and Collin get, from the same grocery-store-slash-department-store-slash-toy-store where they got their pots and pans and the pork chops we had every other Friday for dinner. These things were convenient, and I just didn't care.

"The only thing that's me are these shoes," I say, moving to my closet and tossing my white Converse out to Henry a shoe at a time.

He bends down and picks one up, holding it in his palm and turning it from side to side, memorizing its form.

"Okay, so..." He lets that word drag out while his brow indents with thought. He chews at the inside of his mouth for a second then flits his gaze up to me. I'm a little breathless and coming down off my madness, also realizing that getting rid of everything means I won't have anything left. I pick up the denim shorts that slipped onto the floor and I fold them over my arm. I'll keep these, and maybe one of the shirts, until I can get out to buy new things. Not that I have money for a shopping spree, and calling Collin and Alice to ask them for some...that sounds awful. And these shirts aren't really bad. They're perfectly good actually.

I walk back to the bed and pick another one up, folding it over my arm. I start to pull out a pair of pants that have tangled with the other things, and suddenly my spontaneity feels overwhelming.

"This is stupid," I breathe out. I drop everything from my arms and look down at my hopeless style. The one way someone my age can express herself, and this is the best I've got. I let a heavy breath in and out.

"What is it you like about the shoes?" Henry asks.

I shrug.

"Don't do that. Don't quit on me after...after acting out some awesome HGTV show," he says.

I chuckle and hold my right palm up against my cheek, rubbing my eye and tucking my hair behind my ear.

"I guess..." I stop, pursing my lips together in hesitation as I turn to slowly face Henry. He's tossing my shoe lightly from palm to palm, regarding me with curiosity and a slight curl to his lips that makes me think he knows the answer.

"When I wear those, I feel like I belong wherever I am." I nod slowly, letting that idea sink in. It's maybe the truest thing I've said in a year—and it's about a pair of freaking shoes.

"Okay. We can work with that. These shoes give you power."

I roll my eyes but he stops me, picking up the second shoe and holding them both out for me to take. When I feel their weight in my palms, I shake them lightly. He's right. These stupid shoes make me feel tough. I could run in them if I had to, or walk over glass. When I wear them, there's a little bounce to my step, and it isn't arrogance or glee, it's just...confidence.

"In these shoes," I say, lips parting with a suddenly emotional breath. "I know that everything is going to be okay. No matter what."

I look down at the off-white color, the dinge from a few years of dirt and wear, and the fray on the end of one of the laces sheathed with packing tape. I bought these shoes with my dad. I bought them because he said they were his favorite. He owned three pairs just like them, only different colors. When I wear them, I feel like him—like someone who gives his wife the last slice of pizza and who holds his daughter on his shoulders for an hour just so she can see fireworks better.

"We should get you more things that make you feel like that then. Maybe…" I glance at Henry mid-sentence, and he shrugs before continuing. "Maybe we go downtown tomorrow. I've got some cash."

"I don't want you buying me things," I say, my head falling toward him and an uneven smile on my lips.

"Yeah, but I do. It makes me happy, and I don't need anything, so maybe just let me?" He squints and holds my stare through a long, quiet breath. My heartbeat echoes in my head, and I wonder why this stupid boy is so good to me sometimes.

"Okay," I whisper finally. He picks up one of my shirts and takes it to the closet, putting it back on a hanger.

"Good," he nods, his expression pleased without bragging.

I pick up my entire stack of shirts and walk them to the closet where Henry helps me get each one back up where it was. I move onto my shorts while he puts my container of photos up on the shelf where Nicki keeps her many pair of black, leather boots. He's quiet behind me while I fold and stuff shorts and pants back into drawers, and when I turn around finally, I expect to see him doing something goofy with Nicki's things. Instead, he's leaning inside the closet door and staring at the floor.

I dip my head to get his attention, and his chin lifts with a flash of a smile when he meets my eyes. We stare at each other for a few long and slightly uncomfortable seconds, and a tightening sensation starts to grip at the space under my ribs.

"You like Caleb?"

He asks me pointedly, his gaze unrelenting and his eyes clouded with secrets. His teeth grip at the inside of his cheek, his jaw movements small as he chews, all the while staring with the intensity of a poker player who is suddenly all in.

My brow draws in under the pressure, but I give a small shake to my head.

"I don't really know Caleb," I say.

His glare softens just a little, but he keeps his focus on me, reading every small tick I give. I don't give many. I've never really thought about it beyond that one page in my notebook where I wrote about Caleb after the day I saw him on the lake with Henry. I wrote about Henry on that page, too—about how much I wish he would just kiss me sometimes.

I wrote about them both.

And he read every word.

CHAPTER 12

SOPHOMORE YEAR, FALL

The first month of school has gone fast. I'm acing my classes, which is why I've been able to put off my second-year check-in with the counseling office. I could not cancel it completely, though.

I've been dreading my next meeting with Ms. Manning. I knew that it would be uncomfortable, cringe-worthy, in fact. I've been replaying our awkward run-in at Mischa's concert over and over

Our meeting now is exactly as I pictured it.

She's coughed through nearly the entire twenty minutes we've been sitting in here together, fumbling my paperwork, spilling her water cup and forgetting her place mid-sentence at least twice. I'm pretty sure she's been dreading this more than me.

"Do you have any questions about this semester's schedule, or any…requests?" She stares at me with tight lips, knowing that I don't because she's asked me this question already.

I start to stand, taking my progress report in my hand, relieved that my straight *As* are holding up so far—even with French this semester —when she says something that drops me right back in my seat.

"Elena is my sister."

There's a lot of blinking going on now. I'm blinking...*she's blinking.* And staring. We're doing a great deal of that, too.

"I'm sorry..." I cough pathetically and leave my open palm flat on my chest. More blinking and staring.

"What?" I croak.

Ms. Manning draws in a deep breath through her nose as her gaze slides away from me in thought. I take it as a sign that this is complicated. I'm not sure I want to know complicated things, at least not when I'm ensnared with them too, which I am—very much ensnared.

"We're not...*full* sisters. Step, really. My mother married her father, both widowed with one child. Her father, of course, is the man who built Havisham up into an empire, and I'm...well..." She folds her fingers together and rests her hands on her chest as she leans back, chuckling to herself. "I'm the daughter of a world-class pianist."

My mouth falls open slightly and a faint sound escapes with my breath, like a "huh" but not fully coherent because...*what?*

Ms. Manning leans forward again, pulling herself close to her desk, then scratching at her head with wide fingers while she wears a severe wince on her face.

"I know, I know...it's...it's confusing. And you really didn't need to know, but then I saw you at the concert, and I just thought maybe you had questions. I know Elena would never say a word, and it's maybe I just..."

"You're sisters." I break into her manic stream of words, still stuck at square one. I set my schedule back down on her desk and lean forward, tucking my chin to my chest while I breathe in slowly.

"Does Henry know?" My voice is muffled since I've now dropped my head between my knees.

"Yes," she says.

I widen my eyes at the floor and nod where nobody can see. I didn't expect that. Of course, I didn't expect this either.

"So, you're his...aunt." I put the one logical step together.

"On paper, yes. I guess so. But Elena would never let me claim that. We're not really close, I'm sure you can tell," she says.

I chuckle once and bring my head upright, the blood rushing down my body in a *whoosh.*

"I guess the first clue would be the fact that you keep this all a secret," I say, laughing through the end of my words.

Ms. Manning laughs a little too, but her eyes slant with a defeated kind of sadness. We both sit quietly and stare off into space near one another but not looking each other directly in the eyes. A full minute passes before I snap my gaze to her and call her attention.

"Your mom was a concert pianist?" I pick up on the one good part of all of this, figuring maybe there's something here that's useful for me. Perhaps Ms. Manning has a secret family heirloom tucked away that she wants to give me so I can play on a piano that *isn't* held hostage inside that crazy house.

"She was," Ms. Manning says, her eyes glowing with the same reverence I get when I think of my parents. Her faint, pink lips drift into a sweet smile. "She used to travel back and forth to Europe for performances, and sometimes she would take me. Elena didn't like to travel, but she doesn't like to believe that's why she didn't go. She thinks I was just favored. It wasn't like that, though. My mom accepted her as family, and she wanted us to be close."

She shakes her head and draws her lips tight.

"We just weren't meant to be, though."

Her cheeks fall with her frown as her eyes drift down to the top of her desk. She begins to stretch out her hands, her fingers forming as if they're on a keyboard. "My mom spent so many hours teaching her to play. I was never very good, but Elena...well, you've heard her. She taught you."

"She's remarkable," I say softly.

"She is."

My gaze flits up to my advisor, and our stares meet for a moment, a secret understanding passing through in that instant.

"You stole Mischa from her," I say, regretting the harsh way my conclusion comes out the moment I utter it. The guilt drops into my gut when I see Ms. Manning's forehead dent, a pained expression lowering her eyes.

"He was never hers. Not really. But she loved him...*loves him*." Her eyes drift back up to mine.

"I could tell," I admit. It's the one thing that was painfully obvious from the concert. Elena was gushing, and she also wasn't a welcomed guest.

"Mischa and I have been married for nineteen years. We have two daughters. You saw me with one of them that day—in the rain. I was leaving Elena's house. I had found something in the attic while going through old boxes, and it was her father's. Just old photographs. I figured she'd want it, so I brought it over."

She pauses to chuckle sadly.

"All these years, and I still get caught up in the notion that an olive branch might solve everything. I was in her house for all of eight seconds. I think if she had a secret trap door, she would have dropped me down it in a blink."

I smile on one side, amused because I've felt that way before too. Elena has mastered the art of making people feel just on the outside. I have no idea what draws me in over and over again, though.

That's a lie.

Henry. I come back for Henry. He's this just-out-of-reach schoolgirl crush, the one I'll tell stories about someday. He's so arrogant most of the time, and he has all of these parts to him that are just like Elena's worst parts, but then sometimes...sometimes he's also sweet.

The sheet music—*that was sweet.* I also found out it was rare. The writing was from the conductor who first played the arrangement at the Chicago Symphony in 1936. It's the same arrangement Mischa played, how it was meant to sound.

"If you're sisters, how come you don't have half of the Havisham fortune?" I twist my lips and look at her sideways, knowing in my gut that there's no way Elena would share her brand with anyone. She may have loved—still loves—the same man as Ms. Manning, but not at the risk of losing her empire. Empires...they last forever.

"I wasn't in the will. Not for that stuff, anyway. It all went to her one-hundred percent." Her lips purse while she delivers the explanation, and I read the half-truth that exists somewhere in the gray area.

If I were bolder, I would come out and just ask, but for now, I'm left to wonder if it was a trade. Elena got the company all to herself while her sister got the man.

"Lily...I wouldn't really let Elena know I've told you this. It's not that I care as much as I'm afraid she'll get hostile toward you. She might use it to manipulate you, and really, she'll tell you horrible things about me. Some things I probably deserve, but most of it would be lies—bitter, broken lies from a woman who defines narcissism."

I nod as I stand, offering no such verbal contract, but giving my understanding. This information is big, and it's an insight into something, I'm just not sure what that something is yet. And I'm not sure if I should talk about it with Henry or not. I do know one thing—I'm not asking for permission.

Henry's birthday is Tuesday, but we're celebrating tonight because "Fridays are better for celebrating." Henry's words. What he means is Fridays are better for sneaking out of Satis and coming back way past curfew.

Slipping away should be easy. There's a huge bonfire party planned for the entire school out on the main lawn, and it lasts until eleven. Nicki and I left our room in the perfect state—soft music that can barely be heard through the door, beds stuffed with the dim light on so it looks like our bodies are there and we just fell asleep listening to music. The music was my touch, because inside I'm actually scared shitless about this entire thing.

"Did you guys put fake people in your beds?" I whisper to Anya and Ava who both look at me like I'm a moron.

"She made us find things that looked like hair. For a minute or two, I thought she was going to cut a chunk of mine off and use that to stick out of my blanket." Nicki rolls her eyes at me and goes back to sipping on her hot chocolate while Anya and Ava laugh at my expense.

"I've just never really snuck out before. I mean, what happens if we get caught?" My heart is pounding at just mentioning the possibility.

Anya wrinkles her face a little, as if my fears are absurd.

"They'd probably just bring us back and make us do community service on campus for a month or something," she says. "But relax—we're not getting caught. They don't look in the rooms. They aren't allowed without some sort of just cause, like if they think you're doing drugs in there or something. But even with that, they'd need to have the police with them to inspect."

I hold her gaze for a few extra seconds, lowering my eyelids to really study her and read if she's telling the truth. She tilts her head slightly after a breath, a signal that I really am being paranoid, so I let go of my breath and allow a little of the tension to relax from my shoulders.

"Okay," I give in.

"There you go," Ava says, squeezing my shoulders as if she's about to send me into a boxing ring.

The fire is roaring, and Henry and Caleb—along with a few other crew members and rugby players—are loading more wood in to keep it going. Just a few days shy of sixteen, Henry has gotten bolder than he was before. His rebellious side seems to guide more of his decisions. While, as my birthday looms a month away, my cautious side seems to be gathering more steam.

It's not that I don't like adventure, but I've started to question risk a lot. Like tonight—the risk terrifies me. I've been working so hard, and I audition for a solo at the winter showcase soon. I have things to lose. Henry, though…he seems to want to dare fate. I'm not sure if he thinks he's invincible or he just doesn't care.

The boys growl as they heave the logs into the flames, and Henry tugs his shirt from his body, pounding his chest with fists. His jeans hang on his hips, and his skin glows from the fire. He's taller than the others, even the juniors and seniors. He looks down at them like a wild thing claiming his crown, and they seem to obey without question.

With his arms over his head, his long-sleeved black shirt stretched between his hands and gripped over his body, Henry marches around with his face tilted toward the night sky. He's howling—and some of the others join in. It's obnoxious to the teachers here as chaperones but it's harmless enough that they can't do anything to stop him, and it's that little bit of power that he seems to thrive on.

His eyes land on mine mid-howl, and I can't help but stretch my lips into an inspired grin. I waggle nervously as he starts to approach, and I flash through a short fantasy where he walks right up to me, hand cupping my face as his lips cover mine in front of every single student at Satis. I know that won't happen, and really, it's enough that he's walking up to me. And we're friends, even though he did read my girl-crush diary. Still…friends.

"No howling for you, young cub?" He says, unfurling his shirt and opening it to place over my head. My arms had been wrapped around my body most of the night, the chill from the lake breeze a little colder than I expected. His shirt swallows me up, and I willingly push my arms through, glad to be wearing something so him.

Friends…just friends.

"Thank you," I hum.

Nicki breathes out a snarky laugh and turns her back to me, talking to Ava and Anya, and Henry's gaze sticks to her back for a second while a smirk paints his lips. My cheeks flush, but I'm grateful that the fire hides it.

"I'll run up and grab something else to wear really quick so you can keep that tonight." He steps closer and grabs both of my arms, running his palms up and down my biceps to warm me up. Heat wraps around me quickly, but it has very little to do with the friction and more about the boy giving the touch.

"Thanks," I say again, noticing a few girls nearby stare at me with envy. It feels good and terrifying at the same time. I don't want to be anyone's target.

I blink my gaze back to Henry.

"We're going to leave in five minutes. Tell the others to be ready, and let's meet by the maintenance gates." He leans in to whisper that last part, and the faint smell of alcohol hits my nose. He seems fine, so maybe it was just some dare or something with the other guys. I rationalize it with myself by the time he's jogged back to Caleb and the two of them are heading into the dorms.

"I swear to god, if you wear that to bed every night without ever washing it I'm going to be sick," Nicki says, slurping the last drops of her drink and crushing the foam cup with her sharp thumb nail.

"You're so jaded." I pucker my lips at her and dare her with my stare. Nicki's been trying to toughen me up. She says I'm too quick to hide how I really feel, and I apologize for being me too much. She's right. And I almost made an excuse up now, telling her I was just cold and that I was going to give this back as soon as we got inside of the place we're going, but instead I stood up to her. Her glare holds on until I almost break, but her face shifts into a proud expression, and she slings her arm around me in a sort of bro-hug before escorting me toward Ava and Anya.

"Look at little Lily…your balls are dropping, you sweet thing," she teases, sticking out her tongue and squishing me against her a few times as we walk.

Nicki got her tongue pierced over the summer, and she likes to stick it out more now. I'm fascinated with the stud, but more about the logistics of it all. On move-in day, I grilled her for an hour about the process, and asked her dumb things like if she tried putting a straw through it when she drinks.

She has not. Also, that apparently is a stupid idea. I bet Henry would do it.

I share Henry's plans with the other girls, and we all casually start to walk toward the maintenance area. Because I'm super paranoid, I make Anya stay back with me while Ava and Nicki leave first. I just feel like a group of four is more suspicious than two pairs a few minutes apart. Of course, because of my plan, Anya and I get to the gate just in time for the last group of boys to be hopping over a fence.

"I was starting to think you chickened out," Henry says, his eyes wrinkled in that teasing way along the corners. His lip tugs up on one side as he pulls on the sleeve of his shirt, which I'm wearing.

"Just taking precautions," I say. He laughs and ushers me closer to him, folding his hands together to give me a boost over the fence. I grab at the top and work to swing my right leg over while he thrusts my foot up with his hands. I'm glad I wore jeans, and I'm sure Ava gave everyone an eye-full in her skirt. She has tights on underneath, but still—I know where Henry's hand is right now on me, and if it was there on her, it was definitely more intimate.

I brush that thought off quickly, strangely getting jealous over the idea of him touching her over nylons, and instead I focus on the way his hand is gripping my thigh to hold me steady while I find my balance on the top of the gate. I glance over to the bonfire since I'm up high enough to see. Nobody is facing this direction, so I hold my breath and jump down to the other side while I'm clear.

"Hurry, it's clear!" I whisper to Henry through the fence. There are more people gathered behind me than I thought were coming with us. A few girls I don't know that well, but I do recognize, and the entire crew team.

Henry scales the gate easily, lifting himself up with his arms and bringing his feet up one at a time until he's perched on top of the metal bar, but he stays there for just a beat too long.

"Okay, now jump!" I whisper-shout. His lip curls and my gut sinks.

"Henry, come on! They'll see you!" My voice grows louder, more urgent, but still not full.

Henry lets go with his hands, his ankles wavering to hold their balance as he slowly lifts himself up to a stand. My eyes widen and Nicki cackles behind me.

"You're hating this," she says, grabbing hold of my arm and hugging it with her hands.

"You have no idea. He's going to get us caught," I say, only looking at her for a blip because I'm too afraid to take my eyes off Henry.

"Relax," she says, which only makes me sicker.

Everyone behind us is starting to laugh and cheer, and a few of Henry's crew mates start to chant: "Howl, howl, howl!"

"Oh my God," I mutter to nobody really. It makes Nicki laugh even harder.

Now fully stretched into a stand and with his hands cupped around his lips, Henry's eyes glimmer from the fire and the moon as he tilts his chin and does just what his fan club asks of him.

"Ow oww aww woooo!" His howl echoes through the small breezeway between the maintenance yard and the school, and I'm sure there's no way it wasn't heard by someone near the fire. My only hope is that they assume it's him howling somewhere else.

His hands fall away from his face slowly, out to his sides with his arms stretched wide, and his crooked grin finds me fast. He isn't sorry. He's never really sorry about anything. That's the man he's becoming, and I hate that I still like him so much.

Henry finally leaps to the ground, pulling me into a bear hug and pressing his forehead to mine after he spins me around once. The smell from before is stronger now, and I think maybe I missed just how bad it was the first time. Maybe I just convinced myself.

"I know you hate that, but I had to. It's my birthday," he says, a deep dimple forming in his cheek with his amused grin.

"It's not your birthday yet," I remind him, my tone flat and as opposite of him as it possibly can be. I swallow while he stares at me, eyes hazed as he saunters backward for a few steps to taunt me.

He looks up enough to still hold my gaze then howls one more time, giving me his answer. It's more like a big "fuck you." I feel it right in my chest.

I follow along in the back alone, even my girls are keeping up more with Henry and the guys. We jog through the dark park and cross a few quiet streets until we get up to the busier roadways and Henry pulls out his phone.

"They don't have a car big enough for all of us, so I'm ordering two," Henry says, waggling his finger over his phone screen and laughing at something I can't hear that leaves the lips of a girl I don't really know. I hate her. Whatever.

"You don't look good," Ava says, coming back to me. She holds the back of her palm on my head for a minute to check if I have a fever, but I back away, embarrassed.

"I'm just a little out of shape, I guess. That jog got me," I say. I give her a tight-lipped smile and inwardly beg her to leave it alone.

The cars arrive quickly, and I'm saved from any more questions, but the ridesharing plays out just as I feared. Henry waves the older girls into the back of the large SUV, climbing in with two of his team-mates after them. The rest of us pile into a van, and the moment the door slides shut next to me, I imagine Henry making out with them all at once, in one big-fat-not-really-your-birthday orgy.

I stew at my imagined torture for a few minutes before Nicki leans into me and whispers, "Stop."

I blink to her.

"Stop what?" I ask.

Her head tilts to the side and her eyes narrow.

I know exactly what she means, and she's right. My shoulders sag as I let out a heavy breath and I gather up the sleeves of Henry's shirt into my palms, covering my knuckles.

"You should probably just tell him how you feel about him," she says.

I shrug.

"Yeah. But I won't," I admit.

"I know," she says, reaching her hand down to mine and squeezing it through the fabric of Henry's shirt. I tuck my face against my shoulder and draw in the scent of him—wood and cinnamon, just like his Crew shirt smelled. I still have that one.

We pull up to a glass building, the bottom floor glowing with strobing lights. It's underage night at this place called Gala, but most of the people standing in the line look like they're twenty-four. We spill out of the van after everyone's exited the SUV Henry was in, and nearly everyone that was out of my sight has changed. Subtle changes, like sweaters tucked away in purses that were concealing barely-there shirts before we left, and skirts put on instead of jeans. One of the crew guys is carrying a backpack, which I'm pretty sure is holding the discarded clothing. I glance around with worry that I missed something with my friends, and I'm relieved Nicki, Anya, and Ava are all dressed exactly as they were when we left.

Henry's wearing a gray shirt that hugs his chest and arms, arms that have become more defined and bigger from a summer of rowing practice. I noticed before, but for whatever reason I'm mesmerized by them now. I follow his form through the doors of the club, past the line, as if he's a steak scent and I'm a junkyard dog. The analogy is fitting because while the girls near him are dressed to match every other person in line, I look like the youthful girl on the poster outside advertising tonight's Youth Night in the City.

"I didn't even wear better shoes," I say, tugging on Nicki's arm and looking down at my plane, white tennis shoes. I could have worn my Converse at least. I bought these with Henry, and they're worn and dirty. I didn't even think.

"You look fine, Lily," my friend says, tipping my chin up to look her in the eyes. Nicki doesn't have to compare herself to others like me. She's absolutely unique, and in a place like this, her dark goth style makes it easy to believe that she's eighteen or nineteen. I'm almost sixteen, but I swear I pass for twelve.

"Do you have any eyeliner? Maybe you can…"

She sighs but takes my arm and moves me through the thick crowd to the ladies room.

"My black shit is going to look really weird on you," she says, plopping her purse on the sink counter and stretching it open wide in search of her makeup. She pulls out a clear bag, stuffed with all types of lipliners and mascaras. Every color in her bag looks like winter.

"I love the way you always look," I say, and she presses her finger on my mouth.

"Shh. Let me do this," she says.

She pushes the wisps of hair around my face back and tilts my head back so I'm looking up, toward the light. The pencil makes a popping sound as she yanks off the cap, and I blink wildly as she gets closer to my eyes. I don't wear a lot of makeup, and the things I do wear are more in the *nude* family of colors. My skin is pale and pink, like my mom's, and she was always very minimal. *She was beautiful.*

"Are you done playing butterfly?" I flit my gaze to Nicki's frustrated face.

"Sorry," I utter. I pull my lips in tight and hold my breath while she colors and shades. She works fast, and when I look back at myself in the mirror when she's done, I do feel a little transformed, maybe even…older.

"Thanks," I say, my smile growing.

Nicki pulls the tie from my hair and ruffles her hand through my waves, giving my hair a little life.

"I look less like I've been working a yard sale all day, right?"

She blinks at me twice.

"Uh huh," she says, turning quickly and leaving me there to wonder if she was telling the truth or just irritated with me.

No matter what, I still have Henry's shirt on, and somehow that makes me better than every other friend he brought with us tonight. I push through the bathroom door and the wall of thumping music hits my chest. It takes me a few minutes to find familiar faces out on the dance floor. I find Henry first, body launching into the air over and over again like he's at a rave and high on…

Shit.

I slip through the thick crowd of people near the DJ booth and push myself up on my toes, using the platform stage to gain height, and I spend the next several minutes just watching him move. I should have known something was wrong, that he was *off*. His eyes are so empty, zoned out and unable to focus, and his head just keeps waving from side to side with the heavy beat. He's on something. I might be a good girl, but I'm also from the southside, and we have lots of things on our streets to get high on. Kids got kicked out of Public all the time for using, dealing, and holding for a friend.

I'm nauseated just watching him sway. Eventually, this has to make him sick.

"There you are. Come on, we're all dancing," Ava says, slipping through a group of guys who all part just so they can stare at her. Glancing to each side, she grabs my arm and yanks me out to the floor with her quickly, leaving me little choice but to bounce along with her.

"Those guys were creepers!" she shouts.

I glance over my shoulder to get a good look at them and instantly agree by the way they're gawking at my friend. I take her hand and lead her deeper into the crowd with me so we can get lost, but I make mental notes of the creepers' distinguishing features—goatees, a man bun, and flair on their jeans.

"Henry was asking for you," my friend says, leaning in so her mouth is nearly touching my ear. The music is so loud, I feel it in every organ of my body.

"I doubt it!" I shout back to her. Her brow furrows, like she didn't hear me, so I shout it again. She shakes her head at me and turns me around until I'm literally chest-to-chest with Henry.

"He really was asking about you," she says at my neck.

Her words and his nearness sends a surge of panic through my chest. His shirt is damp with sweat. We've been here for twenty minutes and he's already danced the equivalent of a marathon. He reaches out to my arms and drags his fingers down the length of them until he finds my fingertips, and when his hands connect with both of mine, I'm instantly grounded.

And heartbroken.

He's not really looking at me. I mean, yes, his eyes are on my face, but I'm not what he's seeing. He's touching just to feel, and looking because everything to him right now is foreign and probably bright like candy.

"What did you take?" I lean into him, wishing I had a time machine so I could zip back to whatever moment it was that he swallowed whatever shit he did.

Henry brings one of my hands to his chest, flattening it against his heart, and I feel it racing underneath my touch. My brow pulls in tighter. As he takes my other hand and moves it around his neck, I form a fist with my other hand and pound against his chest. The sensation only makes him laugh wildly.

"Dammit, Henry what did you take?" I shake loose of his grip and move my hands to his jaw, trying to force him to pay attention to me—to look me in the eyes. I only get glimpses of him, though. His focus is lost with every third beat, and as bodies gyrate around us and the crowd moves like a heavy undertow of the ocean, Henry slips away from me and into the arms of one of the girls he rode here with. Her eyes are just as detached as his.

My friends are nowhere I can easily see, so I push and shove my way through the thickest part of the mob and come up for air at a group of seats on the opposite end of the venue. My chest is damp with sweat, and my bra straps are digging into my shoulder blades. I'm miserable, and worried, and really fucking sad.

"This is nuts, huh?"

It takes me a few seconds to recognize Caleb's face, and not because he looks different. It's that the world looks different right now—in here. It looks twisted and disappointing.

"I miss the days of birthday cakes and pin the tail on some shit," I shout at his shoulder. He tilts back with a laugh and nods, knowing I won't hear him speak.

I keep my eyes on Henry, on the girl he's grinding with and her hands messing up every strand of his goddamn perfect and stupid hair. I torture myself with the view for an entire song, and as one rhythm morphs into a new one, I realize that while I've been watching Henry, Caleb's been watching me.

"You wanna go?" he asks when I look to him.

"Oh…no, I'm fine," I say, tempted by his offer. More than tempted. I do want to go.

I let the vision of Henry fill my everything for another full minute, until his eyes clear just enough to focus on mine, not that I can be certain from fifty feet away. At least from this distance, I can't make out the dilated pupils and lost expression. I can remember him howling earlier in the night—I can remember him giving me this shirt.

I run my hands down the soft cotton until I get to the hem where I grip it tightly and squeeze.

"Let's go," Caleb says against my ear.

I turn to him quickly, ready to protest until I settle on his sympathetic eyes. His crooked smile falls into a frown, and I can tell that Caleb…he doesn't really want to be here either.

"Okay," I say, a weight lifting the moment I give in, but a new one clinging to my heart. My first few steps are to the side so I can keep my guard on Henry, and I swear he's watching me leave. I almost give in to the temptation to force my way through the crowd so I can get to him, but his eyes look up and his hands follow, and with one turn, he's lost again.

Caleb and I bump and push our way through the stream of people coming in, stopping to get a stamp from the man at the door. Apparently, we can't get back in without one. The cool air finally hits my body at the curb, and even though the constant stream of traffic rushes by me from only a foot away, the air is suddenly so much cleaner.

"I literally felt like I was drowning," Caleb says, taking giant breaths while he holds his arms over his head. I meet his gaze and start to laugh.

"Same," I chuckle.

We both turn in circles, looking first at the L curving along the track above us, then to the line of people still waiting to get in. I guess we opened up two more spots. Good deed for the day—*check!*

"Wanna just...sit, I guess?" Caleb asks, nodding toward the wet gutter and littered curb.

I sneer at the ground before softening my bunched lips as I look to Caleb.

"I wanna go home." With an arched brow, I silently pray as I will him to tell me he wants the same thing.

"Done," he says with a single nod. I'm not sure if he's just being a gentleman or not, but his smile sets me at ease a little more. While Caleb pulls out his phone to get us a car, I type a message to my friends telling them I'm not feeling well but that I'm heading back with Caleb. I don't want to ruin their fun.

Nicki is the only one to reply before our car arrives.

I know. Do you need me?

I stare at her words for a few seconds. I'm not sure if her harsh honesty is the right medicine right now, even though I know she sees right through my lie. I decide to stick with Henry's preppy friend, good old Ice Eyes.

I'm ok. Have fun. PLEASE!

I add that last part so she doesn't waver or feel guilty. Caleb holds the back door open for me to climb into the car, shutting it for me and jogging to the other side to get in. I hold it together for almost five whole seconds, and when the car pulls away from the club—from Henry—I cry so hard I shake.

Caleb pulls me to his side, and my head falls on his shoulder. We ride like that until the car stops a street away from school, blocked by a row of cypress that flank an old, catholic church. My hair stinks of sweat and smoke, and my chest hurts from all of my effort to breathe. I think maybe I had a panic attack. I also think maybe...*maybe I'm a little in love with Henry Alderman.*

"I say when it's his actual birthday, on Tuesday, you and I kidnap him as soon as he gets out of weight training, and we go have happy jacks at that lame breakfast place over by the kiddie land near the lake." Caleb skips a little with his idea, but all I can do is offer a half smile that slips from my face as soon as my breath leaves my nose.

"I'm sorry. I know you're trying," I say, looping my arm with his.

He pats my bicep, but soon his fingers curl against my skin in a soft tickle that scratches the same tiny place again and again. My body is zapped with instant fear, and I panic in anticipation that Caleb's about to kiss me. I ready myself for it, pulling away a little and tucking my chin into my chest as we walk. When Caleb stops abruptly, I slip away completely and cover my face with my hands in the lamest of all defensive moves ever.

"I'm so sorry, Caleb, but I just wanna be friends!" I shout, but my words mix with his at the same time.

"Lily, I'm gay, and I just have to tell someone here."

My reaction is bad, but not for the reason Caleb thinks. I was waiting to be kissed, and then his personal share was…well…it was huge! And a little like whiplash. His mouth pulls in tight, his face washed with instant regret, as if by sucking in his lips he can somehow suck back in the words and never tell me.

But he did. And I really like Caleb—like a really good friend. Just like I said.

"I'm not sure what to say next," he says, chewing at his lip anxiously while his eyes dart from mine to anything else but me. His hands sink into the pockets of his black jeans and his dark hair falls over one eye. He flicks it back with a jerk of his head, then stares at me, waiting, while his shoulders crawl up to his ears.

"You say, 'I'm really glad we get to be friends.'" I pull my shoulders up to match his. I twist my body from side to side a few times, in recognition of our mutual anxiety and poor posture, and Caleb starts to laugh, then does the same. Soon, we're both doing some form of the robot in a celebration of awkwardness, but then Caleb just stops and lets his arms fall to his side.

He blinks.

It would be so easy for me to wallow in the embarrassment of thinking he was into me. Kinda self-indulgent, sure, which is what would make it easy, but this moment is about Caleb. Of everyone in our tiny circle, Caleb chose me. I'm his person.

I'll *be* his person.

I step into him with open arms and he falls into me quickly, his arms wrapping around me tightly while I cling to the back of his shirt. I can feel the vibration of fear and relief travel through his bones, and I squeeze tighter. We rock a few times in our embrace, and when he pulls away, my own sadness feels a little duller now.

Our feet shuffle along the gritty sidewalk until we reach the Satis House grounds. Caleb helps me clear the same gate we escaped through, the smell of burnt embers from the bonfire still lingering in the air. The charred remains pop and glow in the middle of the court-yard, and I take in the view before I leap down to the ground on the other side.

We're not so far past curfew, which gives me a little relief. Too much relief, perhaps. In my tired and distracted state, I walk face-first into the boobs of the women's dormitory guardian. I could have sold it if maybe I ran into her inside the dorms, but I didn't. I was two feet on the other side of the gate we escaped through, and my co-conspirator was straddling the high fence behind me.

My tired heart is out of beats, and my legs give way along with it as I fall to the ground in a limp and graceless collapse.

CHAPTER 13

I wasted an hour trying to learn how to say *I am frustrated* in French. *Je suis frustré*.

This is, of course, not on my test. I'm still glad I know how to say it, given I have said it about seventy-four times now. I slam my book closed, sending a flurry of notecards in all directions around my table and to the floor.

"*Je suis frustré!*" It feels good to shout. I crane my neck to the hallway behind me and wave an apology to the two guys who have been studying for their physics test in the room opposite me.

"Sorry," I mouth. They just glare.

"*Pardon.*" I say the French word aloud, then giggle to myself because I've crossed over into insanity. They still aren't amused, but they go back to their own studies. I bet they ace their test. I, on the other hand, know every word that will not be on my exam. I am completely incapable of stringing words together into a sentence. Why is learning a language so hard?

With a groan, I push out from the rolling chair and get on my hands and knees to gather up my study cards. When the glass door behind me swings open, I lift up and bump my head on the bottom of my desk.

"Shit!" I rub the sore spot and fall to my ass to turn around to see my company. I was expecting Nicki. She promised to bring me a snack if I was here later than six. It's seven. But those aren't Nicki's shoes.

"What is...*palm*?"

My eyes glaze over on Henry's damp shoes. He's wearing his white Vans, and sweatpants that he probably sleeps in.

"*Pomme*," I say, correcting his pronunciation for *apple*. At least I've got this much down. Maybe if I string together enough partial credit, I can pass the unit exam.

I crawl out from under the table and rip the notecard from Henry's hand without looking him in the eyes. I haven't been able to look at him since the night we snuck out a week ago.

"Awe, come on. Is it still gonna be like that, Lily?"

I stuff my tongue in the side of my mouth and pause halfway between him and the table. A cynical laugh puffs from my nose.

"I spent the last six days re-striping the track. Even though it's nowhere near track season. Today...it rained. You think that Caleb and I got a pass because of the rain? No. You know what we had to do?"

"Paint in the rain?" Henry laughs at his own dumb joke, and it irks me so much that I shift my gaze to him just in time to see the shrug that accompanied his response. His expression is smug, or maybe that's just the way my mood colors it. His hands hang in his pockets, pants pushed up to his calves and an old Cubs T-shirt with the bottom ripped hanging loose on his body. His hair is just wet enough to make the waves curl tighter. It's been pouring all day.

"We scraped gum. Because *the rain should soften it*," I say, putting on the voice of Dean Orson. I let my head fall to the side and tip my chin so I can glare at him one more time before shaking off a laugh of my own. "I guess we're still doing this," I breathe out, frustrated with him. Angry at him.

Je suis frustré...furieux!

He's not going to leave. It's been like this all week. I've gone through four half-ass apologies with him. The first the next morning —*late morning*. I got a hungover phone call that I let go to voicemail. I made it halfway through the message, all the way to the part where it was *Lexi's fault because she gave him a pill and he didn't know it was Molly.*

I didn't delete the message. That's on me. I kept it with the hope that there's something in the rest of it that redeems Henry. I haven't listened to it all the way through yet because it more likely doesn't. I'd rather stay optimistic.

The next three apologies came in person. One at my door, with a flower that I'm pretty sure he picked from the landscape outside. It was wilted. Henry said it was winterized.

It was dead.

The other two were ambushes, much like this, only Caleb was with me, walking from one class to the next. Caleb forgave Henry right away. He lives with him so I guess he has to, but he can't give me a compelling reason to let go of my grudge, even though he wants me to. I'm not done grudging yet—even if Henry smells like wood and rain, and is still picking up my cards with me.

"You can go," I snap, standing with half of the cards in my hands. Henry freezes on one knee, holding a small handful of my notecards in his right hand. He taps them against his leg and glances down at them before picking up the last card and straightening the small pile. He stands, still holding them in front, fidgeting nervously and moving his feet inches at a time as if he's trying to find solid ground.

"Lily," my name hangs between us for long, quiet seconds, and the more neither of us speak, the more anxious I get—about everything.

"Henry, I have a test tomorrow, and I've been studying every night after the service hours I have to do because I got caught sneaking out. If I don't get this...*this*..." I toss my cards back on the table and reach forward ripping all but one of the cards from his hands. I hold them up and fan them out in front of him. "If I can't get this stuff in here..." I tap the side of my head and toss his cards with the rest of mine. "I'm going to fail. Epically...fail."

His lips tighten as his gaze travels just below my eyes.

I hold my hand out for the final card and he glances at the words then hands it to me.

"Thank you." I blink my gaze to him briefly, then turn my focus back to the angry mess I left on my desk. I scoop the cards together in a pile and slide the chair out from the desk so I can regroup and focus. I can feel Henry behind me. I haven't heard his feet move once, and I don't think he's taken a deep breath. I do, lifting my shoulders high and holding them scrunched up against my neck before I release the tension and blow out heavily through my lips.

"Do you still get to audition? For the showcase?" His voice vibrates. I wonder if my worst fear has just now hit him. How selfish of him.

"No. They took it away," I lie, feeling instantly guilty for playing a game like this with him. That's not who I am—*a liar.* I glance over my shoulder and catch a hint of his guilt-ridden features from the corner of my eyes.

"I'm kidding. It was a reprimand. Because sneaking out, it seems, happens all the time," I add, moving back to the French cards I'll never memorize.

He's still there. And as long as he stands behind me, silently, I won't be able to read a Goddamn thing.

"I really am sorry, Lily." His apology is whispered this time. It's pathetic, but for once, I think it's honest. I'm not sure if he's sorry because of how I'm treating him, or because he feels bad about dragging me out and acting like a fool.

I don't like that version of him that I saw.

"I know you are, Henry." I sigh. "Look, I really need to study."

I turn to the side with my arm over the back of the chair. The rain outside is pelting the library roof, nearly drowning out the roar of thunder that vibrates the walls.

"If you're going to stay…at least help." I shrug, and my inner voice calls me weak. I won't memorize anything with Henry in the room. I'll just sit here and vacillate between being mad and forgiving him.

"Elena took me to France when I was eleven. We spent the summer there. I know a little." His lips twist into a half smile that falls into a slight one, the kind that begs to stay.

I nod my head toward the table and turn back to face my studies. A second or two later, Henry pulls up a chair across from me and begins to gather my cards in his hands.

"Do you want to try colors?" He's flipping the cards around so much that they start to spill again. I flatten my palms on the table with a heavy slap, startling him frozen. His eyes flash to mine.

"I don't know any of it. And if you're going to bring nervous energy in here, you have to go." I deflate with the weight of hopelessness tugging down my shoulders.

Henry's nod is short, and incredibly jittery. It makes me laugh because it reminds me of the time my mom tried to train a dog we rescued. The poor thing was so frazzled by her slur of commands that he just kept peeing on the floor. We gave him to our neighbors. I bet they still have him.

Inhaling slowly through my nose in an attempt to calm my own racing pulse, I force an apologetic smile on my lips and look him in the eyes.

"I'm stressed. I'm sorry."

He gives another jittery nod and smiles through gritted teeth.

"Colors sound great. Let's start there," I say, letting my head fall forward to rest on my now-folded arms. I close my eyes and listen to nothing but the words, and I fail—over and over again.

The first half hour is a worthless string of him asking me phrases and me not getting any right; the next thirty minutes shows some progress. Somehow, despite the massive distraction that Henry Alderman is, I retain about half of the things he quizzes me on the first time. We go through them four more times, and with each pass, I get something new right. I slip up on a few, but he corrects me, and I'm almost always able to finish the sentence on my own.

It's almost eight, and my stomach is beginning to rumble. I can tell Henry's hungry too. I've heard his stomach growl.

"*Je suis un pain à la banane.*" I stumble through a sentence of my own making, and Henry's face pulls in tight, one eyebrow high as he looks up at me from the cards in his lap. He's become more relaxed, but I'm still not certain of his expressions.

"You're...a banana bread?" He pauses with his brow quirked, laughter perched at the edge of his lips.

My mouth tightens to hold my amusement in, but it spills out quickly.

"Is that seriously what I said?" I ask.

Henry nods through a belly-shaking cackle. He works to regain composure, looking down at the table top with his palm spread out in front of him on the wood. His hair flops down over his forehead and he takes three or four deep breaths so he can be serious. His mouth keeps trying to hold its form, but it just continues to break into a grin that brings his eyes to me again.

"I'm sorry," he says, holding his palm out to excuse him.

His lips are thin, stretched and working so hard. His dimples are deep, and his eyes blink rapidly. He's suddenly my Henry—the one who loves to slide on wooden floors late at night.

"*Je veux du pain à la banane,*" he finally says through a straight face.

I blink at him twice.

"*Je suis un pain à la banane.*" I repeat it the way I said it the first time, knowing it's wrong. I do it because I love the way Henry laughs, and he reacts exactly as I hope. His head falls forward to the table and his voice goes an octave deeper with a dramatic groan.

"You're hopeless."

"I'm hungry," I respond instantly.

"Oh God, same," Henry says, leaning back in a massive stretch that lifts his shirt up his stomach just enough to show off his skin. I look, and he notices, so I quickly look down at my book and tuck my hands under my knees in my chair.

"Let's get a snack at the hall. I have credits. And it's still open," he says. I glance up, and he cocks his head enough to send a trickle of hair down over his brow. He blows it back with a crooked smile, and I realize that I'm no longer mad at him. It isn't fair, but it's the truth. He charmed his way right back. The French didn't hurt.

"Okay," I say, sliding my book into my bag and taking my stack of cards from Henry so I can tuck them inside too. I zip it up while Henry hits the switch for the lights. My neighbors are still hard at work on their physics studying, and Henry knocks on their glass wall, giving them a thumbs-up when they look our way.

"I'm pretty sure they hate me," I grumble without moving my lips.

"Yeah, well, they're geniuses. Geniuses are assholes…so they hate everyone." He doesn't even mask his voice, and I wonder when their eyes flicker if they heard him. When one of them flips Henry off, I assume so. We both laugh under our breath and wave as we walk toward the exit.

The rain is a steady sprinkle now, so we only have to jog to the dining hall to stay semi-dry. Henry gets to the door first and holds it open for me, catching my arm when my feet slip on the wet tile.

"Whoa there," he says as I stumble to get my balance.

I titter nervously, a little embarrassed but more flustered because he's touching me. Twelve hours ago, I pictured his face as I scraped away gum as a punishment, and I stabbed the sidewalk heatedly, dropping F-bombs every few breaths. And now he's touching me, and I...I like it. How can I be angry at him when his touch gives me butterflies?

"I'm good; I'm good," I say holding my arms out. He drops his hold and steps away with his hands out, ready to catch me as if I'm a balanced tower of tea cups. I smirk at him bashfully and he chuckles before leading the way into the snack bar. Henry grabs a pack of white-powdered donuts and I get a small bag of trail mix and a banana. I hold it up and repeat the French words that led to this snack run, getting it right this time. Henry claps lightly and whispers, "*Bravo.*"

"You mean, *très bien,*" I correct, setting my snacks down for the clerk to ring up.

"Touché," Henry says, picking up his things and walking backward to lead me out to the tables near the windows. His teasing draws out a tight smile on my lips, and it stays there while I sit down across from him and catch his gaze still on me.

I busy myself with my banana first, breaking off the end and setting it on a napkin before taking a bite.

"Something against that part of the banana?" he asks.

"Oh," I mumble with a full mouth. I shrug and chew down my first bite. "The little hard part on the tip bugs me. It's...gross."

I take another bite of the soft center and try not to blush when Henry bunches his brow at me, amused by my quirk. I have lots of them when it comes to food, like picking away nearly every piece of orange rind, and working the skin off beans. It's tricky, and it means that it takes me forever to eat. Alice won't serve chili anymore.

He reaches toward the napkin and pinches the banana tip between his thumb and index finger then holds it up to inspect it.

"You know, they say spider eggs might be in the *bananus,*" Henry says, squinting as he draws the dark little bit closer to his eyes. I actually have heard that—it's what led to my banana-tip protest. He turns it in his hand a few times then, without warning, pops it in his mouth, grinning as he swallows.

I just stare at him with my mouth open in awe.

"What?" he chuckles, tearing into his donut package with his teeth and following the spider bite with an entire donut, white powder dusting his lips.

I shake my head and fold the peel over the rest of my banana, opting instead for my trail mix.

"It's urban dictionary stuff. Nobody really knows what that thing is called. I would know—I did an entire paper on it in sixth grade." He grabs my banana and unpeels what's left, eating the rest whole—other black bit and all.

"You're full of shit," I say, leaning my head to the side and glaring with one eye smaller than the other.

His mouth moves in slow circles, chewing and smirking all at the same time. I try to judge the look in his eyes but give up under the intensity, letting him win. He's too good at bluffing to know anything for sure, and lord knows I can only stare into his eyes for so long without acting goofy and forgiving him more than I want to.

After our initial gorging on snacks, we both begin to pick at our food quietly for a few minutes, his whole bites getting cut to halves and quarters until he has two donuts left. I separate out the raisins in my trail mix, saving the chocolate flecks for last. Henry steals one, and I swat at his hand playfully. He turns in his seat, protecting his shins from my swinging feet, so I clutch the rest of my trail mix in my palm, losing a few sunflower seeds in my haste.

"You can have those," I say, waving them off like I'm royalty tossing him bread.

"That's bird food. I don't want that," he says, brushing the seeds to the floor.

"Is not." I squint my eyes and shake my head. I pinch a handful of my mix and push it in my mouth, and Henry lunges across the table at me. I react by holding my trail mix closer but I also blare out a loud, "Ahh!" My pulse races with my nerves, and Henry's hand stops, fingertips just short of my arm.

Playful laughter slows into a hum, and eventually…silence. I'm left with nothing but his stare. Those eyes get me into trouble. They make me break rules, but they also make me try things I probably never would. They make me care more than I should. They make me feel like maybe I'm just a little special to the guy looking at me, even though I know I'm not.

Henry's lip ticks up with a faint laugh and he slides a few inches back, his hand dragging along the table. I let my hands fall to my lap, the last few berries and seeds stuck to them along with the small bits of chocolate. I look down at my open palms and laugh at my mess, then reach up for the napkin and begin wiping it all away.

"I really am sorry, Lily."

My jaw automatically flexes at his apology. I've heard it so many times this week that I don't know if it can feel legitimate at this point.

"I know," I say, my mouth falling into a soft line while I continue to clean my hands. The napkin is beginning to shred but the stickiness is still there, so I start to rub my palm on my jeans. I know when I look up again, Henry's eyes will still be waiting. His hands haven't moved anymore.

"I knew I was taking Molly," he confesses.

I swallow and look down at my lap. I ball my fists together and nod, only vaguely knowing what Molly really is. Alice told me over the summer that if she caught me with it, she'd pull me out of Satis House and put me back in Public.

"Okay," I say.

"Lily," his voice is quiet. The shadow of his lowered head moves on the table. My eyes flit to his profile in shadow first, then to his actual face.

His eyes are weighed down at the sides, heavy with guilt. My parents used to look at me like that when I wanted something we couldn't afford.

"Why did you even invite them?" My shoulders inch up high with discomfort and I barely look at him. I'm almost warding off his answer before he can give it, terrified he's going to say it's because they were pretty or because he likes them. It's the question I really wanted to ask, but yet now I wish I didn't ask it.

"To be an asshole, I guess," he says with a short laugh. His mouth retreats back to the same soft line—the guilty one. I didn't laugh back. Nothing about any of this is funny.

"You think they're pretty." I look down at the crumbs we've left on the table. I didn't ask, instead just stating it for him. It's easier that way.

"I guess...yeah," he says.

It isn't easy to hear at all.

I nod slightly and run my teeth over my bottom lip, sad there's no more chocolate. Nothing sweet to be found.

"You want to know what Elena gave me for my birthday?"

I look up and he draws his hands away from me, sitting up straight before looking off to the side, shaking once with an amused chuckle.

"Keys to the kingdom!" he bellows, his voice filling the empty dining space and drawing the attention of the clerk counting down until her shift ends. She goes back to counting the money in her drawer.

"What does that mean?" I'm not good at Henry's riddles.

He leans to the side and pulls his wallet from his pocket, unfolding it and slipping out a black card. He slides it over to me and turns it for me to read.

"It looks expensive," I say, taking it in my fingers and feeling the thick card stock. Gold lettering impressed along the front reads HAVISHAM and Henry's name is embossed below, along with the words CHAIRMAN OF THE BOARD.

"Wow." The word just slips out because I'm pretty sure the only card I'll get for my birthday will have a fart joke printed on one side and a check for twenty bucks along with a note not to cash it until Friday.

"Youngest board member of any major Chicago holding company ever. My future is written, and Havisham Industries is my ship to drive as soon as I graduate from Harvard Business School or Yale or whatever other college Elena has lined up for me."

He takes the card back into his hand and stares at it while I spin his words around in my brain.

"Henry...that's amazing," I say, quickly realizing he doesn't agree when I catch the ghost-white color on his face. His eyes gloss over, still staring at the card.

"Yeah," he eventually says, sniffing and running his arm over his face before putting the card back in his wallet. He shakes his head a few times and flits his gaze up to me. His eyes show traces of red. He isn't happy about any of it. The world served up to him, but he doesn't want it. I don't get it.

"You're not happy…" I state the obvious, and Henry just glances up at me, the same straight dash on his lips.

"I know, right?" He leans back in the plastic cafeteria seat and stretches his arm across the back of the open chair next to him, thrumming his fingers along the edge. "I got a car too. Multi-million-dollar company…car…cash, and a credit card."

"Okay, you can quit now," I say, laughing it off like I'm not offended by any of it, but really—it's so much that it is a little offensive.

"I'm just hoping to teach music somewhere, like a grade school, I guess," I say.

Henry's mouth forms an instant crooked smile.

"Yeah…that would be just about perfect. You…you would be a great teacher."

I settle into his gaze for a minute, shifting in my seat under his attention. His eyes do this thing with me sometimes—they move around tiny parts of my face, taking in one eye at a time, a cheekbone, my chin, my lips, an ear. He's doing it now, and I find my chin tucking into my chest a little to hide from his affectionate scrutiny, even though I do like it. I guess I just don't want him to start finding flaws.

"You know the moment she brought me home, the first thing Elena did was sit me down across from her in her office, at that big desk…"

"The one with the quill?" I pipe in with an amused expression.

Henry chuckles.

"Yeah! I mean, who has a quill on their desk still, right? This is not the revolution!"

We both lean forward and laugh at Elena's idiosyncrasies. She has so many, and we spend the next few minutes running through them all, from the way she wears gloves when she goes out for a drive, to the actual teapot she uses to brew in every afternoon. It whistles, and the sound is infuriating when you're trying to concentrate because she lets it just go on and on. She has a name plate on her desk at home, even though nobody, other than Henry, me and Alice, ever seem to come inside.

The jokes at her expense keep tumbling out, and every little kernel Henry uncovers for me is more peculiar than the last, driving my laughter so deep that my stomach starts to cramp. Eventually, he gets back to that moment where he was a little boy, adoption ink still wet, staring at his new parent across a quill-topped cedar desk.

"'Young Henry,' she said, 'you will never feel pain or abandonment in your life again. Nobody will own you, because you will own it all. You'll keep your heart, too, because giving that away is cheap, and we have to look out for ourselves. If you let your guard down in this life, someone will come in to steal what's yours, and you want what's yours...don't you Henry?'"

His laughter has stopped. His smile is gone. There's a shadow to his eyes, too, from the way his head is tilted down in his stare at me. He says it all with a deep, commanding voice that echoes Elena's, and I imagine a young Henry hearing it all while he sits in a chair too tall for his feet to touch the floor in a room gilded with gold.

"She told me she would make every decision for me for the rest of my life, and you know what?"

I can't seem to speak. I only let out a tiny breath that begs for him to say the rest.

"Up until I met you...she has."

The quiet is instant and thick. I know my heart is throbbing inside my body because I can feel it but there's no sound, not even the expected rush over my eardrums or pounding in my head. It's a choking silence.

And then the last little fact he drops on me.

"I called her *Mom* once. I was six, and I thought...ya know." He leans his head to one side and smiles on the opposite, not a bright smile at a fond memory but the kind that comes with a lesson learned. "It seemed like enough time had passed, and other kids had moms or dads."

His eyes sink into mine, a long, hard stare that squeezes my heart more with every passing rise and fall of his chest.

"She beat me with a carbon-steel piano string. Two lashings, here..." he draws a long line along his left shoulder, then reaches behind his neck to indicate where the second one was. "And there."

"Jesus," my voice is barely audible. Henry's eyes go void of anything. It isn't a mask; it's just emptiness, and I think maybe he's a little shocked to be sharing these details.

His eyes dart around the table between us, and his lips keep parting to speak, but nothing comes. Before he can cancel everything out, attempt to take it back and run from me, I try something desperate —I compliment him. No...*I fucking fangirl!*

"You're amazing at everything you do. When you row with the team...I mean...Henry," I laugh out, bashful and sort of lost in my words. It's too late to stop them from coming now, though. "It's just really great. That's all. You...*you're really great.* At rowing, I mean! And...at other things. You know French...kinda. I mean, better than me. And everyone wanted to be at your birthday party..."

I wince and start waving my hands in the air between us, as if I hold some sort of magic eraser.

"I mean, you're popular. But, not like a dictator, like someone people want to be around."

He hasn't run away, but he's also not moving...like, at all. I squint, realizing how much gibberish flew out of my mouth in under thirty seconds.

"Dictators are popular?" Henry finally says, shaking lightly with his laughter at my expense, leaning back and rubbing his chin.

"Gah! No, but..." I look down to my lap and bring my hands together so I can pick at my thumbs. I'm going to have sores by the time this night is over if I keep this up. I want to say something real to him, something that matters, but I know that it's also going to need to be real for me. But maybe...just maybe that's okay now. He said he chose me. I was a decision he made, and I'm not sure what that means, but it has to mean I matter.

I matter to him.

"It's just, you're saying all of these things, and I feel like maybe you don't think you're worth anything, or whatever. And I just wanted you to know that I think you are. I think…" I lift my chin and lock onto his eyes. They're pained and hopeful, and he looks like he might bolt at any second. "Henry, I think you're worth everything."

I shrug, my left eye starting to twitch, and my lips buzzing into numbness. My nerves are in defensive mode, ready to zap anything that touches them, like an electric fence. Yet, all I can seem to do is sit here like a schoolgirl, my ankles crossed and my hands folded in my lap, while I stare at the boy I want more than I've wanted anything in my whole entire life, more than I wanted to play that damn piano in that cold, dark house.

"I think you're great, and smart…and," my lips shut tight, and I feel like I might vomit so I pause for a moment then keep going, ignoring the sting of tears pushing at the corners of my eyes. "I think you're handsome. I came here…to Satis House…because of you. Not that I followed you, but I wanted to be near you. I wanted to know you more. It's been two years, and I still hardly know you, Henry. But everything I *do* know—gah! You aren't just the sum of Elena's decisions, Henry. You're more."

His eyes darken on me and don't blink, and his mouth stays in this half-shocked, awe-struck position that I can't quite read. His lips part, and his breath comes in and out at a steady pace, but quiet—soundless. I'm not sure if he pities me, or if he's amused, but the longer he just holds me hostage with that stare, the more my knee threatens to bob me right out of the room, if a heart attack doesn't take me first.

"I am so fucking broken, Lily. You're better off never knowing me at all." He levels me with his words, blinking only when he's done speaking. His expression stays ice cold. It isn't cruel, but it hovers in the same territory.

"No, you're not." I shake my head in defiance, and he blinks again, his lids closing slowly this time as his mouth bends into a practiced smile. It's the smile Elena put there by force. I can tell the difference now.

His head falls back as he looks up at the tiled ceiling and florescent lights buzzing above our heads.

"Whatever you think you feel for me Lily…" His chin falls back to his chest in the small pause he makes. His eyes sweep around my face, just like before, but then they stop square on my gaze, and they become cold and rotten. "Don't. Because I will never be able to feel anything for you."

His words wound me, surprisingly. I've heard him be mean before, but it's never felt quite as personal as this. My forehead dents, betraying me, and I know he sees the little break in my armor.

"I'm not like you, Lily. You...you're always putting other people first. You didn't want to go to my party, but you did...*for me.* You change your clothes for Nicki and me. You take French because Anya did and said you'd like it. You study the fucking piano, Lily! You do that because you were too afraid to tell Elena no when she insisted you learn!"

I shake my head, a tear slipping out along my right cheek. I catch it with my palm and push it back into my hair.

"No! That's not true. I love the piano. I wanted to learn," I say.

Henry nods, a maniacal laugh bubbling out of his chest.

"Sure, now you do. But none of that was your original thought. You are whatever we gave you—"

"Fuck you!" I shout back at him before he can lash out at me anymore. I cup my mouth in shock and shake my head in tiny movements while his eyes lower on mine. His tongue makes a short pass at his lips, and his jaw works as if he's sorting out the order for his words. My heart is beating so strongly that I feel it in the bottoms of my feet that are pressed hard against the floor, my legs flexed and ready to flee.

Another tear forms, and I let this one go. I don't want to uncover my mouth because I'm afraid if I do, more ugliness will come out of it.

Henry's eyes catch the movement of the beaded tears that form along my bottom lashes. The world begins to blur, forcing me to blink it away. Once I let it go, it falls down my face in a slow trail that feels like it's slicing me open at every inch.

"I should go," Henry says, standing while he holds me down under the weight of his dark eyes. He dismisses his chair with a kick of his leg, sending it sliding into the table with a loud, *clanging* sound that draws the worker's attention again. I start to shake my head, but he turns to throw away his uneaten donuts.

The room lights up with a bolt just as he stops at the door, and the rain picks up outside, plastering the window until even the campus lights outside can't shine through. It's still inside this room—still in time.

"Henry…" I croak out through my parting fingers.

His shoulders sag, but he doesn't move from his place by the door.

"I feel nothing, Lily." He shakes his head and holds out open palms to either side of his body, pressing his back into the door to push it open. "Just like Elena always wanted. I love nothing but myself."

He backs through the door to the roaring sound of thunder, water pounding his body like bullets. It doesn't slow him down. Nothing does. The door latches shut behind him and a second later I can see his form passing along the sidewalk outside.

I struggle to slow my breath. My fingers buzzing with energy, and unable to work properly. I follow his path until he turns around a corner, and then I hurry to gather my own trash and my book bag. My entire body is teeming with fear, and I can't tell if it's telling me to stay or go. Once I'm on my feet, though, giving into the chase is inevitable. It always has been—that part he was right about, sort of. I do things for Henry. But Henry also makes me do things for me.

Shoving my arms through the straps of my backpack, I rush by the trash and discard my wrappers, then bust through the door, feeling the weight of it fight my push, the wind and rain barreling into it from the other side. My face stings from the rain slapping into my skin, and I shield my eyes as I begin to run down the same path Henry took.

I see him the moment I round the corner, his legs taking long strides, his T-shirt plastered to his skin and pants weighed down, drenched with rain.

"Henry!" My voice crackles out his name. I run faster, slipping and catching myself on my knee, ripping a hole in my jeans. I rub the raw spot and keep going, limping a little with my run.

"Henry!" I shout his name again.

This time he stops, and for whatever reason, so do I.

His hands come up to his head, threading through his wet hair and pushing it back out of his face as he turns to me, body nearly drowned, just like mine. My hair is sticking to my face, and my sweater is heavy on my arms and back, the weight of the water pulling everything down.

"What do you want, Lily?" Henry points to his chin, quirking his head a little as if he's giving me a clear shot. He takes a few steps back in my direction. "You want to tell me to fuck off again, then slap me?"

I shake my head.

"No," I say, not loud enough for him to hear. He cups his ear and takes another long stride, anger radiating off him. He's a beast right now, wild in the elements and recovering from his honesty. He's raw— I see it now. The dark eyes and stiff jaw are his way of shutting down, just like running is.

"Go on, Lily, hit me," he says, patting his hand along the side of his face. Water flings from his fingertips and chin, and he spits to clear his lips as he talks. The rain is so heavy it threatens to drown us where we stand, and the lightning is getting closer, his form glowing with a strike and the boom only a fraction of a second after the flash.

"Henry," I shudder, squeezing at the wet sweater smothering my chest.

Henry closes the distance between us completely, hands outstretched again as he looks down on me, rain pulling his hair down to his face. He pushes it away as he bites the tip of his tongue then grits his teeth, practically daring me.

"What do you want, Lily?"

His chest rises and falls at an almost inhumane pace, rabid with emotion and his desperate need to run. There's no abandoned house to go to now, though, and his rooftop is probably streaming with runoff water.

"You...asshole!" I slam my fists against his soaking, wet chest and stare into his shocked face. His eyes move from my right to my left, a constant battle of his focus. His breath comes in hard and suddenly stops. I slam my fists into him again, this time leaving them there and opening my palms to grip at the wet threads of his shirt.

"I want you! And I don't believe anything you say. You aren't those things, Henry. You just aren't." I step into him and let my head fall against his chest, a mix of cold and warm simmering right there on the surface. I turn my head so my cheek is flush with his body and I open my mouth just enough to let my lips drag open as I tilt my head to look up at him.

"I want you…" I say when our eyes meet again—this time, his undeniably broken. The red is more defined, and his lids are heavy. His mouth pulls down at the corners, but his lips part in a desperate breath, the first sound of my name escaping in a whisper, "Li…"

His fingers graze along my chin, tipping my head up more until his other hand finds the other side of my jaw. His thumbs sweep away droplets of rain from my cheeks, and his head falls down to meet mine.

"I don't know how to care about anybody but myself, Lily." The heat from his breath warms my face and my mouth aches to meet his.

"That isn't true, Henry. I know it isn't because you care about me," I say, and his body shakes under my grip. I slide my palms up his chest to his neck, finding his jawline and running my thumbs along the edge. He turns his head enough to kiss the inside of my wrist, and my eyes fall shut at the feeling.

I'm dreaming. This must be a dream.

His head turns in my hold and I lift myself on the tips of my toes as he brings my mouth to his, inches turning to dust in a swift motion. His mouth closes on my bottom lip with a rushed and needy taste, holding on and sucking me in while he steps forward a few more inches. I walk back under his lead, moving from the force of his kiss, and we dance like this in the rain between bolts of lightning.

Henry's hands push my wet hair back and he cups my cheeks and covers my mouth completely, his tongue takes possessive passes against the soft skin of my lips. I let him devour me, learning with every movement of his mouth against mine. I've only kissed two boys in my life, and they were both seventh-graders who wore retainers. This kiss is different. It's my *true* first.

Henry's mouth dips to my neck, kissing the area where it curves into my shoulder as his hands weave through my hair until they're locked down in soaking wet, golden strands. He backs away enough to look down at me, his thumb wiping away the water collecting on my forehead before kissing there.

"She won't allow this, Lily. None of it, and I don't know how to be anything else," he says, rocking me slowly and holding me tight. A flash reflects off his eyes and the corresponding crackle makes me jump. Henry pulls me tight in his arms, but keeps my chin turned up against his chest so he can hold onto my gaze.

"I wanted this," I say, throwing his words back at him. "This was for me." I lick my lips, feeling them tingle as my mind catches up to what just happened.

"Okay," Henry nods, resting his head on mine again. His thumbs make small circles along my jaw and his lips open just enough to kiss the bridge of my nose.

"This is what you wanted," he breathes out, and somehow, even though I'm right where I wanted to be, I start to question everything.

CHAPTER 14

I didn't want to make a big deal out of it, even though Henry and me...kissing—that was a big deal.

He walked me to my dorm, up the stairs to my floor, and kissed me again in the freezing concrete stairwell for another thirty minutes. Not just the *everyday, oh-they're-a-couple-now kisses* either. He pressed my back against the door, and framed me between both of his arms, working my mouth in every single direction until I knew Nicki was going to start to wonder where I was. She'd texted a dozen times.

My lips were raw. I didn't know raw lips was a thing.

Nicki did.

She never teased. In fact, she never actually spoke the words out loud. She just gave me this look, like the one Alice makes when she knows Collin and I are lying about drinking the last soda or eating donuts from his restaurant. It's wisely suspicious, and if Nicki hadn't already toughened me, I probably would have immediately broken under the pressure of her leer.

But she did. I have graduated from the Nicki Roman School of Resilience, and for nearly a month, Henry and I have snuck out to meet on his rooftop every night without Caleb or Nicki or any of our friends uttering a word about it.

"They all know. You know that, right?"

Henry slides into the small space between the utility wall and the edge of the roof, his legs wide for me to sit between them. It's October, and the chill has come to the city. I'm not sure where we'll hide after this month. Perhaps we won't anymore.

"I know they do." I kneel down between his knees and turn so my back rests against his chest and his legs tighten against my thighs, his arms around my stomach like a safety belt. Henry's mouth finds its usual spot at the curve of my neck, and just as it has for days, the skim of his lips against me causes goosebumps to rise all over my body.

I giggle and lift my shoulder, squeezing at his chin. His warm breath laughs against me.

"Always so ticklish," he says, a low growling kind of whisper.

He nuzzles into the crook of my neck and breathes out, shifting his arms and legs a little to hold me closer and keep me warm.

"I told Caleb."

I squeeze my eyes closed at his confession.

"Why?" I whine.

"Because it's weird not telling your roommate that you're sneaking out to hookup. And he knew. You know they all know, Lily." He chuckles and I flush.

I'm not sure why I've been so insistent on keeping Henry and me a secret. I don't see him much during the day, so keeping our nights private hasn't been hard or felt strange, really. At first, I was afraid of hurting Ava's feelings, and facing Nicki's ridiculing and teasing about how it's "about time." Anya would be honest. She's the one who I really don't want to know because she might tell me that he's using me just like he does every girl he's made out with or "hooked up with"—*his words, actually.*

But I know this is different. It's lasted. A month! And there's just something about our conversations up here between all of the kissing and touching. Henry shares things with me, and I feel…important. Even if it's only to him.

"What did Caleb say?" I run my hands along Henry's arms then tuck them under his hands to stay warm.

"He said they all know," he laughs.

I fold into him a little, sad that my bubble—*our bubble*—is bursting. He leans to the side and turns my chin to him, though.

"You know I'm not ashamed of you, don't you?" His eyes grow heavy with his question, and my breath catches.

"Well, I didn't really think that until you said that word, but—"

He grimaces, bunching his face and shaking his head slightly.

"I didn't mean it like that. I'm not...ashamed. Lily, you're fucking beautiful. And really..." His mouth twists. "I don't give a shit what people think. That's maybe the one good quality Elena gave me. I know it's arrogant sometimes, but it's also comforting as hell not to feel like you have to pretend."

My eyes move to his lips, wanting him to just kiss me instead of talk about this more. He eventually leans down and dusts his mouth against mine, suckling on my top lip in my favorite way. He stops suddenly, though, pausing with our mouths attached until my lip slips free.

"You give a shit what people think."

My chest curls in on itself a little and he lifts his head enough to peer down at me with hurt eyes. I swallow, because now that he says it out loud I realize how shitty it is of me. I'm the one that's not all in with this.

I feel guilty under his stare, but no words are coming to me. Eventually, his expression lifts the slightest bit and his head falls against the side of mine as he wraps me up tightly again.

"I get it," he says, mouth right at my ear. His breath is heavy and drawn out, strangled by the burden of being him. "This way...if you get hurt, at least nobody will have to know."

My lip quivers instantly and I tuck my chin. He's right.

Long seconds tick by without a breath from his chest. It doesn't move where it meets my back, and his hands stay still and flat over my own. His mouth is silent as he's frozen with this reality, and I mentally prepare myself for him to tell me how I'm right, how he is a risk because he could never feel anything that I do.

Not for me.

And then...

"I won't hurt you, Lily." His chest finally fills. His grip tightens and his mouth tucks back into the hidden space beneath my ear. His lips part for a whisper. "I'll try really hard not to. I don't want to, is the point. I don't want to, I don't want to..."

I know his words should comfort me, but my chest squeezes with an ominous sense. I know that he hasn't told Elena. We both know better than that. Her judgment on how close we've become is already apparent every single time I see her. It's in the small ways she makes note of how I look at him.

"You're quite fond of him, aren't you?" she always says. I never give her a verbal answer. Normally, it's just a polite smile so I don't give in to her trap, not that it stops her from making more digs.

"He's just so charismatic. Girls have always been attracted to him, even when he was a child." She added that one last time, when I suspect she sensed I had some envy over other girls. She's manipulative that way—finding tiny threads to pull until my armor unravels.

"If I didn't come to Elena's to play the piano over the summer..."

Henry shifts to look at me while I talk, so I lean forward and turn slightly to face him. His face is curious, maybe a little cautious.

"Maybe I could just travel up here, I mean. To practice. Would you..." I leave it open-ended because there are plenty of words to fill in that blank.

Would you still listen?

Would you find a way to see me?

Would you care?

"I would come here every single day." His answer is swift.

"Yeah?"

"Yes, Lily! I would come here right from the office, and I'd make you stay longer, come up here to our place with me. We could watch the sunset and look at the stars and..." He leans forward and runs his nose along mine gently, a guilty grin stretching across his lips before he kisses me with them.

"Lily, I love watching you play. I really do. And you're getting so good. You're better than me now. God, that first day! Remember how I played the piano?"

"I thought you were amazing," I say, the goofy grin tickling my cheeks.

"You just thought I was cute," he says with a tilt of his head. Arrogant and adorable. "I was awful. I know, like…six chords."

He takes my hands, urging me to my knees in front of him as he places my hands on his chest. He spreads my fingers out and looks down.

"You can play Chopin." He runs his thumbs over my knuckles, and I fan my fingers along his chest, then play what I remember of the most recent piece I've tried. I'm not nearly as good as he says, but he seems so convinced and that makes me think maybe I'm better than I say.

My fingers drum along his chest while his hands hover just above them with the occasional light, feather touch.

"What is this called?"

His lashes are like deep flecks of gold as he looks down at his chest. I love looking at him from this angle, the playful tinge on his lips and new stubble aging his young cheeks. He smells like aftershave sometimes when we're up here on the rooftop. I like it.

"Polonaise-Fantaisie," I say, drawing the word out with a curl to my tongue. Henry's face lifts and his eyes glimmer, narrowing on my lips first, then lifting to my gaze.

"Can you play that for real?"

I move my hands to the right along his body for a run, then lift briefly and move back to the center to tap, just as I would on the keys. My teeth grip my top lip and I shrug.

"I'm working on it. I'm not smooth yet, but it's getting better."

I keep thrumming my fingers on his body as I stare at him, but eventually his gaze begins to make me flush, so I look back to my hands. His cover mine when I do, flattening them against his chest and bringing them together so he can hold on with his right hand and move his left to my chin.

"I'd like to hear it tomorrow." His eyes penetrate, and while I know he truly would, I also know that he isn't thinking about the piano anymore.

I nod lightly.

"Okay," I whisper.

Leaning forward, my mouth finds his, and he opens for me just enough to let me slip my tongue inside. I've gotten daring with him, with how I am when we make out. So many things he had to show me the first few times, like how to sit together so our mouths fit just right, or when to kiss hard and when soft.

Before Henry, my kisses were by lockers around the corner from busy hallways or outside playgrounds that I had long outgrown. I know he's had many kisses like ours before, but I've never let that bother me. He's kissing *me* now. And he kisses me often.

Last night, his hands held my thighs and he cupped my ass while I straddled his lap. I liked the way it felt when his grip was firm, and I've been thinking about him doing it again all day.

I lift myself up on my knees and bite on his bottom lip, giving it a soft tug that brings a smile to his lips against mine that I can't help but mimic. His right hand lets go of mine as I brace against his chest, and he runs them both along my hips, looping his thumbs in my jeans teasingly. His fingers curl, the nails scratching against the denim as they flex and crawl to my hips then ass, finally pulling me to him so his chin is flat against my ribs as he looks up under the cascade of my falling hair.

I giggle and sweep my hair over one shoulder so I can see him better.

"I had such a mad crush on your hair the first time I saw you," he admits, reaching up with one hand to grab it like a rope where it lies on my shoulder. He squeezes it then lifts it and lets the strands spill out of his fingers.

"Really?" I blush.

"Oh God, yeah. You're like this...California blonde," he says, a deep and raspy chuckle in his chest.

"Surfer girl?"

I'm coy.

He stares up at me for a few seconds until his crooked smile forms.

"Yeah," he hums, bringing his head up to face my chest and sweater. He opens his mouth and bites a few of the threads, pulling it up a few inches with his teeth as he looks back up at me. "Surfer girl," he muses.

I lick my lips. I think I know what he's insinuating, and I'm all right with it. I just don't know how to encourage him to continue inching up my sweater and the shirt that's underneath. I bite at my lip and stare down at his eyes, glancing toward my chest then back to him. He repeats his pattern, biting more of the fabric and bringing it higher again, this time his hands lowering back to my hips and sliding up underneath.

My breath holds when I feel his fingers graze along the side of my ribs. This time when he looks up to me for permission, I lift my chin and close my eyes, more swept away in the moment.

His fingers travel higher, thumbs just under the lacey band of my bra, and they draw along the sides a few times, testing me. His thumbs run over the fabric next, making wide circles that get tighter and tighter until they reach the very peak of my breasts.

"Ah," I slip out. My body shivers in response, and Henry does it again.

My chin falls down just as his lifts until our eyes meet, his with question and mine begging. One pass of the tip of my tongue along my bottom lip is all he needs and soon his hands begin to gather my shirt and sweater together at the bottom, lifting up my body as I raise my arms and let him pull them over my head to discard to our side.

It's a new bra. I bought it a week ago when I was home for the weekend. Collin needed to buy new serving pants for work, for his promotion, and I picked up a few things. I knew Collin wouldn't ask because he liked leaving girl stuff a mystery with me. I wanted one grown-up, nice thing…for a moment like this. And I am *so* glad that I got this bra.

It's pale pink, see-through lace everywhere, which means Henry's eyes are about to see more of me than I've shared with anyone—*ever.* His fingertips trail down my back first and I sit back a little, getting braver with every heartbeat. His mouth practically pouts, the way his bottom lip falls open, hungrily.

His hands begin to circle around to my front, tracing along the sides of my bra until his palms are flat along my ribs as he faces me. He draws a slow path upward, covering lace slowly, thumbs running along the hard pebbles underneath them on their way to the straps of my bra. In sync, each hand slips a band over my shoulder, and as the straps begin to slide down my arms, I reach behind myself and unclasp the back. The lace falls slowly, and Henry doesn't miss a single movement it makes.

He doesn't look up to me this time. His eyes steely and focused on my bare skin, dark-pink nipples and rising chest. He leans forward in one breath, his mouth covering my breast as his tongue swirls around the peak, and he pulls it into a hard suck that makes me squeak in pleasure.

"I'm going to leave a mark on you," he says, glancing up and drawing a tiny line with his finger along the soft flesh of the inside of my breast. "Just a small one, so you'll remember me being here."

His right hand moves to my other breast where he pinches, then softens my pink skin with his thumb, kneading it while his mouth suckles kisses all around my chest. My head falls back and I grin at the sky with closed eyes, almost unable to believe that this is me, right here and right now.

When Henry leaves his mark, I feel it bruise under his lips, the pull hard and raw on my skin. He presses his fingers on the spot when he's done, then wipes his chin, proud of his work. His eyes find mine, and he pulls me into him, hands digging into my back pockets as I straddle his lap, heat between my legs.

"Naked surfer girl," he whispers, laughing lightly when I bunch my lips at him and scowl teasingly. He tips my chin up with his thumb and draws my face close, kissing me slowly at first, then exploring my mouth more with his tongue. My lips will be pink and raw again, to match other parts of my body. I'll have to fess up, which is fine. I'm proud of the marks he leaves behind.

"Lily!"

Alice's voice cuts through my fantasy like lightning. I flatten against Henry's chest, and his arms wrap around me tightly as we both jerk our heads to the side. My...*aunt*...is standing with her arms crossed and a hardness to her jaw that I've never seen. Nicki is standing a few feet behind her, and when I spot my friend, my heart cracks open with betrayal. She shakes her head, fervently, and begins to repeat "I'm sorry. I'm so sorry, but she was pounding on our door. She was looking for you!"

"Get your clothes on!" Alice shouts.

For the first time in a month, shame washes over me. My back curves and I begin to shelter myself away from not just Nicki and Alice, but Henry too. I no longer want to be seen—by anyone.

"I'll meet you downstairs. Grab your things. You're leaving this school—*now!*"

Alice turns her back to me and marches back to the service door without even giving me enough time to loop my sweater over my head. My hands are flustered and shaking with nerves, and Henry is trying to get to his feet while helping me get dressed and get to my own.

"Lily, what's going on?" he asks.

"I don't know." I'm trembling, and my first attempt at my sweater is backward, so I switch my arms without taking it off. My gaze flashes up to meet Henry's when his hand wraps around my wrist. "I don't know why she's here, Henry. I don't know…I…"

My lip quivers, and I feel a panicked cry trying to break in. My eyes move to Nicki, who is still apologizing, and I start to question her angrily.

"Why is she here?"

"Lily, I swear. I don't know. She just now showed up, and she was waking everyone up. She made the guardian let her in. She dumped her whole purse out trying to show them ID, and before the guardian could even verify her security she was knocking on doors asking which room was yours. I heard her down our hallway, so when she knocked, I opened."

"She saw…" My breath hitches and I cup my mouth.

More shame.

"No, Lily. Don't do that," Henry says, his fingers fighting to get a grip on more of my arm. I'm stiff, and fighting him, but he forces me to face him eventually. "Our time up here is just for us. It's not for her. Or Elena. Or Nicki…sorry Nicki."

His mouth bends with a short smile, but I'm not in the mood. He quickly shifts and dips his body so he can meet my gaze and force my head back up even though I want to hide.

"Don't you dare think any of that was wrong, Lily. That meant too much. And you are too good of a person for her to let you think you're anything otherwise. Do you hear me?" His hands move to both sides of my face and his eyes drill into mine, waiting.

I nod, but barely.

"No, Lily. You are good. And she's...fuck, she's just crazy." His eyes glance to the doorway Alice left through, then back to me. He stares at me again, waiting for me to agree. I nod a little bigger this time.

"That's right," he says, leaning forward and pressing his lips to mine in a chaste, but long and sweet kiss. He gathers me into a hug and does it again before holding my head to his chest and rocking me.

"That's right," he says.

CHAPTER 15

I did not pack my things.

Alice was in a car parked out front by the time I got downstairs. I walked up to her window and motioned for her to roll it down. When she did, I told her I was not going. Then I walked back to Nicki and Henry, and we all went inside and stared at her through the security door window.

Nicki Roman School of Resilience 101.

There was yelling. And she also bothered to get out of the car and order me to leave with her, but I knew she wouldn't physically drag me out of the building. I'm sixteen in four days, and I'm an inch taller than she is.

Collin would have handled this differently. He would have called and just asked me about it. But he was at work when Alice sorted through the mail and opened up a tuition bill for fourteen thousand dollars. Alice doesn't pause in the face of a challenge; she barrels right through with zero information and leaves tornado-like destruction in her wake.

M aybe I would have ended up here in Ms. Manning's office on a Saturday anyhow.

"Did you do something to make Elena angry?"

This is the twentieth time Alice has asked me this question. I quit responding at number ten or eleven.

"Ugh!" Alice growls, standing from the spot between Collin and me on the bench outside the counseling hall. Ms. Manning is dealing with a discipline case this morning, too. One of the seniors was caught selling essays. I can overhear the conversation between her and his parents through the thin doorway beside us. He's being expelled.

I'm surprised Alice hasn't asked if I can be expelled for a refund. Maybe she will?

"It's probably just a mix-up, Alice. Elena wouldn't just refuse to pay or take away her support." Collin is trying to be reassuring, but it's like throwing Pepto-Bismol at a plague.

"You've met Elena once, Collin. This is *exactly* the kind of thing she would do if Lily did something to make her angry." Alice's gaze jerks to me in a beat. "What did you do?"

I simply stare at her. Answering is futile.

The doorway opens and an angry-faced couple doesn't bother to respond to any of the offerings Ms. Manning is shouting to them as they hurriedly drag their son down the marble hallway. My counselor mentions something about giving a recommendation to another school, but that only results in a mumble from the man. The woman's heels *click* at a rapid pace, and the student—or I guess now *former* student—drags his undone tie along the floor as he walks behind his parents.

"At least he doesn't have to wear that ugly suit anymore," Collin whispers at my side. I smile at him, but put on a straight face when I catch Alice's eyes on me. She's not in the mood to joke.

The doorway at the end of the hall slams behind the family, and Ms. Manning flinches a little where she stands. Her eyes then shift from that scene to mine.

"Lily," she smiles. "Come on in."

She stands to the side to let Alice and Collin enter before me, and

I'm tempted to mouth, "I'm sorry," as I pass by. Like Collin, though, I'm sure all of this is a misunderstanding, so I doubt we'll be in here long.

Alice takes the seat closest to the desk, so Collin and I sit off to the side of her, against the window.

"You mentioned something in your call about billing? What's the issue?"

Before Ms. Manning can finish her questions, or even sit in her chair behind her desk, Alice pulls a thick envelope from her purse and flops it down. She's taken it in and out several times and has written on most of the pages with red pen, circling numbers she doesn't like. She doesn't like all of them, really—especially the bottom line.

"Ah, yes...I see..." Ms. Manning pulls the forms apart and chuckles to herself while she looks through everything, her expression amused, as if she's seen this happen before.

"We can't pay that," Alice says, leaning forward and tapping her finger vigorously on the statement.

"And you don't have to," Ms. Manning explains. Her words inject instant ease into the room.

We all lean forward as she spins the pages around and points to a line of text—fine print.

"This is a thing the school sends out strictly for their taxes and to show off, for a lack of a better way to put it," she explains.

"Oh," Alice says, clipped. None of us really understand, but the important part is that we don't have to pay money. That's the part Alice cares about. *The only part.*

"We have to show what your scholarship is worth so we can write it off and show we're giving a certain amount of aid to our more modest families." She's practiced that line, the use of the word *modest*. It's a really nice way to say poor.

"So Elena didn't request to have Lily's scholarship revoked or whatever?"

Collin's question languishes in the open for several long seconds. A deep crevice forms in Ms. Manning's brow, and eventually she leans back in her chair and lets her hands fall to her lap, palms along her thighs.

"Why would that *ever* be the case?" she says.

I glance to Alice, her face puzzled with thought before she tries to answer.

"I don't know. I just figured since she was her sponsor or whatever, that she was sort of in control of how that money was spent. It...it doesn't work that way then?"

Ms. Manning's brow draws in tight as she holds back what looks like laughter.

"Lily, I'm sorry you weren't aware, but I was the one who put you in for our scholarship program. That's how it works, though usually we have an application period. You had missed it, but I recognized your name and checked to see if it was you when I saw your phone number on your submission to the school. I was so excited that the kind girl from the street was applying here!"

I'm baffled by this new information, and I can feel the questions piling up to my side and in front of me, where Collin and Alice fake polite laughter when they really have no clue what any of this is about.

"You got me into Satis House?" It hits my chest suddenly—her kindness, and the gratitude I've been misplacing at Elena's feet.

"Well," Ms. Manning leans forward again with a chuckle as she pulls the financial documents back together and hands them to Alice. "I would say that *you* got *yourself* into Satis. I only nudged it along with a little know-how on how the financial loopholes work around this place."

I'm stunned flat to my seat, and I lean back to let my head clunk against the window pane.

"Then Elena..."

"Is a very fine piano teacher," Ms. Manning finishes. She would never openly insult her sister, especially since she isn't sure where Alice and Collin fall on the Elena scale.

I nod in agreement with her, though, picking up on the undertone of her response. Elena is a great piano instructor, or at least she's the only one I would have ever had access to. She's the one I got, and maybe somehow that gives her a role in my self-discovery. Or maybe I get all of that credit. I'll certainly take more of it than I did before I walked into this office this morning.

"So, it's settled," Collin says, his special brand of nerd slipping out as he stands and claps his hands together in an attempt to get out of this office and move on with his day.

"Yes, you have no payment due. And I am sorry that this wasn't explained to you," Ms. Manning says, taking Collin's cue.

"It was very lovely to meet you both," she adds, glancing to me with a brief wink of understanding. I linger behind Alice and Collin, and before I exit the office I grab Collin's arm.

"I'd like to just stay this weekend, and I have a few schedule things to work out with Ms. Manning, so..." I say. Collin's forehead furrows, and I think maybe he's disappointed I don't want to spend a weekend at home. It was his plan, though, not Alice's.

"Oh," he says, looking to his wife who has already started shaking her head and fluttering her eyes in a gesture that says "whatever."

"I'll be home for Thanksgiving this year. *Our* home." I dip my head to stress that word. I don't want to spend this day with Elena again, and if Alice is there for work, she'll just have to endure it alone. Henry already plans to visit me.

"All right then," Collin says, holding an arm out for me in a position I assume means...*hug*? I step into him, surprised—pleasantly surprised. His hands pat at my back awkwardly, but not without their share of affection. Alice has already started to walk away.

"She's just wound differently than us is all. She'll be glad to see you though," Collin says, head leaning toward Alice's path.

I nod my okay, decidedly all right if she's never glad to see me. I became Alice's responsibility in a blink, and for her, that falls on the side of burden. And the more time she spends in that house with Elena, the colder her heart becomes.

Collin leaves me with an apologetic smile before rushing off to catch up. When I turn my attention back to Ms. Manning, she's leaning against her desk with one hand and holding a fist against her mouth with the other. Her color is...off.

"Are you all right?" I rush to her, my hand on her bare arm which feels instantly clammy.

She nods, feverishly.

"It'll pass," she says, her eyes blinking closed as the red returns to her cheeks. I stand next to her, ready to take her weight if she faints.

"Were you ill that whole time? I'm so sorry they insisted on this meeting right now," I yammer, looking around her office for a trash basket. I find one peeking out from under her desk, so I bend down and grab it. That's when I see the enormous bottle of prenatal vitamins sitting in her open drawer.

"Oh…" I react, even though it isn't my business and I'm not sure why it matters to me. She catches the direction of my gaze then takes the basket from my hands, moving to the chair Alice was in a minute ago. She slumps down with the basket in her lap, hands gripping either side while she holds her breath and looks at the crumpled papers inside.

"There're holes in this," she says with a short, manic laugh.

I flash my gaze to her and the bin and realize she's right—it's woven straw with gaps every inch. I twist around and look for anything else that might work, grabbing a canvas bag hanging on a hook in the corner of her office. I hand it to her and take the basket, but the color has already fully returned to her cheeks.

"Thanks," she says, her head falling to the side with exhaustion. I see it in her face now. Her cheeks aren't as full as they normally are, and her eyes are heavy.

"I thought the sleeplessness was supposed to come *with* the baby."

She whimpers out a pathetic laugh at my joke.

"It's early still. I've been so sick, though. Poor Mischa has to wake up at three with me every morning so I can vomit. I don't know why it comes then, but it does. Well, and now…at…" She leans to her right to glance at the clock on her wall. "Nine forty-seven."

I nod sympathetically and sit on the edge of her desk. Her eyes slip from mine and look off to the side. I bring my hands to my front and pick at the remaining flecks of silver polish left on my nails from when Nicki painted them a week ago. The silence is thick.

"Don't tell Elena," she finally says.

"Oh no…I wouldn't," I answer fast. I lift my head to meet her gaze. Her expression is instant relief.

"Good, good," she mutters, her eyes moving around again

nervously. Elena will find out, eventually, unless she plans to disappear before she begins to show.

"Why have you never moved away?" The question just sort of falls out.

Ms. Manning laughs silently, leaning back a little and looking at the ceiling.

"God, I would love to. But Mischa loves it here. His parents were immigrants. They owned a meat shop."

"They're…passed?" I ask.

She nods.

"We did not carry on the meat shop," she laughs. "But we do still have their apartment. It's beautiful, and it's near the university. If I ever made a change, I'd do what I do here…there."

I smile, but also study her. I thought Mischa was older. His hair is grayed, and I guessed he was maybe in his fifties, like Elena, when I met him briefly. I don't think Ms. Manning is much younger. They have two daughters already.

"Is it easier this time around?" My questions are naïve. I'm an only child, and my guardians seem to have zero plans to have a *real* child of their own. I don't know that I've ever actually been around someone who's pregnant.

"What you mean is aren't I too old," she says. I blush and give a small shrug.

"It wasn't planned. Hell…it wasn't supposed to be possible!" I laugh with her.

"Is it…dangerous?" I ask.

Her head wobbles side to side as her eyes squint.

"I'm forty-six…and I know that this might end badly. But we both decided I had to try. *We* had to try."

She takes in a long breath and shifts to sit up taller as her eyes flit to her lap, her palms slapping down lightly to signal that she's done sharing. She stands, so I move from her desk, closer to the door. So many thoughts and facts in my head.

"Thank you!" I rush out the words, suddenly remembering the real reason I wanted to stay behind and talk with her. I'd almost forgot.

"For helping me to get in at Satis House. This place is everything to me."

Her smile is fast and genuine, glossed lips curved into a satisfied line.

"You got in on your own merit, Lily. I only made sure things like money weren't in the way," she says.

My chest fills with a fast and heavy breath. I didn't realize how worried I'd been over the bill and the thought of not being able to stay here.

"Elena and I both went here. I could leave…like you said. But I don't think it's fair that I have to just because she wants to have it all, you know? This place is mine, too. She can have her fancy boards and fundraisers. I'm happy helping young people think about their futures."

The future. Ms. Manning is really the first person who made me see a future. It's probably not appropriate for me to do, but neither is asking probing questions of my high school counselor's pregnancy, so I give in to my urge and embrace her. Her arms slowly collapse around me in return, and while our hug is brief, it's meaningful.

I miss my mom and dad. I feel like maybe they sent her.

Henry is waiting in my room with Nicki when I return. He's lying on my bed, his body taking up the entire length, and his arm folded over his eyes so he can sleep.

"When did he show up?" I whisper to my roommate.

Nicki is sitting on the edge of her bed, legs folded and her hands holding the pleats of her plaid skirt around her thighs. She's the only one of us who wears that thing on non-uniform days, probably because on her it looks so completely non-uniform.

"You hate me," she says. She hasn't even bothered to draw the thick, black line under her eyes yet this morning. It's strange seeing her like this—like her alter-ego, or something.

"I don't hate you, Nicki."

We talked about it two nights ago, when Alice left, and I forgave her then. We talked about it last night when I couldn't sleep because I was too anxious about my meeting this morning. It looks like we're talking about it again.

"I swear I wasn't spying on you guys. I just wanted to know where you went, so—"

"You followed me a couple weeks ago, and you didn't see anything. Okay, maybe you saw us make out a little, but that's it. You swear." I drop my chin and glare at her, reciting what she's told me a dozen times word-for-word.

"You hate me," she says.

"Oh my God!"

I pretend to choke her then crawl up on the bed next to her and rest my head on her lap. Her body gets stiff, and I know she has a bit of a thing about personal space. I don't care; she needs to open up for me right now.

"Go on, stroke my hair," I say, picking up her hand and resting it on the side of my head. She leaves it there, not moving it for several seconds until we both start to laugh.

"This affection thing is weird," she says.

"You're being weird, so I didn't know what else to do," I say.

She scratches at my scalp a little then gives in and pulls one of my curls out to the side, rolling it in her fingers.

"You're so blonde."

I wrinkle my forehead and smile crookedly; I let her make a disgusted face at my natural hair color for almost a full minute in complete silence.

"I get to stay, by the way. It was a misunderstanding."

Nicki's reaction is slight, but I notice her nuances. Her lips twitch and her eyes brighten.

"I really am sorry," she says, finally, her gaze still on the same lock of hair.

I reach up and grab her hand, and my touch brings her eyes to mine.

"I know you are, and I'm telling you it's fine. We are fine." I squeeze her hand and she slips into an innocent smile.

"Are you two ever going to make out?" Henry's voice ruins our moment, and Nicki's expression returns to the disgusted one she likes to put on for him. She lifts my head up from her lap and shoves me from her bed.

"Why you like this pretty boy so much, I have no idea." Nicki grabs her makeup bag and shoves her feet into a pair of slippers, pointing at us as a reminder that she can spy on us anytime she wants as she leaves us alone and goes to the bathroom down the hall.

Henry cracks one eye open at me and his mouth forms a pouty grin.

"You were supposed to be sleeping. I can't believe you heard that," I say, moving to his side and pushing him until he's forced to move. He pulls me toward him, and as he rolls, my body fits with his until my back is against the wall and he's lying on his other side, just inches away while I'm caught in his arms.

"It all worked out," he says softly, his nose close enough to nudge mine.

"I'm staying."

"You're staying," he echoes. His grin is undeniable, and I think maybe he was actually a little worried too.

"Was Alice mad about…ya know—*how she found us?*" he asks.

I punch out a short laugh.

"She was mad about having to pay an enormous bill. I honestly don't think she gives two shits about walking in on our make-out session," I say.

He's wearing deep blue jeans and a dark-gray sweater with a white collar from a fairly wrinkled shirt poking through the neck. I reach up to straighten it and breathe him in. His hair is still damp from a shower.

"You're going somewhere," I say, focusing on my hands and his collar.

He reaches in and stops my fidgeting, bringing my hand to his mouth. He presses his lips on it.

"Just for a little while. Elena made plans." His eyes dim, and I can tell he's ashamed that he's doing something for her. Ever since he opened up to me about his frustrations with her rule on his life, he's seemed guilty whenever he follows her orders.

"Henry," I say, waiting until he meets my gaze. "It's fine. I'll see you when you get back. Maybe you'll learn something."

He laughs a little, lips twisted with doubt.

"Yeah, maybe," he says, moving his hand back to my waist. He flirts with the bottom of my shirt, tickling me lightly along my midriff and pulling my shirt up enough to see my bra. I push it back down and blush.

"Nicki's makeup doesn't take *that* long," I say.

He groans, jokingly, then brings my head close to his chest, tucking me under his chin. I'm not sure why I'm so comforted there, but I am. Maybe too much so.

"Ms. Manning is pregnant."

I still. Henry's hold becomes stiff, and his breath stops. I focus on finding the thump of his heart. I can't.

Shit. What did I do?

"That's...news." He doesn't use an adjective to describe it. I know the details of his life and his relationship to the woman I met with all morning. Henry and I haven't talked about what I know, yet still my mouth opened and this one, vital secret fell out.

I close my eyes tightly and practice it in my head first.

I know she's your aunt. She's your aunt. She, and Elena...they're...

"I won't tell Elena," he says. My mouth falls open against the knit of his sweater and my eyes blink.

"I'm sorry. She told me about how you're related a while ago, but I never knew how to talk to you about it."

"It's fine," he says, his hand finally moving against my arm. His touch feels robotic, though.

"Henry," I begin to lift my head but he cups it against him and strokes my hair.

"I mean it. It's fine. Kinda hard to call her my aunt when I can't call Elena my mom."

His words singe at my chest, and everything inside of me tightens. He's right, but hearing him say it—acknowledge it—is terribly harsh.

"I actually should go. I'm getting picked up soon, but I'll be back Sunday," he says, kissing the top of my head and rolling out of my arms until his feet find the floor. My bed is so empty where he was, nothing but wrinkles in my comforter. I sit up and bend my knees, hugging them and wishing I had a manual on how to fix the dumb things I say.

"Lily, I promise...it's fine." He kneels with one knee on the bed, moving close enough to kiss me. I lift my chin and meet his lips, grabbing his bottom lip with my teeth and not wanting him to go. He hums at the sensation and smiles as he pulls away.

"I almost forgot..."

He reaches into his back pocket and pulls a small, folded piece of yellow paper out and hands it to me, but doesn't let go right away, pinching one end while I pinch the other.

Our eyes dance.

"I will be home late for your birthday, but I promise I'll be back in time to kiss you goodnight. And I'll have a real present," he says, letting go of his hold on the paper. "But for now, I got you this."

I look at him sideways and start to open the paper, but he reaches forward and stops my hand.

"No. Oh God, no, not until I'm gone," he says in a nervous laugh. For once, Henry Alderman is the one who's blushing.

"Okay," I say softly.

He looks down and shoves his hands in his pockets as he backs away, a crooked and guilty smile practically ruling his face. My feet start to wiggle with anticipation and it makes us both laugh.

"All right, all right. I'm going. Just...wait until you count to five or something, okay? Five."

He holds up an open palm, fingers wide. I reluctantly nod, and he reaches for my door, lowering his eyes as he opens it, then practically sprinting down my hallway like a fool.

I unfold the paper the instant he's gone. I was expecting a stupid drawing or a heart or something dirty maybe, based on how he was acting. Instead, to my dismay, I'm faced with a tiny sentence written in French.

"Dammit!" I blurt out, giggling at his cruel joke.

I fly to my desk and fling books out of my way until I get to my French dictionary. I recognize a few things immediately, but some of the translations give me trouble. After almost five minutes, I'm nowhere near certain of what this says, but I know it's sweet. The words he used are all sweet. I just don't know how to put them together.

The idea smacks me in the face when my eyes land on my phone. I pull up an online translation and nervously type, getting it wrong several times until my hands settle in and start to work the right way.

Je me suis épris de toi.

I fell for you.

I backpedal to my bed and collapse on my back the moment my legs hit the mattress. With my phone held out in front of my grin-stained face, I say the words out loud as good as a first-year French student can.

"Je me suis épris de toi."

"De toi to you too!" Nicki grunts as she pushes through the door, letting out an obnoxious "ahh" when she realizes Henry's gone.

I ignore her. I barely even hear her. In fact, I may not hear anybody for the rest of the day, because Henry Alderman fell for me, and he said so—in French!

CHAPTER 16

Collin and Alice are getting a divorce. Most teens my age, home for the holidays their sophomore year and relieved to be spending time with their families, would be devastated by this news. If I sit still enough and listen to the hush of the snow falling outside, I barely remember that it's a fact.

"I want to live with Collin."

That was the only thing I said, and it was agreed upon instantly. He's staying in the house, and Alice is moving to the city, to an apartment near her work. She's going to be closer to Elena—quite the protégé she's become.

She's her slave, though she doesn't see it that way.

Alice and Collin never really seemed to like each other. They got married young, and then went to work barely making ends meet. I think my parents liked their spirit, or maybe it was the fact that they were the only family we had. Even when they used to babysit me they wouldn't act like real couples acted. They played, sure, which for a kid was freaking spectacular! Outdoor tent parties, s'mores for dinner, and loud music—so much loud music!

I don't think it was the addition of me that made them miserable together. They were miserable anytime they weren't partying like teens, and one can't party forever. I just happened to show up when the *other* pressures of real life were starting to set in. A mortgage, zero health insurance, unsteady work and taxes. Collin and Alice just didn't like each other enough to stick through the thin. I'm actually kind of proud of them for realizing they don't have to stay together just because. I think Collin could make someone really happy.

I've always liked him better anyhow.

I'm waiting for Henry to show up. He's offered to teach me to drive, not that I'll ever get my license—or get a car of my own. I'd still like to know what I'm doing behind the wheel. The snow is starting to pick up, though, so our lesson might have to be put on hold.

I'm shivering by the time I spot the front end of his Maserati. It's a ridiculous-looking vehicle to be pulling down my street, and when he lets it idle at the curb in front of my porch, the sound draws the neighbor from his house just to get a closer look.

"You gettin' in that thing, Lily?" George is on a fixed income and lives alone. He always threatens to set me up with his grandson, but I've done the math and I'm pretty sure his grandson is forty-five.

"I'm drivin' that thing today, George!" I wink at him and give him a thumbs up. He can only seem to stare at me, puzzled. He's also terribly old-fashioned and doesn't quite understand why a woman needs to know how to drive. Alice can't stand him. I feel like I can teach him.

Henry gets out of the car before I make it halfway down the walkway, a medium-sized silver giftbag dangling from his finger now outstretched toward me.

"You already gave me my Christmas present," I say, pinching the golden heart hanging from a chain against my chest.

"I got you another one. Just open it," he says, thrusting it forward and forcing me to catch it at my chest.

I give him a suspicious look and reach my hand in the bag. The stiff bulkiness throws me off, so I spread the bag open wide enough for my eyes to peer inside. Whatever it is, it's bright orange and wound up with an ugly brown belt. It looks like those vests hunters wear.

"I don't get it," I say in a flat voice. Henry laughs and takes the bag from me, pulling the gift out and unraveling the cord around it.

"Life vest. We're going rowing. Well...*I'm* rowing. You're sitting. And you are *not* drowning because it's fucking cold out!"

Tongue stuffed in my cheek, I tentatively take the vest and mutter, "Okay." Henry guides me to the passenger side and I climb in, not bothering to tell either of my soon-to-be-divorced, fake parents that I'm leaving. They knew Henry was coming, and at least one of them paid attention. They'll sort it out.

I buckle up and hold the vest in my lap while Henry slides into the driver's side, closing the door with a satisfying *clunk*. Even the way the door slams shut sounds expensive. The jet-black hood looks like an arrow stretched out before us against the snow-covered road.

"They don't plow much here, so careful when you..."

Henry grins and revs his engine, spinning his wheels into a fishtail as we pull away from my temporary life and race off toward my preferred one. I grip at the ceiling and door handle, my nerves shot up to the same level as his RPM.

"You just got your license. You wanna lose it already?"

He chuckles but slows down at the end of my street.

"I've been dying to do that. Some of the older guys I used to hang out with on the crew team used to let me drive out in the country. I've been spinning my tires and sliding on ice since we met."

"Comforting," I say.

Henry's head tilts with amusement, but he slows way down just the same. He wanted to impress me, not scare the shit out of me. He did both.

It takes Henry about thirty minutes to get us out to a suburban channel deep in the southern suburbs. It's the kind of neighborhood where quaint restaurants line cobblestoned walkways along a forest preserve stream. Since it's freezing, though, the restaurants are all either empty or closed, and nobody is out for a walk.

The sky is a thick gray, the clouds so dense they look as if one could reach up and cut into them. The flakes are falling like dust, not leaving much behind yet but threatening to do more damage as the night comes.

Henry stops along a set of concrete stairs that lead down toward the water, across from a row of historic homes. People live here, in this place that looks like a holiday card. There's literally a warm candle glowing in one of the windows. I laugh at it and Henry catches me, lifting a brow.

"It's pretty here," I say.

"Yeah. Me and the Richmod Prep kids used to take the train all the way down here and do dumb shit in the water in the summer. My first kiss was Katy O'Neil, and it was somewhere behind that big green dumpster in the alleyway between the Italian place and the bakery."

He points down the street but I don't bother to look. I stare at him until it sinks in.

"She was a terrible kisser," he says, trying to make it better.

I shake my head, and he gives up, taking my hand and my life jacket and leading me down the stairs to the river.

"My first kiss was Tyler Olmstead, and it was outside of my English class right before lunch, so his breath was amazing. His lips were soft like butter and I called him my boyfriend for the entire month of March."

Henry doesn't even flinch, and when we get to the shoreline, he turns to me and gestures for me to lift my arms so he can wrap me in my safety jacket. When he clips it snug, I hold out my open palms, and offer a "what the hell?"

"Oh, I'm sorry…was I supposed to be jealous of butter lips? Or good breath? I couldn't tell." He maintains a serious expression for exactly five seconds before sweeping his arm around my back and pulling me flush against his chest and pressing his lips to mine possessively.

"I've never met a Tyler who wasn't a dick," he says against my lips. I can feel his mouth bend into a smile, and I give one back.

There. He was a little jealous. Also, I made Tyler up. My real first kisses weren't even close to butter-lips good, and their names were highly unhip.

Henry kisses me for several minutes, and I almost forgot the whole reason I was wearing a ridiculous vest and standing by a small river. When he steps away, I cling onto his deep red sweater and suck in the taste of him left behind on my bottom lip.

We're both in jeans and sweaters, and I've managed to stuff my coat over the thick fabric on my arms. The safety vest is holding every-thing on, I swear. Henry should be freezing, but he pulls his sweater from over his head, the long-sleeved black tee underneath lifting up a little to show his waist and the plaid band of his boxers that peek out of the top of his deep-blue jeans. Nicki is always calling Henry "Preppy" like it's a bad thing, but I don't know—if she saw the little things I did, I think she may form a different opinion.

"Here. You climb in first," he says, taking my hand and holding my elbow, too, steadying me while I step from the wooden sideboard along the bank of the water and into the thin rowboat. It wobbles under my weight, and I crouch down on instinct, desperate to steady it.

"You're okay. I got you," he says. I flash my eyes up to him, comforted by the complete lack of worry.

Once the boat stops rocking, he lets go of my hand and climbs in on the opposite side, tossing his sweater to the space between his knees and pushing us out into the middle of the water.

"How far are we going?" I ask, already mesmerized by the move-ment of his arms. He's barely even gripped the oars, and already he looks like a god.

"I don't know. 'Til you get sick of it, I guess," he shrugs, then pushes back and pulls the oars to his chest, gliding us across the snow-frosted water.

I manage to tear my eyes away from him for a few minutes as we drift away from the area with homes and businesses, and far off from the noise of the highway or nearby roads. I'm so bundled, I can't feel the cold anywhere but the place where my face isn't wrapped in my hood. My nose feels like it must be a bright shade of red. Henry, in the meantime, is beginning to sweat.

"What's the name of the person who gets to shout out to the rowers? You do that sometimes…what are they called?"

"You want to be my cock?" His eyes lower as he slows his rowing just a little and pauses, oars up and arms rested at his knees.

My eyes flair and my brow shoots up to the fur of my hood.

"I'm sorry…your…your what?" Now I'm starting to sweat, and I'm also trying not to glance down at his zipper. Jesus!

Henry roars with laughter, breaking through the silent paradise we're rowing through.

"It's called a coxswain, but sometimes it comes out like that. I just wanted to embarrass you."

"Yeah, well—good job. Mission accomplished. Oh my God." I lift my mitten-covered hands up to my face and cover every inch.

Henry's laughter continues through several more strokes, until his rhythm settles in. I pull my hands away from my face one at a time, and I do glance to his waist—his zipper—a few times when he isn't looking. There are parts of him I've wanted to explore, but I always cut our make-out sessions short. He lets me, but I can tell he wouldn't stop if I didn't.

We're starting to approach a thick bridge made of piled stone with a pair of tunnels running underneath. It's dark inside, and we've gone plenty far. Henry never seems to get tired, but he's slowing. I can tell he's feeling the elements.

"We can head back," I say, sensing our speed slow as his arms relax.

"Okay. We'll switch ends," he says, locking his oars in place and moving toward me slowly. I begin to shift but he puts his hand on my knee, sitting on one of his few inches in front of me. "Wait there. Before we head back...I...I have something I need to talk to you about."

It feels like my actual heart has lodged in my throat. I try to swallow it down not once, but twice, and Henry can see my panic.

"It's nothing bad," he says, taking my hand in one of his and rubbing his other thumb along my jean-covered knee.

"Okay," I say, still on edge.

His head falls forward, taking his hair with it, and he lets go of his hold on my knee to pinch at his brow and mumble to himself. I can't make out the words, but it's basically "how can I say this."

"Lily, I'm going to Germany for my junior year."

That's how you say it. You say it just like that—a simple sentence, prefaced with my name to make sure I'm paying attention, and then you drive the staple right through the center of my chest.

"You're…wow." My hand moves to the back of my neck and I instantly try to imagine my junior year at Satis without him.

"I know, it's…it's not ideal, but it's also a huge opportunity. I'll get to study process engineering."

"Process engineering," I repeat. This is a career goal I've never heard Henry mention. Of course, he's also never mentioned any goals that aren't of his own making.

"Did Elena set this up?"

His weight shifts away from me and his expression morphs into something rather offended.

"She got me the interview. That's where I went the weekend of your birthday. It's a really special honor, Lily. I wanted this." He's saying the words, but it's also not the same voice I've been listening to night after night for the last three months. He's different now—he's Elena's Henry.

I pull in my bottom lip, mostly to keep myself from sounding hurt or suspicious. I'm ruining this fairytale moment. Henry's ruined it already.

"I'm excited for you," I say, not a single hint of excitement in my tone.

"Sounds like it," he says, scooting forward and looking down as he takes my hand. "Let's just head back."

He guides me to the opposite side of the boat and begins rowing before I get situated in my seat. The motion makes me lose my balance a little, but my foot gets caught in the long strap of my safety jacket, which jerks my body to the left just as my balance is starting to go. I'm in the water before I can scream.

"He…Hen…" My throat has closed, and my stomach is seizing from the ice-cold rush pushing me away from the boat. My feet are kicking in search of a bottom, and every now and then I feel something hard against my leg—boulders, maybe.

"Hen!" I can't get his whole name out, so I just begin making sounds.

"Lily, I've got you!"

My hood has grown heavy and cold with water, and it covers half of my face as I flail my arms, trying to push against the current. It isn't a rapid, but it's steady enough to make it impossible for me to swim, especially wrapped in layers and layers of freezing clothes.

"Grab it!" I can feel the oar against my elbow, but I can't seem to make my limbs work. My breath is growing thinner and thinner, and my adrenaline is so high I feel slightly blinded by it.

I somehow manage to grab onto the paddle under my arm, hooking my elbow around it and finally hugging it tightly as Henry pulls me toward him. I nearly pull him in with me, but he manages to work me back into the boat, and begins feverishly removing wet layers from my body. He pushes my coat and sweater from my body, up over my head, and then covers me in his sweater in an instant. I'm convulsing, long past shivering, and we're maybe a mile away from his car.

He begins to row as quickly as he can while I lay in a crumbled, shivering ball between his feet. I hear small phrases escape his lips, all amid frightened breaths and grunts.

"Hang on, Lily. I'm so sorry, Lily. It's going to be okay. It's okay. We're almost there."

I think of warm things, like Henry's arms and my bed at Satis House, and I slow my breathing as best I can through chattering lips. I force the cold air in, and let it out slowly, the steam escaping my nose like a dragon. My fingers look blue. My lips *feel* blue.

Thoughts rush out of order, skipping from how much pain I'm in to the awful fact that I'm going to have to miss Henry for an entire year. We've barely docked at the bank when he's lifting me under my arms. The boat's rocking sparks a nervous yelp from my gut, but Henry wraps both of his arms around my soaking body and holds me tight until, somehow, he and I are both on solid land.

He scoops me up in his arms and carries me to his car, setting me down long enough to get the back door open, and he puts me inside then shuts the door, rushing to the driver's side so he can turn the engine on and get the heat cooking. He leaves the front seats and opens the back door again, sliding in where my head is, lifting it to his lap and then shutting his door. My body won't stop wiggling, every muscle spasming with the constant signals of *danger* and *cold*.

"I got you, Lily. I'm so sorry," he says, his hands rubbing my arms, chest, cheeks, and legs. He works to warm me inch by inch, and it takes nearly an hour for the uncontrollable shaking to stop.

My cheeks finally begin to feel warm from the heat blasting from the vents, so I reach forward and close the one closest to my face.

"That's a good sign," he says, his voice cracking with regret.

I stare at the back of the driver's seat and replay my fall again. I've done this for an hour straight. And it's always the cold that hurts the least. It's the words I remember—it's Henry telling me he's leaving. And then it's the blame I instantly assign.

"Worst driving lesson ever," I say.

Henry's body moves with his laugh. It's hesitant, but also grateful. I look at him sideways, from my spot on his thigh and in his arms, and I lift the right side of my mouth.

Truce.

Henry is going to Germany. I'm going to become a concert pianist. And Elena will get her way—for now.

CHAPTER 17

S ome of the guys on the crew team are hard to look at in their uniforms. It's a tight singlet, all black with maroon and navy stripes down the sides. It's an unforgiving material that leaves very little to the imagination, hugging every muscle and curve—*and every lack thereof.*

Henry is hard *not* to look at. Other than the two seniors on the team, he's the only one who was somehow born to fill out what is otherwise a ridiculous-looking piece of sporting wear. He may as well be the guy the company uses to model these things.

"Those girls are staring at you."

He glances out to the grass hill where a few groups of freshmen girls have spread out blankets to watch today's race.

"That was you last year, you know."

"Ha! Hardly," I laugh.

"Yeah, you were more brooding and uninterested in me." He loops his fingers with mine and shakes our hands between our bodies.

"I was never uninterested," I confess.

His mouth quirks. Guilty.

"Yeah?"

I don't have to respond. I just lean forward and press my lips to his.

The wind is brutal, so I'm borrowing his school jacket. It was a uniform day since it's the opening day of the spring season. Students are encouraged to dress traditionally for the event, and since my one pair of khaki pants are wrinkled and dirty, and I suck at laundry and ironing, I had no choice but to wear the skirt.

Henry likes it. He likes it because he's a boy, and frankly, even the most prudish girl on this campus gets a little harlot-stamp in these things. Some of the girls roll the tops up to make theirs shorter. I feel like an inch above my knee is just fine. I'm wearing thick winter tights underneath and my snow shoes. Henry bought them for me.

Ah, spring in Chicago.

"Oh, I almost forgot!" I reach into his coat and pull out the folded-up Cubs hat and place it on my wild, wind-blown hair.

"The lucky hat," he says with a grin, tugging on the bill a little.

"I wore this for the one race I went to last year, and you won," I say, proudly.

"We won every race," Henry offers right back.

My smile relaxes.

"Oh. Well, good thing I wore this for that one then. Covers you for a *whole* season."

He scrunches his face and chuckles at me, then reaches up to tap my nose with his finger.

"You're adorable. I gotta go."

He walks away backward, his eyes on me almost like he's proud to call me his. Maybe he is. And maybe one day I won't doubt everything so much, and I'll start feeling like those rich girls who hike up their skirts.

I walk up toward the cabana, to Anya and Ava. Nicki opted to sit the races out. "Skinny boats," she said, "are fucking stupid."

Anya's been wearing her earbuds everywhere she goes for the last week straight. She's trying out for the spring musical, *South Pacific*. Nobody's voice compares to her, but she's up against a few seniors who, well…hike up their skirts and have parents who write epically large checks. She's going to need to blow them away with her audition.

I tap on her shoulder, and she jumps a little then pulls one bud from her ear.

"Really lost in the music that time, huh?"

She makes a wry face.

"At this point, I'm having a hard time discerning the real world to this stuff playing in my ears."

"It will be worth it," I say, not really sure that it will. It's the only response to give though.

Anya pulls the other bud from her ear and tucks them both in the pocket of her cardigan sweater. The teams begin to make their way down the channel, so Anya, Ava, and I move toward the front of the deck that overlooks the route. Elena arrived while I was talking with Henry. I saw her; I saw her see us. She's with some couple I don't recognize, probably someone important whose opinion she's harvesting. It's not the couple that consumes me, though—it's the girl about my age who's standing with them, completely wrapped up in whatever Elena is saying.

It shouldn't matter, but somehow—in my gut—I know it does.

Our boys begin to pass, so the three of us all remove our hats and begin to wave them for good luck. Caleb winks at me from his spot behind Henry, which is funny until Ava notices it.

"He flirts with you a lot," she says.

"It's harmless. Just him being funny," I shake her off. I won't betray Caleb's trust, but I wish he would come out to our friends—to Henry. It's become something that I struggle with between us. I don't like having a secret from Henry, but this is Caleb's to tell or not tell, and only when he's ready.

I feel Ava's stare burn hot on my cheek from one side, but when I shift my eyes just a little, I notice Elena's focus now on me to the right. I'm being squeezed. Choked. I blow a kiss to Henry to center myself, and he breaks his game face briefly, just long enough to glance my way and smile on my side. Goddamn, that dimple. It's magical.

My body shivers at the thought of the water, remembering how ice cold it really is. It's not much warmer than it was when I fell in. We haven't talked about Germany since that night. It's a subject that lingers just off the page, though. It's coming. He leaves at the end of May. I looked the program up online.

"Warning, at three o'clock," Anya whispers from the other side of

Ava. Her words trigger both Ava and me to look, and I have the unfortunate luck of making eye contact with Elena as she gets closer. She's bringing her guests, including the girl wearing a rival school's plain skirt, appropriately rolled up to show off her over-the-knee socks and goosebump-marked thighs. I reach for my waist, shamefully, and while I don't roll the band up one, I slide it up my ribs as high as it will go, gaining a few more inches of leg on the bottom.

Pathetic.

"Lily. I'm glad you're here." Elena's greeting buries so many hidden meanings, most notably the fact that she's not glad to see me, ever, and the hint of surprise that I'm here is totally false. She knew I would be here. In fact, I'm convinced she knows where I am at all times—always. I'm sure she hates how much I'm with Henry.

"Elena," I say, putting on the cursory smile that I've perfected. It's the Satis House smile, or at least, that's what Nicki and I call it. It's how most of the parents interact with each other when they secretly hate one another. That smile gets passed on to their children, and they do the same around campus, making passive aggressive little digs at one another but always with the same, tight-mouthed smile. I'm only missing the sunglasses that hide the truth in my eyes. Elena's good enough to mask hers without wearing glasses. Either that, or she doesn't care that the person she looks at thinks she's a bitch. She thinks it right back.

"I haven't seen you hardly at all this year. You haven't been over with Alice to practice." Her gaze is suspicious, but manipulative. It's like she's always four chess moves ahead of me.

"The Satis House practice rooms are just so nice. It makes it easy for me to focus."

"Yes, and then you don't have to come home on the weekends. I'm sure *that's* been nice." The smirk of a snake appears. "I'm sorry your aunt and uncle are splitting up."

"Alice," I correct. "She's just my…Alice."

Her eyes dim.

"Like you're just Elena. The same."

Her face has no reaction at all this time. Quiet seeps between us, and my friends excuse themselves. I know they have nowhere to go, but they just want to be far away from this. It's hard to watch a dance with the devil. Nicki wouldn't leave. She would try to cut in.

"Have you met Stella, Lily?" Her segue is purposeful, and Stella is beautiful. Long, straight strawberry-blonde hair and green eyes set against the most perfect porcelain skin. She's practically pulled straight from the pages of a private-school brochure, the kind that lures girls like me into the fantasy that we might just look like that if we go to one.

"No, I haven't." I reach forward confidently to shake Stella's hand, and the moment our palms meet, Elena shares the rest.

Checkmate.

"Her family is the one who bought that house next door. You remember that night Henry came home late. Oh, you know him, sneaking out to spend time with pretty girls."

My hand twitches and Stella's goes slightly limp. I know why I'm reacting this way—because this is the pretty girl Elena insisted Henry meet, the ideal prom date, a *real* society girl. And her father is the one she thought Henry could learn from. Stella's reaction makes me wonder what twisted seeds Elena has planted about me.

"I've been giving Stella lessons at the house. Since you weren't using the room anymore, I thought…"

"Oh, I'm sure I'm nowhere as good as you. Henry said you're good enough to play in a concert hall." Stella's eyes dart nervously between Elena and me, and I can tell she's worried that I'm offended by the attack on my talent. She has no idea that Elena is after my heart.

"I'm sure you play beautifully," I say, somehow making my outsides mask the chaos happening in my chest.

"Stella attends Rosenwood. Well…at least she does until May." Elena's lips tighten, the age lines accented by her lipstick deepening with her pleasure.

"Oh, you're going to a new school next year?" I play along, shifting my weight and holding my hands together in front of my body to force myself to stay calm.

"Just for the year. I got into this great program in Germany. I'm a little nervous about being away from home, but it's such a rare opportunity. I had to."

Rare. So very rare.

"Of course, she'll have Henry around, so that should help." Elena says these words for me, but she glances to Stella's parents as if she's saying it to set *them* at ease.

Ease was never her intent. Not for any of it. It never is. Elena thrives off others' mayhem.

"Of course," I repeat, a million shocks firing away at once while I search for an out. I'm drowning in the details—the fact that Henry hasn't mentioned this girl once, let alone the fact that she's going to Germany. He's talked about me to her, though—she knows *my* name. She knows how well I play the freaking piano! She's a complete secret to me, and I am an open book to her, which means that the sick feeling in my gut is exactly what Elena wants to be there.

I simmer in my own anger, my eyes scanning the crowd for an excuse, for a reason to leave this space. I need my friends, but they don't seem to be anywhere.

Then I spot my savior, and I feed her to the wolf. I can't stop myself. Desperation pushes me, but it's the desire to make Elena hurt that makes me act.

"Elena…have you heard the news?"

Her chin dips and her jaw hardens. I step in close enough to make sure I can meet her stare, and I think of every shitty thing that's happened in my life and convince myself that I deserve this one sweet victory.

"Ms. Manning is expecting another child. It was a surprise, of course. She's far enough along now though, and they're so excited."

I see the pain flash over her eyes, but the demon that lives in her soul takes over quickly, the black centers of her eyes spreading until she's practically consuming me with her stare. It takes her a full breath to work her mouth into its well-practiced shape, the harsh line of deep red a sharp warning that I will suffer.

"Seems like a terrible risk." I swear her tongue slithers around that last word.

"Hmmm. Worth the risk for her, I guess."

She closes the distance between us, ensuring privacy, and Stella and her parents have given us space. I wonder if these types of conversations are common in their circle, or specific just to Elena Alderman.

"Are you really that taken with him?" Her eyes shift from my right to my left, and then fall into pity. "Aw, you are. You weren't careful with your heart, were you, Lily? Poor girl. You're playing a game you aren't bred to win."

"Pity." She tacks on that last part just to be cruel. I sold out Ms. Manning's trust and barely grazed her ego.

I'm dizzy from falling so low, dizzy from guilt and shame. I let her make me just as rotten as she is. Here I thought Alice was the minion and I was just learning to play the piano.

When I couldn't find Ava or Anya, I left to walk along the shore behind the chairs of nearby residents who just like to come out to watch. I didn't want to be near anyone who had anything to do with Satis House or Elena's circle, so I went to the starting line. I got there just in time to watch Henry's first push, to watch the way his body switches between man and machine.

I waited here, hundreds of yards away from everyone, until Henry grew frustrated that he couldn't find me. I answered his first text and told him I'd messed up. Then he called and asked where I was. I didn't expect him to get here so fast, and I'm equal parts devastated and relieved to see his form getting closer and closer along the shore. He's pulled on his sweatpants, and his Satis House hoodie looks perfectly huggable with him inside. When he finally reaches the park bench I've glued myself to—figuratively—I decide to indulge in his warmth before I confess my sins then grill him on his own.

"I didn't peg you for one of those drama girls who got into fights with her friends. What's going on?" He knows it isn't something trite like that, and when I meet his gaze, I'm unable to hide just how messed up Elena left me. I try to bury my face in his chest, but he holds me away and forces me to look him in the eyes.

"I told Elena about the baby. I betrayed Ms. Manning." I tear up, mostly from a release of stress.

Henry chuckles and brings my body into his, finally, wrapping his arms around me and rocking me like an infant.

"She won't be mad, and if it comes up, I'll say I was the one who slipped up. She'll understand. It happens; you get talking and things just come out."

He's being so comforting, but I shake with a mixture of laughter and whimper because he's giving me way too much credit.

"I told her because I knew it would make her feel bad. I did it to be mean, Henry," I peel back from his chest, running the butt of my palm under my eyes.

His brow pulls in.

"Yeah, see? I was mean. I did something to be mean, and I broke the trust of my favorite person on this whole damn campus...besides you." I laugh at my stupid joke, but Henry doesn't.

His fingertips lift my chin when I try to duck, and his eyes lock onto mine.

"You are not mean, Lily. You know how I know?"

I don't speak. I'm not sure I want to know. It won't be true. I'm mean. I am so mean. And Henry is going to Germany...with porcelain girl.

"You aren't mean because if you were, you'd never feel bad about it," he says, and the strangest expression paints his face. He's so resolute about it, and I think maybe it's because guilt is not something Henry Alderman understands very well. He's felt it before. He's felt it for me. He did when I fell into the water. Does it have to be something extreme? Physical? Would he feel remorse if he knew I would be jealous? Or would he like it, just like he's been taught to.

"Why didn't you tell me about Stella?" I had to ask, even though every fiber inside me was working to push this question back inside. I wanted to bury it because it lets Elena win. But really, she's right—I never stood a chance at her game.

Henry's reaction is blank, and I wouldn't anticipate the pain that was surely coming if it weren't for the slight jolt in his muscles. His bicep twitched as I asked. His cheek lifted just a hair when one eye squinted. If I had blinked, I would have missed it, but I did not—it was there. I saw it...*felt* it.

His chin lifts and his gaze moves to the space behind me, to the city's skyline and the thick park trees. His forehead is wrinkled with the glare from the sun, and his mouth pulls in on one corner the slightest bit.

Maybe he's also guilty when he's caught.

"I hardly know her..."

"You're going to Germany together," I butt in.

Henry lets out a laugh then looks down at me. My grip loosens on his sweatshirt.

"We're both going to Germany. Not together." His head falls to the side just a little.

"But you will be...together? I mean, it's the same program. It's not a coincidence, right?" I ask.

Henry sighs and steps away, enough that I have to let go.

"No, Lily. It's not a coincidence. Is that what you want to hear?" His tone is ugly, and I wince at it, which makes him bow his head and pinch his brow.

"Henry, she knew things about me."

"Yeah, because guess what? I talk about you." His answer is sharp.

"You never talk about her. Is that because she isn't important? Or is it because..."

"Because I'm hiding a secret affair with another girl from another school who I rush off to Germany with because you, Lily...you're just not enough for me." His face deadpans, and I know he's being sarcastic to try to jar me out of envy, but there's this looming sense I can't shake. I won't be able to if I don't just ask.

"Have you ever kissed her?"

He blinks a single time. I laugh out to the side, caught somewhere between surprised and expected.

"We weren't a thing then," he explains.

I nod. He's right; we weren't.

"You guys just break into her parents' liquor that night? Hide in the basement playing spin the bottle?" I'm only partly joking, but the way my accusation causes his eyes to flicker squeezes my breath away.

"Did you...do more than kiss, Henry?"

My skin starts to actually crawl. I flash through the mental portrait

226

I've stowed away of Stella, her perfect hair and tiny figure and long legs. I think of the things I've done with Henry, his confident touch and the way his hands know exactly where to be on me, to make me feel.

"Did you..."

"Don't ask questions you don't want to know the answers to, Lily."

I swallow. Hard. I don't have to ask because that right there was enough of an answer.

"Was she your first?"

His head falls more to the side. Finally, there's the guilt in his eyes. Of course it's there—this is extreme.

I fall back into the bench, sitting with my fists on my knees and disbelief swirling around my head. My God, Elena is the master of mind games.

"You want me not to go?"

I shake my head after a full second, not sure he really said that or I dreamt it. I would be lying if I said I didn't have that exact fantasy once or twice since I found out he was going to be gone. Henry shifts his feet and moves his hands into the front of his hoodie.

"I won't go. Will that make this better for you?" I'm looking at him when I hear the words this time. They're real.

I nod yes, but I speak, "No."

"That's a confusing response."

I flash a wry smile, but he's not in the mood for my jokes.

"No, of course you need to go. I just feel like this is all so convenient, and Elena really sold it to me." My shoulders slump, and Henry takes another step forward, kicking his foot into mine. I glance down at it and leave my focus there, off his perfect lips and tempting eyes. I can think better when I'm looking at the dirt.

"If it isn't Stella, it's going to be someone else, Lily. I told you that Elena likes to pair me off. It's like a social experiment for her. I mean, you have to know that Alice didn't get that job because she was this amazing personal assistant."

My face wrinkles at what he's suggesting, but I keep my eyes down.

"Lily...Elena saw that you entertained me, and so she took Alice on as a package deal. She hooked you with the piano but it was all about her letting us interact. She thought of you as practice, as someone whose heart I could break a thousand times! Someone I could learn to be both kind and cold to, just like she is with everyone else."

"That's horrible," I utter, eyes fluttering down.

"Yes," he answers. "But it's how Elena is. Always playing match-maker and instilling some sort of twisted lesson. She didn't bargain on how impossible it would be to not let you in, though."

My heart pauses as I soak his words in, my gaze diving deep into his, swimming in the honesty soaked into every bit of what he said. It scares me to like him so much.

"I'm not like Stella. I don't come from some big family with important last names. My last name is from dead people." My eyes flare with those last words, and I realize how cold and honest what I just said was. Henry moves to sit next to me, but not close enough to touch.

"Maybe that's why she wanted you around. You're different, and maybe she thought different would be good for me, so I would never be caught off guard." He shrugs, and I instantly feel like a human supplement. My stomach is sick.

"Like an experiment," I say.

"Don't," Henry says, finally reaching for my hand. I grab on loosely, and he squeezes me to encourage me to grip harder. I think about shaking Stella's hand, about how her grasp changed when Elena brought up their late night of getting in trouble. She was remembering the innocence they lost.

"Don't sleep with her again," I say, realizing my question sounds like a lunatic, jealous girlfriend. I own it, though, because at this moment, that's what I am.

Henry's lips twist to hold in a laugh, and I scoot into him, giving him a slight shove.

"I'm dead serious. You better keep a journal over there, and I want you to sign a pledge every single day that you did not sleep with her."

Henry laughs. I don't.

"Oh, you're...you're serious."

I lift my shoulder. I'm not, entirely, but if he's really willing, then yes, I want a journal—a big, fat, chaste, good-behavior journal.

CHAPTER 18

THE FIRST WEEK OF SUMMER BEFORE JUNIOR YEAR

J ust once, I want to be excited about summer again, like I was when I was a little kid. I never wanted this summer to come, but it did. It's arrived.

The flight to Frankfurt is a little more than eight hours. Henry leaves for the airport in three. Stella is already there. I'm not sure if Henry asked for a separate flight or if the heavens graced me, but I'm glad they're not traveling together. Jealousy is strange that way. It throws rationale out the window. I trust Henry more than I trust my betraying imagination.

I'm also not a naïve dreamer. Losing my parents at the critical age of thirteen gave me a stark perspective on reality. I know that Henry and I might not be the same couple we are now when he gets back. I know I'll change—*he'll change*. But it doesn't mean I don't hope we change in a way that still fits together…somehow.

We fit together now.

I didn't miss a single crew race this season. I even traveled to the ones way down south, and up north to Wisconsin. I refused to go with

Elena, so I made friends with other parents, including Caleb's. He's out to his parents, and he told them how he confided in me. They spent the road trip to Wisconsin picking my brain on whether or not I thought others would accept Caleb for who he is. It was hard for me to answer.

"No one is really who they are at Satis House," I said. "They're all pretending."

I was wrong about that, though. Not everyone pretends. Henry is real most of the time, when Elena isn't in his head. And Nicki is the most real person I've ever met. She is the physical definition of *unabashed*.

I hope I'm a little real, too.

"If I don't head back soon, Elena will send someone here to get me," Henry says, my head resting on his chest and our feet hanging off the end of my twin bed. Our fingers twine together. We've been playing this silent game for several minutes—the rules that we have to squeeze hands with each other at exactly the same time, but we can't speak to let each other know when. We're perfectly in sync, and we never seem to mess up.

"I know. Just a little longer?" I said that thirty minutes ago and he stayed.

"Okay," he says, rolling to his side and pulling me in close. We're facing each other now.

Collin is at work. He probably wouldn't like that Henry is in my bedroom, but we've never really crossed that strange parenting bridge over rules like boys in rooms and such. I'm probably taking advantage of that fact, but Henry's leaving soon, and I want time with him in a place that doesn't feel like we're being watched and judged.

"I like the way your bed smells," he says, nuzzling his nose against mine. I turn my head and breathe in my pillow and sheets.

"I'm pretty sure that's just soap," I say.

"I like it just the same," he says.

Henry draws in a deep breath and moves his chin above my head, a soft moan vibrating his throat. I make the same sound. We're both sad that our time is dwindling.

"Are you sure Collin can take you to the airport?" he asks.

"He promised. He's getting off in one hour," I say.

I refuse to ride with Elena, but I also won't miss seeing Henry off.

My jaw hurts from spending a straight hour kissing him, but even so, I keep moving to taste him one last time, my mouth touching his chin, his neck, his chest. There are things I wanted with Henry—things I wanted him to be my first for. I'm not ready now, though. I know I'm not.

"I wanted to make this last time special, but…" I finally eke out a confession.

"Shh," Henry says, kissing the top of my head. "It is special," he adds.

I close my eyes tight and sigh against him. I still want to feel him. Even if it isn't *all* the way.

"Do you think…we could maybe…" I drag my hand down his chest, pausing at the place where his jeans button. My hand is buzzing with nerves, and not because I don't want to feel him but because I'm too embarrassed to try.

"Lily," he leans back just enough to look at me with one slightly lifted brow.

"I just want to…before you go…" I scrunch my face, mortified and uncomfortable. Henry lets out a quiet laugh, then moves his hand until it covers mine and holds me still.

"Lily, I'm so happy just lying here and holding you," he says.

I bite at my lip because God, that's sweet. But it's also not why I'm being so forward, though probably the most awkward forward there has ever been.

"I'm…not." I suck in my lips and watch for my words to sink in. Henry's eyes haze slowly and his head turns ever so slightly in this seductive suspicion. Slowly, his hand pushes mine along his pants, half inches at a time, until I feel how hard and warm his body is down there. I suck in a sharp breath when I feel him flex under my touch, and his hand puts more pressure on mine, pushing me into him and encouraging my fingers to curl around his form.

My chin lowers against his chest so I can see where my hand meets him. His hand loosens its grip, and his fingers tickle along my knuckles until they move from his jeans to mine, stopping along my inner thigh, inches away from a place where I feel wet.

Emboldened, and wanting Henry to do the same, I run my hand up and down the bulge in his jeans a few times before stopping at the button above his zipper. I tug it loose before my nerve leaves and Henry's stomach sinks in fast with surprise. His hand grips at my leg harder, moving just a little closer, but not close enough.

I take his zipper down slowly, as if making too much noise or rushing too fast will ruin this sensitive and quiet balance in my room. I don't want anything to ruin this, and I don't want to hurry, yet I'm in a rush all the same.

My hand works to open the flap in his jeans, and I let my hand feel his size over his boxers. His body is much hotter through the thin layer of cotton, and his hips push upward into my touch as another moan leaves his lips.

I rock my own hips, giving him permission, and his hand works quickly, pressing up between my legs with a firm hold that eases the pressure that was nearly boiling inside me. My lips part and I pant, and as I do, Henry rocks his hips into my hand again.

No longer ashamed of wanting this, I move my hand to the band of Henry's boxers and dip inside until I'm touching him bare. My hand wraps around him completely, and I can feel his pulse under my touch.

"Oh God," he groans, sliding his hands up to the top of my jeans.

I reach down with my opposite hand and help to unbutton the top and slide my zipper down. Henry's touch is much faster than mine, his fingers diving into my soft, pink panties and finding the aching spot between my legs. I squeeze him with my thighs and begin to move with his touch, his fingers sliding up and down while my hand does the same to him.

We explore each other with closed eyes and held breath for several minutes, and when I can't handle not tasting him anymore, I shift and glance up to find his hungry eyes waiting for my kiss to hit his lips. My mouth reaches for his, and he grinds against me, touching me roughly, just how I need it. Henry's teeth drag across my bottom lip, and the feel of it makes me whimper.

And then he pushes one finger inside. The stretch is surprisingly easy, and he touches me deeper than I thought he'd be able to, his hand moving slowly at first, but picking up speed as something between my legs begins to build.

I feel Henry grow thicker under my touch, so I begin to squeeze and run my hand up and down him faster. His breath matches my movement, and mine copies his. Our lips gasp between kisses, and when the feeling inside my body becomes too much to hold onto, I let out a very loud "ahh" and shivers run through my body. Henry's hips work against my hand, and I close my legs around his touch on me, squeezing him to me and not wanting to let him go. His release comes a breath later.

My body feels worn, but every nerve ending is teeming with satisfaction. Henry's mouth curls into a crooked smile as his hand leaves my body and drags up to the center of his chest.

"Well...shit." He laughs once, almost surprised. "I did not expect any of that."

He cracks one eye open, and I blush now that he's looking at me—after...*that*. He grins, and his eyes laugh at my reaction.

"Lily Ames, that was amazing."

I bunch my lips, not having anything to compare it too, but also still pulsing below.

"Yeah?" I ask.

He chuckles and pulls me into his embrace, rolling me so I'm lying on top of him, our open pants pressed together by two warm bodies, still throbbing and hot. Henry lifts his hips, and I can't help but do the same, still wanting more pressure.

"You want more?" his brow lifts, and I nod and close my eyes, letting him slide his hands down my hips to my ass. He spends the next fifteen minutes pulling me into him and kissing me through what becomes my second and third orgasms...ever.

Henry left about thirty minutes before Collin got home. I cleaned my room, even going so far as to dust, as if somehow that would erase any clues Collin might have about Henry being here and what went down.

I can't make eye contact with him, and it's because he's my parent figure, though I can't seem to call him *dad* yet. I think maybe he would like me to, though. Or uncle, maybe. I might try that first, but not until this summer ends. Not until I can look him in the eyes either.

Traffic is in our favor, and we get to O'Hare shortly after Henry and Elena have arrived. I know I'll have to see her now, so I prepare myself for all of the snarky, hateful things she's no doubt going to say to me. Our last exchange was at Henry's first race. I still don't think Ms. Manning has fully forgiven me for telling her secret. I confessed to her immediately, seeking her out to tell her what I had done, even though Henry offered to say it was him.

She understood because she understands Elena, but I still think she was hurt.

"I'm going to have to circle, I think. Unless you want me to park and come in with you?" Collin almost seems like he wants to. I'm not sure I want my almost-uncle-not-quite-dad watching my mushy goodbye though.

"Maybe just hang out in the cellphone lot." My voice is definitively sad now. This is really happening.

Collin stretches his arm behind my seat, then squeezes my neck in sympathy.

"All right then," he says, slowing to the curb. He bought the car when Alice left. He said he wanted a way to get to me if I needed him. It barely runs, but it's gotten me this far, and so has Collin.

I get out quickly, maybe so I don't change my mind. I toyed with the fantasy that if I didn't show up, he wouldn't leave. That would be selfish, though, and I've decided I'm not a minion. I put others first— maybe more than I should sometimes.

My hands are fists at my sides, and I keep slapping them at my thighs with every step I take, like I'm physically trying to ground myself. I think maybe I'm trying to keep from fainting.

Even in the crowd of travelers all wheeling in various directions, I find him. He's changed. He's wearing a fitted, gray suit. His hands are in his pockets as he pivots and his head turns from side to side; he lifts up on his toes, looking out toward the other set of doors.

He's searching for me.

Elena spots me first, but promptly busies herself by pretending to read something important on her phone. She's dressed to match him. Long gray slacks that swing across the marble floor and a slim jacket that flairs at her waist, longer in the back. She's wearing her black-rimmed glasses today. She does this when she wants to look especially powerful.

Henry makes a final turn, looking behind him to where I am, finally. A sad smile mixes with the relief on his face, and he takes long strides to get to me in a hurry. His hands cup my face at first contact, and he kisses me as if we're saying *hello* instead of *goodbye*.

"Missed you," he hums against my lips.

"Mmmm," I say.

I force a smile on my mouth for his benefit, but he sees through the thin veil. He runs the pad of his thumb over my bottom lip and taps there in the center a few times.

"I know this is really sucky," he says.

"Super sucky," I add.

He laughs silently as his eyes sweep closed. He breathes out and opens them back on me.

"You can't go past security." He sighs hard enough that his shoulders rise and fall sharply.

"I know," I say.

We both wish I could. We both wish for a lot of things. Mostly, I wish for the next ten months to fly by. I also wish for Elena to get abducted by aliens. And then I wish terrible acne on Stella. Not all of my wishes are of good character. I wish them just the same.

"I want to show you something," he says, that goofy smirk tainting his bluff. He's up to something, and he is always bad at hiding it when he is.

He rushes back to where his bags are sitting, stacked at the seats next to Elena. I start to walk over to him, but he hurries back, probably knowing I'd rather not have her ears on our conversation.

Henry hands me a leather-bound book with a ribbon cutting

through the middle. I open to that page, but it's blank, so I sift through the pages backward until I get to the very beginning and recognize the sharp lines of his cursive handwriting.

HENRY'S NOTEBOOK ABOUT NOT TALKING TO ANY OTHER GIRL BESIDES LILY, UNLESS SHE'S A TEACHER, OR IF I'M BEING SUPER RUDE LIKE IGNORING A QUESTION FOR DIRECTIONS. I CAN ALSO SAY THANK YOU WHEN A GIRL BRINGS ME A BEER. OR NO BEER? CUZ IT'S GERMANY, SO IF NO BEER THEN

I giggle and close the cover on his sweet book, handing it back to him but holding on while he brings it to his chest.

"Beer, but only if your drunk lips won't accidentally fall into someone else's."

He spreads his fingers out over the book as I let go, and closes his eyes.

"I solemnly swear. No drunk lips on anyone's but yours," he says, leaning forward just enough to hold my bottom lip between both of his.

Elena clears her throat loudly, and Henry pulls away, glancing over his shoulder to where she stands and literally taps on the face of her watch.

"Yeah," he sighs, turning back to face me.

I stare into his eyes and try not to cry. This is so much harder than I thought it would be. My heart is slapping at my insides. Henry leans into me, bending his head down until our foreheads touch. My eyes close.

"I'll call you as soon as I land. And I'll send letters. Maybe I'll teach you German. Oh! And make sure someone records your showcase for me when school starts up. And..and...if you do go into Satis to practice, maybe play something for me. We can figure out the times and stuff..."

"Henry!" Elena's patience is thin. I hate her so much.

"I'll probably do nothing but play the piano until you get back," I say, whimpering out a sad laugh.

Henry rests his right hand along my cheek and strokes my skin lightly with his thumb.

"Nah. You won't," he says. I flit my eyes up to meet his gaze, a serious note to his expression. His mouth pulls in tight, almost as if he's resolved to this. I wish I could get there. "You'll move on. At least a little. You'll have fun with Nicki and the girls. And maybe you guys sneak out at the bonfire in my honor. Celebrate your birthday, too. Celebrate big! Seventeen. You are going to wreck that number. It won't know how to be anything but you."

I shake a little with a sob, but run my arm over my face and turn it into laughter as best I can.

"Seventeen, huh?"

"Yeah," he says, pulling me into his arms for one final squeeze. I grip fistfuls of his jacket, no doubt wrinkling it in my grasp. If I could hold on tighter, I would. Henry's arms wrap around my entire body, then his hand moves to the back of my head and he holds me against his chest, dipping his chin just enough to kiss the top of my head.

"See you soon," he says, letting go all at once and walking away.

I don't chase after him. I want to, but I let him go. He turns back to look at me, and his eyes don't leave me while he gathers up his carry-on bags and stands straight while Elena fixes his tie and flattens the spots I left behind in his coat.

She pats his chest, the most affectionate thing she's ever really done to him, and then with a small nod to me, he turns and walks through the security line, getting cleared through pre-check quickly and disappearing behind a pain of clouded glass.

"Shit," I mutter to myself, tucking my hand into the sleeve of my thin jacket and wiping away the tears that replace themselves the moment I remove them.

My chest is heavy, breath not coming as easily as I would like, so before I make myself sick, I turn to walk back out to the curb. I text Collin while I walk, and he tells me to give him five minutes. I find a small concrete bench right outside the east departures door, and I slide back until my shoulder blades hit the wall and I can fold my legs in front of me.

Elena, though, gives me no time to recover. She takes a seat next to me, the skirting of her jacket brushing against my bare knee. I didn't really think she would just leave without stopping to gloat. I see her driver parked up ahead, standing outside of the black Lincoln Town

Car. Nobody even bothers to tell him to move. Elena even has the TSA forewarned.

"Oh, dear. I hate that you're so sad," she says.

"I'm fine," I fire back, looking the other direction.

She doesn't hear me, or she doesn't care.

"It was always going to be like this. You know that Henry is just something *more* than you and I are. You see that, don't you?"

I blink away angry tears and keep my gaze away from her as I remain wordless.

"He is exactly as I hoped he would be. Nobody will ever break Henry's heart—he will leave behind the heartbroken, and he'll rule this world because of it. I made sure that he wouldn't suffer from my biggest flaw."

I laugh out loud at her absurd lecture, but I don't turn her direction. I won't give her that satisfaction.

"Henry won't ever love anyone more than himself. And I know you think he loves you, but that's only because you're young, and because there are things he doesn't know."

My jaw stiffens at her clue. It's threatening and calculated.

I turn just enough to be able to regard her from my periphery. She tucks her Coach bag high on her lap, flipping it on its side so she can fan her well-manicured hands over the expensive leather.

"I'm going to tell you something, and you are going to have to make a very difficult decision."

My eyes freeze in their open position. I still manage to keep myself from looking at her fully. My fists tighten and I push my nails into my palms.

"I know Rebecca has told you about how in love I once was with Mischa. I won't deny it—falling for him was my greatest weakness, and when he chose her it absolutely devastated me."

I breathe in as quietly as I can, my entire body on edge in anticipation of where this is going.

"What she didn't tell you, because she's not aware of it herself, is that Mischa was once very much in love with me, too. Men are so weak sometimes…"

My mouth begins to fall open, so I bite my tongue with my back teeth to keep myself from blatantly showing the shock that is starting to overcome me.

"He was not so faithful," she says.

And I know...

"And we were not always careful," she continues.

I know. I know. I know!

"I ended it the moment I got pregnant, and I left the baby in the care of the Catholic Sisters of St. Agatha. I was a driven woman ready to lead her father's company into the twenty-first century. I was not suited for motherhood."

"You still aren't," I blurt out, my chest heaving with the flooding of truths. Elena is laying down her hand, and she's been holding onto aces.

"I don't understand why Henry likes you with that acid tongue of yours. So hostile," she says, her voice thick with its own venom only delivered in the calm slither she prefers.

"Why would you do that? Why would you abandon him only to adopt him again and ruin his life with your...with your twisted games?" I can't help but turn to look at her now. I back away to the farthest end of the bench, and a few people nearby have started to pay attention to our conversation because my voice is so loud.

Elena stands and holds her lips tight, that dreadful smile lingering, but not fully spreading its wings. She reaches into her purse and pulls out a photo, then hands it to me. It's of her, a much-younger her, with a newborn infant held to her chest. I can tell by the look in that woman's eyes that she's going to ruin things for this baby.

"You're sick!" I stand and search the roadway behind me, begging to see Collin's car nearing me. It's nothing but a congested line of taxis and shuttle vans, all maneuvering around her parked limo that gets a pass.

"Henry is never coming back from Germany," she says. My breath comes in sharp and fast, and my mouth opens in protest, but she holds her palm out and talks over me before I can make sense.

"He's not, Lily. Because before he comes home, I'm going to tell him the truth. I'm going to tell Henry that I am his mother, and that Mischa is his father."

"He will hate you! More than he already hates you!" I growl.

"Yes," she says, eyes smug as she pulls her glasses from her face and switches them out for her sunglasses in her purse. "He will hate me so much that he will want to disown this entire life. He will be surrounded with walls and defenses that will make him indestructible. It's the one thing I knew I could do for him—take away this weakness."

"I won't let that happen." The words simmer with my anger, my promise just floating in this standoff and space between us.

"But you have no way to win," she says. There isn't a hint of a smile anywhere near her lips. Her face is just matter of fact. "Even your *heaving bosom* won't be enough to draw him back."

I shiver and sneer my nose. Alice told her how she found us on the roof.

"He won't let that happen," I say.

She shakes her head.

"You have a choice now, Lily."

I hate the way she says my name.

Don't say my name!

"You can live with the secret, which one day he will know you kept from him, or you can tell him before I do. Either way, he will resent you. He won't be able to help it."

I pull my phone from my pocket, silently praying that it's not as late as I think it is. I'll just call him before he boards, or I'll text him. I'll get to him—have him paged from inside if I have to.

But I won't.

Two minutes. I missed Henry's takeoff time by two minutes. Elena wouldn't have told me all of this now if she thought there was a way I could stop it. She waited just long enough.

"He won't run away. I believe in him," I say, meeting the reflection of myself in her sunglasses with a glare of my own.

"Well then, you are weaker than I ever was," she says, turning and walking straight to her car with heavy steps that clap against the dirty ground.

Collin pulls up just as the limo drives away, and I find myself unable to breathe. I rush to his car and collapse into him from the passenger seat, heavy tears blinding me and panicked breath unable to regulate itself.

Thinking I'm just distraught, Collin shifts into park and embraces me, smoothing my hair away from a tear-stained face. And in this one terrible moment, Collin has become my dad.

CHAPTER 19

JUNIOR YEAR

Henry doesn't hate me.
I also think that perhaps Elena was right and he's never coming home.

She took home away, in one clean sever. She made him in her image without any say from anyone. And she gave me no choice but to wield the knife.

By the time I could get the words out of my mouth in a remotely understandable form, Elena was home and Collin and I had been parked in the cellphone lot at O'Hare for an hour. Collin was livid when he finally understood the details. He threatened Elena, first with violence, then with a lawsuit.

I sat in the car while he pounded on her door in the rain, and then I sat at our kitchen table while he berated her with phone call after phone call calling her a child abuser for the manipulation she put me through.

Her only response was to fire Alice, which made Collin's ex-wife and my ex-fake-mom-cousin-aunt begin pounding on our door until neighbors called the police to deal with a "domestic situation."

They were both arrested, and I was driven in the back of a police car to the Southern District Precinct, where I sat for two hours until police could "sort things out."

By the time Collin and I got home, Henry's plane was landing. I knew he was going to call the moment he could, so I sat in my closet and clutched my phone to my chest just like a sniper. And when my phone rang, I put a bullet in his heart.

Our conversation lasted only as long as it took for me to recant everything Elena said and exactly how she said it. I didn't leave anything out, including her endgame. She knew I would tell him the details. What I hadn't counted on, though, was how angry he would be at Mischa—his father. Hate for him was born in an instant. And within the hour, he'd personally brought Ms. Manning into the circle.

So many people keeping secrets. And with one tiny spark, Elena was able to blow up multiple lives. Henry will never trust. Ms. Manning will leave Chicago, and she'll raise a baby on her own as a woman nearing fifty.

So much havoc. All from one woman.

Still...he calls, and when I call...he answers. We didn't go more than three days without talking over the summer.

Talking to me makes Henry think about everything here. He forces himself to anyhow, but I've noticed how distant our conversations have become. It was supposed to be our summer—I was going to hide away in the Satis House practice rooms, and he was going to wait for me on our rooftop. There were going to be sunsets and kisses. Instead, there's a lot of dead air on the phone between us.

Summer is over, though. And I'm moving back in to Satis House.

And I am sad.

"You're really changing the dynamics of our relationship, I hope you know."

It takes me a few seconds to react to Nicki's voice. I've been staring at the last notes in my journal, the one Henry found and read the night we snuck him into our room. I haven't made a single entry since that day.

"I'm sorry...what?" I close the book to glance at Nicki, but keep my finger on the page.

"Dark and gloomy is sorta like *my* thing. Ya know…I wear the black and listen to the death metal and…"

"You don't listen to death metal," I chuckle out, shaking my head.

"You don't know that." She folds her arms and juts her hip as she stares at me. "Maybe I switched things up. You've been so lost in your…" Nicki holds one hand out with a bent elbow and flicks her fingers around.

"What is…?" I make the same, bizarre movement.

"You know. That's your black cloud. The one following you around and making you all depressing and shit."

I grimace.

"You're right. I'm sorry," I say, letting go of the place I'm holding in my journal. I push the book under my pillow and sit with my feet on the floor and my hands in my lap.

"Tell me about this death-metal obsession," I say.

"Pshh, I made that up. I hate that stuff." She turns her back to me and goes back to pulling her collection of boots from her trunk. I throw my Satis sweater at her, and she laughs.

"That's the Lily I know."

Nicki and I finish the afternoon putting our clothes away, and on a whim, we become obsessed with hanging these purple flowers all over our walls. Someone left a bag of them in the common room, and Nicki suggested we decorate with them as a joke. I'm sure she was waiting for me to call her bluff, but the joke's on her because I actually love the way our room looks covered in the deep purple petals. I'm pretty sure she wants to gag.

Henry's call was supposed to come around three. It didn't. It didn't come at four or five either. It's night in Germany now, and his call—it isn't coming at all. He's been late before. And since the fall semester started for him, he's missed a few days. I was sure he'd call tonight though—he knew it was move-in day.

It hurts.

It's the first two days on campus—*the best days to be here*. All I feel is the void of Henry in every corner, though. Karaoke started in the courtyard an hour ago, and we've already listened to Anya sing three Whitney Houston songs. The incoming group of freshmen and sophomores isn't as spirited as our class was, and I think most of the juniors have grown tired of the same Satis House traditions. Seniors never stick around for the activities. Their nights are spent in the city.

"Maybe this event wouldn't suck if people actually participated," Anya says. She's being passive aggressive, which causes Nicki to roll her eyes. It's comforting that at least my friends have stayed the same.

"Give me the book," I sigh, taking the list of songs from Anya and flipping through in search of something I can muddle my way through. I can choose to wallow, which I have certainly been doing, or I can rejoin the land of the living. Henry was never the reason I came to Satis—the piano was. Henry was just a perk, a kernel that piqued my curiosity.

He was a cute boy that made private school a little more interesting.

My thumb passes by the Aretha song I sang two years ago. Henry didn't stick around to watch.

"Hey, who wants to duet with me?" My eyes travel around our small table, first to Nicki who just scoffs at my suggestion. Anya holds up a hand but lowers it to half-mast.

"I'll go with you if no one else wants to, but honestly...I think if these people hear me sing one more song they're going to start to throw things," she says.

My eyes flit to Ava.

"Hard pass. We can all agree that I don't sing, right?" She's quick to pass, and we collectively nod.

Anya starts to stand, her head ducked low in anticipation of groans from the few people still hanging out in the courtyard.

"I'll be the Sonny to your Cher!"

The smile colors my face fast. Caleb wasn't supposed to get here until tomorrow.

"Deal!" I slam the songbook closed and rush around the table to hug my friend. He wraps his arms around me and swings me in a circle, and when he sets me down, I realize how suspicious we probably look to everyone else at the table.

"Well, that sure perked you up," Nicki says. Her tone is snarky, maybe a little accusatory.

"You guys, stop. I just missed him, that's all," I say.

"She's a liar. She totally wants me, and now…my love," Caleb says, dropping to one knee. My eyes stretch wide and my cheeks get hot. I could kill him. "Henry is out of the picture, and we can be together *ha, ha, ha…*"

Caleb's pretend evil laugh dies off with zero reaction from the peanut gallery.

"He's kidding," I say, my head leaning to one side.

"Yeah, we got it. He's a real gas," Nicki says, dragging the songbook toward her to flip through the pages.

"Oh, now you want to sing," I sigh at her.

She pauses with a page turned halfway and her eyes slowly pan up to meet mine. She blows a bubble with the gum she's had in her mouth since about noon, I swear. It snaps against her lips and she pulls it back into her mouth.

"No, I don't want to sing. I was just looking at this book because I didn't want to have to fake like I didn't think it was weird that you and Caleb flirt all the time."

She blows another bubble, and I reach forward and pop it with my finger then flip her off. That makes her smirk.

"Atta girl," she says.

Ignoring my judgmental friends, I turn to Caleb.

"We're singing Aretha." His saunter stumbles a bit.

"Wow. I probably should have asked before I signed on for this."

"Too late. There is no going back from an offer to be someone's Sonny," I say, curling my finger and calling him to join me on the center stage.

I tell the DJ what song we'd like to do, and he puts it in the queue. One of the new students, probably a freshman, is singing Gaga. She's good—she's their year's Anya. It seems I have a thing for following epic performances.

Caleb's dressed like Henry would be if he were here—khaki shorts and a form-fitted black T-shirt. His skin is bronzed from an entire summer in California, and his bright-white shoes stand out against his sockless feet. Preppy.

We look like twins, only my shirt is a light green. It's an outfit I bought on a shopping trip with Henry—part of what we called "project un-tight." I put my hands in my pockets and sway a little with performance anxiety.

"How are you doing?" Caleb whispers, leaning into my side.

"Fake it 'til you make it, right?" I respond.

His lips settle into a comforting smile and his eyes blink once, slowly.

Caleb became the person I talked to over the summer when I couldn't sleep, and *that*—the faking it bit—became our inside joke. I don't even remember the origin now, but it's evolved into this cure-all, magic eraser. We say that, and all of the gross feelings eating me up inside have to go away. Same goes for Caleb.

This is the year he wants to come out at Satis. We practiced for all outcomes, and just now with our friends would have been the perfect time to test the waters, but then again—easy for me to say. I just have a broken heart and a long-distance boyfriend-ish...*sorta*. Caleb has part of who he is that might get judged.

The singer before us hits her final note, and that rush sinks into my chest. It's the performance rush; I get it even when I play the piano, something that I am way better at than singing. I love the feeling, though. I love the triumph of it, when I'm in the middle of it and actually *doing* it.

"We're up," Caleb says, taking my hand and leading me to the mic, which the girl before us left on the stand.

Caleb spins me so I'm facing him and takes both of my hands. We look like a couple at the altar, and I'm sure our friends will continue their gossip about us. Is it really gossip, though, when it's to our faces?

I'm so busy musing about the question that I don't even realize Caleb has switched our songs. The familiar Motown I was expecting is instead a steady seventies *oom-pah-pah*, and when I realize what I'm hearing, I rock my head back and laugh.

Caleb has to start without me, I'm laughing so hard, and the comedy of it all prompts our friends to join in. Soon, the courtyard is filling up, and everyone is howling out the chorus of "I Got You Babe."

I reach for the mic, taking it from the stand, and I lean into Caleb as we both sing loudly together. Our voices are obnoxious, but nobody seems to care. He takes my hand and twirls me out for the next verse, and I sing the first two lines, then give the mic to him. We switch off and on like that until the end, when the song is basically the same proclamation, over and over. What a simple pledge—they got each other. We got each other.

"I got you..." I say through my uncontrollable giggling. Caleb wraps me in his arms from behind, and I hold the mic close to my cheek so he can lean over my shoulder and sing along. We're rocking, and Satis House student arms are swaying. The scene is ridiculous and corny.

And then it suddenly isn't.

"Nice!" Henry bellows a single word. He's standing just outside the glass doors to the study room for the boy's dorm. His eyes level me, and the music drones on without a single person singing along.

He's here. He came back.

Right now.

I'm so in shock at the sight of him, I don't register the visual he's getting until I feel Caleb's hands slip loose from their hold on my waist.

"Shit," I say, dropping the mic to the floor and walking right off the stage toward him.

The glass door rattles as he lets it go. His stride is long and fast, and I find I'm beginning to jog in an effort to catch up. I'm not interested in shouting his name as I rush out in chase, but if I don't do something, he's going to sprint or climb into some car and dash away without giving me a chance.

I weave through the dark halls of the boy's dormitory, around the mailroom area and lobby desk until I'm faced with the heavy metal doors that lead to the main walkway on campus. I can see Henry distancing himself across the lawn, so I open the door and call out his name. In a breath, Caleb shouts his name after me.

"It's my fault. I'll fix this," Caleb says, squeezing my bicep as he picks up into a run and rushes by me. Our friends have caught up, along with a few nosey underclassmen who need to mind their own business.

I begin my march across the grass, but before I can catch up to Caleb and Henry, my Boyfriend-*ish* cocks his arm and sends his fist into the jaw of Dark Hair and Ice Eyes.

"Henry!" I break into a run, and my friends aren't far behind me.

Caleb is holding the side of his face, wobbling a little bit on his feet, while Henry is circling him like a Mike Tyson in his prime. He rotates his wrist and rubs his palm over the knuckles of the hand he took the swing with.

"What the hell, Lily!" Henry shouts. His eyes flash with hurt, but I'm too pissed to feel sympathy. I rush at him and flatten my palms in the center of his chest, shoving him off balance for a step or two. He's bigger than me, and hard to move, so I push him again, this time using more leg power.

"You're being an ass, Henry!" I slap at his arm, my fingers leaving a stinging, red slash on his skin.

He holds up his palms quickly and starts to back away, as if we've trapped him and he's terrified. The more he mutters the same phrase over and over again—*what the hell?* —the more empathy forms in my gut, until I realize that right now at this moment, what Henry feels is my worst fear.

Betrayed.

"Henry, man…look. We were just goofing around," Caleb says.

"They were," Nicki adds in. "We were all messing around. It's Karaoke Night!"

Henry's eyes snap to Nicki and they see right through her fake enthusiasm. It probably should have come from anyone but her. His feet begin to prowl again, and Caleb starts to work in opposite directions. I continuously keep my body between them both, my hands stretched out in both directions as if I have some mighty strength or superpower.

"You've always been flirty with her. Face it, Dude," Henry scoffs. He leans to the side and spits at the ground. "And you," he points at me. "Ice eyes, dark hair…"

His brow lowers a little, and his eyes dip away from the light.

"I'm gay, Henry."

The first time he utters the one thing he's been terrified to say, his voice gets lost in the breath of flared nostrils and pleas from my friends on my behalf. I begin to wave my hands, urging everyone to hush—to just fucking listen.

"I said *I'm gay*, Henry," Caleb says more forcefully this time.

His voice cuts through the anger and commotion, and just like that, everyone is perfectly still.

"Lily's the only one who knew. And I'm sorry if you're not okay with that. But that's who I am. Take your caveman shit somewhere else, because, while Lily and I are good friends, she is *so* not my type romantically."

We all gawk at one another, nobody sure what to say next. Henry struggles to let go of his rage, to make sense of where it fits with this new feeling. Caleb stares at his friend—his best friend—and I watch as his eyes fall as hope slips away that things will ever be anything like what they were before he let everyone know.

"I'm sorry, but what?" Nicki's eyes squint, and she steps closer to Caleb.

He turns a little, shifting his stance, and looks my goth friend in her eyes.

"I'm gay," he says, the tiny sentence coming out with more confidence this time.

"Yeah, yeah...I got that. But you said you were *sorry*. Don't say that part. You're gay...and you're *not* sorry." Nicki moves closer to Caleb, one careful step at a time, and the closer she gets, the more both of their smiles grow.

"You're not my type either," he jokes when they're standing toe to toe. Nicki flips him off.

"I'm everyone's type," she says, lifting up on her toes and kissing Caleb on the cheek. He pulls her into a hug, and his shoulders visibly lower from the burden they've been carrying around.

"You're not...messing around," Henry says, his finger drawing an invisible line that dashes between Caleb and me several times.

"No, Henry. We're not messing around," I say, moving close

enough to him that we could touch if I felt like it. At the moment, though, I feel like folding my arms over my chest and narrowing my eyes.

"You let me hit him," Henry says to me, nodding toward his friend.

"I didn't let you do shit. You hit him all on your own. Because you're an asshole." I add on that last part and Nicki makes a rebellious fist behind Henry's back.

"I only thought…" Henry pauses, his expression relaxing as his pulse settles in. Realization of everything is hitting him, and his hands move to his temples, his fingertips rubbing in small circles.

"Shit, man…I'm sorry," he says, his hands holding still for a beat as his gaze moves to Caleb.

"Did you hear the part about the fact that I'm gay?" Caleb lifts his brows, still waiting for some verbal acceptance.

"Uh yeah…a little late, but I did. And I don't really care. I mean, I support you, but you're not hitting on my girlfriend, so…"

"Excuse me," I say, waving my hand in his line of sight to bring his attention back to me. "If I'm your girlfriend, why didn't I know you were coming?" I lean to the side with my question, cutting off more of Henry's view. His eyes blink away from me for a moment, then meet my questioning gaze. He stares at me without words for several breaths.

"Elena's sick."

And in a single heartbeat, I wonder if somehow, I made this happen.

CHAPTER 20

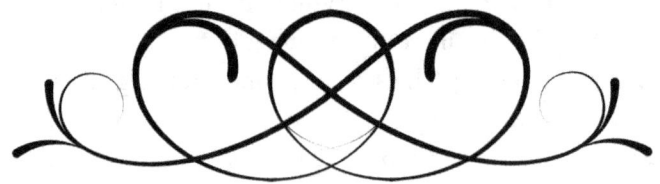

Most cases of acute kidney failure can be treated and reversed. Elena's kidneys, though, would have none of that. Naturally, she wanted a new one.

Elena never really wanted Henry to know. Her driver Phillip, though, thought maybe if he just reached out...Henry would come home.

He has no idea why he did.

We've lived in melancholy for the last eight hours back here at Elena's home. Henry spent an hour apologizing to Caleb, and another hour apologizing to me before we left campus. We were all sitting outside in the grass where the fight broke out. Then finally, Henry just got up and started walking without another word to anyone. I followed him, forcing his hand in mine and his grip felt cold—lifeless. We came here and walked right into the music room. We haven't left it once. It's the same conversation being spun over and over, and mostly Henry has it with himself.

"Why did I come here? Why do I want to help yet never want to see her again at the same time? It's like I'm programmed," he says, eyes lost in the glimmer of dust lit up by the sun just now streaming through the window.

My eyes are heavy. My heart is weak. I'm out of things to say.

She broke him. And now she's going to die and leave him this way.

"It's like you're human," I say.

Henry doesn't even nod.

I try again, crawling on my hands and knees on the floor to where Henry sits with his back against the wall and knees up. My hands grip his knees as I settle in front of him, then place my palm on his chest. He's unresponsive. I don't quit, though. I move on to his face, stroking his cheek and brushing away his hair. It's grown over the summer, long for him even. It's beautiful and sad.

Henry didn't even bring anything with him. He got on a flight Phillip helped arrange and came here, not even letting the school in Germany know he would be gone. When he landed, he came right to me. He's still wearing the gray pants and white button-down shirt he was wearing yesterday in an entirely different country. It's untucked, and wrinkled, and the tie is stuffed in his pants pocket. I grab the end that's sticking out and pull it, flattening it on the floor beside us to smooth out the wrinkles. Henry's head falls to his shoulder and he watches my hand stroke the silk.

"I should probably shower." His mouth forms a wry smile that only lasts a beat.

"Probably," I echo.

I abandon the tie and turn my focus back to him, holding his chin between both of my palms and righting his head so he's facing me.

"Or not. Maybe you don't have to go to the hospital. Maybe we just stay here, we sit right here, for as long as it takes for you to be able to move on."

My eyes work his, waiting for them to accept or to flinch. His gaze flits from my right eye to my left before falling away again.

"She's still my mother." He takes a deep breath and lets it out in a rush, then glances up to me again. "If I don't go, I'll regret it. Even if I hate her."

I suck in my top lip then nod.

"Okay, then."

I back onto my heels and stand, reaching down to take his hands in mine, helping him to his feet.

"I'll wait right here," I say, seeing him out into the hallway and watching until he disappears up the stairs.

I move to the window seat and pull back the heavy drapes, sneezing from the flyaway dust that shakes loose. Elena has been living in a frozen moment, no more Alice around to keep things at her house in order, and no care to the cold lifelessness that's consumed the walls of this place. She's been slowly dying here, not telling anyone until it was too late.

I rest my head against the nook and bring my legs up to the seat, my knees bent and arms hugging them. I drift away in seconds, only coming to when I feel the cool touch of Henry's hand against my arm.

"Huh?" I startle, glancing up to see his freshly dressed body standing right next to me. White T-shirt, gray shorts, and wet hair combed back out of his face, minus the one curl that falls on his fore-head. I may be dreaming him. I almost see a smile on his lips.

"You're tired. Why don't you stay here, and I'll be back soon? I just need to put this behind me. Then I'd like to maybe actually spend time with you. Maybe go apologize to Caleb about six more times."

I take his hand, and his fingers curl just a little. He's thawing, but he's still frozen.

I shake my head and yawn, swinging my legs around and standing so our bodies are touching, just barely.

"I'm coming with you," I say, fully embracing him, my arms squeezing around his form tightly, hands firm on the muscles of his back. I hold him for long seconds, until I feel his chin fall onto my shoulder and the tension begin to ease in his body.

Then I feel him start to cry.

I hold Henry to me while he sobs, and I know this is the first time I've heard him do this since I delivered the awful news to him over the phone. I doubt he ever cried when he was alone. He held everything in, stored it in a box just outside his heart, swallowed his existence and walked through life like a ghost.

"I hate her, Lily," he says, mouth against the skin of my neck.

"I know you do, Henry. And it's okay," I say. She made sure he hated her. She wanted him to hate everything. But Henry's heart beats, even when it's nearly dead. It beats, and he isn't her. He somehow grew despite the barren, loveless world she raised him in.

The sobs taper off after several minutes, and Henry packs his pain away again, but this time without so much armor. It's still there, and I think it's going to take a while for him to remove all of the pieces, but I believe he will. I believe he wants to.

We leave the house and make our way to the car waiting at the curb. Phillip has been outside all night, loyal to both Elena and Henry. I don't know how he can be, but I resolve to believe that he just doesn't want to see Henry left with any loose ends.

The ride to University Hospital is short, and the floor that Elena's room is on is buzzing with activity from the new morning shift. This is what I always pictured the scene to be like in the emergency room where my parents died—lots of beeping devices and nurses in scrubs rushing around. People here are smiling though, and their rush is only to get caught up or to clock out for the day. The people in their care aren't dying soon, but many of them are dying.

Her room looms in the very back, the door slightly ajar. It's symbolic of the woman resting inside; it lures one in, but doesn't make them feel welcome. Henry's fingers thread through mine, and his grip tightens. I look up to him, his focus on the room about sixty feet away. His jaw flexes with indecision.

"We've come this far," I say.

He nods with tight lips.

"Yeah," he hums. "I just can't seem to do it. Give me a minute."

I rap our tethered hands against my body and his gaze drops down to meet mine. I give him a reassuring smile.

"As long as you need," I say.

His nod is fast and jerky. He's scared. I'm scared too. I'll go inside that room with him, and when I see her, I'm going to want to choke her. I'm going to want to say horrible things, all things she'll deserve to hear. I'm going to want to gloat that her plan didn't fully work, that her son is still whole, even if he's stalled because of what she's done.

I'll keep it all to myself though, and just hope that Henry says it all to her face.

When her door opens, both of us jerk. My heartbeat spikes with adrenaline, fear that I'm about to come face to face with her, though I know she's too sick to leave her bed. The face that greets us is familiar, but not Elena. It takes me a few seconds to right my mind with it, and I can tell by the way Henry's body has stiffened that he's feeling the exact same.

"Hi," Ms. Manning says in a hoarse whisper.

I look to Henry and his brow furrows.

"Lily," she says, glancing to me.

I nod my hello.

The three of us stand silently by the nurses' station while a flurry of activity happens around us. I wait for Henry to speak, but after several seconds of quiet, Ms. Manning reaches for his arm and gently places her hand on his elbow.

"Why don't we move to the waiting room." She tips her head to the right, and we follow her lead down the side hallway into a small room with a flat screen playing the latest headlines on CNN. She reaches down for the remote on the coffee table and mutes the sound, then encourages us to take a seat on the sofa opposite the chair she sits in.

"I know why I'm here, but why are you here?" She leans forward and clasps her hands together, arms resting on her knees. She's dressed so informally, it's strange to see—an oversized sweatshirt, leggings, and running shoes. She's already lost most of the baby weight. I wonder where she's living now, and how her baby is.

"I had to come," Henry answers.

Ms. Manning dips her head, her hair spilling over one shoulder. She nods.

"You think you did, but I promise Henry, you didn't."

"Is she…not really sick?" I question because staging something like this is perfectly in her character, though I think the presentation would be more egotistical and dramatic. Elena likes the villain drama.

"She is," Ms. Manning confirms. "But it doesn't matter. She needs a kidney, so I'm giving her mine."

"But you've just had a baby." I question fast.

Ms. Manning nods.

"And I truly do not plan to ever be pregnant again," she says, a cynical chuckle. "They've tested. I'm a match, and my health checks out."

"Why would you give something so big to her?" Henry's question surprises us both, but only because he asked it.

She sits back in her chair and draws her hands to her belly, looking down in thought.

"Because if she dies, Henry, then everything she is becomes yours," Ms. Manning says. Her gaze shifts to me briefly, then moves back to Henry. "And you don't want it."

He blinks, digesting what she just said.

It seems ludicrous, not to want to take over a major company in the Midwest, to inherit her power and name. But Ms. Manning is right, and Henry knows it.

"I don't," he agrees. "But I don't have to take it on. It doesn't mean you have to do this, donate life to the woman who ruined yours... mine...your baby's."

"Henry, I don't do this without malice. I assure you." Despite her tired eyes and dull hair—from likely days she's spent here in this building, near that room—something in her brightens as she stands. We follow her lead, standing too.

"You're saving her life. I don't get how that's a very big *fuck you*, pardon my bluntness," Henry says.

Ms. Manning bites her bottom lip mid smile, a short laugh escaping through her breath as she slowly starts to nod.

"Elena gets to live, and she gets to see you become whatever you want—without any ties to her other than the legal ones on paper. And she will live every day of her life knowing that it's *my* kidney inside that's keeping her alive. She's too weak to refuse my offer. She's already accepted it. But I will hold this over her, in my own subtle way. I will raise my daughter, Rose, to be the opposite of everything she is. And I will make sure she lets you live your life, your way, Henry. If she ever threatens that, I'll launch a PR stunt about the ungrateful matriarch who went against her sister's wishes even after she gave her a kidney. Her social status will be ruined, and for Elena...that is real death."

I can almost hear the internal, evil laughter echoing in Ms.

Manning's mind when she finishes speaking. Elena has made her cold and calculated, but somehow it feels justified this way, like she's still doing good though it's manipulative in nature.

"Go home, Henry. Let me be that family member you never had. You can repay me by becoming someone good. And my Rose will look up to you," she says.

"And continue to play, Lily. Elena had zero to do with where you are right now. You got into Satis House. She had no idea you were accepted until you told her. Everything you have achieved, your talent —that's yours. She's not the one who makes that music. You are."

Her words sink into my chest and squeeze my bones. My breath falls away, but my mouth aches to smile. I nod to her, and Henry reaches out his hand. She takes it with both of hers, and I can tell that she would prefer it to be a hug. I think maybe soon, it will be—when it's no longer a hospital and Henry's had a chance to really cope with his feelings and what was done to him.

I don't question him when he takes my hand and leaves the waiting room, turning left and out toward the elevators rather than back into the area just outside Elena's door. His stride accelerates when we leave the hospital completely, and he doesn't wave for Phillip to give us a ride, instead flagging a cab and tugging me inside with him quickly before anyone notices.

The color begins to return to his cheeks with every block we pass on our way back to Elena's home, and he's almost laughing when the car slows up to the curb outside the giant iron gate.

"Come on," he calls after me, slamming the car door and pushing through the gate as he practically leaps up the stone path. He opens the heavy door and kicks away his shoes in one, fluid movement.

Arms pumping, he rushes down the dark, cavernous hallway, his palms slapping at the light switches along the way until the runway is aglow and then his feet stop, and he slides another ten or fifteen feet until his balance fails and he crashes into the glass-paned doors of Elena's home office. They fly open and he rolls on his knees, laughing wildly as he falls onto his back.

"Are you okay?" I shout.

More laughter booms from his chest and his arms and legs fall out to the sides with a heavy flop.

"I'm free, Lily!" he shouts up to Elena's vaulted ceiling.

My brow wrinkles. I think he's gone mad.

He sits up quickly and flattens his palms on either side as he leans back and stares down the long hallway to me.

"Slide with me, Lily! Run with me, and let's just laugh. Let's fill this house with the sound of pure happiness." He draws in his knees and pushes himself up to a stand, holding out one hand and curling his fingers to me to come.

"Just run." The first true and honest smile to reach his lips in months speaks to me, and I follow suit, smiling back while my pulse races with hope.

"Catch me," I shout, kicking my shoes free and pounding my feet along the floor while they slide wildly as I make my way down the corridor. I break when I'm a dozen feet away from Henry, and I glide to him along the dust-covered floors that ruin my socks and push laughter from my chest.

Henry's arms wrap around me and he spins me in circles until finally pressing his lips on mine. Our kiss is desperate, two mouths holding onto one another without breath for almost a full minute. We hardly move our lips, but our hands grasp at the side of one another's faces until finally we both need air. Henry's head tilts so his forehead is resting on mine, and happiness radiates from him as his smile stretches wider.

He pulls back eventually, but takes both of my hands in his and begins to rush back toward the main door, towing me behind him as both of our bodies spin and slide into walls along the way.

"I'm free, Lily!" His gaze locks on mine as he says the words again.

"You're free, Henry!" I smile back at him.

We're both free. Such a tragic route to get here.

Such a gift not to be wasted.

EPILOGUE

SENIOR YEAR

Performing here is an honor. My mother's best friend sang on this very stage. It was the last beautiful thing my mother saw before her life ended. I've never been very spiritual—despite taking a theology class...*twice*—but I swear I can feel my parents looking down on me now.

Senior year. The first two days at Satis House. The freshmen and sophomores are moving in and planning parties and routes to escape after curfew. The juniors have lost interest and are hiding in the city. My class is focused on our futures, at least most of us are.

Caleb is sitting in the front row. Henry's open seat is next to him, and Anya, Ava, and Nicki are all in the row behind. Even if I blow this performance, I know that five people will be clapping for me, shamelessly. This is assuming Henry isn't late, of course.

His flight got in an hour ago. When he gets here, it will be the first time we've seen each other since he left to go back to Germany after Elena's surgery. Neither of us have spoken to her, not even when she was in recovery. Henry uses her financial support, but nothing else. Kidney guilt—and the looming threats from Ms.

Manning—keep his accounts full. I have been by the house. I walk on the other side of the street, and sometimes I sit on the curb and just stare at its dark, dirty windows and dull-gray brick. The only proof I have that Elena is inside and doing well is the fact that smoke billows from the chimney and Phillip still sits in a car parked outside on most days.

She's left with a driver who is beholden to her for his overpaid job. She pays him so much so he'll stay around, remain loyal. I don't know that for sure, but my gut tells me it's so. She can't even hire Alice back. My cousin-aunt remarried and moved to Brooklyn, to a man three times her age with grown children and a yacht. Elena has nothing more to offer her. Alice is living her best life.

I asked Henry once, just after he found out the truth, how he felt about Mischa—his father. His only response was "what father?" I haven't asked since. The man lost out on knowing a great son, and he lost a great family. The marquee at the Chicago Symphony Center still dons his name, and his portrait still hangs in the window, though, so perhaps that's enough of a life for him. Seems hollow to me.

I pull the curtain at the side of the stage back just enough to gaze out at the next few rows in the audience. The room is only half full, which is still not bad for a regional high school musical showcase. The best in Illinois, Indiana, and Iowa are here for two hours of music. My performance is first, thank God! I'll be able to enjoy everyone else once I'm done.

My eyes trace along the rows looking for Ms. Manning's familiar face. I finally catch her waving to me, and she holds up her phone, waggling it and encouraging me to read mine. I pull it from the pocket of my skirt—a new dress made of tufted black satin and lace. Nicki picked it out with me, and it is somehow perfectly both of us.

My phone buzzes with her message, and I smile at the gif of some cartoon bunny breaking its leg. I send her one back of two bunnies high-fiving, and I watch her face until I see it smile. Our eyes meet, and she holds her hand to her chest, patting a few times to show me her love and support.

So much family lost and yet we all somehow found each other. She's saving Collin's seat for me. He's driving Henry here from the airport, and the last text I saw said they were five minutes out. That was fifteen minutes ago.

The lights lower, and I hear the echo of Caleb's finger-whistle reverberate around the gallery. Dean Orson taps at my shoulder, and I turn to meet his stern glare. He's not an easy man to impress, and the first impression I made on him was when I got caught sneaking back in after curfew with Caleb. He made a joke at rehearsals about adding that to my brief bio he is about to read. I hope he was actually kidding.

"Sorry, sir." I step to the side and let him take the stage, polite applause welcoming him to the mic.

The piano behind him is the nicest I will have ever touched. Elena's pales in comparison. I could probably go out there and play Chop-Sticks and it would sound like Chopin.

I hear my name and startle to attention, listening to Dean Orson read the notes about me just as he did in rehearsal. He doesn't add in the bit about my indiscretion, and for once I'm relieved that he isn't clever or funny. If Nicki were the dean of this school, she would give a five-minute set about all of my most embarrassing moments before bringing me out.

The lights dim as he leaves the mic and moves back toward me. His hand juts out, a fat palm from the sleeve of his tux, and I take it and give it a firm shake.

"Have a wonderful show," he says with a stern nod.

I give one back, and then let out my breath when he leaves and my back is to him.

"Wonderful show," I whisper in repeat, amused.

I step into the dim light, and it brightens as I get closer to the piano. My heart is pounding, and the fear that my fingers won't work tickles the back of my mind. I get jittery when I'm nervous, and as of right this moment, my hands feel nearly numb. I stop at the piano bench, and I bend in a practiced curtsy, which causes Nicki to laugh. I smile while my head is down because I can hear her.

Still suffering from a massive case of tingles, I uncross my legs and breathe out as I stand again, lifting my chin and internally repeating the word *please*. His gaze was waiting for me, and his white shirt and gray vest is exactly as I pictured in my dreams when he described it to me.

Henry said he would come dressed to take me out as soon as my show was done. The best restaurant, and then a trip to the opera down the street. His hands clap long after everyone else is done, and he's the last to take his seat. Always the standout, even when it isn't about him.

My eyes scan the crowd as I begin to turn, and I catch Collin as he slides down the row to sit by Ms. Manning. For a little while, I fancied the idea that maybe *they* would get together, but I guess the age gap is a bigger deal to them than it is to me. Regardless, I'm glad they've become friends.

Rebecca Manning moved to a small town in Wisconsin, and she got a job as an advisor at the community's school right away. She was deeply overqualified, but her desperate need for a place with an attached daycare and a quiet, simple life evened the scales. Getting away to come to the city for my performance wasn't easy, I know. It makes it all the more special that she's here.

I take my place behind the keys and spread out my sheets of music, though I know I won't need them. This is all by heart. My hands know their way. I sit back and squeeze my hands into fists one last time, the last nerves being vacated. I turn to find Henry's waiting eyes, and his smug smile, cocky on my behalf this time. His lip quirks as he nods, and so I spread my fingers and let them find their home.

The sound is harsh and instant, and it fills every crevice of this room. My eyes close through the beginning, erasing the enormity of the moment and replacing it with nothing but confidence and loud, thunderous chords set off by the quiet, staccato of my perfect runs. I slay, and when I pound out those final few bars of Chopin's greatest scherzo, the room erupts. It's more than five friends and two pseudo-family members. It's praise, and I earned every beat of it.

I soak it in.

I rush backstage in a wired state. I could easily march out there and do that, what I just did, again. This performance is simulcast. Nobody really watches it but family members and the people who decide who gets into what schools. I'm applying to lots of them, and after that, there better be a fight.

I woke up a little different today.

"You're an animal," Henry says, sweeping me into his arms the moment I leave the space of the stage. He pulls me into a dark corner and kisses me so hard that my body automatically dips back and falls into his hold. He smells like a man of the world, yet home. He tastes familiar, and new.

His lips pull away just enough to let me see his dimples, the perfect smile and wrinkled eyes that shine with pride.

"I missed you," I say.

I wasn't sure how it would be when he got back. I won't lie, there was a lot of relief when Stella didn't stay for the entire program. Even more relief when I heard rumors that her family was moving out of the house next to Elena's. But even without her, we've had a year to change and grow. He's had a year to somehow get taller, his shoulders broader. We're seventeen, staring down eighteen, that year when for some reason society thinks we can handle being adults.

Henry has started applying to schools too, for engineering. Many of our choices are far apart—not as far apart as Chicago and Frankfurt, Germany, but still. There will be lots of decisions, all which we will make, both together and on our own.

Through it all, through every letter and text and late-night video chat while he was away, I knew I still wanted Henry Alderman. I wanted him to come home to Satis. I want to spend this year watching him row, waving my hat at him when he wins, kissing him in front of jealous freshmen and privileged society girls. I want to spend after-noons on the rooftop with him, and I want to give him all of my firsts. I'm ready now, but I'm also in no rush.

Our senior year is exactly two-hundred-fifty days long, and I intend to drain each and every one of them, starting…right…now.

THE END

ACKNOWLEDGMENTS

I have this quote on a magnet that I've carried around from job to job since I graduated from college and got my first newspaper gig. It's one of those quotes that is debated because it's attributed to Eleanor Roosevelt with no real evidence that she said it exactly that way, or ever at all. Regardless, I like it. I always have.

"Do something every day that scares you."

Okay.

Check.

This book scared me.

Us bookish types have flexible lists of our favorites. You know... someone asks you to list your top ten and you give them forty-seven books. I have three solid books that are always on my list: The Outsiders, Forever by Judy Blume, and Great Expectations.

And so here we are—my muse played out by my own interpretation. There are many long nights that turned into mornings that I consumed myself with this story and exactly how I would write it. It changed over the years, but at its very core, it was always the same. Reversed roles. Modern setting. A vintage flavor. It would always end here.

It scared me to tackle, and that is why I must.

Dickens wove a tale that was heartbreaking and bleak yet still steeped in hope. Goddamn did the young, budding writer I was when I first read this as a teenager admire it. I locked away quotes; I memorized whole chapters. I hated characters and loved others, sometimes loving the ones I hated the most.

I wanted to pay homage, and I wanted to take on the challenge. My hope is that this book delivered for those of you who *nerd-it-up* over Dickens like me. I hope it is youthful yet mature and full of the right amount of pain, growth, love and friendship to be worthy of your time.

I must thank several people for pushing me over the hump with this one—thank you to TeriLyn, Jen, Bianca and Shelley for taking the early dive and going all in! Thank you, BilliJoy of Editing Addict, and Tina Scott, for your editing and proofing eyeballs. Thank you, husband, for your patience and for telling me this one is your very favorite. I can tell you aren't lying. Thank you, Carter, for letting me finish the chapter before we took BP. Huge props go out to Phala Theng for helping me make sure my French was on point! And Autumn of Wordsmith Publicity—just thank you, period.

This scary thing I did would have sat on that list for a very long time if it weren't for you, the readers, who took a chance on one of my books the first time or discovered me with this one. Thanking you never gets old, just as creating new shoes for you to walk in doesn't either. I'm already working on another pair.

XO

Ginger

ALSO BY GINGER SCOTT

The Waiting Series

Waiting on the Sidelines

Going Long

The Hail Mary

Like Us Duet

A Boy Like You

A Girl Like Me

The Falling Series

This Is Falling

You And Everything After

The Girl I Was Before

In Your Dreams

The Harper Boys

Wild Reckless

Wicked Restless

Standalone Reads

BRED

Cry Baby

The Hard Count

Memphis

Hold My Breath

Blindness

How We Deal With Gravity

ABOUT THE AUTHOR

Ginger Scott is an Amazon-bestselling and Goodreads Choice and Rita Award-nominated author from Peoria, Arizona. She is the author of several young and new adult romances, including bestsellers Cry Baby, The Hard Count, A Boy Like You, This Is Falling and Wild Reckless.

A sucker for a good romance, Ginger's other passion is sports, and she often blends the two in her stories. When she's not writing, the odds are high that she's somewhere near a baseball diamond, either watching her son field pop flies like Bryce Harper or cheering on her favorite baseball team, the Arizona Diamondbacks. Ginger lives in Arizona and is married to her college sweetheart whom she met at ASU (fork 'em, Devils).

FIND GINGER ONLINE: www.littlemisswrite.com

facebook.com/GingerScottAuthor

twitter.com/TheGingerScott

instagram.com/authorgingerscott

goodreads.com/GingerScott

bookbub.com/profile/ginger-scott